"Victory number one to me," he quipped

Devon controlled her escalating emotions with difficulty and refrained from lashing out at him physically. "Has anyone ever told you just what a hateful, callous and unbearable animal you really are, Hunter Kincaid?"

"No, can't say they have." His indifferent reply was accompanied by an equally negligent shrug. "Why, has someone told you just what a selfish, intractable and thoroughly wayward little jade you are?"

He was the only person to have ever accused her of having such faults, and the knowledge that she had displayed every one of them that morning made her feel ashamed.

Since his arrival she felt as if everything familiar to her was being inexorably swept away—especially her control over her emotions.

Books by Kerry Allyne

These books may be available at your local bookseller.

Don't miss any of our special offers. Write to us at the following address for information on our newest releases.

Harlequin Reader Service
P.O. Box 52040, Phoenix, AZ 85072-2040
Canadian address: P.O. Box 2800, Postal Station A,
5170 Yonge St., Willowdale, Ont. M2N 6J3

KERRY ALLYNE

tropical eden

Harlequin Books

TORONTO • NEW YORK • LONDON
AMSTERDAM • PARIS • SYDNEY • HAMBURG
STOCKHOLM • ATHENS • TOKYO • MILAN

Harlequin Presents first edition May 1985
ISBN 0-373-10783-8

Original hardcover edition published in 1984
by Mills & Boon Limited

CHAPTER ONE

WITH one hand raised to shade eyes the same colour as the aquamarine sea she was looking out on from the verandah of her large, rambling guesthouse home, Devon Matthews' vision concentrated on the luxury powered yacht navigating the narrow channel through the coral that surrounded Cowrie Island. Situated in the northern section of Australia's Great Barrier Reef, it was a popular safe anchorage for many privately owned vessels, but the one now entering the inner lagoon was obviously of a class that normally preferred the docking facilities available on the mainland, and with a slight frown of curiosity marking her forehead she turned to the deeply tanned, white-haired man sitting on the steps just beside her, mending a sail.

'That's the same boat that was cruising around here about a week or so ago, isn't it, Dad?' she mused.

Leaving his labour of love for a moment Granville Matthews lifted his head in order to cast a searching gaze across the glinting, dazzling water. 'Mmm, that's the same one all right,' he nodded as his hazel eyes came to rest on the gleaming vessel. 'She's a beauty, isn't she?'

'You certainly won't get any arguments about that,' Devon half laughed wryly. 'But I wonder why she's calling in here instead of Northport.' Their nearest harbour and town on the mainland. 'It's only another few hours' sailing time away.'

Her father shrugged, his attention returning to the

sail spread about him. 'Admittedly, it's not the type of boat we usually have mooring here and camping down with the rest of the yachties, but who knows, maybe they've got a spot of engine trouble they want to attend to, or perhaps they just don't want to go on to Northport today.' He looked up again, his expression humorously quizzical. 'Does it matter? And why the interest, anyway?'

Devon shook her head, wondering much the same herself, her wavy golden hair bouncing about her own smoothly suntanned shoulders that were only covered by thin straps of a clinging lemon sun-top. 'I don't know, just because I didn't expect to see them this way again so soon, or for them to call here, I guess,' she grinned, her widely curving mouth shaping ruefully. 'Anyhow, they'll probably be off again in the morning.' The prediction was accompanied by a dismissive movement of her hands as she began descending the steps on bare feet. 'Meanwhile, I'm off for a swim before I have to help Aunt Violet fix dinner.'

'Garth not going with you?' Her father's brows rose enquiringly.

'No, he's engrossed in some book he wants to finish reading and said he'd give it a miss this afternoon.' Garth Wilkinson was her fiancé from the mainland who was holidaying with them for a month.

Granville Matthews nodded, his wiry, weather-beaten fingers resuming their stitching. 'Well, don't be late, you know we've got a couple more guests than usual at the moment—plus Garth, of course—and Violet needs your help.'

'Don't worry, I won't forget,' she promised with a smile and turned for the rear of the wooden, colonial-styled building where she collected a towel from the washing line before proceeding down the decidedly rocky path that led to her favourite swimming venue.

Coming out from between the shading palms and casuarinas some minutes later, Devon stopped momentarily on the creeper covered dunes above Careen Beach, the view spread before her never failing to impress her with its beauty, despite having seen it so many times before.

Sheltered between two small headlands the area was completely secluded, the white sand sparkling beneath the blazing sun that was beating hotly against her back. Inside the protective reef the waters of the lagoon were an incredibly clear yellow-green, while those washing over the coral were pure azure. Further out the sea changed colour again, this time to a deeper, more intense blue, as the grooves and buttresses of the reef front dropped sharply to the ocean floor below. Towards the horizon the scene was repeated again and again where each successive reef, washed over by white-capped waves rolling in from the Pacific, had formed its own picturesque lagoon within its coral ramparts—to the delight of airborne sightseers and photographers, if not always to sailors, for the very aspects that made them such a sight to behold also created hazardous conditions at sea.

Not that any such troubling thoughts were on Devon's mind as she presently stepped on to the beach and dropped her towel on the coral sand before divesting herself swiftly of her ribbed cotton top and shorts. She never bothered donning a swimming costume when she came here alone, preferring to experience the silky sensation of the water gliding unhindered along her darkly golden length, and knowing that the rugged track leading down to this particular beach was an ample deterrent to any of the rather elderly visitors staying at the guesthouse, and the high tide meant no one would be reef-walking around the headland that afternoon either. The yachtsmen who came ashore and camped on the other side of the island she had no worries about whatsoever. They had always respected her father's request that they remain within the generous area allotted for their use, unless there was some specific reason for them to come to the house. It was a privately owned island, after all.

Now, as she dived cleanly into the warm inviting water, she swam leisurely for a few strokes, her eyes automatically seeking any changes brought about by the changing tides, any new inhabitants that may have made their way into the lagoon from over the reef or from somewhere else around the island. Having lived there for the whole of her twenty-two years, no one knew the island or its fringing reef better than Devon did—except perhaps her father—and she never tired of watching its underwater life forms. The variety was so great, and in many instances so colourful, that it often captured her attention for hours. A recollection that had her abruptly, determinedly, rising to the surface again and smiling ruefully to herself. If she wasn't careful she *would* forget all about the time and that wouldn't exactly put her in her aunt's good graces at all—as well as being unfair to that very industrious lady, she owned honestly. So with a regretful grimace she made do with merely swimming the length of the lagoon a couple of times, before returning to the beach to dry off in the sun. Lying back on her towel Devon pulled her cotton top over her face to provide it with some protection from the burning rays and closed her eyes, her thoughts lingering on her aunt as her shapely body relaxed in the hot, still atmosphere.

Violet Matthews, Granville's younger, unmarried sister, had resigned from her position as assistant chef at a large hotel on the mainland and had moved on to the island more or less uninvited, though no less appreciated for all that, when her sister-in-law had died as a result of complications setting in after she had given birth to Devon—her first and only child, if one discounted three previous miscarriages—at the rather late age of forty-five. Since that time Violet had made herself indispensable, helping to rear her niece and run the guesthouse.

In those days Cowrie Island had catered to a far greater number of visitors than it did now, for as more and more resorts opened on other islands—and with easier, more comfortable forms of access than the weekly trading launch that serviced Cowrie—the guesthouse's popularity had waned considerably, so that now their guests were mainly in the retired age bracket who had no objections to making their own amusement during their stay. Of course the consequent drop in revenue had been very noticeable but by careful budgeting, supplemented the last few years by the income Devon earned with her designs for T-shirts and other souvenirs that were sold in a tourist shop in Northport, the family had been able to get by, and as none of them was really interested in seeing the island overrun with visitors they considered the financial hardships that did occur from time to time to be well worth it in order to retain their way of life.

With a pleasurable sigh Devon pulled her top from her face, preparing to roll over on to her stomach, but as she did so her eyes suddenly snapped wide open in dismay, and indignation, on seeing a tall male figure standing no more than a few yards away, his deep blue, assessing gaze totally unabashed in its thorough scrutiny of *her*! Gasping, she flipped her towel across her slender, flaring hips and clutched her sun-top to her chest as she rapidly gained a sitting position.

'Get out of here!' she blazed furiously even as her cheeks burnt with a mortifying heat at having been so discovered. 'How dare you come peeping and prying! This is private property and you've no right being on this beach!'

Strong, square hands came to rest on lean, shorts-clad hips above which a navy T-shirt outlined a broad and powerfully muscled chest. 'I wasn't peeping—just admiring the scenery. It's quite—umm—spectacular, isn't it?' the stranger drawled in a drily expressive tone that brought new waves of embarrassed colour to her face.

Having expected an apology, at least, Devon's ire mounted uncontrollably at the thought that he found both her predicament and her embarrassment amusing—as manifested by the dancing lights he didn't bother to disguise in the depths of his ebony-lashed eyes.

'It's no different to the scenery on the other side of the island!' she claimed heatedly, if a little distractedly. 'And that's where you yachties are supposed to stay! You're not permitted, and *you* especially are not wanted over here, and if you don't leave immediately I'll have my father ban you from Cowrie altogether!' She drew a heaving breath. 'Which boat are you from, anyway?'

'The *Kanandah*,' he supplied negligently. 'We arrived this afternoon.'

The luxury one she had watched making its way through the reef. He was probably one of the crew. 'Well, couldn't you read the signs saying this part of the island's off limits? Or did you just think it didn't apply to you because yours is the most expensive vessel there?' Her voice became strongly overlaid with sarcasm.

His firm, sensuously shaped mouth sloped crookedly. 'Not exactly. We were simply told that if we wanted to see Granville Matthews we could find him at the house.'

We! There was someone else with him? Devon spared a hasty, anxious look around but thankfully could see no sign of anyone else. 'Then you don't appear to be a particularly competent navigator because the house is that way!' she retorted on an acid note, pointing back over the dunes. 'It's a large wooden building I wouldn't have believed anyone could miss!'

'Oh, I didn't miss it,' he advised casually. 'I just came on past it in order to have a look around.'

Devon pressed her lips together infuriatedly. The gall of the man when he was aware he was trespassing! 'Then I hope you enjoyed your look, mister, because it's the last one you'll ever get of this island, believe me! When I get through telling my father about this you'll be off of here so fast your feet won't touch the ground!'

Surprisingly, he grinned unconcernedly at that, his teeth shining whitely against the bronze of his skin. 'I doubt it. And as for enjoying my look round . . .' he paused, his glance significant as it roved deliberately over her only partially covered form, 'well, there's certainly no question that I did that.'

Devon grudgingly averted her gaze. It was impossible to appear dignified and in control when one was almost naked, and particularly when a boorish intruder purposely reminded her of the fact.

'Besides . . .' she suddenly realised he was continuing in the same lazily mocking voice, 'it was Granville Matthews—your father, I presume?—who gave his consent for my coming this way.'

'That's a damned lie!' Her wide-spaced and darkly fringed eyes locked fiercely with his again. 'He'd never do such a thing!'

'Because he's aware of your liking for sunbathing in such a—er—natural state?'

'No! He doesn't even know that I. . .' Flushing once more she came to a halt, biting at her lip in annoyance for having been nettled into making even such a fractional disclosure. Knowing her prim and proper aunt would never, never have approved of such behaviour had always kept her silent on the subject. That was, until this unwelcome, insensitive lout had come along! She began again with a disparaging snap, 'No, because he also values our privacy, and because he's got no time either for those who come pushing in here as if they own the place just because they happen to be on the biggest yacht! So as I said, when I tell him. . .'

'That I disturbed his daughter while she was in the altogether?' he inserted tauntingly. 'Or perhaps we could tell him together, hmm? That way he may understand why you're so incensed at my presence.'

'He'll understand anyway!' she glared at him balefully. 'But now, since you've had your look round, you can just clear off! I want to get dressed!'

'So don't let me stop you,' he shrugged indolently,

remaining exactly where he was. 'I've already seen everything there is to see, after all.'

Did he have to keep reminding her! 'As well as all you're going to!' she gritted. 'So you can leave—right now! Or would you prefer it if I started screaming for help?'

'What, and allow whoever comes to see you so charmingly unclothed too?'

She hadn't considered that, and if it should happen to be Garth who arrived she was positive she would never hear the end of it. At times he could be almost as straitlaced as Aunt Violet. 'Then you might at least have the decency to look the other way instead of—instead of. . .'

'Being honest enough to admit appreciating what I see?'

She sucked in a stormy breath. 'Instead of trying to humiliate me for your own amusement, you—you ill-mannered creep!'

Not even that seemed to perturb him, or have him experiencing an attack of consideration. 'I wouldn't precisely call you gracious either, sweetheart,' he merely countered in wry accents.

'Why should I be? *I'm* not the one who's trespassing!'

'And neither am I.'

If she had been in a position to do so, Devon might have thrown something at him. 'Says you! Now are you going to leave or not?'

'And thereby spoil my unmannerly image?' He flexed a wide shoulder, his gaze mocking as it held hers. 'I see no reason why I should.'

No, he probably didn't. His overly assured type always did think they could act as they pleased, regardless of anyone else! But if he didn't intend to depart, just how *was* she going to get dressed without revealing more of herself than was already subject to his openly assessing, aggravating perusal?

With another glare for his insensitivity she swivelled around as best she was able until her back was to him and then proceeded to drag her lemon top over her head with fumbling fingers, cursing inwardly that it should choose this particular time to stick to her heated skin and, as a result, make the exercise that much more difficult and lengthy. Thankfully, however, her shorts and pants were rather more accommodating and by managing to wrap the towel around herself a little more securely she was able to hitch these more or less into place with a few hurried movements.

Feeling decidedly more comfortable now, Devon promptly sprang to her feet, gave her shorts a couple of righting tugs before tossing her towel over one shoulder, and stalked past her audience with her head held high but without saying another word. Actually, she was so furious only physical retribution would have served as a release for her feelings, but as the man—even taller and more solidly built than she had previously thought, she noted on drawing level with him—had already proved to possess no finer instincts, she considered such an action on her part could be just a touch imprudent. There was a distinct possibility he might respond in kind, and having no doubt just who would come off worst from such an encounter she had to be content with picturing her father ordering him off the island for good once she informed him they had a brazen trespasser in their midst.

'If you're going back to the house I'll go with you,' the casual declaration was suddenly made behind her, and had her spinning about wrathfully, her already seething temper threatening to boil over. Oh, yes, he was willing to leave now, wasn't he?

'No, thanks, I'd rather go on my own!' she snubbed between clenched teeth. 'I'm rather particular about who I'm seen with!'

'One wouldn't know it if that patronising excuse for a man up at the house is your fiancé,' he returned with a contemptuous half laugh.

Devon gasped, hardly able to credit his effrontery. 'How dare you!' she exploded. 'What would you know about Garth, anyway? And for your information, there's more to being a man than just muscles and a macho attitude, you know!'

'Sure,' he agreed drily, closing the gap between them leisurely. 'But just being male doesn't necessarily make him one either, beautiful. As for what I know about him. . .' He paused, his lips twisting eloquently. 'I met him . . . that was enough.'

'Oh?' Her winged brows peaked caustically. 'And when would that have been? When he discovered you trespassing and informed you in no uncertain terms that your presence was unwelcome? Is that why you're trying to belittle him now?'

'Uh-uh.' He shook his head as he came to a halt just before her, and making Devon feel her own five foot six height relatively stunted in comparison. She guessed him to be six foot two at least. 'It was while Royce and I were talking to your father. He introduced us.'

For a moment she could only stare at him indecisively as doubts began to creep into her mind for the first time. He sounded so positive that it was becoming more and more difficult to continue gainsaying his contention. The Royce he mentioned she presumed to be the companion he had spoken of earlier.

'And—and why would he do that?' she consequently stammered on a rather less confident note.

'Because he happened to be there at the time, I guess,' he drawled whimsically. His darkly blue eyes filled with lazy goading. 'Although why he would be when his fiancée is disporting herself down here like a free-spirited child of nature, God only knows. I certainly wouldn't be if such a long-limbed and shapely sea nymph wore my ring on her finger.'

'No, I'm sure you wouldn't!' Devon retorted acidly, attempting to ignore the unbidden colour his description had brought to her cheeks. 'You'd have neither the good taste nor the consideration to behave in any other fashion than the offensive one you've already displayed! Just like others of your kind, you're doubtlessly only capable of a "grab and subdue" approach with regard to the opposite sex!'

One corner of his mouth tilted sardonically. 'You mean, like this?' he quizzed, and before she realised what was happening two tanned hands had indeed grabbed hold of her and dragged her disconcertingly close to a hard chest.

Devon's lips parted involuntarily in a mixture of shock and fury, but before she could close them again they were captured determinedly by a mouth she discovered to be incredibly seductive in its skilful exploration of their soft contours, and not forcefully quelling as she had anticipated at all. So persuasive was it, in fact, that she soon found to her horror they were beginning to soften pliantly beneath the tantalising contact, and her breathing was erratic as she belatedly wrested herself free.

'Ex-exactly!' she finally answered his facetious question with as much sarcastic conviction as she could muster. 'You've proved my point!'

'And you mine,' came the impenitent, mocking return.

'Meaning?'

'If your fiancé was really worth his salt, you wouldn't be so receptive to another man's kisses,' he drawled lazily.

Devon crimsoned. 'I was not r-receptive!' she spluttered embarrassedly, defensively. 'I—I was surprised and shocked, that's all. I'm not accustomed to being grabbed and kissed by total strangers!'

'Nor by your fiancé, at a guess,' he proposed on the driest of notes.

'Not in that manner, no, I'm glad to say!' she derived considerable satisfaction from refuting hotly. 'And I'll thank you to keep your unwanted comments concerning Garth to yourself! He's nothing whatever to do with you!' And with a defiant toss of her head she began heading for the track leading up to the house once more, and at a pace she hoped would leave him behind. The man's audacity appeared limitless!

Unfortunately, it was a hope doomed to disappointment because his longer, muscled legs could cover the ground even faster than hers could, leaving her no recourse but to studiously ignore him instead as he followed her up the narrow, uneven path.

'It's a real tropical Eden, isn't it?' he remarked at one stage where the lush vegetation, filled with fan palms, twining vines and flourishing ferns, encroached to within inches of them.

Devon remained silent for a few seconds, but the opportunity was too good to pass and she flicked him a grimacing glance over her shoulder. 'Mmm, complete with snake too, unfortunately, at the moment!' she gibed meaningfully.

His ensuing laugh was amused and as they continued on their way she strangely, annoyingly, found her thoughts waywardly centring about him. She surmised him to be in his early thirties, around thirty-four probably, and with his roughly handsome features and disturbingly flagrant disregard for the proprieties, she didn't doubt he could spell disaster for any female unfortunate enough to arouse his interest.

Not that it wasn't apparent some hapless members of her own sex hadn't already suffered for having done so—just the confident, experienced fashion in which he had kissed herself had demonstrated he was no stranger to success where women were concerned—as well as it being equally obvious he considered all women fair game, whether attached or not. His presumptuous behaviour towards herself when he was fully aware she was already engaged had more than adequately shown that!

While as for his remarks regarding Garth . . . well, so what if he was of a rather more scholarly than active disposition, or that his emotions were a little restrained. At least that was preferable to not bothering to control them at all, wasn't it?

Reaching the end of the track first, Devon hurried across the intervening lawn towards the front verandah of the house where she could see her father seated in a cane chair, deep in conversation with a rather distinguished looking man of some fifty years who was dressed neatly in a pair of fawn slacks and short-sleeved, cream shirt. They made a somewhat incongruous pair, she mused absently as she bounded agilely up the steps, for her parent was still wearing his old, stained working shorts, his weather-beaten chest devoid of any covering at all.

Their conversation ceased and they both rose to their feet at her approach, but with only a faint half smile of acknowledgment for his companion—that he had some connection with the younger man negligently following her made him almost as unwelcome as far as she was concerned—she headed straight for her father.

'Dad, did you give. . .'

'Ah, Devon!' He started speaking at the same time, causing her to break off. 'I'd like you to meet Royce Attwood. He's from the yacht we noticed coming in this afternoon.' And with obvious pride to the pleasant-faced man beside him, 'My daughter, Devon, Royce.'

'How do you do?' she responded cursorily, and a little hastily, to the older man's subsequent greeting, anxious only to return to the question she had been about to ask, but merely to find her father hadn't finished yet.

'I see you've already met Hunter,' he went on with a smile that encompassed the T-shirted man now beside her.

'Regretfully!' she gave vent to her feelings, and accompanied it with an emphasising glare at the subject of her simmering resentment. She also wasn't averse to hoping that if his associate should just happen to have some position of authority aboard the yacht, her annoyance at one of the crew's presence might not go unreported.

'Oh?' Granville Matthews looked from one to the other of them in obvious surprise, and just as obviously at a loss for something to say.

It was left to Royce Attwood to prompt, wryly askance, 'Hunt . . .?'

From his position where he now leant casually against the verandah rail, his arms folded lightly across his broad chest, Hunt gave an indolent shrug. 'It appears I upset the—umm—lady by abruptly interrupting her solitude when she . . .' pausing, it was he who spared Devon a glance this time—a glinting, taunting glance that had her eyes widening in dismay and unconscious pleading at the thought of what he had the power to reveal in retaliation, 'definitely wasn't expecting any company,' he turned back to the others to conclude in dry tones. And to Devon's heartfelt relief!

'Oh, I see,' nodded Granville understandingly, his smile returning. Then, to his daughter curiously, 'Although I must admit I find it hard to understand why that should apparently have annoyed you to quite such a degree.'

'Yes—well . . .' She hunched one shoulder diffidently, and feeling obliged now not to disclose all that had infuriated her in return for her own secret having been kept, 'I—I just couldn't bring myself to believe you'd given someone permission to explore Careen Beach, I suppose. You never have before.' She still couldn't help sounding just a trifle accusing.

'No, but then I didn't expect you to resent it so vigorously this one time either,' he chided gently. 'It wasn't as if I allowed a whole party of people down there when all's said and done.'

It might have been better if he had! And she was still puzzled as to why he had permitted *anyone* to look over the area anyway. In the past he had always insisted on retaining their privacy as much as she had.

'No, but perhaps if I hadn't been quite so unprepared. . .' Her voice trailed away uncomfortably, her awkwardness increasing as she caught sight of Hunt's humorous expression, knowing he was remembering just *how* unprepared she had been. Briefly, a woman appeared at the far end of the verandah to water a couple of hanging baskets of brightly flowering cacti and Devon sighed gratefully for the legitimate excuse it afforded her to escape. 'Oh, there's Aunt Violet,' she exclaimed. 'She's expecting me to help with the dinner so I'm afraid you'll have to excuse me.' She turned more towards the older of their two visitors. 'I don't imagine I'll be seeing you again,' most of the yachtsmen who came to the island usually only stayed a couple of days before moving on, and she couldn't envisage a yacht like the *Kanandah* being any different, 'so I'll. . .'

'Oh, I'm sure you'll be seeing more of them,' interposed her father with a smile. 'They're not really anticipating leaving for a while yet.'

It was all Devon could do not to grimace despairingly at the totally unexpected information. Theirs was a boat she would have been delighted to see depart as soon as possible—along with one especially unwelcome member of its complement! 'I see,' she acknowledged weakly, disappointedly. 'In that case, it appears I may see you again later, after all.' And with a half smile in Royce Attwood's direction she headed for her room and a shower.

Twenty minutes later, and wearing a lime green and black, thin cotton sunfrock this time, Devon arrived in the large kitchen at the back of the house where her aunt, trim and prim as always, had already begun preparing the evening meal.

'I'm sorry if I'm late,' she apologised sincerely as she immediately set about washing some of the salad vegetables they would be requiring and which had already been laid on the sink. 'I got caught up with those men talking to Dad.' Pausing, she sent a frowning look across to the table. 'How come he seems so friendly with them, especially on such short notice? I mean, he even allowed one of them to explore our side of the island, and he's definitely never done anything like that before.'

Momentarily, her aunt stopped what she was doing, her greying brows drawing together thoughtfully. 'No, he certainly hasn't,' she agreed. 'Although I've no doubt he had a good reason for it.' With a slight shrug of her thin shoulders she resumed peeling some carrots. 'He wouldn't give such permission lightly, I'm sure.'

Devon didn't think he would either, and that was what made it all the more enigmatic. 'Mmm, but what reason? And on such short acquaintance too!'

'As to that I couldn't say, dear. I only met them very briefly—I had too much to do in here to stay and talk—but they both seemed very likeable, and very taken with the island, so maybe that's why.'

Both likeable? There was no way Devon could endorse that claim! 'We've had others here, though, who would fit that description equally well, but they were never able to prevail upon him to relax the rules,' she pointed out.

Violet bustled across to rinse the carrots in the other bowl of the sink prior to tipping them into a saucepan. 'Yes, well, I think you'll just have to ask your father about that later. Or perhaps Garth knows,' she added as an afterthought. 'He was also talking to them for a while when they first arrived.'

So she had been told, Devon recalled testily, but at least it sounded a little more promising that her fiancé could be able to throw some light on the subject before too much longer. He usually put in an appearance just as they were concluding the dinner preparations, whereas her father normally liked to put in some work on his own small sloop at this time of day and as a result was invariably late for the meal.

'And just where is Garth, by the way?' she quizzed lightly. 'I couldn't see him when I returned from my swim. Don't tell me he's back in his room again doing more reading.' With a partly disbelieving laugh.

'I wouldn't be at all surprised,' said Violet, turning her attention to some broccoli now. 'He rarely seems to do much else while he's here.'

'Oh, I don't know about that,' Devon defended staunchly. 'He climbed to the top of The Pinnacle,' the highest point on the island, 'with me this morning.'

Her aunt gave her an old-fashioned look. 'Then complained all through lunch about how his legs ached in consequence.'

'He's just not used to it, that's all,' Devon smiled excusingly. 'He does only have an office job, remember.'

'Hmm ... I suppose there is that to consider,' Violet allowed. Then, with her lips pursing speculatively, 'Although I suspect that wouldn't apply to that fit-looking young man out there with your father if the positions were reversed.'

Devon's aquamarine eyes rounded incredulously. It was such an uncustomary kind of comment for her aunt to make. 'Do you mean Hunt—Hunter ... or whatever his name is?'

'That's right,' was the decisively nodded confirmation. 'That's the one I was referring to—Hunter Kincaid. And if you were talking to them, how is it that you don't know his name?' She fixed her niece with an enquiring gaze. 'Didn't Matt,' the nickname for Devon's father used by just about all his close acquaintances, 'introduce you?'

'Well, no, not exactly,' Devon shrugged evasively. 'You see, I—er—met him during his explorations but we sort of didn't get around to introductions.' As she recollected, at the time she couldn't have cared less about his name! 'Then when we arrived back together Dad just assumed it was only necessary for him to introduce me to Royce Attwood. I merely picked up the Hunt and Hunter from their conversation afterwards.' She began meditatively drying the tomatoes she'd washed. 'In any event, I think you're being a little unfair comparing Garth with someone like that who obviously leads a much more physical, outdoor kind of life as a yacht crewman.' Not only that, but she really would have preferred to try and forget the man entirely!

'Oh, well, if you say so, dear,' her aunt smiled vaguely, her concentration obviously centred on the food again. 'I expect you know your fiancé best.'

As well as Hunter Kincaid by the sound of it! added Devon tartly to herself. He really must have put on a good act in her aunt's presence for that usually so perceptive woman to have been taken in by him to the stage where she was now comparing him favourably against Garth. Previously she had never had anything but praise for Garth's rather studious demeanour, his fastidiousness—and his lack of preoccupation with more athletic pursuits, she recalled a little piquedly.

Whereas, on the other hand, *she* was only too aware just how contemptible Hunter Kincaid could be!

For a while silence reigned in the kitchen as both Devon and her aunt went about their tasks with a minimum of fuss. After so many years of practice they had it down to a fine art now and by the time Garth put in his regular appearance everything was well in hand and they were able to relax a little.

'Oh, hi!' Devon greeted him warmly. With his mid-brown hair slicked back tidily and clad in dark green pants and an oyster-coloured shirt he looked extremely well-groomed, she thought. 'What have you been doing this afternoon?'

'Beginning a new book mainly,' he answered offhandedly as he took a seat by a large antique dresser. 'There didn't appear much choice with you gone and then being informed, civilly but succinctly, that *my* presence wasn't required for the discussion taking place on the verandah.' In a somewhat huffy tone.

It didn't require much for Devon to guess just which discussion he was alluding to, but... 'You mean, Dad actually asked you to leave?' she gasped, finding it almost impossible to believe.

'Perhaps not in so many words, but the inference was plain enough!' His rather narrow lips pressed together in patent disapproval. 'And that when I would have thought my presence, more than any other, as the partner in my father's firm who deals with all Cowrie Island's business affairs, would have been imperative if business was to be discussed.'

'Business?' she echoed, even more surprised now than after his last revelation. 'What sort of business?'

'How should I know?' he countered on a now

markedly peeved note. 'I wasn't allowed to hear what
was being said!'

Stranger and stranger, pondered Devon confusedly,
and half beginning to wish now that she had stayed
around a while longer herself in order to have
discovered just what was going on. However, to try
and mollify her fiancé's obviously injured pride, she
tried to dismiss the matter lightly.

'Oh, well, maybe Dad was simply attempting to save
you from having to listen to a dreary discourse
concerning something he knew would be of no interest
to you,' she suggested, albeit rather lamely.

Garth merely gave her another aggrieved look.
'What happens on this island is of interest to me. Not
only as your father's accountant, but also as your
fiancé.'

From across the room, Violet now glanced at him
swiftly. 'But I understood your father was Matt's
accountant.'

'Since they've been friends for such a long time, and
because he was originally, technically I suppose he still
is, Miss Matthews,' he conceded formally, if a little on
the fractious side. 'Nevertheless, I'm the one who
actually audits the island's books and handles all the
paperwork now.'

'I see,' Violet nodded stiffly, taking his touchiness
amiss, and it was left to her niece to return the
conversation to their original topic.

'So you know no more about the whole matter than
we do,' she sighed disappointedly.

'If you also know absolutely nothing, it would
appear not,' Garth acceded in clipped accents, clearly
still put out by the whole episode.

Devon sighed again. It seemed she was just going

to have to wait for her father to divulge the reasons for his unexpected and uncustomary behaviour after all.

CHAPTER TWO

THROUGHOUT the meal that evening it was extremely difficult for Devon to stop her increasing curiosity from getting the better of her and begin questioning her father at the table, but as she knew he would never discuss business of any kind in front of their guests she had no choice but to contain herself as best she could.

By the time the guests had been served coffee in the sitting room, however, and her father stated his intention of taking a walk down to the yachties' camp—as he often did in the evenings for a drink and a chat around the camp fire—she could stand it no longer and promptly followed him as he headed for the doorway.

'I'll go with you,' she declared, even though on this occasion she would really have preferred to give it a miss. The less she saw of Hunter Kincaid the better she would like it!

'So will I,' said Garth firmly and earned himself a rather exasperated glance from his fiancée as a result.

If, as he had implied, her father hadn't wanted to discuss the matter in his presence before, it was possible he wouldn't want to now either. Besides, since he had previously always considered a visit to the bottom camp somewhat below his dignity, he was making it too obvious as to why he was willing to make an exception tonight.

'You don't have to if you'd rather not,' she therefore proposed as they reached the steps, hoping he would

28

take the hint. 'I know all that nautical talk doesn't greatly interest you, and I don't expect we'll be away all that long.'

Ignoring the hint—purposely, Devon suspected— Garth kept pace with them doggedly. 'No, that's all right. Perhaps I should take more interest ... in preparation for the time when we're married and I take over the running of the island.'

Devon squirmed inwardly at his choice of words. The idea had been mentioned for them to have a larger say in Cowrie's management but it definitely wasn't a foregone conclusion as yet. 'Yes, well, nothing's actually been formally decided along those lines yet, Garth,' she felt obliged to remind him. 'In any event, the proposal suggested was for *both* of us to take charge,' she emphasised indignantly, 'and then only if Dad decides to relinquish control.'

'But I thought it was all settled that he would be off on this trip he's been planning once his boat is ready,' Garth put forward, his own voice sounding rather resentful now. 'Has that idea been scrapped, then, Mr Matthews?' He looked across to the older man intently.

'There's some who would like to see that happen,' Granville disclosed eloquently, his eyes straying towards Devon.

'And you know very well why!' she retorted. 'You're seventy-one years old, and at your last check-up even your doctor advised you to start taking it easier. Nor do I consider your sailing off on your own on that little boat of yours particularly well-advised!'

'But if that's what he wants to do ...' interposed Garth with a shrug and received a positive glare for his efforts this time.

'That doesn't necessarily make it right!' she snapped. 'I mean, anything could happen, and at sea is quite likely to. It wouldn't be so bad if there was someone with him, but to even contemplate going off completely on one's own on that old boat. . .' She shook her head disbelievingly.

'And if it was in a new one?' Her father crooked a quizzical white brow.

She hunched one shoulder deprecatingly. 'Well, naturally I suppose that would put it in a slightly better light, although I still wouldn't be in favour of it . . . and nor would Aunt Violet,' she added in order to lend more weight to her argument. 'Besides, we all know the island's finances aren't in a position to cover such a purchase so there's not much point in discussing it.'

He exhaled slowly. 'You're probably right,' he allowed, and they continued along the smooth, downward path leading to the island's mooring area in silence, each of them occupied with their own thoughts.

Devon still felt somewhat annoyed regarding both her fiancé's assumption of his role once they were married and his virtually endorsing remarks concerning her father's proposed lone sailing trip around the continent. He knew as well as she did that the doctor had recommended her father not to undertake anything too strenuous from now on, she fumed. Moreover, he was also making it extremely difficult for her to question her father about the events of the afternoon. If he hadn't stubbornly insisted on accompanying them she would have been able to have sought some answers by now instead of having to keep them bottled inside her until an appropriate time presented itself when she could manage to get her father alone!

There were five yachts apart from the Kanandah anchored in the lee of the low promontory that curved westwards, their crews talking desultorily as they sat around a blazing fire—used to provide light rather than heat—in an open area between the trees just a short distance from the beach and the old wooden jetty where the trading launch off-loaded the island's house guests and supplies.

The majority of those present Devon and her father already knew from other visits and were accepted into their midst readily, but Garth was a stranger to all of them and it took a while for the necessary introductions to be completed. When they were finally over and the three of them had been companionably provided with drinks, Devon heaved a sigh of gratitude for having been spared another meeting with one person in particular. In fact, neither of the men she had met that afternoon were present, she noted, and presumed they had chosen to remain aboard for the evening.

No sooner had the general conversation resumed, however, than Devon felt a hand drop lightly on her shoulder and she looked up to find Hunt, his other hand resting similarly on her father's shoulder, bending towards them.

'Mind if I join you?' he enquired smilingly of Granville.

'Please do,' replied the older man genially, already moving in order to make more room for the muscular figure to fit between his daughter and himself—to Devon's irritation. Did he have to be quite so accommodating where this man was concerned? 'Is Royce planning on coming across too?'

'Uh-uh.' Hunt shook his head. 'He retired to his cabin immediately after dinner to do some work. He's got a few notes he wants to make.'

'But you haven't?' hazarded Granville. Disappointedly? wondered Devon in bafflement.

'No, I prefer to keep all my information up here,' laughed Hunt, tapping a finger against his temple. 'Notes can have a habit of getting lost.'

'Isn't that the truth,' Granville averred in a seemingly almost relieved voice that had his daughter's forehead creasing anew as she tried to fathom the reason why her father should be evincing such an emotion—if indeed her suspicion had been correct.

Not that she was allowed much time for her speculations because she now found herself the object of Hunt's somewhat disconcerting attention as his vivid blue eyes took in her puzzled features lazily.

'And how are you tonight, beautiful?' he drawled with just enough taunting humour in his tone to have her pressing her lips together vexedly.

'Do you mean now . . . or before you arrived?' she gibed bittersweetly, softly, under cover of the voices surrounding them, and finally managing to dislodge the hand that had still been touching her shoulder.

He merely grinned, his head tilting closer to hers. 'Your animosity is still showing, sweetheart,' he admonished drily in an equally quiet tone. 'And all because I happen to know what you look like unclothed.'

'Which, to my mind, is quite reason enough . . . even without your certainly less than gentlemanly behaviour in refusing to leave when it was pointed out—sufficiently succinctly even for you, I would have thought—that your presence was neither wanted nor appreciated!' she muttered vehemently.

'So can I help it if you made such an enchanting picture I was unable to tear my eyes away?' he countered in assumed innocence.

'Yes!' she ground out unequivocally. 'And you can stop referring to the matter all the time as well! Or is that also too much to expect of someone as insensitive as you?' Her arching brows reached an expressive peak.

In return, one of Hunt's own brows lifted sardonically. 'As to that, I guess it would all depend on just how I was *asked*,' he stressed significantly.

His inference was obvious enough and, consequently, did nothing to improve Devon's feelings of resentment. 'And you'll be dead and buried before I ever *ask* anything of you, Hunter Kincaid!' she seethed.

'Even though you've already done so once?'

'When?'

'This afternoon—on the verandah—when I was explaining to your father the reason for your being so—umm—displeased at my intrusion on your privacy. Your eyes, at least, were more than willing to seek my silence then, as I recall,' he reminded on a wry note.

Devon shifted restively. She'd forgotten that! 'A—a favour I more than repaid by keeping quiet myself,' she claimed defensively. 'Because if I had told Dad all that did occur on the beach, I very much doubt he would now be treating you as hospitably as he is doing.'

'Mmm, you could have a point there,' he surprised her by allowing with a slow, rueful smile that had her catching her breath involuntarily. 'Shall we agree to call it quits, then?'

'I fail to see why I should,' she refused his offer of

peace uncharacteristically. Normally she didn't like to prolong disputes of any kind, but for some unaccountable reason she suddenly felt a need, quite distinct from his initial unfavourable impression, to keep this man at a distance. 'You're the one at fault! Besides, since I have no intention of making the mistake of ever being in your vicinity again while you remain on this island, I. . .'

'An intention that could be a little difficult to achieve,' Hunt interposed in a somewhat mocking tone.

Her head lifted challengingly. 'I don't see why.'

'Probably not . . . at the moment.'

'Meaning?' A flicker of apprehension had her staring at him warily. She hadn't liked that significant pause before his last words.

'Cowrie's a relatively small island,' he shrugged. Evasively, she suspected.

'So . . .?'

'It's more than conceivable we could run into each other again.'

'Because of the business you were discussing with Dad?' she chanced a stab in the dark.

'You could say that, I suppose,' he owned, although certainly not as informatively as she could have hoped.

As a result she was forced into debating whether to continue questioning him—which, under the circumstances, went very much against the grain—or to pretend to an indifference she was far from experiencing. Eventually, her desire to know just exactly what was going on overcame her reluctance.

'And just what business would that be?' she queried as nonchalantly as possible.

Before he could reply, however, a voice sounded on her other side. 'If it's not too much to ask, Devon, do you think you could possibly spare me some of your attention also?' Garth put in a little irritably.

Devon could have hit him in her frustration at his inappropriate timing, and something of her annoyance must have shown on her face because Hunt promptly grinned. An action that had her swiftly turning her back to him—just in case he mistakenly believed her aggravation had come about because she preferred talking to him—and forcing an apologetic smile on to her lips for her fiancé's benefit.

'I'm sorry, Garth. I didn't realise we'd been talking so long,' she said contritely.

'Obviously!' he sniffed. 'So just what were the two of you whispering about?'

'Oh, we weren't whispering,' she denied with a light, and hopefully convincing, half laugh. 'We just weren't talking loudly, that's all.'

He grimaced, but didn't press the point. 'Well, what were you discussing so quietly, then?'

'As it so happens, I was attempting to discover what he and Mr Attwood were talking to Dad about this afternoon——' she said, carefully omitting to mention the earlier part of their conversation.

'And?'

'You interrupted me at the most relevant moment,' she relayed with a meaningful grimace.

'How could I have done?' His expression registered his disbelief. 'You'd been talking to him for God knows how long before then!'

'Yes, well, I was attempting to worm my way around to it,' she parried.

Garth uttered a disparaging snort. 'What on earth for? You're entitled to know, aren't you? So why waste time beating about the bush?'

'Because I considered that was the best approach to take, and as it worked out, I'm sure I was right.' Pausing, she chewed at her lip thoughtfully. 'Even then I wasn't exactly given any direct answers. In fact, he was quite uncommunicative.'

'Oh?' His brown eyes narrowed suspiciously. 'So there is something going on that we should know about.'

Devon gazed at him askance. 'I'm not sure how you came to that conclusion. After all, I'm certain Dad's not being deliberately secretive. He just hasn't had an opportunity to mention anything about it yet.'

'Hasn't he?' Garth clearly thought otherwise. 'Then why was I summarily dismissed from the verandah this afternoon, eh?'

Mmm, there was that to consider. 'Oh, I don't know!' She shook her head defeatedly. 'Maybe because. . .' She came to an abrupt halt as a sudden recollection came to mind. 'I wonder if Royce Attwood has any connection with the boat-building industry,' she mused. 'I mean, I thought it was a strange remark for Dad to have made when he mentioned something about a new boat on the way down here, and that would definitely explain why he didn't want you present at their discussion. He knew you'd tell Aunt Violet and myself about it and that we'd both try and talk him out of it. Yes, that's got to be it!' Her voice strengthened with conviction. 'He's considering buying a new boat for that damned trip of his!'

'Oh, well, in that case there's nothing to worry about,' Garth shrugged, noticeably relaxing. 'Although I don't know where the money's supposed to be coming from. The island's barely in credit as it is.'

Devon's mouth levelled exasperatedly. 'Of course there's something to worry about!' she contradicted, concentrating on his first indifferent statement. It wasn't the island's finances that concerned her, it was her parent's health. 'If he did somehow manage to get himself a new boat there'd be no stopping him from going off on his own.'

'A decision for him to make, surely,' proposed Garth negligently. 'Besides, he's always seemed to me to be very capable with boats.'

'Oh, naturally he is!' she retorted in impatient tones. 'Good lord, why wouldn't he be? He's been sailing in them ever since he was old enough to walk! But in case it's escaped your notice, it's rather difficult to be capable if you have a heart seizure or something similar!'

'That's still no reason for you to be sarcastic,' he complained on a rather querulous note. 'That achieves absolutely nothing, and particularly when there's no guarantee he'll suffer anything of the kind anyway.'

Devon made a determined effort to moderate her tone somewhat. 'All right, I'm sorry, but I happen to be very concerned about him, while you don't even appear to care.'

'Only because I think you're making mountains out of molehills,' he offered appeasingly.

Was she? Devon wasn't so certain. After all, she spent more time with her father than anyone else did, and during the last couple of years especially she'd noticed a sad but inescapable deterioration in his physical ability. Not that it was entirely unexpected at his age, and if he hadn't wanted to go off on his sailing trip she doubtlessly would just have accepted it, but as it was she felt *someone* needed to sound a warning

regarding the inherent dangers in such a proposal in
the hope of dissuading him.

Presently, a few of those around the camp fire began
drifting back to their boats; a couple because they
planned to leave on the early morning tide—at low
water the passage through the reef was still navigable,
but not quite so comfortable; others because they
wanted to be up early in order to effect repairs or just
generally check over their equipment before heading
off for a day's fishing on the outer reef.

Of course, immediately the exodus began, Garth
was anxious to do likewise, this evening's venture
down to the camp obviously not having interested him
any more than his previous few had done, and nor had
he made any effort to lower his dignity sufficiently to
the stage where he would voluntarily participate in any
of the discussions. Devon also rose to her feet
automatically, preparing to accompany him, despite
the fact that she would rather have stayed in the hope
of hearing just what Hunt and her father had been
deliberating upon for the latter part of the evening.

'We're off now, Dad,' she cut in on their discourse.
And in an endeavour to separate him from his
companion, 'Are you coming too?'

'No, love, not just yet. I'll be along shortly,' he
replied. 'You go with Garth and I'll see you in the
morning, okay?'

She sighed and nodded, not really having any option
but to agree, and with Garth at her side, turned to
leave. As she did so a tall, dark-haired girl emerged
from the group on the other side of the fire, her
voluptuous figure accentuated by the bikini top and
brief shorts she was wearing. Pauline Telfer! Devon
grimaced, and it wasn't hard to guess in whose

direction she was headed. Along with her brother, the
other girl had been a regular visitor to the island for
quite some years and one whom Devon knew well. She
also blatantly sought, and more often than not
received, the attention of all the yachtsmen camped
there, and right at present Devon didn't doubt that
Hunter Kincaid was the magnet drawing the older girl
towards the opposite side of the fire.

A last glimpse over her shoulder as she and Garth
began making their way up the track proved her
assumption correct as she saw the green-eyed beauty
sink down with a feline grace beside Hunt—or should
that have been, on top of him? she amended, for
Pauline couldn't possibly have moved any closer if
she'd tried. Unknowingly angling her head higher,
Devon returned her attention to the path leading up to
the house. They were probably perfectly matched, she
decided sourly, since they both possessed identical
characteristics in that they were so self-assured as to
be insufferable, and patently never gave a thought to
anyone but themselves and their own wishes!

On reaching the house they found it in darkness
except for the dim hall and verandah lights that were
kept on throughout the night for the benefit of the
guests, most of whom always retired early, and
entering quietly they proceeded to the door of Devon's
room.

'You know, I can't take to that Hunter chap,' Garth
caught her unawares by abruptly declaring. 'There's
something about him—perhaps it's the way he has of
looking at you, mockingly arrogant it seems—but
whatever it is, he just rubs me the wrong way.'

'Mmm, I know the feeling.' Devon's lips twisted
wryly.

'You don't like him either?'

'Now that you mention it, no, not particularly.'

'I'm glad,' he smiled thankfully. 'For a while there tonight I thought you may have been interested in him.'

'Oh, don't be an idiot,' she reproved with a soft laugh. 'How could I possibly become engaged to someone like you and then be interested in someone like him? You're completely opposite types, and his I would need to be mad to want to have anything to do with. He's vexing, goading, and just plain detestable on occasion as well!'

'Is that so? Well, if you find him being the same again, you just let me know. I'll soon put a stop to that,' he vowed. 'Not that I expect he'll ever get up to the house again. Your father can't possibly have become that friendly with him that he would issue another invite.'

'I certainly hope not,' she seconded on a fervent note. Although if he did, she wasn't sure just how her fiancé would be able to keep his promise should it become necessary. She suspected that there would be nothing at all Garth could do to alter any chosen course of action of Hunter Kincaid's.

'And having got that settled, I guess I'd better say good night,' he murmured, and bending his head, touched his mouth gently to hers.

Devon responded to the slight pressure mechanically rather than spontaneously as her thoughts wandered. Whenever he kissed her Garth was always very proper and controlled, she reflected—somewhat like her Aunt Violet—but at least it meant she was never subjected to any unbidden roaming hands, whereas in the same situation she could well imagine Hunt's hands being extremely exploratory, and no doubt proficiently so too. Abruptly she gulped at the disconcerting turn her thoughts had taken, but fortunately Garth didn't appear to notice anything amiss as he raised his head and smiled.

'So what shall we do tomorrow? Have you anything planned?' he asked.

Recovered now, Devon hunched a slender shoulder offhandedly. 'Well, I've got some designs and so forth for the craft shop in Northport that I have to pack ready for the launch when it arrives in the afternoon, and of course I'll have to be present when it comes in so I can help Dad bring the stores up, as well as make certain the guests who are departing haven't left anything behind. There's four of them going back tomorrow, actually. The rest of my time should be free though. So what do you say to a visit to the waterfall slide? It's a while since you've been there and it's usually fun.'

'Oh, all right,' he acceded, albeit not very enthusiastically. 'I suppose I can always take a book along to read if it becomes too tiring.'

Devon's lips twitched irrepressibly. Him and his books! She enjoyed reading herself, particularly in the evenings, but Garth never went anywhere without arming himself with a variety of reading material beforehand. 'Okay, I'll see you at breakfast, then.'

He nodded, and dropping a last chaste kiss to her brow began making his way towards his own room.

Close to an hour later Devon was still wide awake, her mind so active as to make sleep impossible as she subconsciously awaited her father's return. She just had to know for certain what his discussion with Royce Attwood had entailed—if only to hopefully

prove her own worrying assumption wrong.
Consequently, the moment she heard him mounting
the steps she hastily covered her short nightdress with
a cotton wrapper and opened one of the french door
leading from her room to the verandah.

'Dad, can we have a talk, please?' she enquired
anxiously.

Turning in her direction, Granville nodded slightly,
a wry half smile catching at his lips. 'Mmm, I rather
thought you might be wanting to,' he conceded.

His words had Devon's throat constricting. So there
was something going on! With barely suppressed
apprehension she waited for him to be seated on the
upright chair at her work desk while she perched
herself on the end of the bed.

'You're curious as to my discussions with Royce and
Hunt,' he stated rather than asked.

'Just a little,' she smiled faintly. Not so much
Hunt, of course, since he only appeared to be one of
the crew, but Royce definitely!

He rubbed the tips of his fingers across his forehead
a couple of times, then expelled a long, slow breath.
'They're interested in buying the island,' he disclosed
bluntly.

Devon's eyes flew wide open in shock. That was
something she hadn't even remotely considered! His
'they're interested' only registering briefly. 'But—
you've no intention of selling, though, have you?' she
queried nervously, even as she tried to persuade
herself such an eventuality was totally unthinkable.
When all was said and done, there had been similar
offers in the past that had been refused.

He moved one shoulder in a non-committal gesture.
'They're talking of a seven figure sum, and it would

certainly mean all of us, including you and Garth, would never have any financial worries again.'

The monetary aspect of it Devon discounted immediately. There were other things more important than that. 'But this is our home! It always has been!' she protested. 'And as for Garth and myself, when the time comes what's wrong with us just continuing to run the guesthouse as our family's always done?'

'For you, maybe nothing, you're used to living out here, but Garth isn't, and of late I'm afraid I've begun to have my doubts as to whether he's capable of keeping the place going,' he sighed.

'Oh, of course he is!' she claimed defensively. 'In fact, with his qualifications as an accountant, I'd have thought he was perfect for the position of manager.'

'For balancing the books, he no doubt is,' Granville agreed. 'However, as you know full well, that isn't all he would be required to do, and that's what has me worried.'

'Such as?'

'Firstly, since it hardly makes for a cordial atmosphere, he would need to modify that somewhat distant attitude he shows towards the guests at times. . .'

'Well, naturally he would once they were his responsibility,' she inserted persuasively.

'And secondly,' he continued, 'his apparent aversion to physical activity of just about any kind doesn't particularly augur well for his keeping the place in running order when there's the jetty constantly needing repairs to retain it in even moderately serviceable order; the gardens to be attended to; the generators maintained; the house repainted regularly; the motorboat kept in good order since that's our

only private means of reaching the mainland; genera
household repairs to be effected; plus a hundred and
one other things that crop up from time to time, all o
which involve physical exertion.' He held up a hand
when she would have spoken. 'Oh, I know what you're
going to say—that he'll change when he realises it's up
to him to attend to all these matters—but unfortunately
I'm beginning to wonder if he will. I find it more
likely that after a few months or so he'll either be
leaving most of the work to *you*, or else he'll be
wanting to hire someone to do it for him. The first
prospect is one I intend to do my utmost to see never
occurs, and the second is one which could possibly
mean the difference between the island making a
profit, even though small, and a loss.'

'That's still no reason for considering selling the
place!' Devon burst out anguishedly. 'And if I'm
prepared to take a chance with Garth I don't see why
you shouldn't be too! You can't be certain that'
what's going to happen.'

Granville sighed, his expression sympathetically
understanding. 'No, that's true enough, but at my
age I think I do have a little more experience with
regard to human nature than you do, love, and in
this case can perhaps see matters with slightly more
objectivity.'

Devon bit at her lip disconsolately, her breathing
deep and disturbed. 'But I don't want to see the island
sold—to have to leave here—and nor will Aunt Violet,'
she all but choked. It was just too dispiriting to
contemplate!

'Yes—well—nothing's been finalised as yet, o
course. They're also only considering it at the
moment. It could take weeks before a decision is

ctually made, and then only if it's acceptable to all
concerned.'

He was attempting to make it sound less of a
foregone conclusion, she knew, but the fact that he
was really considering it did little to offer encouragement and her expression remained despondent.

'Anyway, just who did you mean when you said
they're interested in buying the island?' she questioned
moodily. 'I thought Hunt was one of the *Kanandah*'s
crew.'

To her surprise, and resentment that he could find
something humorous at such a stage, her father
chuckled. 'Whatever gave you that idea?'

Did that mean he wasn't? 'Well, he dresses like he
is, and he sure doesn't behave any better than some of
the rougher ones we've had call in here,' she grimaced.

'Oh? What makes you say that?'

Her turquoise eyes flashed stormily. If she could
only tell him precisely! 'Because he couldn't—or most
probably, wouldn't!—even apologise for disturbing me
this afternoon, and—and he's done nothing but goad
me about the incident ever since . . . as if I was the one
in the wrong!' she had to be satisfied with complaining
indignantly instead.

To her added annoyance he appeared to take no
exception to hearing that. 'Your reception of him
having been impeccable, of course,' he merely put
forward drily.

Her chin lifted defiantly. 'I don't know what you
mean.'

'Maybe not, but I certainly know *you*, love, and
what your reaction usually is when someone chances
exploring this side of the island.'

The same as his had been until today! 'Then

perhaps you should have remembered that before
giving him permission to look over the beach,' she
returned huffily.

'I did,' he laughed. 'But Hunt assured me he'd be
able to handle the situation, and ...' he sent her a
teasing glance, 'it would appear he succeeded.'

All too well! recalled Devon, her cheeks warming
involuntarily at the memory. 'Yes—well—in any
event, that's neither here nor there,' she shrugged
dismissively. Not surprisingly, the main origin of her
resentment wasn't something she wanted to dwell on.
'Then if he isn't one of the crew, just who is he?'

Her father's mouth tilted wryly. 'He's Chairman of
the Board of the Eastern Development Corporation.'

Momentarily, Devon stared at him in stunned
silence, and then she was shaking her head in disbelief.
'According to whom? Him?' She gave a lightly
sardonic laugh. 'I think you're being taken for a ride,
Dad. He couldn't possibly be Chairman of a Board.
He's not old enough for a start.'

'He has all the evidence necessary to prove it, as
does Royce,' her father shrugged. 'And I put a call
through to Brisbane this afternoon in order to check
the ownership of the *Kanandah*. It's registered to
Eastern Developments, all right.'

On the surface it appeared convincing, and
yet. . . 'And they just happened to be cruising around
here when they decided they wanted to buy an island,
did they?' she scoffed.

He half smiled at her vehemence and shook his
head. 'No, as a matter of fact they have a report with
them—which I found perhaps most conclusive of all—
that had been submitted by one of their own project
engineers some three or four months ago, in which it

was recommended that the island be studied in depth with a view to purchase and development,' he relayed. Then, with his brows raised enquiringly, 'Do you remember that nice young feller who was crewing on that big ocean-racing yacht that called in here. The— the. . .' He snapped his fingers impatiently as he tried to remember the name.

'The *Drifter*, you mean?' she supplied swiftly.

'Mmm, that was the name of it,' he nodded. 'And you remember the feller I'm talking about too, don't you?'

'Oh, yes, I remember Dean Henderson,' she confirmed with some asperity. Up until then she'd thought of him as being rather pleasant, but now she positively loathed him! 'So that was why he was up here asking all those questions, was it?'

'Apparently—and the reason for the *Kanandah* being in these waters now.'

'I see.' She pulled a disgruntled face. 'And Royce Attwood? Who's he, then? And how come you were doing most of your talking with him?'

'I understand he's Hunt's executive director, and the reason I was discussing the matter with him mostly was because, at this stage at least, Hunt was more interested in actually seeing something of the island for himself.' He paused, eyeing her watchfully. 'He also wants to undertake a thorough exploration of the whole island, as well as its special features, starting tomorrow morning, and I said I thought you'd be the best person to show it to him,' he concluded in something of a rush.

'No way!' Devon ejaculated in horrified accents. 'I can't—I won't do it, Dad! That's as good as asking me to help sell it!' She gazed at him with a hurt expression. 'Besides, I don't even like the man. Why can't he simply go looking on his own if he's so keen to see it? He didn't seem to have any objections to doing that this afternoon! Or why can't you show him? You certainly appear to get on well enough with him.' A hint of bitterness edged its way into her voice.

'I do,' he averred quietly. 'In fact, I happen to like him very much. He's down to earth, he lays it straight on the line without giving you any bull, he's done his homework on the subject, and he's got a great sense of humour.'

'A veritable prince among men, in fact,' she gibed acidly.

A remark that was studiously ignored. 'Nevertheless, as much as I'm sure I would enjoy his company while showing him what we have here, I suspect that these days you're more knowledgeable and definitely more capable—no doubt he'd like to go snorkelling over the reef, and you know I haven't done any of that for years—in that regard than I am, hence my suggestion that you accompany him.'

She sucked in a deep breath. 'And if—if I refuse?' she hazarded shakily, unable to recall the last time she had even contemplated not fulfilling one of her father's requests.

'He'll doubtless manage to see it all, anyhow.' Halting, he glanced down at the floor for a moment, then brought his gaze deliberately back to hers. 'While we both know who'll be the losers, don't we?'

Devon half turned away, pressing her lips together dejectedly. She didn't want him to be disappointed in her, or in herself either for that matter, as she knew she unquestionably would be in the months to come if she didn't accede to his request, but at the same time she felt she had to at least attempt to forestall the inevitable somehow.

'I—I've made arrangements to go to the waterfall with Garth in the morning,' she hedged throatily without looking at him.

The wooden chair creaked as her father left it and walked across to the bed, a work-roughened hand tipping her pensive and misty-eyed face up to his. 'Would it be too much to ask for you to postpone that until the afternoon?' Granville quizzed gently.

She partly spread her hands and then clenched them again in her lap. 'I don't expect there'll be time with the launch arriving.'

'You don't think he would be willing to exchange the waterfall for a few hours' reading?' whimsically.

Despite herself, a rueful smile caught at Devon's wide mouth. 'Probably,' she conceded. As Garth had said, he was planning to take a book along anyway.

'Then you will act as Hunt's guide?'

'Oh, I suppose so,' she sighed resignedly. The look in her eyes suddenly turned urgent. 'If you're sure this is what you really want?'

His fingers lingered softly against her chin for a second before he dropped his hand to his side. 'The only thing I'm sure of at the moment is that I'd like to know all the pros and cons before I make *any* decision,' he assured her. 'That is, of course, apart from being very certain I couldn't possibly love my daughter any more than I do right now, and all I care about is seeing her well provided for, both now and in the future.'

'Oh, Dad!' she cried helplessly. 'You make me feel so ungrateful, and yet all I want is for things to remain the same as they've always been.'

'I know, love, I know,' he smiled fondly. 'But I'm not getting any younger, and sometimes we just have to make the best of things and that includes changes when they come.'

They were words Devon was still turning over in her mind when she returned to her bed after her father had gone, and although she vowed to at least try not to make her father's decision any more difficult than it already obviously would be, where someone else was concerned she felt quite entitled to attempt to influence the outcome—by whatever means she could!

CHAPTER THREE

THE minute Devon walked into the kitchen the following morning and saw her aunt's thoughtful expression she knew someone else had been there before her.

'Dad's already told you, I gather,' she deduced with a faint half smile.

'He has,' Violet nodded as she continued turning the bacon in the pan on top of the range.

When nothing else appeared to be forthcoming, Devon peered at her more closely. 'And?'

Her aunt shrugged indeterminately. 'Well, I'm not in favour of it, naturally, but it's his right to sell if he so wishes, and . . .' she sighed, her lips pursing, 'I must admit I can understand his reasons for considering it—especially since the initial offer is so tempting.'

'Initial offer?' probed Devon curiously.

'Oh, you know how it is, these things are always negotiable. It all depends on the final conditions—ours and theirs,' Violet declared with the knowledge born of other such approaches. 'At this stage you can't even be certain it will come to anything. No doubt they'll want to cost the whole project first—construction of new buildings, improved facilities, faster and more frequent methods of access to and from the mainland, the anticipated number of likely guests and so forth—and only then will it be decided if the deal actually goes through or not.'

Devon touched her teeth to her lower lip in silent contemplation as she began breaking eggs into another pan, her aunt's information surprising her a little. 'Have any previous offers Dad's received reached the costing stage, then?' she questioned. She couldn't remember any herself that had done so.

Violet attended to the steaks already sizzling under the grill before speaking. 'A couple. The most recent while you were away at boarding school, but none of them proceeded any further. When they discovered they couldn't use their costs as a lever for persuading your father into letting the place go for a song they soon disappeared back to where they'd come from.' Pausing, her demeanour turned meditative again. 'As a matter of fact, I rather think that's why he's prepared to be more than usually helpful now to Messrs Attwood and Kincaid. At least it seems they're willing to be fair, and didn't just breeze on to the island as a few others have done and insult his intelligence by treating him like some rustic simpleton who had no idea what the place was worth.'

More or less as her father had intimated the night before, Devon brooded, and on hearing footsteps behind her, turned to find Garth entering the room.

'Morning!' He included them both in his greeting. 'Although I must say you two are looking somewhat pensive today. Anything wrong?'

Since there didn't appear to be any soft way of breaking the news, Devon came out with it flatly. 'Dad's considering selling the island.'

For a second Garth's jaw dropped, so great was his obvious surprise, and then it closed again with a snap. 'But he can't!' he expostulated indignantly. 'What about the plans for us to take over here? Or isn't our future of any importance now? I suppose this is a perfect way for him to get that new boat he's doubtlessly after, is that it?'

Although she didn't doubt such a purchase could be high on her father's list of priorities—if the sale was concluded—Devon was still positive it wouldn't have been a deciding factor in his decision and, as a result, took great exception to her fiancé's unwarranted contention that it had been. Nor did she particularly care for his attitude of apparently only seeing such a sale in the light of how it might affect himself.

'Not as far as I'm aware, no!' she repudiated sharply. 'While as for our future, as it so happens I understand that *was* a major consideration in his decision.'

'Oh!' Some of his indignation began to disappear, but whether because of her last statement, or because of her bristling response, she couldn't be certain. 'You mean, *that's* what he was discussing all yesterday afternoon?' His upper lip curled satirically. 'No wonder he didn't want me around. He knew I would have had something to say about it.'

'In your capacity as the island's accountant?' put in Violet subtly.

A mottled stain coloured his rather pale cheeks. 'Yes—well—in that guise also, I expect,' he blustered. 'After all, it is my place to advise and guide in these matters, and—and I really think my recommendations should have been sought before he consented to discuss whatever proposal has been put to him.' Abruptly, he began to look worried. 'He hasn't signed anything yet, has he? For all we know they could be attempting to rob him blind! Oh, well, even if he has, I'm sure I'll be able to circumvent it somehow.' Sounding considerably more relieved.

'That is, only if Dad wishes you to,' Devon stated succinctly. 'Not that I can imagine him having done anything of the kind so precipitately anyway. He's not exactly senile, you know, Garth.'

'No, no, of course not,' he hastened to placate her. 'I wasn't really intending to imply that he was. It's just that some of these people are very smooth operators, and I don't believe now, with the real estate market as depressed as it is, is the correct time to even be considering selling—as no doubt that Kincaid feller is well aware!' His voice hardened with dislike. 'That's probably what he's banking on. Getting it cheap now and then re-selling it once the market improves, and pocketing the extra profits that should be ours!'

'Well ... Dad's,' she couldn't help amending pointedly. 'In any event, I would hardly call an offer of seven figures attempting to buy it on the cheap.'

'Seven, you said?' Garth queried immediately, his eyes widening. 'And the exact amount?'

'I didn't bother to ask,' she all but flared. She didn't know whether she was being overly sensitive this morning, but to her mind she didn't really think he should have been asking either. 'I wasn't particularly interested. Especially as I hope nothing comes of the whole affair. I'd willingly forgo any financial benefit in order to continue living here. As I'm sure Aunt Violet would too, wouldn't you?' She looked to her relative for corroboration.

'Oh, unquestionably,' that woman promptly concurred with feeling. 'I couldn't imagine living anywhere else now after all these years. It's really become home to me.'

With the last of the hot foods now ladled into covered warming dishes, Devon and her aunt began carrying them through to the dining room where they were placed alongside the fruits and cereals already laid out on a long, polished sideboard. Breakfast and lunch were always casual meals with no stringently set time tables so the guests could arrive as it suited them and help themselves.

Seeing Garth following her, empty-handed, on one such trip, Devon nodded towards the dish filled with triangles of golden toast that was still on the kitchen table.

'Bring that in for me, will you, please, Garth?' she requested. 'It's the only one left.'

'Oh, all right,' he agreed, but to her amazement seeming a trifle aggrieved at having been asked to do something so menial. Then, as he caught up to her again, 'How long do you expect it to take you to pack your designs, etcetera, after breakfast?'

'Not long. Only about fifteen minutes or so,' she replied. The subject suddenly triggered a reminder of her promise to her father—how could she have forgotten!—and she came to a halt just before the dining-room doorway. 'Oh, by the way, I'm very sorry but we can't go to the waterfall, after all. Or at least I can't,' she modified with a grimace. 'Dad's asked me to act as guide for one of our *visitors*,' sardonically, 'on a tour of the island this morning.'

'Which one? Kincaid?' he immediately wanted to know, his tone sour.

She pulled another expressive face. 'Unfortunately!'

'And it has to be this morning? Why not some other time?'

'He apparently wants to see all the island has to offer as soon as possible,' she shrugged.

'In order to provide him with more ideas for making

money out of the place, I suppose!' Garth sneered.
'Well, I think I'll just go along with you. He can't
have any objections to that, can he?'

Considering Hunt's comments regarding her fiancé
the day before, Devon thought it more than likely, and
because of that she found she too was a little reluctant
to have him accompany them. It would be difficult
enough as it was putting up with Hunt on his own,
without having the pair of them needling each other
the whole time as well.

'I wouldn't know, but I'm afraid *I* don't really think
it's such a good idea, Garth,' she owned in as
apologetic a manner as she could. But on seeing him
about to protest, went on hurriedly. 'I mean, it's more
than probable Royce Attwood will be talking to Dad
again today, and surely it's more important for you to
be available to sit in on their discussions.'

'Provided I'm allowed, that is!' pungently.

'Oh, I can't see why you wouldn't be. Not now that
the secret's out, anyway,' she predicted confidently.
'Besides, you know how much you dislike hiking all
over the place, and I intend to set such a pace that he
won't have an opportunity to get more than a passing
glance at anything, and you'd only hate it even more
under those circumstances. Also,' she half smiled
impishly, 'I only mean to show him the worst aspects
of the island in any case. I'm sure not going to make it
easy for him to decide whether Cowrie's suitable for
what he's got in mind.'

'That's the way!' Garth approved with acrid
pleasure. 'If we can't alter your father's attitude,
perhaps we can alter his.'

'Precisely!' Devon nodded in emphasis. 'So while
I'm putting that scheme into action this morning,

you'll stay here and find out what's happening this end with Dad?'

'Mmm, as you say, that's no doubt the best way to play it,' he conceded, and in a mood of complete accord they entered the dining room together.

As soon as the meal was concluded Garth disappeared in search of Granville—who always breakfasted at a much earlier hour in the kitchen—and knowing he would be dogging her father's footsteps for the remainder of the day, Devon couldn't help but smile. Her father's activities had certainly never created such an interest in her fiancé before.

In the meantime she cleaned and tidied the dining room quickly while her aunt attended to the kitchen, and then returned to her bedroom in order to sort and pack her most recent designs in a heavy folder ready for transport to the mainland on the trading launch. She still had a few of them laid out on the bed as she deliberated whether to include them all or not, when there was a knock at the open door that led on to the verandah and on looking round she saw Hunt's tall figure filling the doorway. Dressed similarly to the day before in T-shirt and shorts, he seemed to fill the room with a disturbing aura of unassailable masculinity as he casually ambled inside to take a look at the paintings on the bed.

'Matt said I'd probably find you here,' he said lazily. 'You wouldn't be trying to avoid our little tour of the island, would you?'

Confused slightly, both by his nonchalant entrance and his presence that seemed to totally dominate the femininely decorated room her father had been the only male to enter previously, Devon backed away a few steps in an effort to lessen the feeling of being helplessly overwhelmed.

'N-no, of course not. Why would I do that?' she countered, if a little jerkily. 'I—I was just getting these ready,' she rushed to gather up the colourfully patterned sheets of paper, 'for the boat this afternoon, that's all.'

'I see.' His attractively shaped mouth curved wryly, and before she could stop him he calmly removed the designs from her suddenly lifeless fingers and began spreading them out on her bed once more. 'What are they for?'

'S-souvenir designs,' she stammered—much to her annoyance that she should be permitting him to affect her so. 'I sell them to a shop in Northport.'

'They're very good,' he commended, continuing to peruse them intently. 'I like that one in particular,' Pointing to a palm-silhouetted sunset. And slanting her a quizzical gaze, 'Have you ever done any solely promoting the island?'

She hunched a darkly golden shoulder diffidently. 'I did a couple for some ashtrays and tea towels once, but most of our guests aren't the type to go in for T-shirts, sarongs, beach towels, and that sort of thing.'

'Although you could devise some exclusive designs if there was a market for them?'

'I guess so if . . .' She halted, suddenly realising the direction of his thoughts. 'If I felt like it,' she stressed meaningfully. She was damned if she'd help promote the island for his benefit when it meant she wouldn't be able to live there any more!

Hunt merely grinned and turned his attention to the wall beside her bed while Devon hastily re-gathered her paintings once again. 'You also do murals, I see,' he mused.

Glancing up involuntarily, she surveyed the brightly coloured scene of various corals and sea life she had painted the year before, and which his eyes were now ranging over measuringly. 'Not really,' she denied. 'That's the only one I've ever done and I've never really been satisfied with it.'

'Why not? It looks extremely life-like to me.'

Deliberately excluding the design Hunt had said he'd liked, although she wasn't at all certain just why she retained it, Devon added the rest to the folder and began tying its securing cords. 'Oh, the giant clam isn't quite in proportion, and there's just something wrong with the Imperial Angel fish,' she relayed absently.

'Which one's that?' he smiled down at her drily.

Discovering her own lips to be waywardly curving in response, she clamped them together determinedly and busied herself with inserting the folder within its special waterproof covering. 'The one with the purple and black markings on its head, and royal blue and yellow striped body,' she advised coolly.

'I can't see anything wrong with it,' he declared after a few moments.

'Mmm, but then you didn't even know which one it was either, did you?' she quipped sardonically.

'Which just goes to show how much there is for you to teach me.'

At that, Devon's head lifted swiftly. 'What do you mean . . . teach you?' she demanded, startled. 'Dad only asked me to show you over the island. Nothing else!'

'You could also impart a little information along the

way, though, couldn't you?' His vivid blue eyes met
hers mockingly.

In defence, she half turned away on the pretext of
sealing the folder's cover. 'What makes you think any
such information I might give you would be the truth?
I'm not at all interested in seeing the island sold, you
know.'

'So Matt said, but I still think I'll back my own
judgment as to when you're telling the truth and when
you're not.' He paused, a lopsided smile pulling at his
lips. 'Matt also warned me you could be tempted to
try something of the sort.'

Oh, had he? She was beginning to wonder just
whose side her father was on! That was also the second
time he had referred to her parent as Matt—something
Garth still hadn't been invited to do as yet!—and the
fact that her father appeared to have accepted this
man—of all people—so willingly, and so readily,
infuriated her. But that very same anger did at least
enable her to now face him challengingly.

'Then if you would care to put your judgment to the
test, Mr Kincaid. . .' Leaving the folder on the bed
she indicated the door with an outspread hand.

'Hunt,' he corrected drily without moving.

Since that was how she already thought of him, it
seemed rather senseless not to comply, even though
she considered there was perhaps more reason for
keeping him at a distance now than there had been
yesterday. 'Very well, then,' she consented primly. 'So
now shall we go?'

'After you, beautiful,' he drawled. 'We've got a lot
of ground to cover out there.'

And all of which she would see they did so in as
short a time as possible, she vowed as she stepped out

on to the verandah and began leading the way around to the steps at the back of the house and then across the lawn to a different track from the one they had used the day before.

'Where are we going first?' Hunt queried indolently as he followed her in among the leafy vegetation.

'I thought we'd take this walking track right through to the seaward side and then make our way back around the perimeter of the island from there,' Devon disclosed without turning to look at him. Mostly in order to hide the pleasurable twinkle evident in her eyes. First impressions always seemed to make the greatest impact, so where better to start than the least imposing areas.

As they passed she reeled off some of the names of the trees, although only the exotic ones he wasn't likely to remember, as well as some of the birds her accustomed eyes picked up among the branches. However, after only travelling a few hundred yards, she disappointingly found her rapid pace beginning to slow as the heat of the day—January was always their hottest month—made it impossible even for her, as used to it as she was, to keep it up for too long, and when they reached the point where another track branched to the left of their own and Hunt determinedly brought her to a halt by catching hold of her arm, she wasn't entirely sorry.

'Hold it, sweetheart!' he ordered wryly. 'Where does that lead to?'

'Only The Pinnacle,' she revealed in as unsinterested a tone as possible.

'Which provides a view of the whole of the island?'

'In a manner of speaking.'

'Meaning?' He eyed her speculatively from beneath narrowed lids.

'Only that it's not really high enough to give a decent view,' she lied. In truth, the view from the top was nothing short of breathtaking—and the very reason she didn't want it to be the first place they visited. The fact that there were two sailors' graves—crew members from the ship that gave Careen Beach its name early in the previous century—to inspect along the route, as well as a cave filled with Aboriginal paintings from an even earlier period, she conveniently forgot to mention at all. She merely shrugged and proposed, 'You could always go up there some other time, if you really wanted to. You don't need me to show it to you.'

For a brief moment she didn't think he intended taking her word for it as he looked along the branching path interestedly, and her heart raced, but then to her immeasurable relief he gave a faint smile and indicated they should continue along the track she had originally chosen.

After the short, somewhat cooling rest, Devon set off again as fast as she could, but this time Hunt wasn't waiting until something of interest caught his attention before bringing her to a stop, and no sooner had she gone a few yards than a hand gripped the nape of her neck and effectively brought her to a standstill.

'Okay, sweetheart, you've had your fun,' he drawled. 'Now just let's take it a bit slower, shall we? I'd like to at least take note of something while we're on this little jaunt.'

'Oh, I am sorry if I was going too fast for you. I forgot you're probably more used to travelling everywhere by car,' she apologised, provokingly tongue-in-cheek. 'It's just that I have to get back to help Aunt Violet with the lunch, you see.'

'No, you don't. Matt said he'd help out in the kitchen if you weren't back in time,' he both surprised and irritated her by advising. Her father's co-operation was becoming hard to believe—and even harder to take! 'Nor were you going too fast for me. I'd simply appreciate taking in the scenery a little more. If you have no objections, that is?' His dark head tilted enquiringly, tauntingly.

'Not at all,' she pretended, grimacing inwardly at having her plan partially thwarted. 'Does this suit you better?' She set off once more, but at a veritable snail's pace on this occasion.

'All right! If that's the way you want it!'

There was some nuance in Hunt's voice that had her about-facing warily, and just in time to see him bend before she was slung unceremoniously over a broad shoulder, a bronzed and sinewed arm wrapping around her bare legs, ensuring she remained there. With a muffled cry of surprise and outrage, Devon immediately began to pound clenched fists against his muscular back.

'How dare you! Put me down this instant, you damned great ape!' she half demanded, half panted as he resumed walking—at a normal speed. 'Put me down this instant, do you hear?' Her voice rose wrathfully.

'I hear,' he averred drily, the predominantly amused tone only enraging her further.

'Well, then?' she heaved impatiently, her pummelling action growing weaker as her arms started to tire.

'I'll put you down when you promise to behave, and when you *ask* instead of commanding me to do so . . . not before!' came the decisive return.

'*Ask* to be put down!' she flared. 'Why should I? I didn't *ask* to be treated so—so barbarously!'

'Didn't you?' he countered lazily. 'I figured you did.'

'You would! You obviously don't know any better, you—you. . . .' She broke off as the breath was knocked out of her when he effortlessly jumped a shallow gully that crossed the path, but promptly resumed once they were back on to even ground. 'I knew immediately I set eyes on you yesterday that you were nothing but an inconsiderate, insensitive. . . . Ouch!' A none too gentle slap on her behind had her crying out resentfully.

'Then be quiet,' she was directed on a sardonic note. 'It would be an enjoyable walk if it wasn't for your squawking.'

Her *squawking*! About to begin another tirade, Devon suddenly thought better of it. Against someone like him it obviously wouldn't have any effect, and apart from that, since every step he took jolted her stomach unmercifully she was only making it worse for herself by continuing.

'All right! *Please* put me down!' she was finally forced into requesting.

To her relief that at least had him stopping, although he didn't immediately make any move to release her. 'And are you going to behave, instead of acting like a peevish, spoilt brat?'

'Oh, yes, anything, but just put me down,' she pleaded. It would be altogether too much to bear if they happened to come across some of the island's guests while she was in such a mortifying position.

'Anything?' Dark brows rose graphically above taunting blue eyes as he finally consented to do as she wished, but without fully relinquishing his hold on her as his encircling arms held her loosely, but discomposingly, close to his rugged frame.

Flustered, and unable to answer in kind as a result, Devon broke away from him resentfully. 'God, I hate you!' she gritted. 'I wish you'd never come here! You really think you're a law unto yourself, don't you?'

'Because I refused to passively submit to your contrary little antics?' Up went those expressive brows of his again.

'Because although you may have managed to ingratiate yourself with my father, that doesn't give you the right to mistreat and humiliate me as and when you feel like it!'

'Not even when it's deserved?'

She noticed he hadn't denied it! 'According to whom . . . you?' she countered scornfully. 'Considering your behaviour has been nothing short of disgraceful ever since you arrived, I wouldn't have thought you were in a position to criticise anyone else's!'

His firmly moulded mouth slanted mockingly. 'Except for a certain, obviously over-indulged young female who likes to give out with the orders, of course.'

'Where you're concerned, why wouldn't I?' she sniped. 'And as for my being over-indulged—I certainly am not! However, if that's the way you feel, no doubt you'd prefer to continue your explorations without me.' She spun on her heel and started back towards the house.

'Oh, no, you don't sweetheart!' A hand on her arm brought her up short. 'You agreed to be my guide, and my guide you're going to be.' He tapped a finger against her chin aggravatingly. 'Even if I have to resort to carrying you again.'

He would too, the brute! she fumed silently, railing against the knowledge that she really had no option but to continue with him. Dragging free of his grip, she glared at him impotently. 'Well, come on, then!' she heaved in patent dissatisfaction as she began heading along the track once more. 'I haven't got all day!'

'Your fiancé's anxiously awaiting your return, is he?' came the drawling enquiry from behind her.

'Why wouldn't he be?' she half turned to retort with some asperity. 'After all, we did have plans of our own for this morning!'

'For example . . .?'

Her head lifted fractionally higher, but this time she didn't turn. 'That's our business, not yours!'

'You could have brought him along with us . . . or didn't you want to?'

Now Devon did swing round, rapidly. 'I don't know just what you're trying to imply by that, but you can forget it, whatever it is!' He couldn't possibly think she had *wanted* to be alone with him, could he? 'The reason Garth isn't accompanying us is because he has more important things to do.'

'Such as keeping close to Matt in case he has any more discussions with Royce?' surmised Hunt drily on catching up to her.

She dropped her gaze discomfitedly. His deduction had been too shrewd for her liking, and she really wasn't certain she wanted to admit as much. 'What makes you think that?' she parried therefore.

'Probably because he comes across as the type who has his eyes open for the main chance all the time, and right at the moment I don't doubt he's got the wind up at the thought of his inheritance, via you, disappearing,' he contended on a wry note.

Devon's glance flashed back up to his irately. 'That's not true, and how dare you even suggest such a thing! He just doesn't want to see the island sold, that's all. The same as I don't.'

'Well, not at present, and by your father, at any rate. Once the two of you are married, and he has more say, I suspect it would be an entirely different proposition.'

Devon's anger escalated uncontrollably in spite of the sudden remembrance of Garth claiming now wasn't the time to sell. Did that mean, as her companion had just claimed so obnoxiously, that he wouldn't be averse to doing so at some other time? She gave herself a mental shake. No, of course it hadn't meant that. The man beside her was simply attempting to make her believe it was.

'Oh, yes, you'd like me to think that, wouldn't you?' she jeered contemptuously. 'Setting me against my fiancé would unquestionably suit *your* plans admirably. It's called driving a split between the opposition, isn't it?' She halted momentarily, her breasts rising and falling rapidly beneath her thin cotton top. 'How would you know anything about Garth, or his thoughts, anyway? You've only spoken to him once!' Apart from a nodded acknowledgment there definitely hadn't been any communication between the two of them last night at the camp.

Hunt's lips quirked half wryly, half derogatorily. 'And as I said yesterday . . . that was enough.'

Just his expression was sufficient to have her inhaling wrathfully. 'Due to your being such an infallible mind reader, I suppose?' she scoffed in acid tones.

'No, just practised in dealings of this nature, and consequently wise as to just how avaricious some people can be,' he shrugged casually. 'We meet all kinds in our line of work.'

'And so do I here on the island ... witness yourself,' she smiled with sweet sarcasm.

'Mmm, most of whom you pass a few pleasantries with during their week or so's visit and that's the sum total of your knowledge of them. Hardly a sound basis for judging a person's character, would you say?' he goaded. 'In fact, you've lived such a sheltered and secluded life here that I wouldn't mind betting Garth Wilkinson is the only male under the age of fifty you've ever really been associated with, and that merely because his father's firm has been handling the island's affairs for the last thirty years or more.'

'Oh, that's ridiculous!' she rejected his suggestion disdainfully. 'Naturally I've met other young men. The bottom camp is usually full of them.'

'Except I didn't claim you'd never *met* any, just that you'd never associated with another one for any length of time. So tell me ...' he invited, his head tilting quizzically, his thickly lashed eyes alive with a bantering light, 'just how many of these other younger men have you ever become involved with—in a romantic sense, shall we say?'

Unconsciously, Devon's steps faltered a little. 'I— well—none really, I guess,' honesty forced her into conceding, albeit with extreme reluctance. But on catching sight of the satisfied smile beginning to pull at the edges of his shapely mouth, promptly defended, 'Not that that means anything, anyhow, and—and especially where Garth is concerned!'

'It hasn't exactly provided you with the experience

to make a valid comparison either, though, has it?' he
asserted drily.

'It's only you who's ever suggested I should do so,
and we both know your reasons for wanting me to
doubt him now, don't we?' it was her turn to mock. 'It
would make matters so much more simple for you
with my father, wouldn't it?'

Hunt flexed a wide shoulder dispassionately. 'I
wasn't aware Matt either needed your consent, or even
a lack of opposition on your part, in order to make his
decision.'

Devon abruptly caught at her lower lip with even
white teeth to halt its dismayed trembling.
Unfortunately, he was all too correct. 'How thoughtful
of you to remind me,' she quipped in throaty tones.
'That must really have made your day.'

'No, far from it, as a matter of fact.' He raked a
hand through his hair irritably as his gaze rested on
her despondent profile. 'And I'm sorry. It was a
tactless remark to have made under the circumstances.
Believe it or not, I can understand why you're so
against a change in the status quo here.'

Although her eyes had flickered briefly in his
direction on hearing him apologise—that was definitely
something she hadn't anticipated—they were now
firmly fixed to the track again. 'Nevertheless, anything
so unproductive as personal feelings won't be allowed
to stand in your way, of course,' she disparaged.

He gave a rueful half laugh. 'With the potential I
believe this place to have, I couldn't afford to.'

'Ah, yes, I was forgetting the quest for the almighty
dollar, wasn't I? It means everything to the likes of
you, doesn't it?'

'Does it?' For the first time she detected something

of a bite in his voice rather than its customary
drawling indolence. 'I see it more as providing a
location many can enjoy instead of merely a few ... *if*
it's decided to go ahead and purchase it, that is!'

So there was still some hope, noted Devon in relief,
her step becoming infinitesimally lighter as they
approached the low dunes denoting the end of the
path. 'But it's my *home!*' she still lamented. 'And it's
not as if there aren't dozens of other islands on the reef
people can visit. I would have thought the market was
saturated with them already.'

'Sorry, but our surveys indicate otherwise,' he
contradicted, but this time without sounding at all
apologetic. 'Particularly for the kind of resort we
envisage.'

'Huh! One with music blaring continuously, the day
organised from beginning to end, and an elaborate
swimming pool surrounded by artificial grass no
doubt just so guests can lounge around a garish
complex without actually having to be—ghastly
thought!—contaminated by the salt and the sand, I
suppose,' she derided.

'Vixen!' he surprised her by grinning as he gave a lock
of her blonde hair a lightly punishing tug. 'Actually, it's
just the opposite. My thoughts are to make a true "get
away from it all" resort where people can really unwind
by leaving it in as natural a state as possible, but with
better service and accommodation available, as well as
providing the necessary facilities for a greater range of
activities for those who do wish to participate in them.'

'Such as?' she probed, curious in spite of trying not
to be.

'Oh, scuba diving, sail-boarding, fishing excursions,
trips to the outer reef, ski paddling, that kind of

thing,' he disclosed idly. Then, with a slow, easy smile that unaccountably had her heart pounding, 'What do you think of the idea?'

Annoyed with herself for having allowed him to generate such a reaction within her, even if involuntary, Devon took her anger out on him. 'Since I won't be living here any more if it does happen, what does it matter what I think?' she snubbed before walking swiftly across the dunes and on to the gently sloping beach.

Hunt followed casually, his expression enigmatic. 'You're a real little tiger when aroused, aren't you, sweetheart?' he drawled. 'However, I would recommend you to cool it somewhat or you may find yourself engendering the same feelings in others.'

'In other words, I'm to treat you deferentially while you do as you like, is that it?' she retorted even as she whirled to face him watchfully. Unsure as to his mood, but remembering his threat to carry her in that humiliating manner again, she decided it could be prudent to keep a wary eye on him. Not that it stopped her from continuing on a scornfully gibing note. 'So what are you going to do if I fail to comply? Take my home away from me? You probably will anyway!' She glared at him direfully.

'That's as may be,' he granted with another hunching of his powerful shoulders. 'But until then I could just be tempted to settle for silencing you ... the most effective way possible.'

'Oh, and what way would that be?' she just had time to challenge haughtily before finding out all too swiftly as he abruptly pulled her towards him and set his mouth to hers before she could think of protesting, let alone evade him.

With a smothered gasp Devon immediately hit out at him, only to have her arms pinioned against her sides when his own enfolding arms swept her closer. Frantic now lest the lips that were moving against hers so demandingly somehow managed to induce a response as they had the afternoon before, she tried holding her soft mouth rigid, but to no avail she discovered in despair, as it seemed determined to disregard her efforts at control and traitorously parted in submission.

Again he had succeeded in catching her off-guard, but that was little consolation when she was all too confusedly and embarrassedly aware that her lips were beginning to cling to his with an ardour she had never before experienced, even with her fiancé.

When Hunt finally raised his head, temporarily Devon could only stare at him helplessly until she had regained some of her composure and then she broke free infuriatedly. 'When I tell my father about this . . .!' she threatened on a ragged and resentful note.

His lips twisted wryly. 'That I kissed you—or that you responded . . . again?' he taunted.

'I—you . . . that has nothing to do with it!' she was reduced to contending uncomfortably, her embarrassment complete at knowing full well there was no way she could actually refute such a claim. 'How—how dare you keep a-assaulting me in such a fashion! I happen to be engaged, and—and I would appreciate it if you'd respect that fact!'

'Because your fiancé would object?'

'Because *I* object!' she all but shouted.

'Although only afterwards, hmm?'

Devon flushed hotly. 'No! I. . . . Oh, you're the most despicable man it's ever been my misfortune to know!' she denounced, and turning away, began walking along the beach with her head downbent.

And that was the whole trouble, she deliberated half angrily, half defeatedly. As he had so correctly surmised, apart from her father and Garth, she *didn't* know many other men, at least not well, and where Hunt was concerned that inexperience really had her at a loss as to how to deal with him. He was totally different from anyone she had ever met and he made her feel perturbingly vulnerable on occasion, particularly when he utilised that pointed mockery of his with such telling effect.

'You know, if you keep heading off on your own like this you'll have me thinking my presence is unwanted.' A wryly amused voice suddenly sounded beside her.

Devon half shrugged, but didn't speak, despite the great temptation to do so. It was really too soon for her to want to engage in another confrontation, verbal or otherwise, especially since the last one had been so disastrous from her standpoint.

'Nor was it my intention to silence you completely for the remainder of the morning,' Hunt went on in the same humorous accents.

Starting to smoulder inwardly once more—he really was the most unsettling and aggravating individual she had ever come across!—it was impossible for her to continuing holding her tongue while he enjoyed himself at her expense.

'And it was my understanding this tour was to enable you to see something of the island, not simply to provide you with the opportunity to continually bait me!' she snapped.

'You were the one who began by playing cute, beautiful,' he drawled succinctly.

Unfortunately, that that was another claim she couldn't in all honesty repudiate didn't make Devon feel any better. The more so when she suspected that no matter how she had behaved it wouldn't have precluded that goading attitude of his from coming to the fore.

'Oh, for heaven's sake, stop calling me that!' she directed irritably instead, hopeful of diverting him. It was easier than trying to defend the indefensible.

'Calling you what . . . beautiful?' he quizzed lazily, his eyes roaming over her perfectly formed features and slender, curving shape thoroughly, and bringing a warm wave of colour to her cheeks as a result. 'But you are . . . very! Or hasn't your fiancé ever told you that?'

Actually, he hadn't, but she had no intention of admitting as much. Besides, her Aunt Violet always maintained it was what was on the inside that counted, not the outside, and she said as much to the man beside her.

'Well, I've still always believed in saying what I think, and I don't intend to stop now,' she was informed in leisurely but decisive tones. Suddenly, he laughed. 'No matter if you do apparently find it disconcerting.'

So he'd guessed that, had he? she fumed. All the more reason probably why he continued to do it! 'Unwelcome, is how I would have put it,' she consequently parried in a sardonic voice. And hurriedly seeking a less personal subject, waved her arm to indicate the view to seaward. 'Well, now that you're here, does it meet with your approval?' her enquiry was facetiously made. With the tide almost to its lowest ebb, it was really one of the least prepossessing areas of the island. Only the small patch of mosquito-infested mangroves with its tangled root systems and thick, oozing mud was worse, and that was next on her itinerary for his inspection!

Briefly, Hunt's gaze took in the gnarled ti-trees lining the dunes, their twisted limbs evidence of the force of the winds that could sweep in from the open ocean, and then moved on to the low, undulating ridges of shell-encrusted beach rock that stretched unbroken from high water mark to fifty yards or more out to sea. In this section there was no coral visible at all.

'Not particularly,' he owned at length, giving Devon cause for a surreptitious smile of satisfaction. 'But then I imagine it wasn't supposed to either.'

With her smile fading even more rapidly than it had appeared—her father couldn't possibly have deduced her intentions and warned him accordingly, could he?—she rounded her aquamarine eyes in an expression of innocent surprise. 'Whatever do you mean? How should I know what appeals to you? I'm merely showing you the island ... as asked, that's all.' Her curling lashes lowered a little, her glance becoming taunting. 'Or were you anticipating total perfection?'

'Uh-uh.' He shook his head slowly. 'I've done enough research on the subject to have a fair idea of what I'd find.' Pausing, he added drily. 'As well as harbouring an extremely strong suspicion you wouldn't be revealing Cowrie's best features willingly.'

Devon impulsively gave a disgruntled grimace. He always seemed to be one step ahead of her! Or was she just transparent? Either way it didn't exactly fill her with confidence at being able to circumvent *his* plans.

'We had to start somewhere,' she offered in pseudo deprecation.

'Mmm, so we did,' he smiled easily. In fact, he always had a ready smile, and a far too damned attractive one at that, observed Devon irrelevantly, and much to her vexation as well as consternation. 'Then while we're here we might as well view it in close-up, mightn't we?' Lifting a hand to the nape of her neck he began urging her along with him towards the undulating rock, catching her completely by surprise in realising he was even interested in looking at it more closely. Garth really hadn't been.

Treading carefully as they went in order to avoid the sharp-edged shells that were fixed to the rocks in patches, they made their way out some distance from the shore to where the sandy pools between the ridges were a little deeper, and then proceeded to walk slowly in a line parallel to the beach. Most of the crystal-clear pockets of water contained some forms of life—crabs, small fish, and the like—but it was the occupants of some of the larger ones that had them stopping. A few were temporarily playing host to some young stingarees and manta rays, while at the bottom of others basked some small, beautifully marked epaulette sharks.

'We get quite a number of those,' advised Devon in what she trusted was a suitably warning tone, even though the species was actually harmless. With her home at stake, she'd decided this was to be a no holds barred war and meant to make use of anything and everything she possibly could.

'It's just as well they don't trouble humans, then, isn't it?' Hunt countered with a wryly knowing grin that immediately told her that effort had been unsuccessful. 'How about the other, less inoffensive, kinds?'

'Oh, we see loads of them too,' she exaggerated airily, trying again. 'Black tips, white tips, tigers, whalers, hammerheads. We often find them trapped in the lagoon after the tide's turned and the water's too low for them to get out again over the reef.'

'Often?' A dark brow peaked meaningfully.

'Well, occasionally,' she was prepared to concede, shrugging. More in the order of perhaps one or two a year if the truth were known, but she wasn't about to tell him that.

'Nor do all these species you mentioned happen to be dangerous, do they?'

'Oh, I don't know about that,' she evaded.

'I do,' he returned, expressively dry.

Devon attempted to camouflage her frustration as best she was able. Blast the man! He *did* appear to have done his homework, as her father had claimed. 'Yes—well—I guess it all—er—depends on which book you read on the subject,' she made an effort to pass the matter off with as much nonchalance as she could muster.

Hunt didn't even bother to reply, and not because he was in the process of divesting himself of his T-shirt and draping it around the back of his neck either, she suspected, but simply because his silence showed more adequately than words would have done just what he thought of her explanation. Deciding two defeats were enough, she began heading back to the beach with the surefootedness of long practise.

For a time Hunt continued on their original course, but when the rock began to peter out he too made his way back to shore, and only a little less agilely than she had done, she noted with some asperity. Wasn't there anything he failed at? The only time Garth had been out there with her it had taken him an age to gingerly return to the sand.

'So what's the next delight you doubtlessly have in store for me?' Hunt questioned whimsically on rejoining her.

In the act of studiously trying to ignore the imposing sight he made as the skin of his muscled torso gleamed like burnished mahogany beneath the sun's brilliant rays—good lord, she wasn't an adolescent to be affected so by mere physical attributes, was she? Devon rushed into unthinking speech.

'The mangroves,' she blurted, and then promptly berated herself for having been so informative. She had intended keeping them as a surprise.

'That should be fun,' he drawled on a satirical note. 'Maybe we'll see a few large mud crabs on our way through.'

From having been pleasurably anticipating his aversion at discovering them, it was Devon who now looked aghast. 'I'm not going in there!' she expostulated, pointing to the dense green-leaved mass that suddenly seemed all too close. 'And especially not in bare feet! You have to scramble up and over all their roots—when you're not sinking up to your knees in slimy mud, that is—and besides, the mosquitoes are big enough and ferocious enough to carry you off bodily ... and all while they're systematically draining your full blood supply, of course!'

He merely shrugged imperturbably. 'It was your idea to bring me here.'

'Only in order to show you, not to give you a tree by tree inspection!'

'Well, while I'm having a look around we may as well do it thoroughly.'

Almost to the edge of the area now, Devon really began to hang back in earnest. 'You can if you like, but I'm definitely not!' she declared flatly.

'Oh, yes you are,' he insisted, and abruptly linking his fingers with hers, made certain she could only lag so far behind. 'You're my guide, remember?'

'Not for clambering through mangrove swamps I'm not!' she defied, desperately but futilely attempting to jerk free as she felt the sand beneath her feet already becoming overlaid with a fine film of silt. Then, when he displayed no sign of relenting and she began sinking a trifle deeper, 'Hunt! Please! Okay, I apologise for having brought you along here, but please don't make me go in there. It's dark and creepy, and messy, and I hate it!'

Pausing at last, Hunt turned to eye her measuringly. 'For once, I think you might be telling the truth.'

Devon averted her gaze guiltily, but elected to side-step the issue by querying urgently, pleadingly, 'You're not really going to make me go in there, are you?'

'Well, I guess that all depends on just what you intend to replace it with, doesn't it?' he proposed indolently, but no less implicitly for all that.

'The—the rock pool,' she offered hopefully, even though that was another of the island's features she had meant to conveniently by-pass, but at the moment too relieved at being given an opportunity to avoid the mangroves to really object to such an obvious form of blackmail. Or the fact that he still had hold of her hand.

'Whereabouts is that?'

She waved her free hand vaguely in the direction of a small hill they had just passed. 'A—a little way up there.'

'Something you forgot to mention before, hmm?' sardonically.

Devon flushed. 'I—umm—thought you could see that some—some other time.'

The fingers laced with hers tightened their grip imperceptibly. 'Some other time after I'd decided the place wasn't worth buying after all, no doubt,' he surmised.

Exactly! Although she could hardly admit as much. 'Dad probably would have told you about it anyway,' she shrugged defensively. 'It's formed by the natural spring that provides most of our fresh water.' She stopped, her expression a mixture of defiance and diffidence. 'Well, are we going to—to see it or not?'

He suddenly uttered a light laugh, his deep blue eyes crinkling with amusement. 'Anything would be preferable to mangroves, wouldn't it?'

When coupled with her own thankfulness, his good humour had Devon smiling involuntarily in response. 'I can vouch for that,' she confirmed on a fervent note.

'Besides, I had no intention of going through there, in any case,' he disclosed with a provoking grin as they began retracing their steps. 'I've been in mangroves before and unless one's on a research trip I wouldn't exactly call it a pleasurable experience.'

'Oh, you heel!' Her smile was swiftly replaced with a simmering glare. And to think he'd had her pleading with him not to carry out his threat! 'You deliberately made me believe. . .' Too indignant to continue she now concentrated all her efforts into trying to wrench her hand from his instead.

'Successfully, too, it would appear,' he wasn't above rubbing it in. 'And you can forget about that,' watching her futile attempts to prise herself loose with a patent amusement that nettled her even more, 'because I've decided I like the arrangement. I know exactly where you are and what you're up to this way.'

'Well, isn't that just great for you!' she gibed rancorously. 'However, I *don't* happen to like it!'

'Tough!' he retorted, drily impervious. 'Perhaps you should have been less perverse and un-cooperative.'

Devon's breathing quickened uncontrollably. With someone as arrogant and uncaring of decency as he was, she doubted his attitude would have been any different no matter how helpful she'd been. Moreover, if such a thing were possible, it may even have been worse!

'Well, I wasn't, and I don't intend to be in future either,' she flared rebelliously.

The solid muscles of his back, clearly visible from her determinedly lagging position, rippled smoothly beneath his bronzed skin as his shoulders lifted in a gesture of total unconcern. 'Then our time together could prove extremely discomfiting . . . at least for one of us,' he turned to counsel in mocking tones.

He was meaning for her, of course, seethed Devon, and sent him a fulminating glare in return. He'd done nothing but arbitrarily ride roughshod over her wishes ever since his arrival, but she was damned if he was going to get everything his own way! If it was the last thing she did, she would ensure he received his come-uppance for some of those defeats, somehow! she vowed vehemently.

CHAPTER FOUR

THE rock pool had always seemed a magical place to Devon with its glittering, cascading waterfall and richly tropical surrounds, and where the sparkling water was always refreshingly cool even on the hottest day. As she followed Hunt to its boulder-strewn edge on this occasion, though, she immediately saw that the waterfall wasn't flowing—a sure indication that her father must have been in the midst of refilling the water tanks at the house from a smaller pool located a little further up the slope—and promptly experienced a sense of satisfaction knowing that its loss detracted considerably from the area's charm.

'You look inordinately pleased about something all of a sudden,' Hunt surprised her by abruptly remarking. Hell, she couldn't possibly have been so unthinking as to allow her gratification to show outwardly, could she? she despaired. 'I don't suppose there could be something missing, could there?' His eyes narrowed as they surveyed the pool alertly.

Devon only just managed to suppress an incredulous gasp. Not even he could be that astute, surely! 'L-like what?' her disbelief had her attempt at feigned innocence being voiced in a stammer.

'A waterfall, maybe,' he managed to shock her even further by hazarding. 'That rock face on the far side didn't get that smoothly worn appearance from nothing, and besides . . .' he paused, his lips curving wryly, 'Royce was telling me that Matt had said there was one when he was enquiring about the island's water supply yesterday.'

If her parent had been present, Devon could have hit him as well as the man beside her, for not only having provided the information in the first place but for thereby also putting Hunt in a position where he could both goad and defeat her with the knowledge at the same time.

'Oh, that,' she now had no choice but to pretend to recall, albeit in a somewhat testy fashion. 'Funny, I didn't even realise it was missing.'

'Hilarious,' he quipped. His eyes filled with lazy taunting. 'Victory number one to me, huh?'

Devon controlled her escalating emotions with difficulty, and it was only by clenching her free hand at her side that she did refrain from lashing out at him physically. 'Has anyone ever told you just what a hateful, callous and unbearable animal you really are, Hunter Kincaid?' she lashed scathingly with her tongue in lieu.

'No, can't say they have.' His indifferent reply was accompanied by an equally negligent shrug. 'Why, has someone told you just what a selfish, intractable, and thoroughly wayward little jade you are?'

The very quietness with which he delivered his stricture, as much as the unexpectedness of it, had her biting at her lip doubtfully and her anger suddenly disappearing as less positive thoughts rushed to take its place. He was the only person to have ever accused her of having such faults, and the knowledge that this morning she had unquestionably displayed every one of them made her feel slightly ashamed.

Not that she cared what Hunt thought of her, of course, but she was well aware just how disappointed her father would be in her if he ever came to hear of it, and that she didn't want at any cost. The alternative, though—abiding by his wishes and showing Hunt everything Cowrie did have to offer—would require a degree of willpower on her part she wasn't sure she even possessed. Nevertheless, for her father's sake at least, it was obviously an effort she was going to have to make, she realised dismally, and with a convulsive swallow set about doing just that before what little conviction she did have deserted her.

'I'm sorry,' she apologised miserably, not quite looking at him. 'As you said, it—it's Dad's decision to make, not mine.' Swallowing again, she made herself divulge on a falsely bright note, 'Actually, it's much prettier here when the water's flowing, and—and the rock's so smooth you can slide down it. It's good fun. Just like a slippery dip. The bottom of the pool's all sand too, and. . .'

'Devon, that's enough!' Hunt cut in on her sharply.

'No, there's more yet,' she went on in the same lively tone as if once having started it was imperative she said it all. 'It shelves gently this end as well so it's quite easy for elderly people or—or children to. . .'

'*Devon!*' There was a steely ring of command in his voice when he interrupted this time, and releasing her fingers at last he cupped her head between his two hands and resolutely forced her face up to his. 'What the hell's got into you?'

'N-nothing,' she denied huskily, and blinking quickly on feeling the sting of salt under her eyelids. She wasn't going to make a fool of herself by crying in front of him—she wasn't! 'I've just decided to—to do what Dad wanted me to, that's all, and I don't s-see what you've got to complain about. It's the type of—of information you wanted, isn't it?'

'But not relayed in this manner, for God's sake!'

'Oh, I didn't realise there was a particular way it had to be delivered,' she gibed tremulously. 'I thought getting what you wanted was all you cared about.'

'Then you got it all wrong, didn't you?' he smiled gently, his voice resuming its customary drawling inflection. 'Because all I ever wanted from you was a little reasonable co-operation.' Then, with a disarming widening of his shapely mouth, 'Plus maybe a smile or two.'

Devon licked at her lips distractedly, her mind in a whirl. Until yesterday her life had been calm and uncomplicated, but since his arrival all that had changed, drastically, so that she now felt as if everything familiar to her was being inexorably swept away—including her control over her own emotions— for instead of concentrating on the threat he indisputably presented to her way of life, her senses now only seemed capable of registering an overwhelming and wholly disconcerting awareness in response to that attractive curving of his firmly moulded mouth. A reaction she found so perturbing that it at least had the relieving effect of banishing any likelihood of tears as she fought frantically to overcome it.

'Yes—well—then if you've seen all you want to here, I think it's time we were getting back,' she proposed expressionlessly, her gaze fastened purposely to the strong column of his throat, her features studiously composed to reflect none of her inner turmoil. 'Even though Dad may have said he'd help Aunt Violet, I'd still rather not be too late.'

Momentarily, she thought he wasn't going to release

her and she trembled inwardly—the little control she was managing to portray was still very fragile and she doubted it could withstand any sort of challenge to its stability—but then he exhaled deeply and dropped his hands to his hips.

'Okay, sweetheart, I guess we've gone about as far as we can go this morning, haven't we?' he declared on a vaguely rueful note.

Too far, from Devon's point of view, although she found it somewhat enigmatic that he apparently thought so as well. After all, he'd achieved what *he* wanted. Not that she intended puzzling over it, though. She was only too pleased to know she would soon be free of his disturbing presence, and with that consoling thought in mind she made for the path that led back to the house with eager steps.

'So why wasn't the water flowing?' Hunt broke in on her reverie unexpectedly, causing her to start.

'Oh—er—because Dad's pumping it out from another pool closer to its source, I expect,' she disclosed, grudgingly. In spite of her decision not to go against her father's wishes, it still came hard to actually go along with them.

'You mean, the spring's flow is that weak?' he frowned.

Tempted to endorse his assumption for a second, her shoulders suddenly slumped resignedly. What was the use? Her father would probably only put him wise to the truth of the matter in due course. 'Usually only around this time of the year . . . before the onset of the wet,' she advised finally.

'Has it ever dried up altogether?' His probing became more intent.

'Only once, I believe, a long time ago when the rains

really didn't fall at all in any quantity,' she sighed. She would dearly have loved to have said it occurred all the time.

'So what happened?'

'Water was shipped in from the mainland,' she shrugged. 'We sometimes have to do that now during the summer, in any case, if our consumption goes too high. There's no hassle about it—it's just extremely expensive.'

He nodded thoughtfully. 'You've never considered increasing your rain storage capacity?'

Devon pressed her lips together vexedly. 'Yes, Dad's thought about it, but in comparison to the number of times it's necessary to ship water in, the cost of constructing additional tanks out here is even more exorbitant!' Pausing, she cast him a meaningful sidelong glance from beneath long lashes. 'Naturally, if the number of guests and staff on the island was increased more tanks would be an absolute necessity, as would larger generators in order to provide sufficient light and power.'

'Don't worry, that thought had occurred to me,' he owned wryly, and thereby gave her spirits a much needed lift as she wondered if that wasn't the line she should have taken all along. If he believed the costs involved in developing the island to the standard he envisaged to be too high, he wasn't likely to go ahead with the project, was he?'

Consequently, as they presently neared the house, she deliberately took him past the maintenance area so he might see for himself just how much of the equipment would need to be replaced or upgraded to enable the island to cater for a larger population, and for the first time was pleased to note how obvious it was that even the buildings housing the machinery badly required extensive repairs. In fact, to provide adequate protection for new equipment they would undoubtedly have to be replaced in their entirety, and with the law these days insisting all new constructions be cyclone proof, the expense of so doing could be expected to rise by as much as another third, she reasoned with unqualified satisfaction.

'I'm beginning to see now why the idea of selling appeals to Matt. That equipment's sure only got a limited life,' was Hunt's sole comment as he also viewed the area with assessing eyes, but it was sufficient to have some of Devon's pleasure fading a little.

She hadn't really considered it in that light. If the generators did break down permanently, which was quite a possibility considering they had been doing so temporarily with increasing frequency during the last few years, just where would the money come from to repair, or worse still, purchase substitutes for them? With no intention of permitting her companion to guess at the doubts he had unwittingly raised within her, however, she simply hunched a golden shoulder impassively.

'Oh, I wouldn't exactly say that,' she disagreed. 'They used to build them to last in the old days, you know, and these have been going strong for years.'

'My point entirely . . . too many years!' he had no compunction in emphasising significantly.

'Then maybe you should reconsider your ideas for purchasing the place!' she was stung into suggesting.

'Uh-uh!' he discounted that notion lazily, and dashed her rising hopes as a result. 'There's still a long way to go yet before I'm likely to do that.'

'How long?' she grimaced.

'Hopefully we'll know for certain by the end of this month. If it is to go ahead I'd prefer to have it all settled before the wet begins so we can utilise those months to have the plans, plus all the other necessary arrangements finalised, and then we should be in a position to begin work immediately the rains have finished.'

Time being of the essence because time was also money, she presumed, pulling another disgruntled face. Her thoughts raced on searching for other difficulties. 'And the local authorities? What if you should buy it and then they reject your application for development?'

'We've already had discussions with them to explain our iddeas, and provided we don't deviate from them they can see no reason for it not being approved.'

More was the pity! She began racking her brain once more. 'Well, what about an—an architect, then? You surely can't mean to have plans drawn without one at least having visited the island?'

At the house now, Hunt leant casually against the bottom post of the back steps. 'He'll be arriving next week, as a matter of fact. Along with a couple of surveyors, our construction foreman, and a few others whose job it is to see that nothing's been forgotten and that it all goes without a hitch,' he informed her drily.

'You've got it all down pat, haven't you?' she heaved. Followed by a distinctly more enthusiastic, 'Although once they arrive, I suppose there'll be no need for you to remain here, will there?'

'Sorry,' he grinned and tapped her provokingly under the chin, 'but having discovered the company to be so congenial here, I've decided to turn it into a working vacation and, therefore, don't expect to be leaving until the last of my staff does.'

Devon sighed disconsolately and mounted the first step. So there was to be no relief there either! She half swung towards him, her turquoise eyes troubled as they connected with his. 'And if—if you did buy it, when would we have to—to leave?' Her voice shook in spite of her attempts to keep it steady.

Hunt dragged a hand through his hair roughly, tousling it, and then with a heavily expelled breath trailed his fingers across her cheek softly. 'Don't worry about it, sweetheart,' he urged on a deeper, more vibrant note than usual. 'We'll work something out . . . if and when the time comes.'

With the briefest of nods she hurried up the remaining steps and on to the verandah. Just by his actions he had made it clear it wouldn't be long afterwards, she surmised.

'I'll see you again this afternoon, shall I?' His voice reached up to her from the ground where he was in line with her as he began heading for the bottom camp.

Stopping, she looked down at him with a frown drawing her winged brows together. 'To continue our tour, you mean?'

'Uh-huh!'

'Oh, but I can't this afternoon,' she was pleased to be able to inform him, and it did much to lighten her mood. 'I have to help Dad load the trailer with whatever needs to go back on the launch, and then reload it again with the incoming stores.'

'Wouldn't it be more appropriate if your fiancé did that?'

'Not really.' She shook her head slightly. 'He

doesn't work here yet, he's only a visitor at the moment, just like you. The difference being, *he* isn't as abrasive as you are, thankfully!' she mocked dulcetly.

His ensuing grin was anything but remorseful, although it was totally devastating from Devon's standpoint, as her suddenly racing pulse could verify. 'And are you also thankful he evidently doesn't kiss you as often either?' he dared to taunt in return.

Devon's cheeks flamed as she gasped and looked about her anxiously. It would be even more embarrassing if anyone had overheard his comment, and that he had made it at all . . . well, that just proved how correct her thoughts about him had been.

'Yes, I am!' she threw back at him stormily. Then, realising what she could be implying—as no doubt he had been! 'No! Of course not!' And when that didn't sound right either, 'I mean, there's no evidence about . . . oh, why don't you just go away and leave me alone!' she concluded on a fractious note. The more she said, the more she only seemed to play into his hands.

'When you tell me when our little tour is to continue, maybe I will,' he offered chafingly.

'Oh, in the morning, I suppose,' she retorted flusteredly. Any time, as long as it prevented him from making any other such mortifying remarks and he left right now!

'I'll see you after breakfast, then?'

'Yes—yes,' she acceded swiftly and made good her departure before he could utter another word.

As he had apparently promised, her father was helping his sister in the kitchen when Devon entered and his bushy brows promptly lifted in an unspoken query. When she didn't immediately reply, however, but walked across to the sink to begin washing her hands, he was forced into making it a verbal one.

'Well, how did it go?' he quizzed wryly.

'Oh, super! I can't remember the last·time I had such an—umm—invigorating morning!' she alleged with just enough sarcasm for her own ears.

'That's nice, dear,' smiled her Aunt Violet. 'Where did you go?'

'To Rocky Point, back along the beach to the mangroves, and then past the pool,' Devon relayed with a grimace through the window in front of her for the tall figure she could see heading in the direction of the camp.

'Saving the best for last, eh?' It was her father again. Drying her hands, she turned to face him and knew immediately from his shrewd expression that he was fully aware she hadn't intended anything of the kind, and that he had also picked up her earlier caustic intonation.

'Something like that, I guess,' she shrugged uncomfortably.

His eyes were unwavering as they held hers. 'You will be showing him everything, though?'

'Yes.' Her affirmation was given in a listless murmur. 'I've arranged to take him round the rest tomorrow morning ... even though I would have liked to have spent some time with Garth,' she added a little more spiritedly.

'Well, as it so happens, you wouldn't have been able to do that, in any event,' he half smiled sympathetic-ally. 'You see, his father was in touch with him while you were away to say he was needed back in the office, and he's leaving on the launch this afternoon.'

His news didn't altogether come as a surprise to Devon. Garth had said as much might happen when he'd first arrived a week and a half ago, but she did find it rather demoralising that it had had to occur at a time when she needed an ally most.

To her father, though, all she said was, 'I see. Then that would appear to settle that, wouldn't it?'

'I'm sorry, love, I know how pleased you've been having him here,' he immediately consoled. 'Besides, perhaps he'll be able to make it back again on next week's launch and finish his holidays then.'

She nodded, smiling faintly. If Garth could, it would at least give her *something* to look forward to. As it was, she suspected it was going to be less and less easy to find anything to be happy about as the island became inundated with Eastern Development personnel.

Since it wasn't possible for them to discuss the matter during lunch—there were too many guests around, not to mention her father—Devon had to wait, impatiently, until the meal was concluded and she'd helped her aunt clear everything away before she and Garth had the chance to be alone, and they promptly made for the chairs on the unoccupied verandah.

'So what was your morning like?' Garth was the first to speak once they were seated.

'Even worse than I expected it would be,' she both grimaced and sighed. 'He's the most arrogant and unfeeling brute I've ever met, but even more infuriating that that, he's too damned on the ball!' She sucked in a resentful breath and added disgustedly, 'He *knew* what I was trying to do all the time!'

'Oh, well, never mind,' Garth dismissed her

complaints negligently, to her amazement. 'At least I've got good news.'

Putting aside her own feelings for the moment, she leant forward interestedly. 'You mean, Dad did have more discussions with Royce Attwood and you sat in on them too this time?'

'Mmm,' he endorsed eagerly. 'And you know, it is a tremendous deal they're offering. I doubt your father will ever get a better one.'

Devon could only stare at him in shocked disbelief, feeling as if she had just been betrayed. It was the last thing she had expected him to say, and certainly not what she wanted to hear! 'But—but I thought you intended to find fault with the idea . . . not praise it!' she charged aggrievedly on recovering.

At least he had the grace to shift a little discomfitedly, she noted. 'Yes—well—I was going to, but honestly, if I'd done so it could only have been regarded as nit-picking. What I'm trying to say is, if they keep to their word, your father's got it made, and with our share of. . .'

'What share?' she interrupted sharply. 'Cowrie belongs to Dad, no one else. There are no *shares*!'

'Not at the moment, no, but that's apparently his idea, see. For us all to share the proceeds.'

'Well, I'm not interested in any share!' she flashed. 'I'm only interested in our remaining on the island.'

'And that's just being blindly obstinate!' he retorted in irritable accents. 'Can't you understand? This would set us up for life!'

Which was all the island meant to him, was it? A ticket to an imposing life style! Her gaze unconsciously drifted down to the beach below the house, the sight of gently swaying palms reaching up to a brilliant blue sky, the white sand lapped by crystalline waters that shimmered and danced as the sun's rays bounced off each ripple filling her with an emotion that was hard to describe, but which always brought a smile of contentment to her lips. At least, it always had until now.

'I was under the impression we already were, just by being able to live here,' she dragged her eyes back from the beautiful scene in order to impart pensively.

Garth's mouth pulled into an exasperated line. 'Oh, come on, Devon, be realistic! You know very well the island's been going downhill for years, and it will hardly be the end of the world if you have to live somewhere else—particularly under the prevailing circumstances.'

'Oh?' Her brows arched sardonically. 'I don't remember you thinking that way when you first heard of it. In fact, you were highly indignant at the thought of not being able to manage the place, as I recall.'

He dropped his gaze, abashed, but only momentarily, and then he was looking up again to impress, 'But that was before I knew all the facts. And believe me, managing this place as it is can't even come close to competing with the opportunities that would be available if it was disposed of. I mean, have you any idea exactly how much we would actually get from such a sale?'

'No, and I've not the slightest desire to find out either!' she announced in clipped tones. 'I couldn't care less what they're offering because I'm more than content to remain right here.' She paused, her glance cynical. 'Money doesn't buy happiness, you know, Garth.'

'No?' It was his brows that leapt satirically upwards

now. 'Well, it would sure beat the hell out of the hand-to-mouth existence we'd have to endure if we tried continuing with this place!' Then, moderating his voice persuasively on seeing the hurt look that crossed her face, 'Besides, it's always been in the back of my mind that we'd sell some time in the not too distant future, anyway. You must know yourself, even if you are loath to admit it, that we couldn't retain it indefinitely, and especially with the number of guests gradually decreasing. Times have changed, Devon, and to expect to keep an island like this to yourself just isn't possible, or practical, any longer. So as far as I'm concerned the most logical alternative is to acknowledge the writing on the wall, accept gratefully a far from measly remuneration in recompense, and begin a new life elsewhere. When all's said and done,' he shrugged, 'Northport's not such a bad place and there's certainly a greater variety of things to do there.'

'Except I don't happen to want to live in Northport!' she promptly asserted stubbornly. It was the first time he had ever mentioned to her about having secretly considered parting with the island and as a result it made her wonder if he'd ever really intended to manage the guesthouse as they'd planned. That he may not have, now made her feel even more deceived, and therefore considerably less receptive, if that was possible, to his arguments.

'All right, some other town then,' he allowed obligingly. 'Where would you suggest?'

'Cowrie Island,' she said deliberately, her chin lifting. 'I told you, I'm not interested in living anywhere else.'

'And as I told you, you're just being obstinate!' He

glared at her in obvious aggravation. 'Although you're going to have to accept it some time, you know, whether you want to or not, because unless I miss my guess, your father's going to go through with this deal and there's not a thing you can do to stop it!' Halting, his expression became resolute. 'And all things considered, I say good luck to him!'

'Good luck to him ... or good luck to you?' The bitter gibe was out before she could halt it.

Notwithstanding that he glanced away temporarily, Garth slung out of his chair in a rancorous movement. 'If that's all you've got to say, I can see I'm wasting my time even discussing it with you! You've just got this fixation about the place so that you believe anyone who disagrees with you must have an ulterior motive!' he retaliated before storming off along the verandah. Almost to the front door he stopped and turned to face her again with a heaved sigh. 'I'll see you down at the jetty before I leave, okay?'

Devon nodded mechanically, her lip caught between even white teeth as she watched him pass through the doorway, her gaze both sorrowful and contemplative. No matter how much anger he had displayed at her insinuation, she was still disappointedly aware that her suspicion wasn't as wide of the mark as he would like her to believe. However, it was the thought that that was what may have been in his mind all along that really hurt. That, and his evident incomprehension as to how deeply she felt about the island.

With a sigh, she rubbed her fingers against her temple dismally. Why, even Hunter Kincaid had shown more forbearance than her fiancé had by saying he could understand why she was so reluctant to see Cowrie sold, she recollected. And it wasn't only on her own account that she wanted to see it retained either, as Garth had tried to imply! There was her father and her aunt to consider too. The former, because it would provide him with the means to go off on his sailing trip—which she just couldn't bring herself to believe was an activity he should undertake—and the latter, because she hated being idle, and without her guests to cater to Devon knew her aunt would be lost—irrespective of being wealthy!

In the background there suddenly came the sound of the island's mini-tractor approaching, signalling that her father would shortly be loading its accompanying trailer with their departing guests' luggage ready for delivery to the jetty, and Devon rose slowly to her feet, preparing to go and assist him. As she turned to leave, however, her soft lips took on a rueful curve as recollections of her distressing and disappointing dispute with her fiancé refused to be dismissed. And to think she had considered Garth her foremost ally! she grimaced expressively.

The *Coral Trader* duly arrived just before four and for a time the old wharf was a hive of activity. Since it was Devon's job to attend to all incoming guests the first thing she did was to greet their two new arrivals and by way of the tractor and now unloaded trailer, which had seats constructed along its sides for just such a purpose, transport the middle-aged couple and their baggage up to the house where they were delivered into the capable and attentive hands of her aunt. This accomplished, she then returned down the hill to help with the more demanding work of loading their incoming stores—always greater at this time of year in preparation for the cyclone season ahead when there was the possibility the weather could prevent the launch keeping to its weekly schedule.

Since those people leaving the island, except for Garth who was leaning casually against one of the jetty's bollards some short distance away from the landing steps, had already boarded the boat, the area was a little less congested when she made it back, although as the crew brought more and more boxes and crates ashore it rapidly took on an obstructed appearance again.

Also, she noted with some dissatisfaction, Hunt and another two young men she didn't know had now joined her father and were at the moment engaged in a discussion with the launch's skipper. With their last disconcerting parting still vividly in mind, Devon was even more reluctant to find herself in his vicinity now than usual and consequently brought the tractor to a halt beside the mound of stores furthest away and began stacking them into the trailer.

A few seconds later Garth ambled across to her and seated himself on a crate close by. 'I'm sorry I've had to break up our time together like this, but I'll see if I can get a ride out on a yacht coming this way—if there is one—for the weekend at least. All right?' he sounded quietly.

'Mmm, that will be good if you can,' Devon half smiled as she stopped for a moment to wipe perspiration from her forehead with her forearm, avoiding any mention of their argument. 'We could have a barbecue down on the beach—just the two of us.'

'I'd like that,' he acceded just as carefully. 'It's not often we get the chance to be really alone.'

They would have if he could only be bothered to

bestir himself a little instead of lazing about the house so often, she thought wryly, but judiciously didn't voice her thoughts aloud. 'No, well, that's one of the penalties when there's more often than not guests around, I suppose,' she allowed generously instead, resuming stacking boxes again.

He watched her in silence for a while, then suggested quietly, 'So why don't you come back with me to Northport this afternoon too? You know you're always welcome at home, and at least we'd have more to do.'

Devon ignored his last comment as she came to a halt once more. 'It's a little late to make such a decision now. The launch is almost ready to leave,' she part laughed, part grimaced wryly. 'In any case, I'm sorry but I couldn't possibly leave during the next few weeks. Not with the added work the extra visitors will make for Aunt Violet and Dad.'

'What extra visitors?' he frowned. 'I only saw two get off today to replace the half dozen leaving, and your bookings always fall off for the next couple of months, don't they?'

'Usually,' she averred, nodding. 'But this year things aren't quite the same as normal,' with an expressive sigh, 'and apparently we're about to receive an influx of Eastern Development personnel.'

'Oh! To check the place out and decide what requires doing, I suppose,' he deduced, sounding nowhere near as displeased at the prospect as she had. 'They want to get it finished before the wet begins, I expect.'

'So I believe,' she came close to snapping and returned to her work resentfully. Knowing how she felt about the matter, he could at least have displayed a little more tact by camouflaging his obvious approval!

As if sensing her feelings, Garth left his seat and moved further away to rest his folded arms on the wharf's worn railing and stare down at the water below. 'Well, even you must have anticipated something of the kind happening,' he half turned to claim in a cooler tone. 'After all, they're contemplating investing a considerable sum of money in the place, and they want to be certain it's worth it.'

Devon wrestled with a heavier carton and dropped it into the trailer from a height that made everything shake. 'To ensure they're going to be repaid with a handsome profit?' she couldn't help sniping.

'Why not?' he promptly countered, his lips thinning. 'That's what makes the world go round. All losses do is create higher unemployment, and I can't imagine anyone in their right mind wanting that!'

Implying, she *wasn't* in her right mind because she objected to having her home taken over, she surmised with an angry glare as he moved further along the rail. With her indignation rising, she began grappling with a carton of tinned fruit she would normally have waited for her father to help with, only to utter a gasp of shock when a muscular arm suddenly wrapped itself about her midriff and lifted her bodily out of the way.

'What the hell do you think you're doing? That's far too heavy for you,' an all too familiar, and unwelcome, voice bit out censoriously.

Already in something of a less than submissive mood, Devon's stormy gaze passed over the darkly suntanned chest confronting her to lock defiantly with Hunt's vivid blue eyes. 'And if I don't give Dad a hand with the stores, who would you suggest does . . . Aunt Violet?' she gibed sarcastically.

'So what's wrong with hero back there?' He

gestured contemptuously over his shoulder with his thumb. 'Or is he as incompetent in shifting stores as he obviously is as a lover?'

Temporarily, Devon didn't know where to look as her cheeks burned with a self-conscious heat. She had never encountered such disturbing directness before, particularly on a personal level, and that he should continually make such remarks about her fiancé she found not only annoying and embarrassing, but extremely unsettling as well.

'No,' she finally managed to disclaim, albeit not as forcefully as she would have liked. 'It just happens that he's going back on the launch, that's all.'

With a scornful glance to where Garth was still leaning against the rail, he raised a sardonic brow. 'And it was just out of the question that he might conceivably give you a hand before he left, was it?'

'He—he's not dressed for it,' she excused with a shrug, gazing towards her fiancé herself now and noting his perfectly pressed pale grey trousers and creaseless blue shirt.

'Is he ever?' It was really more of a derisive statement than a question.

A trace of wariness darkened her eyes. 'I don't know what you mean.'

'I mean, I'd be surprised to learn he ever helped with the unloading . . . no matter how he was dressed!'

Now that she actually thought about it, Devon abruptly realised he wasn't wrong and that so used was she to there only being her father and herself to do all the work that she hadn't missed Garth's presence when he had been available to help. And perhaps that was also what her father had been referring to when he'd said only the night before that he feared Garth might not pull his weight if and when he should take over managing the island, the disquieting thought suddenly followed. It was a perturbing notion to say the least, but as there was no way she was going to disclose anything of the kind to the man before her she simply forced a look of suitably demurring amusement on to her face.

'Oh, naturally he. . . .' She broke off as her fiancé chose that moment to glance in her direction, but on seeing who was standing next to her made no move to join them, merely raising his hand in a minimal salute and heading towards the boarding ramp before she could even lift her own arm more than a few inches in response.

'Well, well, that would have to be about the most touching farewell I've ever witnessed,' Hunt immediately mocked. 'Are your reunions equally as passionate, I wonder?'

'Oh, go to hell!' Devon blazed, her eyes following Garth doubtfully. Obviously his acceptance of the scheme to buy the island still didn't extend to the man behind it. 'Not that it's any of your business, but there's a—a reason for this.'

'Had a fight over his sudden change of heart, did you?' And scathingly, in response to the astonishment that had her forgetting all about her fiancé for the moment and wondering instead how on earth he could have guessed, 'Royce told me how his eyes had lit up like the candles on a Christmas tree when he discovered how much he could stand to gain if the deal went through.'

In view of Garth's later behaviour, Devon didn't really feel in aposition to gainsay his accusation, but at the same time she didn't intend to blindly accept it either. 'Then *if* that was the case,' she stressed significantly, 'I'm surprised you're not thinking of him more favourably. After all, that just means there's one less for you to convince, doesn't it?'

'Except for one small detail,' he disputed on a taunting note. 'At present I rather think it's Matt wanting to convince *me* to buy the place.'

She bit at her lip sharply. 'Of—of course. How stupid of m-me to think otherwise,' she granted on a faltering note no amount of effort appeared capable of making steady, and pushing past him reached for the carton she had been struggling with before he interrupted her.

'And how stupid of you to think I've changed my mind about you lifting those!' Hunt retorted roughly as he once again swept her off her feet and dumped her down a few feet away. 'So why don't you just go and give that useless bastard of yours another of those incredibly fervent waves and let me do this instead, huh?'

'No! And don't you dare call him that either!' she stormed, her temper flaring ungovernably at his high-handedness and his derogatory comments as she purposely took a step forward towards the pile. 'I always help Dad with the loading and. . .'

'Well, this time you can take a rest, can't you?' An unyielding hand on her shoulder propelled her back to where she had been. 'Because if you don't,' he went on with a smile, but managing to convey a sense of menace nonetheless, 'you'll finish by wishing you had, I can assure you!'

Devon seethed impotently, aware that his sheer unpredictability made it imprudent for her to force the issue any further, and with her eyes flashing infuritatedly she flounced across to the rail to watch the launch reverse away from the jetty. Shortly, it was heading out through the reef and on its way back to Northport—Cowrie being the last island it put in at—and with a sigh she swung round to observe Hunt as he transferred the heavy cartons from the wharf to the trailer with a speed and ease she knew she could never have duplicated.

He worked with a rhythm that had his muscles flexing and relaxing in an almost continuous play of movement that, to her alarm, Devon abruptly realised she was finding fascinating, and she snatched her eyes away to concentrate on her father instead. He was still further along the jetty and similarly engaged, along with the two young men she had noticed earlier, in loading another trailer he had brought down prior to the boat's arrival. After a moment or two her curiosity began to get the better of her and she glanced back at Hunt quizzically.

'Just who are those two men assisting Dad? I don't remember seeing them before.'

'No, that's Alister and Vince. They're two of the crew from the *Kanandah*,' he relayed without looking up. Then stopping altogether, he sent her a bantering grin. 'Since there was obviously only going to be you and Matt doing the work we decided we couldn't allow one of the fair sex to do any such thing. Chauvinistic of us, wasn't it?' His lips twitched crookedly.

Under other circumstances she probably would have called it gentlemanly, but as it was. . . . 'The way you arrogantly take over, yes it is!' she concurred pungently. 'And what's more, you're filling the trailer too full. The tractor will never pull it all up the hill.' It was her turn to smile now, smugly.

In a matter of seconds he removed four of the heaviest boxes. 'How's that, then?'

'Better,' she allowed primly.

'Then we might as well get it up to the house, mightn't we?' He began striding towards the tractor.

Devon rushed forward to intercept him. 'I can at least drive that!' she protested. Followed by a wry, 'Besides, it has idiosyncrasies it just loves to demonstrate on the unknowing.'

'Okay, sweetheart, I guess that's allowable,' he conceded in an amused drawl, and while she slid behind the wheel, he perched himself on the front of the trailer.

By the time they were half way up the hill, however, Devon was beginning to wish she'd let him do the driving after all, for as he leant forward with his arms resting across his knees, his head was just about in line with her shoulder and she found the experience to be both disturbing and distracting. It was only by constantly telling herself to concentrate that she managed to get them to the house without having permitted him to disconcert her to the extent where she made some unthinking mistake whereby the tractor got the better of her.

No sooner had they pulled up alongside the back verandah than Hunt had effortlessly swung two of the large cartons into his arms and strode into the kitchen with them. Devon followed with two smaller parcels. Not even he could object to her carrying those, surely! As it happened Violet was in the room when they entered, and from her somewhat startled expression evidently surprised to see just who had arrived with her niece.

'Come on, Aunt Vi, there's a lot more where these came from. Where do you want 'em?' Hunt promptly grinned teasingly at the older woman.

Behind him, Devon waited expectantly, pleasurably, for the explosion. No one, but *no one*, called her relative Vi, and as for the Aunt . . . well, considering theirs was such a short acquaintance, and he certainly wasn't any relative, anyway, she could hardly restrain a smile at the thought of him being well and truly cut down to size for once!

When Violet did reply, though, it was to leave her niece open mouthed with shock to hear her aunt chuckle in genial tones, 'You young rogue!' And pointing to the door of the storeroom near the dresser, 'In there on the right, if you would be so kind, please, Hunter.'

'Hunt,' he amended with another smile as he passed her, and once more to Devon's amazement her normally so formal aunt cheerfully complied.

When he emerged from the storeroom, Devon still hadn't moved, and her aunt frowned at her anxiously. 'Are you feeling all right, dear?' she enquired. 'You look quite strange.'

'What? Oh, yes, I'm fine, thanks, Aunt Violet,' she recovered enough to claim weakly. 'I was just—just daydreaming, that's all.' And trying to figure out just what it was about Hunter Kincaid that, to her own unbounded exasperation, had her only relations treating him as if he was one of the family and could do no wrong!

'I expect you're missing Garth already, are you?' Violet hazarded compassionately.

'More than likely,' put in Hunt uninvited and straight-faced, although the sideways glance he directed at Devon was purely goading. 'You could tell just by their tender farewells on the jetty how loath they were to part.'

Violet made a clicking sound of understanding. 'Oh, that's nice,' she smiled, all unaware of the currents that were flashing between the other two occupants of the room.

'Yes—well—it's time we were getting on, isn't it?' Devon cast the man beside her a murderous glare. 'As you said, there's a lot more to be unloaded yet. So if you've quite finished discussing me, perhaps we could finish it!' She thumped her own two parcels on to the table now and, turning round, headed for the door.

'Devon! That wasn't very polite when Hunt's obviously been good enough to offer his help,' she heard her aunt chide disappointedly, but determined she wasn't going to be pressured into apologising, she just kept walking.

'Don't worry about it, Aunt Vi, she's probably just out of sorts because her fiancé's left,' Hunt's whimsically worded excuse that followed certainly brought about a reaction, though. It had her waiting for him by the trailer with her hands clenched and her emotions simmering.

'If you don't cut out those smart remarks concerning Garth and myself, Hunter Kincaid, this time I'm assuring *you* that you'll wish you had!' she threatened irately as soon as he was within hearing distance.

'Oh?' A dark brow quirked chafingly high. 'And just how do you propose to do that, beautiful? By complaining to your father ... or even by exacting physical retribution, perhaps?'

'It could just be both!' she retaliated in as direful a

tone as she could exhibit as she swung herself on to the tractor's seat in a furious movement. His obviously mirthful unconcern rankled unbearably, the more so when she suspected that neither course of action would be likely to have the desired effect and, consequently, made any threat she could utter an empty one—of which he was as aware as she was! Without waiting to see if he was aboard, she thrust the tractor into gear and started down the hill again at a speed that, although not recommended, at least helped to release some of her turbulent emotions.

In all, they needed to make another three trips before the jetty was eventually cleared, and no one was more thankful than Devon when the last of the goods had been put away and she could finally anticipate some relief from Hunt's riling presence. That was, until her aunt apparently decided his assistance deserved some repayment apart from just a verbal one and invited him to join them for dinner, whereupon her pleasure was rapidly replaced by a sinking feeling of despair on hearing him accept.

CHAPTER FIVE

As was customary, the island's guests and their hosts shared the same large table in the dining room for their meal that evening and, on this occasion particularly, Devon was extremely pleased that they did. It provided her with the opportunity to maintain a running conversation with them and thereby ignore the man seated next to her father on the opposite side of the table.

However, in spite of her attempts to disregard him entirely, she still wasn't able to completely subdue her curiosity as to what he and her father were discussing so earnestly, although she wasn't altogether surprised when the snatches of conversation she did manage to pick up proved to be about sailing. It had always been a great love of her father's and from what she could gather Hunt was no novice at the sport either.

What did give her cause for annoyance and concern a while later, though, was to overhear them talking about her father's long-planned sailing trip—with Hunt evidently encouraging him to go ahead with it! Reluctantly, because it was neither the time nor the place for her to be voicing her objections to the scheme, she was forced to bide her time as patiently as possible until the meal was concluded before informing Hunt in no uncertain terms to keep his unwanted comments to himself regarding her family's private affairs.

As it so happened, in fact, she even had to wait

considerably longer than that, because immediately on leaving the dining room both men disappeared into the small office at the front of the house and as her censure was really meant for the younger of the two, once again she had to defer her intentions until she could catch him on his own. It would doubtlessly be self-defeating if she made her feelings known in her father's hearing, especially now that he had some support, and from someone who—although for the life of her she couldn't understand why!—he appeared to regard so favourably.

In the end, it was nearly eleven before Hunt finally took his departure and, after making sure her father had returned inside once he'd seen his companion off, Devon hurried down the back steps and chased after her quarry determinedly.

'Hunt!' she called imperiously on almost catching up to him. 'I want to talk to you!'

He turned to face her slowly, his expression as readily provoking as always. 'Do you now,' he drawled wryly. 'That's a change. So what have I done wrong by your island to cause such a precedent this time, hmm?'

'As a matter of fact, it has nothing to do with the island,' she answered stiffly. 'It's more important than that.'

He gave a short half laugh. 'I didn't think anything was more important to you than the island.'

'Which just goes to prove how little you know me!' she retorted on a slightly less collected note.

'So it would seem,' he granted in apparent seriousness. Then, smiling broadly, 'Although you must admit I've been doing my best to rectify my lack of knowledge in that area.'

'Only in order to increase your knowledge of Cowrie, certainly not of me!' she scorned.

He shrugged, and then before she knew it his hand had snaked out to thread within the silken strands of her hair, propelling her closer. 'Okay, I'll show an undivided interest in you, then, if that's what you would prefer,' he proposed lazily.

'No!' Devon immediately protested in a panic even though she was unsure, whether he actually meant to do anything of the kind, or whether he was simply being annoying again. Pushing away from him, she heaved a sigh of relief on finding herself at liberty. 'And—and that isn't why I came after you! It was in order to tell you to mind your own business and to stop encouraging Dad in his foolhardy idea of sailing off on his own!'

His deep blue eyes, several shades darker now in the dim light, swept over her sardonically. 'That sounds more like you. Just because the idea doesn't find favour in your eyes, you consider it an unwarranted interference if anyone else disagrees.'

'No, that's not it at all!' she denied half defensively, half indignantly. Once again he was insinuating she was selfish, when actually all her concern was for her father. 'I'm against it because he doesn't happen to be well enough to undertake such a trip, if you must know!'

'Only in your opinion, apparently. Matt appears to consider he's well and able enough.'

'Well, his doctor doesn't!'

'Oh? That's not what I was told. In fact, according to Matt the doctor simply advised a break from his heavy workload here,' he emphasised meaningfully, 'and then to take things a little easier.'

'And you think a solo yachting voyage comes under the classification of taking it easy, do you?' she scoffed caustically.

'If he approaches it in slow stages there's no reason why it shouldn't be. He's obviously competent enough to know what he's doing.'

His last remark was much the same as Garth had made while they were down at the camp, and so was her reply. 'It's also very difficult to be competent if you're not even capable of standing on your feet!' she snapped. 'I mean, you do realise the reason the doctor advocated he try not to do so much was because he thought a heart condition could be developing, don't you?'

Hunt's shapely mouth firmed somewhat. 'I also realise "could be" is a long way from "has"!' he countered succinctly. 'And perhaps if he is relieved of both his financial worries and his workload, you may even find the "could be" in doubt also.'

'Oh, yes, it's in your own interests to say that, isn't it?' Devon accused, disparagement uppermost. 'After all, the thought of his being in a position to afford the type of boat he's always wanted is just another lever for you to use in order to achieve your aims, isn't it?'

'No, it is not!' His sharply voiced denial was catergorical. 'And I wouldn't be making too many of those wild accusations either if I were you, sweetheart, or you may really find yourself with a battle on your hands!'

A battle he would somehow ensure she had no hope of winning, no doubt! she surmised wrathfully. However, the thought did have her moderating her tone a little—although not appreciably the astringent intonation contained therein. 'Then why *are* you supporting the scheme so adamantly?' she challenged.

'Mainly, because it's obviously been a life-long ambition of his, and it's just as evident he feels that, due to his age, if he doesn't make a move shortly, then he very likely never will be able to fulfil his dream . . . which, I might add, clearly means a great deal to him!' he stressed forcefully.

Devon touched even white teeth to her lip diffidently. She also knew how much her father's plan meant to him, but that still didn't necessarily make it advisable, did it? 'Yes—well—it's also been a life-long ambition of mine to have my father live for as many years as possible,' she retorted in defence.

His eyes didn't waver from hers by so much as a fraction. 'Even to the extent of being willing to sink the ship completely in order to put out the fire, it would appear.'

'And just what's that supposed to mean?' she flared, sensing more criticism.

'It means, that because you fear he *might* suddenly die at sea, you would rather kill him for sure by preventing him from going at all!' she was informed in hard-edged accents.

'That's not true!' she cried resentfully. 'And—and you have no basis for claiming his not going would bring about anything of the kind! It hasn't in the past, so why should it in the future?'

'Because the difference is, the minute he leaves this island he's going to have nothing to do . . . except pine for what his over-protective daughter is wanting to deny him!' He paused, his expression unrelenting. 'And don't try telling me he won't, because even if you are too obstinate to admit it, you know damned well he will!'

Just as leaving the island would create a similar void in all their lives! 'But with you accepting none of the blame, of course!' she gibed bitterly.

Hunt shook his head in disbelief. 'Why the hell should I?'

'Because it's all your fault! If you hadn't come here none of these decisions would be necessary!'

'No, he'd be considering sailing off in that old sloop of his instead! At least this way he can afford to have a decent boat under him fitted out with the best equipment available!'

Devon stared at him fiercely, her breasts rising and falling rapidly with the strength of her feelings. 'Oh, God, I detest you!' she choked. And not only because all her troubles had begun with his arrival, but because he also seemed to have an answer for everything! Abruptly, her eyes misted. 'You don't care how many lives you ruin as long as you can *develop*,' with tearful acrimony, 'an area, do you?'

Apart from a muscle that flickered briefly beneath the sun-darkened skin of his jaw, Hunt's demeanour didn't alter. 'I'd hardly call it ruining a person's life to rescue them from obvious financial straits, and at the same time provide them with the means to achieve what they've always longed to do!'

Okay, so maybe there were a number of reasons her father wasn't averse to the deal, but there were others concerned too, weren't there? she reasoned defiantly, blinking away her tears. 'And Aunt Violet? She doesn't want to leave here either—as you probably already know, and was doubtless the reason you were so busily buttering her up this afternoon! She won't know what to do with herself once there's no guests for her to feed up and fuss over.'

He nodded contemplatively. 'Hmm. . . . Except in that regard I could have plans for Aunt Vi,' he caught her offguard by suddenly musing.

'Oh, and what sort of plans would they be?' she demanded on a suspicious note. Now what was going on in that contriving mind of his?

'W-e-ll,' he lengthened the word thoughtfully—or was it deliberately suspensefully? fumed Devon, 'naturally we'd require staff if everything pans out as I envisage, and if that meal she provided tonight is any indication, then with an increased and more modern range of equipment plus a few helpers, I suspect we would really see Aunt Vi's true colours come to the fore and we'd find ourselves with one hell of a fine chef on our hands.' Halting, he tilted his head quizzically. 'Think she'd be interested?'

Oh, yes, she'd certainly be interested all right! Would probably jump at the chance, in fact, Devon admitted with a sigh. And there would go any opposition she may have been able to extract from her aunt concerning the sale! To the man with her, though, she merely offered a deprecating hunching of her shoulders.

'I wouldn't know,' she alleged listlessly. 'You'd have to ask her that yourself.' Then, with her voice strengthening, 'But we appear to have digressed. I came out here to talk about Dad, not to discuss any new plans you may be hatching.'

'You're not interested in learning if I have anything in mind for you too, then?' he drawled.

Devon's fingers clenched. 'I already know all I want to in that regard. You're doing your best to deprive me of my home as soon as possible. Isn't that enough?' And inhaling deeply, 'Now to return to. . .'

'You wouldn't prefer to work here rather than leave altogether?' he broke in on her idly. 'After all, you do have a thorough knowledge of all the attractions here that would be hard, if not almost impossible, for anyone else to duplicate.'

Momentarily, her heart leapt at the thought of remaining, and then it spiralled downwards again. 'That's the carrot that's supposed to hopefully put paid to all my opposition, is it?' she jeered. 'Well, you can forget it! Cowrie means more to me than simply somewhere to work! Besides, since you put it that way, yes, I would rather leave than ever be employed by you, Hunter Kincaid!' Especially if it meant all her special places on the island would be private no longer.

'Oh, don't be so childish!' he slated. 'That's just cutting off your nose to spite your face, and you know it. Nor was it an attempt to stifle your opposition. I figure I can already do that without resorting to such means,' with his lips twitching wryly. 'It was simply an offer I considered would benefit us both.'

Perhaps he was telling the truth, perhaps not. It really didn't matter. 'Well, whatever the reason, my answer still isn't about to change,' she shrugged. 'The island just wouldn't be the same, and I'd rather n-not be here to see it h-happening.' Her voice began to shake ominously and, looking away, she drew a steadying breath before continuing. 'In—in any event, there's still Garth to consider.'

Hunt made a contemptuous sound deep in his throat. 'I don't know why! What consideration has he ever shown you?'

'You wouldn't know!' She swung back to face him

now, balefully. 'And whether you approve of him or not, he still does happen to be my fiancé!'

'You wouldn't know it from looking at the pair of you,' he declared drily. 'Just because you've evidently known each other all your lives doesn't mean you're supposed to act as if you've been married that long as well, you know. Instead of that half-hearted apology for a wave he gave you on leaving, *this* is what he should have been doing!' He suddenly swept her against his hard, muscular outline, his arms imprisoning her as a hand reached up to cradle and immobilise her head, his lips claiming hers with a sensuousness she was helpless to overcome.

In no time at all it seemed her initial flustered struggles had given way to an even more disturbing response. It was as if she had lost all control over her emotions whenever he kissed her, and all they wanted to do was answer in kind the drugging demands of his possessive mouth. Compulsively, her lips parted, inviting his further exploration, a shiver of unexpectedly fervent feeling shooting through her when he did so. Then without warning, and just as abruptly as he had pulled her to him, Hunt now put her away from him.

'That's how engaged couples usually say good-bye,' he drawled in a roughly bantering manner.

Striving desperately to appear as unaffected by the encounter as he apparently was, despite experiencing an overwhelming need to take to her heels, Devon returned his indolently scanning gaze as steadily as possible. 'You speak from the experience of having a fiancée yourself, do you?' something quite unaccountable made her challenge.

'Uh-uh!' he grinned and gave a negative shake of his head. 'Promises to marry have never been in my line.'

Meaning, no doubt, that he'd never found it necessary to offer marriage in order to get what he wanted! she deduced with a grimace. Her chin angled unconsciously higher. 'In that case, as far as engaged couples' behaviour is concerned, it would appear my knowledge is greater than yours, then, wouldn't it?' she asserted, sweetly mocking, and took her leave purposefully, while she was still on top.

'Although obviously not in experience,' she heard him laugh after her.

'Thankfully!' she retorted implicitly over her shoulder, but didn't stop until she reached the verandah. Then, involuntarily almost, she cast a swift look back, and received a taunting salute for her pains, whereupon she promptly spun about and hurried into her bedroom.

It wasn't until some time afterwards when she found herself mulling over their conversation as she prepared for sleep that she suddenly realised in some surprise that, in the main, there had been a complete absence of his normal goading, and she spared a thought to wonder why. Moreover, she couldn't make up her mind whether it had been an improvement or not. When all was said and done, the lack of it definitely hadn't appeared to make her any more successful in winning an argument against him than she usually was when it was present! she noted with a disgruntled expression as she punched her pillow into a more comfortable shape with unnecessary vigour.

In the morning Devon awoke somewhat earlier than usual and deciding it would be pleasant to have an early breakfast alone with her father for a change, showered swiftly and donned a pair of red shorts

together with a white strapless, midriff top, and set off
for the kitchen. On passing the dining room, however
she came to a stunned halt on seeing Hunt calmly
ensconsed at the table with her parent and partaking of
a hearty meal.

Since her appearance had obviously caught their
attention she then had no choice but to enter the room
and respond to their greetings, although now she
would have preferred to keep going and eat alone in
the kitchen.

'Come to join us, love, have you?' Granville smiled
fondly. 'That's nice. Pull up a chair.'

With nothing for it but to do as he suggested,
Devon took a seat opposite them, reluctantly, her gaze
expressive as it came to rest on the younger man.
'Have you moved in here?' she enquired with a forced
smile for her father's benefit, but with just enough
causticity for the recipient of her query to get the
message.

Hunt's mouth took on a wry curve. 'It's a tempting
thought, but as it happens I arrived early, so my
adopted aunt invited me to have some breakfast.'

'They don't feed you on the *Kanandah*?' Her eyes
widened, eloquently gibing.

'Mmm,' he owned laconically. 'But it's hard to
refuse one of Aunt Vi's meals.'

Besides which his sizeable frame would undoubtedly require some filling, she speculated sardonically, and not a little put out by his continued
reference to her aunt as Vi. Why should he be
permitted such familiarity, particularly when Garth
hadn't even been invited to progress beyond a
formal Miss Matthews after all the years he'd known
her? Moodily, she poured herself a cup of tea from

the pot already on the table and began buttering a piece of golden toast.

'So what made you arrive this early, then?' she asked of Hunt at length.

Beneath their dark green, tank top covering, his shoulders flexed powerfully. 'Seeing we've got a lot of ground to cover today, I thought an early as possible start would be expedient.'

'In fact, Violet's packing a lunch for you both right now so there won't be any need for you to interrupt your tour,' put in her father informatively.

Devon would have preferred the welcome respite a return to the house for the meal would have provided! 'That is thoughtful of her,' she smiled hollowly. 'Although she really needn't have bothered. I mean, I have to return to help her with the guests' lunches, in any case.'

'Oh, no, not now there's only four of them. Violet says she'll be able to manage on her own without any trouble at all,' he unwittingly destroyed her hopes. 'No, you and Hunt make a full day of it, then you're not likely to miss anything.'

Uncertain whether anything had been intended by that last comment, Devon slanted him a searching, sideways glance. 'As if I would,' she murmured, though somewhat tongue-in-cheek.

'Oh, I wasn't suggesting that at all,' he hastened to assure her earnestly, although she couldn't quite keep a light flush from staining her cheeks when she intercepted a graphic, brow-raised gaze from the man beside him. 'It's just that you've seen it all so many times before that what you might now consider unexceptional could prove to be very interesting to someone who hasn't seen it previously.'

'Mmm, maybe,' she was prepared to concede, meditatively. Her glance shifted so that it centred fully on Hunt. 'I can see I shall just have to point out to you every solitary thing I can think of, won't I?' And thereby fill his head with so much trivia that he would hopefully tire of his tour very swiftly! 'So where would you like to begin? With a climb to the top of The Pinnacle?'

'Uh-uh!' His ensuing veto may have been brief, but at the same time it was unmistakably decisive. 'I think the reef first, while there's still sufficient water covering it to enable us to do some snorkelling, otherwise the tide will be low again if we leave it until after we've seen The Pinnacle.'

Foiled again, grimaced Devon in disgust, but refusing to allow her disappointment to show. 'The reef it is, then.' She gave a creditably indifferent shrug. 'Although I do hope you have your own gear because we don't have any spares except Dad's, and I doubt his flippers, especially, would fit you.'

'No worries,' he averred on a dry note. 'As a matter of fact I did bring mine with me. They're outside the back door.'

'That's fortunate,' she lauded with extremely suspect pleasure before concentrating her increasingly vexed thoughts on her meal once more. Already she could tell it was going to be one of *those* days!

Immediately breakfast was concluded, Devon returned to her room in order to slip on an ice blue and cerise bikini before replacing her shorts and top, and to gather up her snorkelling gear. Hunt was talking to her aunt in the kitchen when she arrived at that room, and from the unquestionably delighted look on that woman's face it wasn't difficult to guess just what had been the topic of their discussion.

'I gather you've spoken to Aunt Violet about her staying on,' she consequently said to Hunt as they left the house and she retrieved a couple of towels from the laundry as they passed.

He nodded. 'Apparently the idea appeals to her greatly.'

Exactly as she had thought it would! 'Another one to you, huh?' she quipped with as much feigned unconcern as she could evince.

'You would rather she was miserable too at having to leave just because that's what you're determined to do?' He was back to being his mocking, as well as reproving this time, self again.

'Of course not!' she denied, but a little uncomfortably. She supposed that was how it could have sounded, although naturally she was glad for her aunt's sake. She simply hated to see him have yet another victory, that was all! With a dispirited sigh, she led the rest of the way down to the beach in silence.

Once there, Devon peeled off her outer garments and, catching up her apparatus, walked quickly down to the water. If she was going to have to go through with this, she may as well get it over and done with as rapidly as she could. A few moments later Hunt joined her, his hip-hugging swimming shorts revealing an even longer length of strongly muscled, brown leg than his covering shorts had done, and suddenly aware her covert gaze was turning into an interestedly assessing one, she hurriedly cleaned and rinsed her mask before pulling both it and her snorkel into place, and then moved out into slightly deeper water to dispose of any sand in her flippers before sliding them on to her feet.

'Ready?' she asked flatly as soon as he had followed suit, and immediately he nodded pushed herself off from the bottom and began heading out through the lagoon without waiting to see if he was as accustomed to this type of swimming as she was.

It soon became apparent he was by the ease with which he caught up with her, and as they slowly propelled themselves through the glistening water side by side she discovered, as she had many times before, that the tranquillity of the scene below seemed to have the power to clear and soothe the mind until all that remained was a limitless wonder and enjoyment of her surroundings.

As they swam, myriad varieties of fish glided past tamely; shoals of silvery black-spot sea perch, peacock wrasses, brown, blue and black-banded tuskfish, large red coral cods with their distinctive blue dots, yellow and black butterfly fish, together with a host of others. But it was to the numerous blue and green parrot fishes, gnawing at the massive boulders of coral that were interspersed across the lagoon's sandy floor, that Devon impulsively pointed and, by signalling, indicated that Hunt should stop and listen. In the absolute quiet that followed the noise of the fishes' beak-like jaws scraping at and breaking off pieces of coral to obtain the polyps and worms that lived within was easy to hear, and Hunt gave an almost disbelieving shake of his head before they continued on.

As soon as they were above the mass of the surrounding reef itself, Devon began a series of duck-dives in order to point out other things of interest; velvety mantled reef clams, each one a richly different colour; orange and white anemone fish sheltering within gently swaying, brightly tinted tentacles; fat, sluggish-looking *bêche-de-mer*; exquisite wine-red, orange and green feather stars; royal blue starfish and needle-spined sea urchins; large brown cushion sponges, bright yellow inside, and a red hermit crab in a large triton shell; brilliant blue and black tangs, blue-green damsel fish, Moorish idols, and gloriously marked angelfish; and of course the breath-taking beauty of the multi-hued coral itself in both its hard and soft forms.

Everywhere they went there was something different to be seen, perhaps the best part being that, due to no fishing ever being permitted on the inner reefs, none of the so very varied life forms hurried away at their approach but allowed them to swim among them, even to hold some of the fishes in their hands, and because Hunt's interest was so oviously genuine, to the extent of indicating things to her that he thought she may have missed—and so completely opposite in attitude to Garth when she had attempted to share such an underwater paradise with him—Devon found herself revealing much, much more than she had originally intended and, to her amazement, deriving considerable pleasure from doing so.

However, as they neared the reef front where the coral plunged steeply thirty fathoms or more to the seabed below, she still couldn't quite bring herself to warn him of the, to some people, startling sight that was about to confront him. It was one of those few chances she had to catch him unawares for once and she was curious, if nothing else, to see how he would react to it. As she recalled, ruefully, one look had been sufficient for Garth and he hadn't been able to return to the security of the lagoon quickly enough, and subconsciously, she was half hopeful that would be the response of her companion today as well.

As it turned out, Hunt demonstrated no such desire on seeing the reef abruptly drop away beneath him, leaving him in the deeper blue waters of the open ocean, although after continuing seaward for a few yards he did surface. With a partly disappointed, partly ill-concealed impish look on her face, Devon did the same.

Pushing his mask to the top of his head and removing his snorkel, he fixed her with an askance gaze. 'You'll keep, young lady, you'll keep!' he vowed in a, not altogether pseudo, menacing drawl.

'Why? What did I do?' she queried innocently, but unable to entirely restrain the humorous curve playing about her lips. 'You said you wanted to see everything, and some of the best corals are always found on the outer edge of a reef.'

'I think perhaps you'd better show me then,' he advocated drily, almost as if he didn't believe her.

'I was going to,' she claimed as she re-adjusted her mask. Followed by an irrepressible, 'Provided you stayed around long enough to have a look, that was,' just before inserting her snorkel and swiftly diving.

Hunt followed her just as quickly and found she hadn't been exaggerating. Some of the most attractive coral growths were located along the sides of that nearly straight-sided drop. Among them the fiery red, lacy fan coral, while here too even greater varieties of multi-tinted fish darted and whirled amidst the coloured stems, and in and out of hidden crevices.

This was also the habitat of most of the larger species of reef fish and on this occasion it was Devon who received a shock on suddenly turning and discovering the enormous head of a giant Queensland groper—its great maw of a mouth opening and closing slowly—not more than a yard or so away from her. It wasn't the first time she had come across him—in fact, a pair of them had made the island's reef their home—but it was the first time she had come face to face with him so abruptly. Normally the species wasn't aggressive towards humans, its diet consisting mainly of crustaceans and other fish, but they were exceptionally inquisitive, and to have its eight-foot long form nosing around for the whole time you remained in their particular territory was somewhat unnerving, and so, with an expressive signal to Hunt advising him of their unwanted company, she reluctantly headed for the surface once more and set off for the shallower water above the reef.

By now the tide had receded noticeably, and as they made their way back leisurely towards the reef flats Devon began directing Hunt's attention towards the many and varied shells that seemed to carpet every sandy space; red-lipped and purple-mounted strombs; pale orange and coffee coloured spider shells; volutes of every description; delicately patterned, but poisonous, cone shells; ram's horns that had been washed up from deeper waters during storms; Bailer, trochus, and cockle shells; and of course numerous examples of those that had given the island its name, including egg, tiger, and small ring cowries in all their different variations of colour.

'Well, what did you think of it?' she asked when they at last returned to the shallows and removed their gear, and for the first time speaking to him in a totally natural vein.

'Incredible!' Hunt's reply was short but sincere.

'And so are you as a guide. You really know your subject and what you're doing out there, don't you, sweetheart?'

The unexpected compliment had her executing a deprecating half shrug as she began leaving the water. 'As a Chairman of the Board, you don't make a bad skindiver yourself,' she quipped wryly. And with her gaze resting on him quizzically as they ambled across the sand, 'You've done quite a bit of diving before, haven't you?'

He nodded. 'Like you, I was also born and raised close to the sea and I've been mucking about in boats and diving for almost as long as I can remember.'

So that explained his expertise! Finger-combing her hair into place, she didn't quite look at him as she probed diffidently, 'Whereabouts by the sea?'

'Mooloolaba, on the Sunshine Coast just north of Brisbane,' he relayed casually, shaking the water from his own hair and then raking a hand through it before dropping down on to one of the towels she had brought along.

Devon spread the other towel out a short distance away and sank down on to it in a thoughtful pose with her arms linking loosely about her updrawn legs, her chin resting on her knees. 'You must miss it, then, now that your business is conducted from Brisbane,' she ventured. Her father having informed her that that was where the Eastern Development Corporation was based.

'Uh-uh!' He moved his head lazily. 'Our main office is in Brisbane and I commute by helicopter when I have to, but our head office is still on the Sunshine Coast. It's one of the fastest growing areas in the State and we still get a lot of work from that district ...

apart from the fact that I prefer to continue living there.'

She gazed out to sea for a moment, her thoughts confused. She didn't know why she should be interested in his background, but strangely she was. 'And—and your firm is a family concern, is it?' She couldn't think of any other circumstances that would permit him to reach the position he had at such an early age.

'No, all my own work,' he advised matter-of-factly, but with a humorous tilt to his mouth as if he sensed the reasoning behind her question. 'When I was a kid it always used to alternate between feast and famine in our house—with famine predominating.' The upward curve of his lips became more ruefully pronounced. 'My old man's passion for punting on the horses saw to that.'

Devon's eyes shaded with sympathy. Just by what he left out she suspected his early years had been far rougher than she could ever imagine. 'Th-then how . . .?'

'Did I make it to Chairman of the Board?' He hunched his wide shoulders in a deprecating gesture. 'With a little hard work, and a lot of good luck, I guess.'

After what he'd just had to say, she was inclined to think it was more likely to have been vice versa. 'For example?'

'For example . . .' Hunt suddenly reached across to wrap a hand around the far side of her neck and by exerting pressure on it pulled her off-balance so that she half fell towards him, 'I'm still deciding just what punishment you deserve to have meted out to you for that little trick of yours out there,' he smiled mock-threateningly into her wide-eyed and somewhat startled features.

'Why, did it frighten you?' she dared to taunt as she laughingly struggled to regain her previous position, in vain.

'No, it didn't frighten me,' he declared wryly as he pushed her down on to the sand and kept her pinned there by a hand on each shoulder. 'Nonetheless, as you damn well know, it is a trifle unsettling to be looking at vividly coloured fish and an assortment of coral one moment ... and then staring into a seemingly bottomless blue pit the next!'

Her turquoise eyes sparkled impenitently. For some unknown reason she appeared to have lost her nervousness of him this morning. Perhaps because the mood of affinity that had developed between them while viewing the reef hadn't yet dissipated.

'I—well—since you were obviously an experienced skindiver, I thought you would no doubt know what to expect,' she alleged mirthfully.

'Just like you were anticipating the appearance of that groper that had you nearly jumping out of your skin, hmm?' he teased in turn.

She could hardly deny it. 'He is huge, isn't he?' she grinned expressively instead.

He raised his brows slightly at her wording. 'You've seen him before, then?'

'And his mate,' she nodded. 'They've got a cave down there somewhere where they've set up home. In fact, they've been here quite a few years now. Just about all the reefs have their pair of guardian gropers.'

'Mmm, so I've heard.'

Her lips formed a disappointed pout. 'So you were expecting to see something of the kind?'

'Not entirely,' he owned, eloquently dry. 'Originally, I was under the impression we would only be exploring the top of the reef. However, immediately we moved into deeper water I knew there was a distinct possibility some of the larger species could suddenly put in an appearance.'

'The first time I saw him I nearly swallowed my snorkel in shock,' she now confessed with a grin. 'I'd been told what large heads and mouths they possess, but until you actually see one for yourself nothing can prepare you for just *how* huge those gaping mouths are!'

The whole time she had been talking Hunt's gaze had been fastened to her softly contoured lips, and now he brushed his thumb across her lower one slowly. 'While yours is quite beautiful, particularly when you smile like that,' he murmured with a more resonant nuance than she had ever detected in his voice before.

All at once Devon tensed warily, her expression faltering beneath the intensity of his. In almost as many minutes he had twice changed the direction of their conversation, but this time his demeanour had altered perceptibly too, and thereby resurrected all her previous feelings of disturbing vulnerability.

'Hunt—I . . . no!' Only the last was unhesitatingly voiced as his head lowered to hers and she began to struggle in earnest now. 'Stop it! You have no. . .'

His lips closing inexorably over hers effectively brought an end to her partly commanding, partly panicking protest, and as he slid a pillowing—or restraining?—arm beneath her head and drew her slender form closer to the rugged masculinity of his, her heart began pounding raggedly. She was only too aware of the response he was capable of engendering within her, but even more disconcerting was the knowledge that he was unquestionably aware of it also! He appeared to totally disregard the fact that she was engaged, and he therefore had no right to keep kissing her as he did, but, oh God, did he also have to be so skilfully practised that he made her ignore it as well? she despaired on feeling her senses start to swim as his warm and knowing mouth trailed a scorching path to the throbbing hollow at the base of her throat, and knew herself to be surrendering helplessly once more.

Hunt smoothed an arousing hand leisurely over her hip and upwards, seeking the deep indentation of her waist before, with fingers spreading, moving it unhurriedly across her ribs until, finally, bringing it to rest cupping a tautly swelling breast. Feelings she had never before experienced pulsed through Devon, shocking her with their depth so that she trembled and gave a gasp that was somewhere between a moan and a sob. Nothing she had shared with her fiancé had prepared her for this fiery, uncontrollable leaping of the emotions in response to an exploring touch, and she clutched desperately at the sinewed shoulders leaning over her as if seeking something stable in a suddenly rocking world.

Lifting his head, Hunt surveyed her flushed and bewildered features with rueful eyes, his sensuous mouth sloping crookedly. 'You really are an innocent aren't you, sweetheart?' he mused wryly.

A deeper, brighter stain of embarrassment joined the colour already tinting Devon's cheeks and she averted her face swiftly. 'So you keep inferring!' she heaved. He made her feel like some gauche and maladjusted adolescent! Forcing herself to look back at him, her eyes smouldered resentfully. 'Because it's a supposition that enables you to amuse yourself at Garth's and my expense, no doubt!'

'I don't know about amused, but I sure am amazed,' he amended drily. 'What kind of a man is he, this fiancé of yours, that he can be engaged to someone with your looks and so very shapely figure and yet apparently make no attempt to make love to you?'

'One who *is* capable of exercising some self-control, obviously!' she sniped explicitly.

'Much to your disappointment, presumably, if your response a while ago was any indication,' he immediately mocked on a drawling note and had her face reddening anew. She should have known better than to attempt to put him in his place when her own inexcusable behaviour had left her open to just such mortifying remarks. 'Perhaps I could do you a favour by telling him what he's missing.'

'Don't you dare!' she burst out, aghast. She could believe him capable of doing it, if only to discomfort Garth.

'He wouldn't understand?' came the innocent-sounding, but subtly toned question.

How could she expect him to? She didn't even understand herself why she appeared to have no defences whatsoever against this man. 'Would you, if the positions were reversed?' she countered with some asperity.

He smiled indolently. 'Sweetheart, if I was engaged to you I'd be making damned sure there'd be no reason for you to be looking to another man to cater to any of your needs because I'd be well and truly seeing to them myself, believe me!'

He probably could too, she conceded, grudgingly, even though she hadn't meant if the position had been reversed specifically with regard to Garth. Nonetheless ... 'And—and neither am I looking for someone to cater to any of my needs now, as you put it!' she protested heatedly. 'You're the one who keeps grabbing hold of me, not the other way around!'

'You, merely employing the most novel method of rejection I've ever encountered, hmm?'

Devon turned her face away again, chewing at her lip discomfitedly. Did he always have to be quite so ruthlessly forthright? 'I—well—since you keep implying I suffer from a lack of it, maybe I just figured I should make the most of the opportunities you so obligingly present me with to gain more experience,' she parried with a protective flippancy.

Hunt's sable-framed eyes glinted with lazy provocation. 'In which event, it's doubtless just as well I don't practise such a rigid self-control as your inestimable fiancé.'

'No, it is not!' she refuted in no little dismay. Oh, lord, what had she done now? Unwittingly insinuated the very opposite to what she really wanted? 'I'm more than content with matters as they are—or as they *were* until you arrived,' she inserted hastily in order to make her position quite clear, 'so—so now, if you feel you've amused yourself sufficiently for one morning, I'd be glad if you would let go of me.' Her voice became tinged with defensive sarcasm as she began straining away from him. 'Thanks to you I'm now covered in sand, and I'd like to wash it off.'

With an unruffled grin, he resumed his sitting position, but continued to eye her humorously as she scrambled hurriedly to her feet. 'I could always brush it off, if you would prefer,' he drawled.

Devon simply replied with a nettled glare and set off for the deepest water available in the lagoon now that the tide was just about at its lowest. It wasn't only the sand she felt in need of washing away now, but also the disturbing image of his hands moving freely over her smooth skin which his last bantering offer had waywardly implanted in her mind.

Later, after having returned their snorkelling gear to the house and collected the picnic lunch Violet had prepared, they began the climb towards the top of The Pinnacle. Only now Devon's former feeling of companionship towards the man accompanying her had dissipated entirely, and although she didn't attempt to deliberately hide anything from him, the spontaneity and enthusiasm that had been present during their exploration of the reef weren't in evidence, her information brief and supplied in an offhand manner.

As ever, the panorama visible from the peak was magnificent, providing as it did an uninterrupted view of the whole island together with its surrounding coral, as well as the long, foam-swept ribbon reefs in the far distance that denoted the outer barrier as the incoming swells from the misnamed Pacific broke over them rhythmically. Behind their protective edges, to landward, the azure water was calmer, with only an occasional surge of white to indicate the presence of other formations that could prove so treacherous to the unknowledgeable, while to the south a few smaller, uninhabited islands could be seen on the horizon, the whole outlook glittering brilliantly beneath a cloudless blue sky.

They had lunch in the shade of a young coconut

palm a little way down from the peak, and as he bit absently into a crisp apple afterwards, Hunt looked over the seascape again contemplatively before settling his gaze on Devon's slightly moody countenance.

'So you don't really get much of a view from up here, huh?' he reminded her on a sardonic note of her original contention when she had taken him out to Rocky Point.

'Just a case of familiarity having bred contempt, I suppose,' she excused with a shrug.

'And the graves, and the cave paintings? Was it familiarity that made you forget to mention them too?'

'I guess it must have been,' she wasn't above claiming. 'Although you've seen them all now, so I really can't see what difference it makes.'

'Except that from here I can also see another two or three coves north of Careen Beach that, to date, I also haven't heard mentioned or seen.'

Devon glanced towards the area herself, as much to avoid his penetrating gaze as anything. 'You hadn't heard of the mangroves either until we went there but you didn't particularly want to see them,' she temporised evasively.

'Meaning, those coves don't have much to re-commend them?'

Aware his eyes were still focused intently in her direction, she shifted restively and studiously made certain their glances didn't connect. 'Well, no, not exactly,' she admitted awkwardly. Then, on a more defiant note, 'I just thought you'd be able to discover at least some of the island without my help!'

'Despite knowing Matt was expecting you to show me *everything* Cowrie has to offer?' Hunt's expression assumed a satirically disbelieving cast.

Devon heaved a disgruntled breath. 'I didn't realise that would mean my spending almost every waking minute in your company, though!' she grimaced.

Her mutinous outburst brought a disarming smile to his lips, and had her wishing inconsequentially that he wasn't so damned good looking. However, instead of making some goading retort, as she was half expecting, he merely concentrated his attention on what apparently interested him most by assuming, 'Both coves being much the same as Careen Beach, then?'

Relief, that he hadn't commented on her last rankled remark—with disastrous results from her standpoint, no doubt—plus a certain lingering disconcertion, had her answering unthinkingly and, in consequence, more informatively than she had done for some time.

'Sandy Bay, the first one is, but Shell Beach—it's only one really, not two—is a little different. It has only a narrow passage between the reef and the beach, which means of course that it's not so good for just swimming, but not surprisingly in view of its name, that's really the one to go to if you want to see the largest variety of shells, and especially after a storm when different ones are washed up from the deep,' she relayed.

'I see.' Hunt's mouth took on an oblique slant. 'It would appear your services as a guide don't finish today, after all, then.' And when she didn't reply—wouldn't was more like it, 'Matt was also telling me this happens to be a favoured turtle breeding ground. Something else that just slipped your mind?' A sceptically quirking brow spoke volumes.

Now Devon did deign to answer, challengingly. 'Yes, as a matter of fact, it did!' she flared, and quite truthfully. 'Even though the season's almost finished, some late ones have still been arriving on the night tide during the last couple of weeks in order to lay their eggs, but due to having a considerable amount on my mind this last few days,' tartly expressed, 'I haven't checked for signs of any more of them having come ashore and, as a result, clean forgot about them!'

'Okay, one to you this time,' he laughed, holding up a hand in a gesture of submission. 'That should make us square for the day . . . and be reason enough for a return of that smile of yours, shouldn't it?'

Struck once again by his ready good humour—she suspected Garth wouldn't be prepared to forgive and forget anywhere near so easily—it was impossible for Devon's normally sunny nature not to assert itself in response and the corners of her soft mouth suddenly started to curve upwards.

'That's more like it,' Hunt promptly approved, and creating within her an oddly pleased feeling she could only be rid of by giving herself a severe mental shake. With his folded arms resting across updrawn knees, he went on idly, 'Matt also informs me you have quite an extensive array of shells at the house. I'd be interested to see them if I could.'

The beginnings of Devon's smile faded abruptly. 'They're not for sale, if that's what you've got in mind,' she informed him tightly.

'So who suggested they were?' He rubbed a hand part way round his neck and shook his head in patent incredulity. 'Hell! What have I done to make you so suspicious of everything I damn well say?'

Thinking about it, she couldn't have said for certain. In fact, if she was really honest, she'd concede that any underhand tactics so far had all been perpetrated by herself, not him. A subconscious ploy just to hopefully keep him at that safe distance? she now wondered. Not that it seemed to have been particularly successful, the rueful thought immediately followed, and had her dipping her head uncomfortably.

'All right, I—I'm sorry,' she apologised in jerky accents. But feeling obliged to at least try to be as pleasant in defeat as he had been, half smiled whimsically, 'I guess that makes it two to one in your favour now.'

His answering smile had her senses reeling. 'I'd rather just see your collection of shells,' he averred gently.

'That too, then,' she suddenly found herself allowing.

'Now?'

'If—if you like, and if there's—there's nothing else you want to see round here.' She waved a hand about her somewhat distractedly as she fought to recover her equilibrium.

'It should finish the day off very nicely,' he contended, swiftly consigning the remains from their lunch to the basket before rising lithely to his feet and extending a helping hand towards her.

Accepting it, Devon released it again as soon as she was upright. 'I noticed before that the *Kanandah*'s not at her mooring. Where's she gone?' she enquired in an effort to camouflage her still inexplicably unsettled emotions.

'To Northport, for extra supplies. We're giving a barbecue tomorrow night and everyone on the island's invited,' he informed her, casually.

'To celebrate . . .'

'As return hospitality for all that's been extended to us since our arrival,' was the purposeful interposition Then, as an addition, as if guessing what her reaction would be, 'And I don't want to hear any excuses from you about not attending.'

'Well, I—umm. . .'

'Or I'll be up to the house and carry you down there myself, kicking and screaming all the way, if necessary,' he broke in again to threaten drily.

He would too! Devon knew only too well, and sighed. At the moment both her thoughts and her emotions were far too confused, and confusing, for her to want to spend more time in his company than she absolutely had to, but simultaneously, he obviously didn't intend to take no for an answer.

'Not that I would be kicking and screaming, anyway, but . . . you don't exactly give a person much choice, do you?' she gibed quietly.

Hunt's teasing grin made an indolent appearance. 'How could I when, whether reluctantly given or not, your assistance has probably aided us most?'

'I see,' she acknowledged with a faint nod. Strangely, she found it a somewhat depressing reason.

CHAPTER SIX

ALTHOUGH she had spent a quite uneventful, but once again unexpectedly enjoyable, morning with Hunt exploring Sandy Bay and Shell Beach by walking over the exposed reef at low tide rather than swimming over it on this occasion, Devon was still not looking forward to attending the barbecue at the bottom camp the following evening—as indicated by the slowness with which she dressed for the affair. Her aunt had long since left together with their guests—though she strongly suspected that woman's early departure was most likely to have been prompted by a desire to lend a helping hand if it was needed—so that only her father and herself still remained at the house.

A knock on her door a few minutes later, however, showed that even he was ready to leave now and with a resigned sigh she pulled her comb through her lightly waving blonde hair one last time before joining him.

'You look appropriately nautical tonight,' Granville smiled as they made their way down the back steps.

Involuntarily, Devon glanced down at her navy blue trim-fitting shorts and matching blue and white striped top. 'Mmm, I suppose I do. I hadn't realised,' she returned ruefully.

'It was very nice of Hunt to think of putting on something like this, though, wasn't it?'

'Mmm.' Her answer was as laconically, as grudgingly, made as her last. She kicked absently at a stone on the path with a sneakered foot, her expression thoughtful. 'He's lucky to be in a position where he can do such things at his age.'

'Fortunate, maybe, but I don't think there was much luck, as such, attached to it. More like a lot of damned hard work as far as I can make out,' he amended on a wry note.

Much as she herself had surmised the day before? 'Oh?' She raised her brows quizzically, promptingly.

He expelled a meditative breath. 'Well, from what Royce was telling me I gather Hunt had something of a hard beginning and that he's been working ever since he was eight or nine. First, after school hours, and then later working for a builder during the day, while also starting up his own industrial cleaning business at night. The latter becoming extremely lucrative in a very short time because he was willing to take on anything and everything, including the dirtiest and at times distinctly dangerous work that no one else was interested in doing. From there he could then begin to utilise that inborn sense he obviously possesses for being able to recognise potential when he sees it, and moved into the development field with a couple of purchases of land that at the time were considered to be almost worthless backblocks, but which now happen to form the centre of a new, thriving community.' He paused, a broad smile shaping his lips. 'And of course, once having made your first million, it becomes progressively easier to make the others that follow.'

Devon nodded silently. Except for the details, it was more or less as she had suspected. Nevertheless, even though she could admire him for his achievements, that didn't make the knowledge that his discerning eyes had now alighted on her island any more acceptable!

'You know, I suppose, that he's already asked Violet to stay on here if he does buy the place?' he now turned to enquire in an evidently pleased tone.

She nodded again. 'While you're envisioning sailing off on your own in a lovely brand new boat, no doubt!' She couldn't stop all signs of her antipathy towards the idea from showing.

He didn't deny it, but merely suggested quietly, 'You could always come with me.'

The temptation to do so was strong, if only in order to keep an eye on his health, except for one thing. 'And Garth? What's he supposed to do in the meantime, wait patiently for his fiancée to condescend to return?' She slanted him a sardonic look. 'Or are you now going to suggest that he comes too?'

'Hardly!' he half laughed, half snorted. 'You know as well as I do that Garth doesn't know the difference between a jib and a gybe, and we'd be lucky to even clear the channel with him giving a hand. That is, if we could manage to part him from his books long enough to join in to that extent.'

Unfortunately, he wasn't wrong, and she couldn't restrain a wry smile in acknowledgment. 'Besides, I thought your whole idea was to do it single-handed,' she put forward with a sigh.

'Well, yes, it is really,' he conceded. But with a quickly added, 'Although I'd have no objections to you coming along if you really wanted to.' His eyes twinkled abruptly. 'I never have particularly liked preparing food, as you know.'

'Oh, thanks!' she retorted drily. 'In other words, you'd only want me along as head cook and bottle washer, is that it?'

'No, I was only joking,' he chuckled. 'You should

know you're the only one I would want with me, in
any capacity. Although as Hunt was only saying this
morning, with a new boat. . .'

Devon didn't hear the remainder of his words. She
was too occupied in seething over the fact that Hunt
was still apparently encouraging her father in his
scheme. How dare he continue to override her wishes
just because he didn't happen to see the matter in the
same light she did! It was purely a family concern and
should have had absolutely nothing to do with him! It
was *her* father at risk, not his, so it was easy for him to
blithely dismiss the inherent dangers involved and
urge her father into fulfilling his ambition. If anything
untoward did occur, it certainly wasn't likely to cause
him any heartbreak! With her head angling higher by
the second, she now approached the brightly lantern-
lit camp in a less reluctant, but decidedly more
belligerent, frame of mind.

The first things they noticed as they entered the
clearing were three long tables surrounded by chairs—
something else the *Kanandah* had collected from town,
Devon deduced—already laden with bowls and
platters of salads, cold meats, and seafoods of every
description, and the two permanently fixed gas
barbecues being industriously supervised by two men
she didn't know, but whom she presumed were part of
the *Kanandah*'s crew, their cooking plates literally
smothered with sizzling, succulent steaks, chops and
sausages, which filled the warm night air with an
appetising aroma.

Somewhere a stereo was providing background
music, anything from disco to classical, a few of the
mingling crowd already moving energetically to a
currently popular tune, some merely standing or

sitting around talking in twos and threes, others handing out an assortment of drinks from huge ice-filled containers.

Observing Royce seated with Stan Noonan, a long-time friend and frequent visitor to the island, Granville was soon heading in their direction once Devon had indicated she would join her aunt, whose help evidently hadn't been needed after all, and a couple of their guests. From where they were seated beneath a long-leaved pandanus she would be close enough to see what was going on, yet just far enough away to remain a little apart from it.

So far, she realised, she hadn't been able to distinguish Hunt's commanding figure among the crowd and she wondered if, for some reason, he was still aboard his yacht. Then no sooner had she finished mulling over his whereabouts than he came into view beside one of the barbecues, his arm draped loosely about attractively sarong-clad Pauline Telfer's bare shoulders, his shapely mouth curving appreciatively in response to what she was laughingly saying.

Oh, yes, now she'd shown him everything he wanted to see on the island, doubtless all his attention would be reserved for the dark-headed girl from now on! Devon denounced acidly, and then gave a horrified gasp, a wave of dismayed colour washing all the way up to her hairline. Dear God, why should she care who he bestowed all his attention on? She was engaged, wasn't she? And not only that, she didn't *want* to have anything more to do with him! By rights, she should have been relieved to see him with the other girl, certainly not nettled or—or resentful! she hesitantly supplied the most accurate word, and promptly wished more than ever that she hadn't come.

As a result of her perturbing reaction, Devon thereafter did her utmost to keep Hunt in sight—solely in order to ensure that wherever he was, she wasn't, and thereby prove to herself, at least, that she was satisfied to be without his company—but only when she had successfully managed to install herself the furthest distance possible away from him at the table for their meal did she feel able to relax a little and thus deliberately ignore his presence altogether as she concentrated, if somewhat uninterestedly, on the food in front of her.

Afterwards, though, it became rather more difficult to retain a watch on his movements, as more of those present began to engage in the, of necessity, casual dancing, and especially as she herself wasn't exactly an unpopular partner. At the conclusion of one such humour-filled circuit of the clearing, Devon stopped to get herself a drink before returning to her seat and suddenly discovered Pauline beside her intent on doing the same, but without Hunt in tow, she noted thankfully.

'So what do you think of the new man in my life? Spunky, eh?' the brunette smiled almost gloatingly as she poured herself a glass of champagne from an already opened bottle standing in an ice bucket.

Devon swallowed convulsively. 'You mean, Hunt, do you?' she queried tautly.

'Well, naturally! Who else?' Pauline smirked in amusement. 'We've been practically inseparable ever since he arrived. And that yacht of his! Have you seen it yet? I have . . . on a number of occasions, actually,' with an archly meaningful look, 'and I can tell you it's out of this world!'

'Yes, I should imagine it would be.' Devon strove to

act unconcernedly. Why should it matter to her how often the other girl had been on the *Kanandah*, or for what purpose? 'It's certainly a beautiful looking boat.'

'As is the owner!' Pauline rolled her eyes expressively. 'I'll bet you've regretted being tied to your fiancé this last couple of days while you've been showing him over the island.'

So she knew about that, did she? But then, it was more than likely everyone did, Devon supposed. 'Not in the slightest, as a matter of fact,' she now answered with a smile of her own, forced though it may have been. 'Personally, I've never cared much for the kind who make it so obvious they're averse to committing themselves.'

'Meaning?' suspiciously.

'Only that I prefer the more reliable type.'

'I meant with regard to Hunt, not what you prefer!' came the impatient clarification.

As Devon had deduced. She gave a vague shrug. 'Well, he is in his early thirties and still very much unattached, after all, and I'd be very surprised if there hadn't been a considerable number of women in his life on the way there. As you said, he *is* good looking, and when coupled with his obvious wealth, I'm sure it's a combination he's become extremely adept at using to his own advantage over the years.'

'Yes, well, I don't know how you, of all people, could make a judgment like that,' Pauline asserted with a dismissive toss of her head. 'I mean, as I was explaining to Hunt only yesterday, stuck way out here all the time as you are, you wouldn't know anything about men with only your father and Garth to gauge by.'

Devon inhaled furiously. They had been discussing

her! 'Oh, and just why would you be explaining anything about me to him?'

'Because he asked me about you, that's why,' the other girl laughed insouciantly. 'I don't think he knows what to make of you. You being so prim in your outlook at times where men are concerned, and all. At least, either that, or he just feels sorry for you, I guess.'

Sorry for her! Well, not for trying to deprive her of her home, that was for certain! So what did that leave? That he pitied her for her lack of experience and had therefore set out to do her a favour by broadening her horizons in that regard, and probably providing himself and Pauline with some amusement by discussing them with her afterwards too! She squared her shoulders determinedly.

'Well, you can tell him from me there's no need for him to concern himself on either count,' she declared, refusing to show that in reality she was crying inside with both shame and disappointment. 'As it so happens I couldn't care less whether he can make me out or not, while as for feeling sorry for me . . . well, I suggest he reserves that emotion for himself! With his attitude, I'd say he needs it far more than I ever have!'

'Okay, if that's what you want,' Pauline agreed obligingly.

'I do!' Devon confirmed with a positive nod and, replacing her can of fruit-flavoured mineral water— her throat felt too tight to get anything down it now— she turned on her heel and left the clearing altogether instead of returning to her seat.

Momentarily, she wasn't even aware of which particular direction she was headed, but then the feel of sand underfoot brought her back to her surround-

ings and, tossing her sneakers on to the ipomea-
covered dunes, she continued walking away from the
camp along the beach.

'And just where do you think you're going?' Hunt's
unmistakable voice suddenly sounded some distance
behind her.

'To look for turtles,' she said the first thing that
came to mind, without stopping.

'It's a bit early for that, isn't it? The tide won't be
full for almost another two hours yet.'

She wasn't sure but she thought his voice sounded
closer that time and she increased her pace a little.
'I'm in no hurry,' she shrugged.

The stifled expletive that ensued was definitely
nearer, but just how near she didn't realise until she
was abruptly spun around to face him. 'Okay, so
what's been bugging you all evening, hmm?' he
demanded on an exasperated note.

Devon took a step backwards, her eyes flashing with
a militant light, her breathing quickening uncontrollably. How dared he stand there acting as if *she* had
something to answer for, when in actual fact it should
have been just the opposite!

'For a start, your continuing interference in my
family's affairs!' she exploded tempestuously. 'I told
you the other night why Dad shouldn't be considering
that trip!'

'And I told you why I thought he should!'

'That doesn't make it your business to be
encouraging him to. . .'

'He asked for my opinion, and I gave it!' he
interrupted peremptorily.

She rounded her eyes sarcastically. 'And why would
your opinion suddenly be so important to him?'

'Maybe because he knows his self-absorbed daughter's would be too biased!' he shot back in unsparing tones.

Her chin started to tremble and she clenched her jaw resolutely to stop it. 'In that case, I wonder why he invited me to go with him, then!'

'And are you?' Hunt probed watchfully instead of replying.

'How could I?' she flared. 'I've got a fiancé to consider too, remember?' Halting, she sent him an acrimonious glare before going on bitterly, 'But of course you do! After all, discussions concerning Garth and myself are apparently nothing new for you and your latest girlfriend! What do you do, give her a rundown on each day's proceedings so you can laugh about it together? That m-must really top off y-your evenings!' Her voice began to break and she swallowed painfully. 'Or perhaps that's when your unwanted pity comes to the fore, is it? That is, if it's possible for anyone as utterly ruthless and contemptible as you to even know the meaning of the word!' Now an ungovernable sob did force its way out, and with her eyes misting treacherously she took to her heels.

It appeared Hunt didn't see that as the end of the matter as she did, however, for within a few strides he was level with her again. Wanting only to escape him, Devon swerved and raced for the dunes, an action which immediately proved to be a mistake as her foot caught in one of the creepers and she went sprawling to the ground. Hunt promptly sank down on to his haunches beside her, but when she would have scrambled to her feet again a hand catching hold of her ankle had her collapsing unceremoniously once more. A hold that was then exchanged for one around her wrist, which accordingly guaranteed any other attempts to flee were out of the question.

'Now perhaps you'd care to tell me just what the hell that was all about!' he suggested at his satirically mocking best.

Nor surprisingly, it wasn't an approach that appealed to his captive. 'As if you don't know! But that's all you like to do, isn't it, Hunt? Make fun of people!' she charged, striking out at him with her free hand.

In next to no time that wrist was securely imprisoned too, and as he also lowered himself into a sitting position, he pulled her around so that she was at right angles to him.

'No, not all,' he refuted finally, but with some subtle nuance evident that had a slight nervousness mingling with her rancour. 'Right at present I can think of a number of things I'd like to do to you, sweetheart, believe me! And quite possibly might . . . if I don't soon get some answers!'

'I thought that was purely your domain!' she dared to gibe heedlessly. 'You surely don't expect me—the naïve misfit you apparently can't figure out, so in your patronising arrogance you decide to pity instead—to have anything to say that would be of interest to you!'

'Yes, that's exactly what I'm expecting!' he asserted roughly, his brows snapping together in a frown. 'Because I only wish to God I knew what on earth you're talking about with all this "naïve misfit" and "pity" rubbish!'

'Is it?' Devon attempted to counter in derisive disbelief but was unable to prevent an edge of despondency from creeping in. 'Your girlfriend tells a different story!'

'Well, that's enlightening, to say the least!' he retorted, caustically dry. 'I wasn't even aware I had a girlfriend!'

'Oh? Then what else would you call someone you've evidently been almost inseparable from ever since you arrived?'

To her anguish, he laughed at that. 'Sweetheart, if you cast your mind back, I believe you'll find the only person I've been almost inseparable from since I arrived is *you*!' he pointed out wryly. 'Although somehow I get the feeling that's not who you were meaning.'

'As you very well know!' she retorted resentfully, although in a somewhat more moderate fashion now that she understood the reason for his amusement. 'We're talking about Pauline!' Her tone began to strengthen again. 'You know, the girl you like to discuss—ridicule, more like—Garth and myself with.'

'Do I?' His brows peaked graphically in unison. 'That's the first I've heard of it.'

'Well, it obviously isn't for her! And if you weren't discussing us, then why would she be explaining anything about me to you?'

'Oh, yeah, I remember now,' he drawled on an ironic note that did nothing to appease her smouldering feelings. 'I asked her if you'd ever dated any of the yachtsmen who called in here. She said, no, not to her knowledge. End of conversation!' One corner of his mouth lifted with mocking eloquence. 'Big discussion!'

Devon gazed at him dubiously. 'Pauline implied differently,' she put forward, but in somewhat less assured tones.

'And because I'm automatically on trial every time

open my bloody mouth, you believe her unquestion-
ingly, of course!' For only the second time since she
had known him there was a decided sting in Hunt's
voice. 'And that, despite the fact that, any idea of
yours to the contrary, I've hardly spoken to the girl
more than half a dozen times, and then usually only
briefly!'

'I—well—she's got no reason to lie!' Devon
abruptly found herself on the defensive.

'And I have?'

The hard deliberation with which the question was
delivered had her stirring discomfitedly. She supposed
not, and yet . . . 'Well, you certainly appear to be on—
er—very close terms with her! Every time you were
together back there,' nodding towards the clearing,
'you had your arm round her!' she recalled tartly, and
a trifle reproachfully too, she noted in gathering
dismay.

Hunt flexed a broad shoulder dismissively. 'The
way Pauline inserts herself beside you, it's difficult to
do anything else.'

'And is that also why she's been out to the
Kanandah so often?' She pulled a disbelieving face.

'I wouldn't know.' He shrugged again. 'I've only
been aboard once when she's been out there.'

That once having been sufficiently satisfactory,
though, from Pauline's viewpoint! 'How disappointing
for you!' she couldn't restrain from gibing, then
immediately wished she hadn't on seeing the shrewdly
speculative look that came over his face.

'Oh? What makes you say that?' His head tilted
lazily and he ran a disturbing finger along the fragile
line of her jaw. 'And in such an—umm—accusing
fashion too!'

'Accusing!' she just managed to get out with an appropriately humorous tinkle of laughter. 'Don't be ridiculous! Why should I care what the two of you do?'

'That's what I wonder ... because you do seem to be dwelling on the matter, don't you, sweetheart?'

'O-only in order to discover who's telling the truth! And—and only in so far as it concerns myself, of course,' she added hastily, judiciously.

Leaning forward slightly, Hunt slid his hands slowly up her arms and across her shoulders to cup her head securely. 'Then perhaps this will help make up your mind,' he proposed softly as his head lowered to hers.

It wasn't hard to divine his intention and Devon strained frantically away from the touch she knew could turn her bones to liquid and what little defence she did possess into a disquieting, unconditional capitulation. 'No! Stop it! That proves nothing!' she contended desperately.

'It does to me.'

But what? That she could no more resist him than could Pauline? The humiliating thought gave her the stimulus to remind, albeit with a jerky breathlessness, 'Be-besides, there's G-Garth.'

'So?' Hunt enquired with indolent indifference against her quivering lips.

She swallowed despairingly, guiltily. 'He is my f-fiancé, after all.'

'Then maybe he shouldn't be!' came the disconcerting opinion, and with none of the irresolution she had evinced, as his mouth finally, sensuously claimed hers.

No, maybe he shouldn't, Devon was forced into conceding on finding the hands that had been meant

to be pushing at Hunt were instead spontaneously
linking about his neck, and her lips responding
unreservedly to his tantalising possession of them. Not
while another man was capable of making her forget
everything but himself and awakening such potent
feelings within her as this man could, and was doing—
and as Garth never had.

With her lips willingly returning the demanding
pressure of his, Devon swayed towards Hunt's virile
frame unknowingly, and offered no resistance when
his encircling arms drew her down beside him on the
sand. His mouth was warm and compelling as it
moved with unhurried thoroughness from her lips to
her throat, her shoulder, and back to her eagerly
waiting mouth again; his hands strong but gentle as
they traced her curving form; the hard male shape of
him stimulating as it pressed against her invitingly
pliant body.

Gaining courage, Devon slid her hands under the
silk knit of his shirt, feeling the corded muscles of his
back tense beneath the experimental play of her
fingers. She had never touched a man in such a
fashion before and the emotions it galvanised into life
were entirely new to her too. As were those that soon
after had her pulse racing erratically and her breath
coming in ragged gasps when first Hunt's hands and
then his stirring mouth found and explored the
rounded contours and throbbing nipples of her sun-
gilded breasts.

With a groan, Hunt clasped her to him even more
tightly, his fingers tangling amidst the silken strands
of her tousled, golden hair as his mouth sought hers
one last fevered time. 'Oh, God, you could drive a
man to distraction!' he declared huskily against her

parted lips. 'Much more of this and you won't have any innocence left at all.' His lips twisted ruefully. 'You learn too fast, I'm afraid, little sea nymph.'

Still floundering in a sea of newly rioting emotions, Devon flushed self-consciously. In other words, she had shown herself too willing, too uninhibited, she deduced, cringing inwardly at the humiliating thought. Obviously he hadn't minded indulging in a few harmless kisses, but just as evidently he hadn't anticipated, or wanted, it progressing any further. Easing away from him she dragged her top back into place embarrassedly.

'I'm sorry,' she offered stiffly, her features held no less tautly as she attempted to disguise her feelings of shame.

Hunt gazed at her strangely. 'For what, for crying out loud?'

Saved the added mortification of answering by a familiar female voice suddenly calling, 'Hunt! Hunt, where are you? It's unkind of you to disappear like this. You know you're the only one I like dancing with. We fit together . . .' there was an expressive pause, 'so cosily.' Devon took the opportunity to gain her feet with alacrity.

'It would appear your girlfriend feels deserted,' she sniped bitterly.

In a matter of seconds Hunt was on his own feet. 'And I told you, I don't *have* a girlfriend!' he denied on a rough note.

'No, it doesn't sound like it!' she scorned and, just managing to evade the arm he flung out to stop her, fled between two bushes of sea lettuce just before Pauline made her appearance via the beach.

By the time Devon had cut through to the path

leading up to the house her cheeks were wet with tears of pain and abasement. Tears that were still falling when she reached the safety of her bedroom. Never, *never*, would she allow him to make her feel so degraded again! she promised herself vehemently.

CHAPTER SEVEN

DURING the next couple of days Devon kept herself as busy as possible at the house, ostensibly to help her aunt prepare for their coming influx of Eastern personnel, but also in the hope of avoiding giving herself time to think, as much as anything. Nevertheless, the frequent sight of her father, Royce and Hunt either checking certain aspects of the island's equipment, or else just merely conversing, made it very difficult for her to exclude Hunt from her mind completely for any length of time, and particularly when, after seeing him return to the *Kanandah* each day, she made her way down to Careen Beach for her usual swim.

Then she found it almost impossible to keep him out of her thoughts at all. Perhaps because the beach continually reminded her of the one occasion when they had seemed to be in total harmony, she reasoned pensively. Although that really didn't satisfactorily explain just why she should also find herself, despite all her motives for not doing so, missing his mostly aggravating presence to quite such an extent, the perturbing thought usually ensued.

Because miss him she certainly did, she finally had to admit, even if only to herself and with the greatest reluctance. The same as she had to concede, after many days spent desperately fighting the notion, that she also missed those arousing kisses he had bestowed on her daily and which, subconsciously at least, she grudgingly acknowledged, she had eventually come to expect. The reason why she should miss them, though, wasn't one she cared to delve into too deeply, however. It was sufficiently discomposing, not to say alarming, to discover she missed them at all!

Hunt, on the other hand, didn't appear to miss her company in the slightest. In fact, he gave the appearance of being quite content with matters as they were, treating her with a casualness that probably troubled her all the more due to its sheer nonchalance, on those rare occasions when they did accidentally meet, although without any diminishing of his customary mockery, she noted, but definitely without displaying even the smallest desire to spend any time alone with her again. A circumstance that only added weight to her supposition that he had merely been amusing himself previously, first by seeking to prove she was no more immune to his indisputably proficient brand of love-making than any other female probably was, and then by making her feel an abandoned wanton once he had succeeded in his aim.

No less depressing either, Devon discovered, was that his last thought-provoking remark concerning her fiancé also refused to be dispelled from her mind so that, as a result, when Garth did manage to get out to the island on a locally owned yacht for a few days, she greeted him with an enthusiasm and demonstrativeness that hadn't characterised their relationship before in an attempt to prove that he was as capable of stimulating the same fervent feelings within her as Hunt was.

When he not only didn't, but also remonstrated in a somewhat annoyed tone, 'For heaven's sake, Devon, I hardly think it's necessary for you to be quite so—so unrestrained! After all, I've only been away for a couple of days, and when all's said and done, I don't really consider it's very feminine of you to make your feelings known in such a fashion. I've always believed that to be the man's sole prerogative!' she had no choice but to dismally accede that he wasn't the man for her as she had previously believed.

At the same time, however, and against everything that told her it was only fair that she advise Garth of her decision immediately, she still had no intention of actually breaking their engagement and returning his ring while Hunt was still on the island. The idea that he would promptly deduce, correctly as it might be, that he had been the cause of such an action and thereby doubtlessly provide him with even more humorous satisfaction, was just too humiliating to contemplate, and so she did her best to portray the role of one entirely complacent with their lot during the remainder of her fiancé's stay.

The day after Garth's departure the *Coral Trader* arrived again, this time with Hunt's staff aboard together with all their equipment, including a water drilling rig—something Devon's father had also often thought of having shipped out to the island, but the cost had always been beyond him. Apparently, though, Hunt was of the same idea as he was, that as with the Great Artesian Basin which covered over a million square miles of the mainland, after millenia of such high rainfall as the north received there was more than likely a good chance that somewhere beneath Cowrie there was an even greater intake bed than the one at present yielding the island's comparatively unsubstantial water supply.

Not surprisingly, Violet was in her element with so

many more, and appreciative, mouths to feed, and after the first few days even Devon lost most of her antagonism towards them in the face of their affable and often hilarious company. Not that she saw much of any of them during the day, but with the evening meal their good-natured bantering, from which neither she, her father and aunt, nor their two remaining guests were allowed to escape, would invariably begin so that by the end of the first week it seemed as if they had all known each other for years instead of merely days.

The only fly in the ointment Devon could see was that two days after the men's arrival—and coincidental with the day that Pauline Telfer and her brother departed in their yacht, she noted caustically—Hunt and Royce also moved into the guesthouse in order to both be on site as the investigations proceeded, as well as because the massive dining table provided far greater space and convenience for their nightly reviews and discussions. It wasn't an arrangement that suited Devon at all, and for the hundredth time wished her father wasn't so damned accommodating where the younger man was concerned, because it was he who had suggested the move!

In the middle of the following week the drilling rig struck the water they had been searching for so diligently, and at a flow rate that predicted Cowrie would never again be subject to a shortage of that precious commodity no matter how many people stayed on the island. Naturally enough, for all those connected with the company it was a result to be celebrated, but not for Devon because she somehow knew that nothing would stop the sale taking place now. Nevertheless, throughout the meal that evening she did her best to keep her disconsolate feelings from showing, particularly when she became aware of Hunt's eyes fixed intently upon her as they so often had in the past. Whatever happened, she wasn't going to provide him with any more gratification by revealing just how despondent she actually was.

Not even after serving everyone else's coffee in the sitting room—their usual nightly conference presumably having been waived due to the day's events—and she took Hunt's in to the dining room where he was perusing a pile of sketches and papers alone did she betray by so much as a change of expression how the discovery had affected her.

For his part, Hunt watched her deposit the cup on the table with the same absorbed gaze that had been present during the meal, but then, as she turned to leave caught hold of her wrist in a loose grip momentarily—just long enough to bring her to a halt—whereupon he immediately released it again.

'I'm sorry,' he said quietly, unexpectedly, his glance unwavering. 'You know what today's discovery means, don't you?'

'That Cowrie will now definitely change hands?' With her features tightly controlled, she nodded. Then, accompanied by a suitably deprecating shrug, 'Oh, well, as has been said before, I guess all good things have to end sometime, don't they? I daresay I'll survive.'

'Even without the extra your fiancé tried angling for?'

Now her demeanour did alter. To one of total bewilderment. 'I don't know what you're talking about. What extra?' she frowned in confusion.

'The additional sum he wanted added to the purchase price which, he assured us, would enable him to guarantee your full co-operation in future,' he divulged bluntly.

'Oh!' Astonishment had Devon sinking on to the chair next to him as his completely unanticipated revelation seemed to reverberate within her head. Suddenly her eyes narrowed and she looked at him sharply. 'You said . . . us? Are you saying you have a witness to this—this supposed proposition?'

Hunt's mouth shaped sardonically. 'Still as doubtful as ever, eh, sweetheart?' he charged. 'But yes, I have a witness . . . Royce, as a matter of fact.' He paused, significantly. 'Plus a tape recording of the whole miserable conversation, as it so happens. When he came out to the *Kanandah* wanting to see me the last time he was here, I thought it could be interesting to have a copy of what he had to say.'

Devon's hopes plummeted, and in their stead came indignation. Even without a tape recording she wouldn't have doubted a confirmation from Royce. He had always struck her as being extremely honest and above board. But that Garth should have had the hide to take it on himself to try and extort, there really wasn't any other word for it, more money from them was absolutely insupportable! And if she had wanted any further reason for convincing herself she was doing the right thing in intending to break their engagement, this was well and truly it! But by having mentioned her, did that also mean. . .

'But you surely don't believe I had anything to do with that, do you?' she gasped. 'I mean, why would I be asking for more money? I don't even know what you offered in the first place!'

His head angled in a manner she could only call sceptical. 'Don't you?'

'No!' she almost shouted. Inexplicably, it was suddenly very important that she convince him of that, as well as having had nothing whatsoever to do with Garth's conniving. 'Just ask Dad if you don't believe me! He can tell you I wasn't interested in knowing! The same as I told Garth I wasn't when he found out what your offer was!' Halting, her head drooped and her voice became huskier. 'I was only ever interested in retaining Cowrie, not in how much we were likely to get for it.'

'As I suspected when Wilkinson came to see us,' Hunt disclosed on a somewhat wry note. He uttered a short, humorless laugh. 'What I didn't expect, though, was that you were *so* against the sale that you didn't even want to know that much about it.'

'But you do believe I had nothing to do with Garth going to see you?' She reached out a tentatively pleading hand, then promptly retracted it before it could actually touch his arm.

'Yeah, well, maybe my judgment of human character is a little better than yours, because I had strong doubts right from the start regarding your likely involvement,' he drawled, not a little mockingly, and had her cheeks colouring in consequence.

It was the second time he had insinuated as much, and because he apparently hadn't believed she'd been a party to Garth's ploy, she now found herself feeling guilty for having suspected him of inventing the story.

'I'm sorry,' it was her turn to apologise now, dolefully. 'It was just that it came as such a shock, and on top of—on top of. . .' She faltered to a stop, trying frantically to regain her earlier expressionless manner.

For a minute or two silence reigned until Hunt broke it with an almost musing, 'I know you said you didn't want to work here if the sale took place, but have you ever considered at least remaining until the resort is ready to open? After all, the constructions crews, etcetera, will all have to be fed and taken care of and not even your aunt, as capable as she obviously is, could manage that without any help. I imagine she'll need at least another two, if not three, to help her, and I'm sure she'd much prefer it if you were one of them, especially as you do already know the ropes here.'

Aquamarine eyes flickered in surprise. 'You're offering me a job?' she sounded cautiously.

'Again,' his concurrence was drily given.

Devon's first thought was to refuse, outright, just as she had before, but then an almost defiant reasoning began to prevail. It was true, her aunt *would* require help, so why shouldn't she be one of those to provide it? Besides, as he had deduced, Aunt Violet would no doubt prefer it if she stayed, she told herself bracingly.

'All right, then for Aunt Violet's sake I will stay on . . . until the resort goes into operation,' she added the last hurriedly, just so he wouldn't think she was having second thoughts about her prior decision as well. 'Th-thank you.' It was an effort to get the words out but she supposed she owed him that much at least.

In response, Hunt's lips quirked expressively, as if well aware of her thought processes. 'Okay, I'll get Royce to advise the appropriate people within the company,' was all he said though.

Devon nodded her acknowledgment faintly and began to rise. She was pleased her time on the island had been extended, and yet, conversely, she was unsure now whether she had actually made the right decision.

Meanwhile, Hunt gathered up some of the sketches on the table. 'Would you like to see some of Clive's preliminary drawings before you go?' he suddenly looked up to enquire.

Once again, her initial thought was to decline, but unaccountably she found herself sitting again without consciously realising she was doing so. 'I guess so,' she shrugged, deciding that now she was re-seated she may as well, and accepted the sheaf of papers he handed her.

Clive Bassett was the company's architect and it didn't take her long to acknowledge, even if reluctantly, that he was obviously not only an able one but an extremely imaginative one also. Although the drawings were only in the rough, they depicted a variety of designs and layouts for the proposed resort, and even at that stage it was clear to see that the buildings were intended to blend in with their surroundings rather than dominate them. One sketch in particular caught her interest and after studying it for a few minutes her mouth began to curve wistfully.

'I like the general idea of that one,' she finally said impulsively. Actually, she hadn't meant to comment on any of them but the words just seemed to slip out of their own volition.

'Because it incorporates the house?' Hunt hazarded wryly.

'Probably,' she shrugged again, not wanting to discuss it further. The whole idea was still too new for her to be able to accept it with complete indifference. Fortunately, an abrupt pounding on the roof acted as a diversion and her expression took on a whimsical cast. 'What with today's discovery, and now this, it would appear you'll very shortly have more water than you know what to do with.'

Listening to the thunder of the rain, Hunt's brows rose quizzically. 'You're saying the wet's begun ... already?'

Tempted to endorse the assumption—it was evident there was still an amount of groundwork he wished completed before the rain did arrive in earnest—she eventually decided against it. The weather itself would soon disprove it, anyway.

'Not quite,' she therefore disclosed. 'It's just the first of our nightly deluges that come as a prelude. It'll be fine again by morning. Just distinctly more humid, that's all.'

'A comforting thought,' he immediately quipped on a rueful note, but obviously relieved all the same. Then, after a slight pause, 'While on the subject of drawings, though ... I hear from Matt that you've been doing some that could be suitable as a logo for the island.'

Devon shook her head vehemently, railing yet once more against her parent's loquaciousness. Wasn't there *anything* he didn't intend to disclose to this man? 'Not really,' she denied tautly. 'I was simply trying some new designs one time and they happened to be of shells, that's all.'

'Cowrie shells?'

'Well—yes—but they're nothing out of the ordinary.'

'Matt seemed to think they were some of the best you'd ever done,' he persisted.

Thanks Dad! she grimaced silently, tartly. 'Even if they are, they're still my property to do with as I see fit,' she opted to challenge instead of defend now.

'True,' he allowed, nodding. 'But since we want a logo, and you've apparently designed one that could be acceptable, don't you think it's a little petty, just because matters haven't turned out as you wanted, for us not to come to some arrangement?'

'Not particularly!' She eyed him rancorously. So now she was petty just because she wouldn't fall in with his wishes, was she? 'In any case, as far as I'm concerned one member of this family coming to an arrangement with you has been more than sufficient!'

'An arrangement, I might point out, however, that hasn't exactly been to your disadvantage!' Hunt retorted, his voice sharpening no less than hers.

'Monetary-wise, maybe!' she granted on a jeering note. 'But what's the use of money when, to get it, you have to sell the very thing you wanted to keep? That sort of defeats the purpose, doesn't it?'

'Except that Matt, as the owner, obviously *did* want to sell!'

His pungent reminder, as always, had her subsiding defeatedly, leaving her feeling empty inside. 'So he did,' she acceded in low, self-mocking tones. 'Your good luck, my bad, it would appear.' And in the same despondently flippant accents as she rose to her feet for the second time, 'Accordingly, I suppose there's no reason for you not to have my drawings either, is there? Especially since you've made me realise how meaningless it would be for me to keep them.' She turned for the doorway leading to the hall. 'I'll get them for you now.'

'Devon . . . for God's sake!' she heard him exclaim roughly behind her, but just kept walking. That was, until her ears also picked up the sound of his chair being thrust back, whereupon her pace increased markedly.

As it was, she reached her room only mere seconds in front of him, and before she could close the door behind her he had pushed peremptorily inside.

'I said I'd get them for you, Hunt! I didn't say you were welcome to come and collect them!' she immediatly gritted.

'aMybe not, but then I wasn't expecting you to react like you just did either! And believe it or not . . .' a captivatingly wry smile began playing about the edges of his attractive mouth, 'I was worried about you.'

Devon swallowed hard as a mute sob rose in her throat. Not so much as a result of what he'd said, but the realisation that if he had beckoned to her at that moment she knew she would willingly have fallen into his arms. Oh, God, what was the matter with her that she allowed him to have such an overwhelming effect on her, particularly after all he'd done? she despaired.

'Oh, I see, so to add to selfish and petty and all the other uncomplimentary adjectives you've described me with, you're now inferring I'm unbalanced too, are you?' she gibed. If her head couldn't rule her emotions where he was concerned, it did at least still have control of her words. 'Well, for your information, Hunter Kincaid, I can assure you you're way off beam because it would take a great deal more than anything you can throw at me to reduce me to that state!' Forcing out a faintly hysterical tinkle of amused laughter she moved across to her desk and picked up a folder which she held out to him. 'Call them a parting gift, if you like. In the hope we never meet again!'

Although he took the folder from her, it was only in order to throw it on to her bed. 'No, thanks! I don't need you doing me any favours, you perverse, petulant little bitch!' Hunt rasped, his eyes snapping with a steely blue fire she had never seen before. 'No matter how good they may or may not be, I wouldn't touch them now if you paid me! Thankfully, no one's irreplaceable, not even you, sweetheart,' witheringly, rather than endearingly, 'so I doubt I'll have any difficulty in finding someone else capable of designing a logo equally as good as, if not better than, any of yours! I merely thought you may have liked to know that something of yourself would be remaining on Cowrie even after you'd left!' He dipped his dark head mockingly, derisively, as he opened the door. 'Sorry! It appears my judgment—regarding you, at least— isn't as accurate as I believed—trusted—it to be!' And before she could even open her mouth he had gone, the door shutting with resounding finality behind him.

For a time Devon stood motionless, staring at the position where he had last been, her eyes blurring uncontrollably. She supposed she should have been happy—after all, it appeared she'd finally succeeded in really putting that distance between them that she'd always wanted—but unpredictably she wasn't. She was the most miserable and confused she had ever been in her life and, with a choking cry, she tossed her folder of drawings on to the floor carelessly before throwing herself on the bed in their place, her tears starting to fall at a rate that matched the rain continuing to drum overhead.

Three weeks later, without there having been more than a dozen cool sentences exchanged between them, Devon watched with an ache in the pit of her stomach as Hunt departed on the *Kanandah* one wet and windy, though still warm day. The rest of the company's personnel had left on the launch the day before, so that now she stood all alone on the verandah—her father having accepted Hunt's offer to take him to Northport in order that the appropriate papers connected with the island's sale might be signed and a deposit paid; her aunt deciding to take the opportunity to accompany them and have something of a holiday while she was still able—the tears that had kept appearing for no apparent reason during the last few weeks once again spilling over her thick lashes to mingle with the rain the wind was blowing unheeded on to her cheeks.

Brushing them away with the backs of her fingers she tried to concentrate on what needed to be done around the place while her father and aunt were away, but it was impossible to do while her eyes steadfastly refused to waver for one instant from the white-hulled boat now receding swiftly into the distance. Not even after it had finally disappeared from sight altogether did she immediately move, because it was only in those last few seconds, knowing it was unlikely she would ever see Hunt again, that she realised she was watching his departure so tenaciously, so anguishedly, due to her loving him with all her heart and soul and actually not wanting him to leave at all!

Now she could at least understand why he had come to have such an overpowering effect on her emotions, even if she did find it difficult to accept. After all, she'd instinctively known right from the beginning that he spelt danger for any female unthinking enough to become involved with him, and if his association with Pauline hadn't endorsed that conviction and made her doubly wary, then his own quite open comment about promises to marry never having been in his line certainly should have.

That they evidently hadn't was more than obvious now, though, and wiping her fingers across her eyes again she turned and made her way cheerlessly inside the house. It wasn't the first time she'd had the island all to herself—quite often when the guesthouse experienced a slack period they would all take it in turns to spend some time on the mainland—but whereas she usually enjoyed the solitude, on this occasion, with nothing to distract her thoughts, she suspected it was going to be intolerably dismal.

As it happened, however, her mind became fully occupied with other, more pressing, matters during the next couple of days because as the wind progressively strengthened, the rain increased, and the barometric pressure steadily dropped, Devon soon began to suspect that something a little more impressive than a mere wet spell may have been forming somewhere to the north. A suspicion that was proved correct when she put a radio telephone call through to her father on the mainland.

That he was also very concerned about being unable to return due to the conditions brought about by that apparent cyclone was obvious too, but after assuring him she knew exactly what to do, and ascertaining the route it was predicted it might take—accurately forecasting the likely direction something as wholly unpredictable as a cyclone might take was an impossibility; sometimes they would meander up and down the coast for a few days before either turning out to sea and dissipating, as the majority of them thankfully did, or else suddenly descending on the mainland, with devastating effect on occasion—she did her utmost to put his mind at rest regarding her safety before ringing off and setting about making her preparations.

By early afternoon Devon was satisfied she had taken every precaution she could, as she explained to her father when he phoned to advise that Cyclone Muriel, now rated important enough to warrant its own name, had definitely started moving southwards and that although not expected, at that stage, to pass directly over Cowrie, its path still wouldn't be all that far distant. A deduction Devon had already made for herself actually because the force of the wind and rain had been increasing drastically hour by hour, and as she surmised they must have been doing all day in Northport too when their line suddenly went dead. Now she really was on her own, she thought ruefully, and hurriedly had a shower and then cooked herself an early dinner while she could still do so before venturing outside in order to turn off the generators and pump—just in case.

Just how much more savage were the elements now Devon promptly realised as she literally had to struggle against the wind that tore at her clothes, while the rain beating so ferociously into her face made it difficult to see and therefore avoid the palm leaves and other assorted natural debris that was being wrested from the already violently buffeted vegetation. Grateful for the brief respite while inside the machine sheds, she delayed her return a moment as she looked out to sea from the doorway. This was very definitely one of those times when the Pacific made a mockery of its name, she thought drily, for now it was a heaving, churning, maelstrom of water that exploded against the reef in mountainous spray-scattering waves that had already filled the lagoon well past its normal high-water mark. Happily, Devon knew the ground the house was situated upon was high enough to escape any storm surge that might occur, but even so it was still rather unsettling to see the normally placid waters of the lagoon pounding furiously higher and higher along the foreshores.

By midnight the wind was a howling, shrieking fiend, the rain such a deafening crescendo on the roof that it completely drowned out the sounds of destruction Devon knew must be occurring outside. The house itself she didn't really have too many worries about. In its seventy-odd years of life it had successfully withstood a number of such storms, and although it was high-set the steel bolts fixing it to its concrete stumps were specifically designed to ensure it couldn't be blown off its foundations, while those securing the roof helped guarantee that wasn't likely to abruptly disappear either.

An hour later her ears, attuned as they were to the noise now, told her that the worst was over and that it had definitely begun to ease; another hour after that and she knew it had moved even further away from the island, and with a thankful sigh she was finally able to retire to her bed.

CHAPTER EIGHT

WHEN she awoke Devon lay still for a moment, hardly able to credit the comparative silence that greeted her. There was only a slight breeze she could hear outside, certainly no rain, and not only that but through her shuttered bedroom windows she thought she could even detect what seemed to be faint flickerings of sunlight. Rolling to her feet she hurried down the hall and threw open the back door, staring in shocked dismay at the view that met her eyes.

The vegetation had been decimated. Trees uprooted, some merely sheered off halfway, while those that had been left standing were completely stripped of most of their branches, together with all their leaves, as had the majority of the other shrubs and bushes about the place. With nothing to impede her vision now, she could also see that one of the outbuildings had lost some sheets of iron from its roof, one of which was deeply embedded in a corner post of the verandah. A quick inspection of the house as she opened the shutters thankfully showed that to be the only damage it appeared to have suffered, though, and with a last eloquent grimace for the clearing up that was ahead of her she returned inside to wash and have something to eat before starting to tackle it.

Half an hour later she was back on the verandah again, shading her eyes against the bright, though still rather overcast sky as the sound of an approaching helicopter broke the stillness. Initially, she thought it must have been one of the emergency services aircraft checking the area, but as it drew closer she could see no such easily identifiable markings and wondered what on earth anyone else would be doing out that way. When it became evident it intended landing she was even more surprised—she couldn't even remember one setting down on Cowrie before—and waited curiously as the machine was efficiently brought to rest on the lawn at the back of the house.

A man's tall form, clad in slim fitting jeans and a maroon T-shirt, emerged almost immediately and Devon's breath caught in her throat as she instantly recognised him. In fact, she even took a couple of involuntary steps down the stairs, but then brought herself to a determined halt. Although her heart was racing ecstatically at the sight of him, she knew that if she wanted to retain any of her pride and self-respect at all she could never allow such feelings to show. Accordingly, when Hunt reached the bottom of the steps her expression was carefully schooled.

'Come to check how your assets have fared, have you?' she gibed sardonically.

'Not especially,' he disclaimed, flexing an impassive shoulder. 'Unlike some, I've always considered people more important than property.' His eyes abruptly lifted to hers and held. 'You're all okay?'

Against her will she found herself responding to the concern in his voice and some of her deliberate antagonism receded. 'Well, I expect Dad and Aunt Violet are. They're still in Northport. The telephone went out yesterday afternoon and I haven't been able to contact them since,' she revealed matter-of-factly.

'You're saying, you were here all on your own last night?' he frowned.

She gave a deprecating shrug. 'Dad wanted to get back, but he couldn't because of the weather. It just came up too quickly.'

'Hell! It never occurred to me that you might still be alone here.' Pausing, he eyed her closely. 'That couldn't have been very pleasant for you.'

'Maybe a little unnerving,' she admitted on a wry note. 'But the house is really as good as cyclone proof these days so I wasn't too worried.' A rueful curve caught at her lips. 'Well, most of the time I wasn't.'

His answering smile of understanding played havoc with her emotions and in an effort to both hide the effect as well as overcome it, she went on swiftly. 'So who else caught it besides Cowrie? Do you know?'

'Oh, Northport to some degree, of course, plus a couple of smaller towns down the coast, but it hasn't actually moved ashore as yet. It's still travelling southwards.'

'They usually do,' she nodded.

'I can't say I'm sorry,' he half smiled expressively, looking at the devastation surrounding them. 'My God, the place looks as if a bomb's hit it!' He began mounting the steps, his mouth shaping with lazy mockery. 'Something else you forgot to mention happens around here?'

'I—well. . .' she began flusteredly as she backed away slightly. 'You must have known this was a cyclone area, and—and it's not as if this sort of thing happens every year. We may normally get a storm or two during the season, but something like this only occurs once in every twenty years or more.' Recovered now, she sent him a not altogether unhopeful glance from beneath long, curling lashes. 'However, if you're having second thoughts about buying the place. . .'

'Uh-uh!' Hunt broke in with a laconic but drily decisive negation. 'The deal stands. Granted, I didn't expect to see it ravaged in quite such a fashion within a week of purchasing it, but simultaneously, it's not entirely a bad thing to have had happen. I've now seen it under its best and worst conditions and that can only assist us with our planning.'

Pulling only a lightly grimacing face—subconsciously she didn't really think she'd been expecting otherwise—she shrugged, 'You'll be wanting to see all over the place again, then, I suppose?'

He didn't actually confirm it, but countered banteringly instead, 'Is that an offer to be my guide once more?'

'No!' she ejaculated in patent dismay. Feeling as she did about him, the last thing she wanted was to be alone with him for any length of time. She would be bound to give herself away. 'You know the island well enough now not to need a guide.'

'Couldn't handle it twice, huh?'

No, she couldn't, but for entirely different reasons than he supposed. At least, she sincerely hoped they were different reasons! 'Whether I could or not has nothing to do with it,' she claimed, trying to inject some firmness into her voice. 'There's simply too much to be done here, as you can see,' with an expressively outspread hand, 'for me to waste time traipsing all over the place.'

Before her hand could drop to her side again, Hunt caught hold of it. 'I also see you're not wearing your engagement ring,' he drawled. 'Why's that?'

With a gulp, Devon dragged her fingers free immediately, clasping them with her other hand as if by hiding the bare untanned mark the ring had left she could deny its telltale presence. 'B-because I took it off, of course,' she quipped shakily, protectively. As she had always intended to do as soon as he'd left. 'It—it kept catching on things while I was working yesterday.'

His intensely blue eyes roamed over her indolently, disturbingly. 'So you're still planning to marry him?'

'Naturally,' she just managed to push out in something like a normal tone. 'There's no reason why I shouldn't.'

'Except that you don't happen to love him?'

The noticeable irony in his remark had her stiffening resentfully. 'No? And what would you know about it? There's more to love than mere physical attraction or—or compatibility, you know!'

'You don't say!' he mocked. 'But you sure as hell can't have a full and satisfying relationship without it ... as you very well know, only you're too damned frightened to admit it!'

'Frightened!' she expostulated in a passably scoffing manner. 'Why should I be frightened to admit anything, *if* I believed it was the truth?'

He took a step closer, his firmly moulded mouth shaping wryly. 'In case you inadvertently betray how you really feel.'

Devon moistened her lips nervously as she promptly increased the distance between them again. 'I've just t-told you that,' she stammered.

'Mmm, I know what you *told* me, but. . .'

'Well, then,' she interposed swiftly with a shrug as if that settled the matter. And desperate to change the subject, 'So now, why don't you have your look round, and let me start on what needs to be done here?' She made to step past him and head down the steps.

'Uh-uh!' No sooner had she begun to move than an arm reaching across to the stair rail was barring her way. 'That can wait. That's not why I flew all the way out here.'

Devon gave up attempting to push his arm away in order to stare up at him with eyes bright with unshed and inexplicable tears. 'Then apart from checking out the island, what is? Just so you can taunt me about my engagement again? Well, thanks all the same but right at the moment I don't need it! I didn't exactly have an enjoyable time last night, and. . .'

'You think I did?' Hunt clasped her by the shoulders, shaking her. 'Knowing you were out here while that tempest was raging, and not being able to do a damned thing about it! God! Maybe it was just as well I didn't know you were here alone . . . otherwise I don't know what I would have done! Gone off my head completely, probably!' Releasing her abruptly, he swung away raking a hand savagely through the thickness of his hair, then turned back with a rueful shake of his head. 'I know you've never trusted me but you don't even trust yourself, do you, sweetheart?'

Still trying to assimilate the incredible fact that he had apparently been worried on *her* account, Devon could only proffer a tremulously confused, 'I don't know what you mean.'

'I mean, just for once, try believing in your own feelings,' he enlightened her on a resonant note as he brushed his hand against her cheek gently. 'Do you think I don't know why you were crying when the *Kanandah* left?'

'Who—who says I was?' she parried jerkily, blinking in her surprise.

'I do . . . with the aid of a pair of binoculars.'

'Oh!' She averted her gaze in consternation. 'It could just have been—been the rain.'

His lips twisted wryly. 'Except we both know it wasn't. Besides, do you always watch people you dislike until they're out of sight? In those circumstances most others wouldn't have bothered to watch at all.'

Oh, God, he knew, he knew! she despaired. 'Y-you weren't the only one on board,' she still had to try and evade in an uneven murmur.

Glancing at her downbent head, Hunt expelled a heavy breath and with a hunching of wide shoulders began descending the steps himself. 'Okay. Then I guess there's nothing more to be said.'

Now Devon did look up, to gaze after him in bewilderment as he headed across the lawn towards the helicopter. He'd as good as said he knew she was in love with him, so why was he suddenly leaving? To show her he didn't care? But then he'd already admitted that's why he was there, hadn't he? In an agony of perplexity and indecision she began chewing at her lower lip.

'Well, Pauline said you were the new man in *her* life!' she called after him part accusingly, part reproachfully, and not a little distractedly.

'Did she really? That *was* nice ... or nasty of her, wasn't it?' he half spun round in order to contend sardonically. 'It's a pity you didn't think to ask her if I'd ever given her any reason to believe she was the new girl in mine, though!' He continued walking.

'Well, wasn't she?' she both charged and cried at the same time.

This time he didn't even look back. He just shrugged, 'I told you the answer to that before. You didn't believe me then, so what's the point of my repeating it now?'

All of a sudden Devon's finely marked brows drew together in a frown. Could that be why he was leaving? Because, as he'd maintained previously, she did tend to unfairly put him on trial every time he opened his mouth? In a matter of seconds she was rushing across the grass after him.

'Hunt!' she shouted desperately on seeing him open the aircraft's door. 'Please . . . wait!'

To her relief he at least closed the door again, even if he didn't exactly turn to face her directly, but merely leant one shoulder negligently against the helicopter as he waited for her to reach him. Once she did, all her courage seemed to desert her and she flushed self-consciously under his unswerving gaze. Oh lord, she only hoped her thinking had been correct!

'Please d-don't leave,' she quavered. 'I really don't mean to make you—make you defend yourself all the time, you know, it's just that—it's just that. . .' She paused to swallow the constricting lump in her throat. 'I know I'm not as sophisticated and "with it" as all the other females of your acquaintance doubtlessly are, so I just had to protect myself somehow because I thought you'd—you'd probably only find me more amusing if I let you know how—how I really felt about you.' She gave a small, shuddering sob.

'Oh, Christ!' It was a groaned prayer Hunt uttered rather than an oath as he gathered her shaking form to him tightly. 'The only reason I tried to keep it light was because it was obvious, right from our very first meeting, just how delightfully innocent you really were, sweetheart! Certainly not because I was ever making fun of you,' he vowed huskily. 'Oh, true, I wasn't averse to having a shot at Wilkinson—it was just beyond me how he could treat you so indifferently when I would've given everything I owned to be able to possess you—but I can assure you none of them were ever intended for you, my love. Or, at least only in so far as to try and awaken you to the knowledge that there were far deeper emotions to be savoured than the dispassionate ones he'd evidently only demonstrated, and thereby hopefully steal you away from him.' His mouth lowered to her forehead. 'I've wanted you from the moment I first saw you in that lagoon, Devon, as naked as the day you were born, and so damned beautiful I couldn't take my eyes off you! I love you, little sea nymph, make no mistake about that!'

Devon tilted her head back, her eyes a radiant turquoise now as they lifted to his. 'Oh, Hunt, I love you too ... so much!' she owned fervently. 'I'm so thankful the cyclone brought you back.'

His arms tightened about her imperceptibly. 'I would have come anyway,' he revealed on a deep note. 'The thought of you perhaps going ahead and marrying Wilkinson nearly drove me crazy. I knew I had to have you, because I just couldn't come to terms with the idea of going through life without you. Cyclone Muriel simply precipitated my arrival.' He broke off, shaking his head despairingly in remembrance. 'Hell, I hope I never have to go through another night like the last! If anything had happened to you. . .'

'But nothing did,' she was able to smile happily. And with her slender arms sliding upwards to link lovingly around his neck and begin impelling his head

down to hers, 'Although I am expecting more of this
morning.'

Her message was plain, and so was the warmth of
desire in Hunt's eyes as he willingly covered her lips
with his in a kiss that shocked her with its depth of
feeling and had her reciprocating more ardently than
she ever had before.

'Oh, God, I want you more than I've ever wanted
anything in my whole life!' he groaned unevenly
against the softness of her mouth some long
electrically charged minutes later.

Devon's breath came raggedly. 'I want you too,' she
breathed with simple eloquence.

Hunt shook his head in a distracted movement. 'Do
you realise just what you're implying?' he queried on a
thickened note.

She nodded, albeit a trifle shyly. 'I'm implying I
love you without reservation, and—and that I want to
be yours in the most complete way possible.'

'But you're so damned. . .'

'Inexperienced?' Her eyes lifted to his achingly
'Then isn't it time that was rectified by the only man
I've ever wanted to make love to me?' she smiled
winsomely, and twined her arms even more tightly
about the strong column of his neck when, with a
muffled sound of helplessness, he swept her high
against his chest and began striding towards the
house.

Some considerable time later Devon roused herself
sufficiently from her state of drowsy contentment to
lift her head from where it had been resting against
Hunt's bronzed and heavily muscled shoulder in order
to gaze down at him adoringly. 'I love you, Hunter
Kincaid,' she said throatily.

With a smile that had her heart turning over, he curved a hand around her nape and bent her head to his. 'No more than I do you, Devon Matthews,' he answered in deep-felt kind as he brushed his lips over hers lingeringly. 'You're all and more a man could ever wish for, and I want you as my wife as soon as it can possibly be arranged.'

As did she! Although in her new-born confidence that didn't stop her from bantering, 'I thought you said promises to marry weren't in your line.'

'Nor were they . . . until a contrary, argumentative, but thoroughly captivating little sea nymph suddenly erupted into my life like summer lightning,' he grinned lazily. 'So perhaps you'd better listen carefully while I make my first and last such vow.' Propping himself up on his elbow, he held her gaze with loving eyes. 'Because I hereby promise to love, marry, cherish, honour and keep you for the rest of my life. Understand?' He smiled again.

'Enchantedly,' she sighed in blissful tones.

'And leaving the island?' he hazarded, his expression growing a trifle guarded. 'What are your feelings in that regard now?'

'You were the one who kept insisting it was the only thing I cared about,' she pointed out lightly. 'It meant a lot, I admit, but even so . . .' she dimpled, 'it can't compete with what I'm getting in exchange.'

A statement for which she was rewarded extremely satisfactorily. 'And Wilkinson? Did you really only remove his ring because it was getting in the way?' Hunt then probed.

Devon shook her head. 'No, I took it off, as I think you suspected, because I knew I couldn't ever marry him feeling as I did about you.'

'So it's finally over between the two of you?' His pleasure at the thought was evident.

'Well, yes and no, actually,' she disclosed with a wry half laugh. 'It's over, yes, but unfortunately I haven't had an opportunity to tell Garth that as yet.'

'You'd better hurry and do so, then, or he's going to get one hell of a surprise to see someone else's ring on your finger, isn't he? That is, if he can bestir himself enough into paying you sufficient attention to even notice!' he added derisively. Then, in a return to his earlier indulgent tone, 'Because I mean to have that mark on your finger covered by a ring of mine, if not by the end of today, then by tomorrow at the latest.'

'So soon?' Devon gasped, although not without some appreciation. 'You really believe in moving fast once your mind's made up, don't you?'

'Uh-huh! And especially when you're involved,' he drawled. 'Besides, I want everyone to know you're very definitely spoken for.' His eyes crinkled engagingly. 'Because I know just what a temptation you can be.'

'One you didn't appear very taken with when you said I learnt too fast that night of the barbecue, though,' she reminded reproachfully.

'Didn't appear taken with!' Hunt repeated incredulously. 'Are you out of your mind? I was hard put not to just plain take you, there and then, I wanted you so much! By that time I was finding it damn nigh impossible to keep not only my eyes off you, but my hands as well!' He paused, his mouth sloping ruefully. 'Or hadn't you noticed?'

'I noticed it more, and missed it worse, once you stopped,' she confessed self-consciously. Then, with a diffident hunching of one shoulder, 'I thought you just meant I was making it too easy for you, and that—that you weren't very impressed.'

'You mean, *that's* why you apologised?' His eyes held hers disbelievingly. 'I never did succeed in working out why you had.'

She nodded.

'Oh, no! Never that, sweetheart!' His dismay was genuine as he pulled her comfortingly closer again. 'As I said, the opposite was more like it.'

'Then why did you ignore me so completely afterwards?' She slanted an uncomprehending glance upwards from under glossy lashes.

He exhaled wryly. 'Mainly, because your attitude was anything but encouraging at the time, if you recall. In fact, freezing would probably describe it best. But also, I guess, because I *was* becoming tired of having to defend my every word and action. I figured I was wasting my time, and so spent the remainder of my stay trying to convince myself I'd had a lucky escape.'

'And did you succeed?'

'I thought I had until I realised you were crying when we left, and then I knew I'd merely been unknowingly waiting for just such a sign. Only by then it was a little late to do anything about it immediately. I still had to sign those papers with Matt in Northport, and although I intended returning straight afterwards, unfortunately no sooner had we berthed than a message came through that necessitated me going down to Brisbane. Then when I did manage to return, and as worried as I've every been about anything, I'm greeted with one of your snide remarks as soon as I set foot to the ground.' He glowered at her with mock ferocity.

'I'm sorry,' she apologised earnestly. 'It was just the only way I could think of to disguise my true feelings because I didn't think you reciprocated them. At least, not until you made that remark about it being pointless in repeating you'd never been interested in Pauline, which then set me thinking.' With a sigh, she buried her head against his smooth chest. 'Would you really have left if I hadn't explained how I felt?'

'I don't honestly know,' he answered thoughtfully. 'Although if I had, I doubt it would have been for long. Being unable to keep away from you appears to have become an integral part of my life,' with a delightfully dry smile. 'But at the same time, I reasoned there was still no guarantee you would admit how I suspected you felt if I told you I loved you first. Judging by the past, I wouldn't have been at all surprised if such a declaration didn't immediately prompt the accusation that I was only doing so in an effort to recoup some of the purchase price of the island.'

'Oh, no, I would never have thought of anything like that,' Devon protested laughingly. 'Well, I don't think I would have. Although I can understand how you could believe I might. However . . .' halting she eyed him mischievously, 'now that you have mentioned it, this does mean you'll be getting Cowrie considerably cheaper than you envisaged, doesn't it?'

'Uh-uh!' he grinned, shaking his head un-equivocally. 'Whatever you receive from the sale, beautiful, is yours! I want none of it! You're worth far more to me than mere money.'

Devon's lips found his unerringly. 'You do have a winning way with you, don't you?' she smiled, and then narrowed her glance expressively. 'When you're not being infuriatingly mocking and purposely aggravating, that is!'

Hunt gave a warm, utterly stirring laugh. 'When you rise to the bait so readily, my love, it's too great a temptation to forgo,' he grinned without the slightest show of remorse.

'I see,' she acknowledged, straight-faced, though her eyes gleamed. 'Then I shall just have to cultivate ways to defeat you, shan't I?' She began trailing her mouth slowly, sensuously, down his throat and across the firm flesh of his shoulder, while smoothing a hand exploringly over his broad chest.

With a convulsive shudder, Hunt moved so that he was leaning over her, his own mouth seeking hers, his hand cradling a rosy-peaked breast. 'You don't need any more than you have already,' he groaned deeply. 'I have the distinct feeling I'm the one who's going to need all the help I can get. You've even had me surrendering regarding Matt already.'

'How do you mean?' curiously.

He hunched a brown shoulder deprecatingly. 'Well, you seemed so worried about this proposed trip of his—even though I'm still inclined to think unnecessarily—that I decided to see if I could find a solution that would suit the pair of you.'

'And?'

'What's his equal love to sailing?' he countered drily.

'Fishing.' Her reply came without hesitation.

'Mmm, that's what I'd gathered,' he nodded. 'So I just casually put the suggestion to him that he might like to consider staying on here in charge of the game fishing boats we'll be providing for guests' use. No one knows the area better than he does, and I figured that since I was already employing one of my, hopefully, future in-laws, I may as well employ both of them.'

'And?' she queried again, but more urgently this time.

'He agreed,' Hunt said with a smile for her ensuing obvious delight and relief.

'Oh, thank you, thank you!' Devon threw her arms around him exuberantly. 'I love you for that more than you'll ever know!'

The curve of his shapely mouth grew teasing. 'I don't suppose I will ... unless, of course you could think of some way which might just help to show me.'

'I do believe I know the very thing,' she sparkled, already moving against him invitingly, and very shortly proved to the unqualified satisfaction of them both that, indeed, she did.

the face on the milk carton

CAROLINE B. COONEY

Published by Laurel-Leaf
an imprint of Random House Children's Books
a division of Random House, Inc.
New York

Originally published in hardcover in the United States by Delacorte Press,
New York, in 1996. This edition published by arrangement
with Delacorte Press.

Visit us on the Web! www.randomhouse.com/teens

Educators and librarians, for a variety of teaching tools,
visit us at www.randomhouse.com/teachers

Library of Congress Cataloging-in-Publication Data is available on request.

RL: 6.0
ISBN: 978-0-440-22065-7 (pbk.)
October 2008
Printed in the United States of America
60
New Laurel-Leaf Edition

Random House Children's Books supports the First Amendment
and celebrates the right to read.

To my mother, Martha Willerton Bruce,
and my father, Dexter Mitchell Bruce

CHAPTER

1

Janie finished her essay.

She never knew what grade she would get in Mr. Brylowe's English class. Whenever she joked, he wanted the essay serious. Whenever she was serious, he had intended the essay to be light-hearted.

It was October.

Outdoors throbbed with autumn. She could feel the pulse of the deep-blue skies. With every leaf wrenched off its twig and whirled by the wind, Janie felt a tug. She felt like driving for hours; taking any road at all; just going.

Actually Janie was only fifteen and had barely started driving lessons. She was having driving fantasies because of dinner last night.

Her parents—as always—had taken opposite sides. Setting themselves up like a debate team, her mother and father would argue until some invisible marital timer rang. Then they would come to terms, rushing to meet in the middle. Until last

1

night her mother had said Janie could begin driving while her father said she could not. "She's just a baby," said her father, in the infuriating, affectionate way of fathers.

"She's *old*," said Janie's mother lightly. "Practically a woman. A sophomore in high school."

"I hate when that happens," her father grumbled. "I like my little girl to stay little. I'm against all this growing up." He wound some of Janie's hair around his wrist.

Janie had fabulous hair: a wild, chaotic mane of red curls glinting gold. People always commented on it. As her best friend, Sarah-Charlotte, said, "Janie, that is *serious* hair."

"I guess you've grown up anyway, Janie," said her father reluctantly. "Even with all the bricks I put on your head to keep you little. Okay, I give in. You can drive."

In English, Janie smiled to herself. Her father was an accountant who in the fall had time to coach the middle-school soccer teams. Today after school he'd have a practice, or a game, but when he came home—they'd go driving!

She wrote her name on her essay.

She had gradually changed her name. "Jane" was too dull. Last year she'd added a "y," becoming Jayne, which had more personality and was sexier. To her last name—Johnson—she'd added a "t," and later an "e" at the end, so now she was Jayne Johnstone.

Her best friends—Sarah-Charlotte Sherwood and Adair O'Dell—had wonderful, tongue-twisting, memorable names. Why, with the last name John-

2

son (hardly a name at all; more like a page out of the phone book) had her parents chosen "Jane"? They could have named her Scarlett, or Allegra. Perhaps Roxanne.

Now she took the "h" out of Johnston and added a second "y" to Jayne.

Jayyne Jonstone. It looked like the name you would have if you designed sequined gowns for a living, or pointed to prizes on television quiz shows.

"Earth to Janie," said Mr. Brylowe.

She blushed, wondering how many times he had called her.

"The rest of us are reading our essays aloud, Janie," said Mr. Brylowe. "We'd like to issue an invitation for you to join us."

She blushed so hotly she had to put her hands over her cheeks.

"Don't do that," said Pete. "You're cute when your face matches your hair."

Immediately, the back row of boys went into barbershop singing, hands on hearts, invisible straw hats flung into the air. "Once in love with Janie," they sang.

Janie had never had a boyfriend. She was always asked to dances, was always with a crowd—but no boy had actually said *I want to be with you and you alone.*

Mr. Brylowe told Janie to read her essay aloud.

The blush faded. She felt white and sick. She hated standing up in class. Hated hearing her voice all alone in the quiet of the room.

The bell rang.

English was a split period: they had lunch in

3

the middle and came back for more class. Never had lunch come at such an appropriate moment. Perhaps she would write a better essay during the twenty-seven minutes of lunch.

Certainly it wasn't going to take Janie long to eat. They had recently discovered she had a lactose intolerance. This was a splashy way of saying she had stomachaches when she drank milk. "No more ice cream, no more milk" was the medical/parental decree.

However, peanut butter sandwiches (which she had in her bag lunch) required milk. I am so sick of fruit juice, Janie thought. I want milk.

She had been eating since the school year began with Pete, Adair, Sarah-Charlotte, Jason, and Katrina.

She loved all their names.

Her last-year's daydream—before a driver's license absorbed all daydream time—had been about her own future family. She couldn't picture her husband-to-be, but she could see her children perfectly: two beautiful little girls, and she would name them Denim and Lace. She used to think about Denim and Lace all the time. Shopping at the mall with Sarah-Charlotte, she'd go into all the shoe stores to play with the little teeny sneakers for newborns, and think of all the pretty clothes she'd buy one day for Denim and Lace.

Now she knew those names were nauseating, and if she did name her daughters Denim and Lace, there'd probably be a divorce, and her husband would get custody on the grounds anybody who chose those names was unfit. She'd have to

4

name them something sensible, like Emily and Margaret.

Peter, Adair, Sarah-Charlotte, Jason, Katrina, and Janie went in a mob down the wide stairs, through the wide halls, and into the far-too-small cafeteria. The kids complained about the architecture of the school (all that space dedicated to passing periods and hardly any to lunch), but they loved being crammed in, filching each other's potato chips, telling secrets they wanted everybody to overhear, passing notes to be snatched up by the boy you hoped would snatch them, and sending the people on the outside of the crush to get you a second milk.

Everybody but Janie Johnson got milk: cardboard cartons so small you needed at least three, but the lunch ladies would never let you. Janie was envious. Those luckies are swigging down nice thick white milk, she thought, and I'm stuck with cranberry juice.

"Okay," said Sarah-Charlotte. Sarah-Charlotte would not bother with you if you tried to abbreviate her name. Last year she had reached a standoff with a teacher who insisted on calling her Sarah. Sarah-Charlotte glared at him silently for months until he began calling her Miss Sherwood, which let them both win. "Okay, who's been kidnapped this time?" said Sarah-Charlotte wearily, as if jaded with the vast number of kidnappings in the world. Sarah-Charlotte patted her white-blond hair, which was as neat as if she had cut it out of a magazine and pasted it onto her head. Janie, whose mass of hair was never the same

5

two minutes in a row, and whose face could be difficult to find beneath the red tangles, never figured out how Sarah-Charlotte kept her hair so neat. "I have approximately five hundred thousand fewer hairs than you do," Sarah-Charlotte explained once.

Everybody turned the milk cartons over to see who had been kidnapped. The local dairy put pictures of stolen children on the back of the carton. Every few weeks there was a new child.

"I don't know how you're supposed to recognize somebody who was three years old when she got taken from a shopping center in New Jersey, and that was nearly a dozen years ago," said Adair. "It's ridiculous." Adair was as sleek and smooth as her name; even her dark hair matched: unruffled and gleaming like a seal out of water.

Janie sipped juice from a cardboard packet and pretended it was milk. Across the cafeteria Reeve waved. Reeve lived next door. He was a senior. Reeve never did homework. It was his life ambition to get in the *Guinness Book of World Records*, and the only thing he had a stab at was the "Never Did His Homework Once but Still Got the Occasional B Plus" listing.

Reeve had gotten the occasional B plus, but he had also gotten a lot of D's and F's. News came from the Academic Office that unless Reeve shaped up, he would not graduate with his class.

His two older sisters and one older brother had gone to spectacular colleges—Cornell, Princeton, and Stanford. They were mortified by Reeve's failures and came home weekends to tell him so.

Reeve had ceased to speak to his entire family. In fact, he stomped away and had supper at Janie's so often that Janie's mother had said last night, "I'm thinking of charging your parents a meal fee."

Reeve did not laugh. In a strangled voice he said, "I'm sorry. I won't come again."

Janie's father punched him, the way, if it had been Janie, he would have hugged. Jabbing Reeve in the gut, her father said, "Meals here, bed there, Reeve. Someday we'll collect our debt."

"Yeah, when I'm a plumber," said Reeve gloomily, "you'll let me clean your drains."

"Now, Reeve. Just start studying, pull those grades up, and—" Her father broke off. "Right," he said, punching Reeve again. "In this house we won't discuss it. Here. Have a brownie and some ice cream."

It was such a trespass on Reeve, that everybody knew the details. Whatever Reeve kept secret, his mother told Janie's mother anyway. Reeve felt cramped by the intimacy of his life: he had always lived in this town, always gone to this school. I want to live in a city, he'd said last night, and be anonymous.

Ruefully Janie thought her name would give her a pretty good start if she wanted to go anonymous.

Sarah-Charlotte was hoping Reeve would ask Janie out. Sarah-Charlotte was not interested in getting her driver's license; she was interested in having a steady boyfriend, who had to be tall, handsome, muscular, smart, courteous, and rich. Reeve was all but one.

"And if Reeve doesn't ask you out," was Sarah-Charlotte's theory, "maybe his friends will."

Janie did not think the boy next door ever came through in real life. Nor would any of Reeve's friends ask her out. Last year's seniors had dated lots of younger girls. This year's seniors seemed annoyed that they had to be in the same building. And Janie felt younger than her age: she had grown later, and grown less. While Adair and Sarah-Charlotte were busy becoming sophisticated and articulate, Janie remained small. Her mother said she was cute. Janie loathed that word. Cute was for toddlers and kittens. Boys didn't date cute little girls. They dated streamlined, impressive women like Sarah-Charlotte and Adair.

Besides, how would she date?

Her parents didn't even let her go to the shopping mall alone. They'd never let her date. Alone with a boy? Hah. Not likely.

Janie waved back at Reeve and he turned to his friends, duty done. If he knew I'm really Jayyne Jonstone, she thought, would he do more than wave?

She felt curiously heavy: like the difference between whole milk and skim. Through the cafeteria windows the sun gleamed, filling the school with golden shafts in which dust swirled.

On her left—so close he was nearly in her lap—Pete drank his milk in one long swig and crushed the carton in his hand. The boys loved doing that.

8

If they had a soda, they stamped the can under their feet and looked proudly at the flat aluminum.

"My mother says none of them are really kidnapped anyhow," said Pete. "She says it's all hype."

It took Janie several seconds to realize he was talking about the face on the milk carton. "What do you mean?" she said. She ate her peanut butter sandwich. Almost anything with peanut butter was excellent—peanut butter and marshmallow fluff; peanut butter and bananas—but a person needed milk to wash it down.

"All it is," said Pete firmly, "is divorce, where one parent gets mad and takes his own kid, but he doesn't tell the other parent where they're going. It's never actually a stranger stealing a kid, like on television."

"You mean they weren't really stolen?" said Sarah-Charlotte, vastly disappointed. She made several dramatic gestures. There was no room for dramatic gestures in the cafeteria, and people grabbed to save the whipped-cream towers on their Jell-O from getting splattered by Sarah-Charlotte's hands. "Nobody wants a ransom?" cried Sarah-Charlotte. "Nobody is being tortured?"

If I drink one carton of milk, Janie thought, is my allergy so serious I'll die? How boring the obituary would be: *Here lies Jane Johnson.* I should leave a note: *Put "Jayyne" on my stone.*

Janie shook her head.

Pete and Jason immediately complained that they had gotten red hair in their faces and would Janie please get a grip on her hair.

9

"What do you want me to do?" demanded Janie. "Wear a net around it?"

"Either that or build an addition to the cafeteria to house it," said Peter.

Everybody giggled.

Janie shook her hair more vigorously. The boys ducked and threw potato chips at Janie, while she reached for Sarah-Charlotte's milk and drank it up.

Perfect meal. Peanut butter sandwich and a glass of milk. Janie set the carton down and sighed with pleasure.

The little girl on the back of the carton stared back at her.

It wasn't much of a picture. After all, how good could a picture be when it was printed on a milk carton?

"You ready for that algebra test?" Jason asked Adair.

"I was ready till I ate cafeteria food. Do you think he'll let me out of the test if I have food poisoning?"

The girl on the carton was an ordinary little girl. Hair in tight pigtails, one against each thin cheek. A dress with a narrow white collar. The dress was white with tiny dark polka dots.

Something evil and thick settled on Janie, blocking her throat, dimming her eyes. "Sarah-Charlotte," she said. She could hear herself shouting Sarah-Charlotte's name, yet her lips were not moving; she was making no sound at all.

She reached toward Sarah-Charlotte's sleeve, but her hand didn't obey. It lay motionless on top of the carton. It looked like somebody else's hand; she could not imagine herself wearing that shade of nail polish, or that silly ring.

"You drank my milk," accused Sarah-Charlotte.

"It's me on there," Janie whispered. Her head hurt. Was the milk allergy already setting in? Or was she going insane? Could you go insane this fast? Surely it took years to lose your mind.

She imagined people losing their minds the way you might lose a penny, or your car keys— accidentally dropping your mind in the cafeteria.

"On where?" said Peter.

"The girl on the back of the carton," whispered Janie. How flat her voice sounded. As if she had ironed it. "It's me."

She remembered that dress . . . how the collar itched . . . remembered the fabric; it was summer fabric; the wind blew through it . . . remembered how those braids swung like red silk against her cheeks.

"I know you're sick of school," said Sarah-Charlotte, "but claiming to be kidnapped is going a little too far, Janie."

Pete retrieved his flattened milk and tried to shape it back into a carton. He read between the folds. "You were stolen ten years ago from a shopping center in New Jersey, Janie. What are you doing here?"

"Yeah," said Adair, giggling. "Why aren't you off yelling for the police?"

"Oh, she's just trying to get out of reading her essay," said Jason.

1 1

"No, she's just trying to steal my milk," said Sarah-Charlotte.

The bell rang. The others hurled their garbage toward the huge plastic-lined trash cans by the door, and missed. Ducking under the plump arms of the lunch ladies, they raced back to class instead of picking it up.

Janie held Sarah-Charlotte's empty milk carton and stared at the photograph of the little girl.

I was kidnapped.

Janie learned that her body could function without her.

She lived entirely inside her mind, searching her memory like a little kid going through an encyclopedia, trying to find the right heading. *Jane Elizabeth Johnson, Kidnapping of.*

Her body, including her voice, her smile—even her knowledge (during sixth period she was actually able to answer questions in biology lab) —continued to work properly.

How interesting, Janie thought clinically. My body doesn't need me.

She had a sense of herself being brain dead: running on tubes and machines.

Inside, her mind spun. It was like having a color wheel for a brain. When it slowed down, things were separate, like primary colors: *I have a mother and father . . . I have a childhood . . . I was not kidnapped . . . kidnapping means bad*

*people . . . I don't know any bad people . . .
therefore I am making this up.*

But when her mind speeded up, the colors
blended dizzily. *That is me on there. I, Janie
Johnson; I was kidnapped.*

But it could not be.

The facts did not compute.

She tried to climb outside her mind and go
where her body was: sitting neatly at a desk, neatly
taking notes.

It was like crawling on glass. No matter how
firmly she resolved not to think such stupid things,
she thought them. She slithered backward into
her mind.

Perhaps it's insanity, Janie thought. Perhaps
I'm trapped in here with this horrible idea and I'll
never get out. After a while people will notice and
they'll lock up my body the way insanity has locked
up my mind.

She discovered that school had ended.

Her body had gone to her locker. Taken the
right books. Put on her jacket. Remembered the
gym uniform that had to be washed. Said good-
bye to friends and foe.

But slowly. Like someone trying to avoid the
muddy parts in the grass. Her small body seemed
to thicken, as if she had real iron in her blood
and weighed several tons. The bus had left before
she even arrived in the lobby. All the buses had
left.

It was pouring rain.

The golden, gaudy-blue October had vanished
and turned black and thundering. The sky at its

richest: full of rage, ready to hit someone. It threw the rain against the pavement and ripped the leaves from the sugar maples.

A car headed for her. She watched the car, realizing that it was going to run her over: that somehow, although she was on the sidewalk, the car was aimed for her. Perhaps I should move, she thought. But nothing happened to her legs. They stayed there, holding her color-wheel brain in place, waiting to get run over.

"Get in quick," said Reeve, "before you get any wetter."

She had recognized neither him nor his Jeep. He had pulled the Jeep almost over her toes. The outside rearview mirror brushed the buttons on her jeans jacket. Janie got in slowly. This is fun, she thought. Now I'm paralyzed and blind, too.

Reeve said, "Let's ride down by the water. See if the tide is up over the road." Reeve loved floods. Two years ago there had been such a wonderful flood the families on the beach roads had to be rescued by the National Guard. Reeve had begged his parents to buy waterfront property so they could be in place for the next flood. They had uncooperatively said they liked it better a mile away on top of a hill. But Reeve kept an old battered canoe ready in the garage in case there should be another opportunity to paddle down the middle of the street. "A deluge like this," said Reeve happily, "a true Noah's Ark–type rain, you should have some decent flooding."

Janie nodded and turned the hot-air vents in her direction to dry her clothes. Her thick red hair sproinged up like a new permanent from the wetting it had taken.

"May I borrow your penknife?" she said.

"Sure." He detached the knife from his belt loop while she steered the Jeep. Then she couldn't get the blade to come up without breaking off a fingernail. Reeve stopped at a red light and opened the penknife for her.

Janie took the empty milk carton out of her book bag. She'd rinsed it out in the girls' room between fifth and sixth periods. She slit the carton open. Carefully she flattened it out. Then she opened her three-ring, blue-cloth English notebook, which had a clipboard on the inner front cover, and clipped the flat carton so that the photograph did not show. All Reeve could read was the logo FLOWER DAIRY, YOUR LOCAL MILK PRODUCER, SERVING ALL COMMUNITIES ON THE SHORELINE.

"That's an interesting hobby," observed Reeve. "You don't find too many milk carton collectors."

Janie thought about Pete's explanation. These so-called kidnappings are really just divorces, where one parent takes the child away and doesn't tell the other parent where they've gone.

Does that mean, she thought, that either my mother or my father is *not* my mother or my father? That somewhere out there is a *real* mother or a father who has wondered *for twelve years* where I am?

Reeve was staring out at the Atlantic Ocean, where the storm was hurling water and sand on the unprotected beaches. Reeve was handsomer than the rest of his family, yet there was a very strong resemblance among them. People could actually recognize Reeve by the smile that so much resembled his brother's, and the ruddy cheeks that were the trademark of his sisters. Now he was making terrible faces, flexing his forehead and lips and nose like Silly Putty because high tide had not managed to go over the road.

Reeve turned the Jeep into the Scenic Overlook, better known among teenagers as the Sexual Overlook because at night you could go there and watch couples in action. To the east stretched the ocean, and to the west, barely protected by thin spits of sand and mud, was the harbor where the wind jostled boats against the wharves. The boatyard was filled with marina employees taking boats out of the water for the winter storage. Even over the pounding of the waves and rain Janie could hear a strange smacking sort of applause. Not rigging hardware, nor waves against docks. "What's that noise?" she said. At least I'm not deaf, she thought.

"Flags," said Reeve. American flags, everywhere: on the docks, at the fuel pumps, on the boats. Each clapped in the fierce wind like a cloth maniac. "I'm sort of like a flag," said Reeve.

"Red, white, and blue?"

"No. A big banner flapping in the wind. YOU'RE DUMB, says the flag. My sisters, my brother, my parents: they don't say it out loud, but they kind of line up my college application forms next to my grades and my SATs and the old flag waves, YOU'RE DUMB."

"You're not dumb," said Janie, although he

was. She adored Reeve. but brains would round him out a bit.

"My parents haven't taken me to see any college campuses," said Reeve. "Nor arranged any interviews. Nothing. For Megan and Lizzie and Todd we spent a year apiece visiting and pondering and drawing up lists and pros and cons. With me, they've already given up. They don't yell at me anymore. You know what my mother said to your mother?"

"No," said Janie, although she did; her mother had repeated it, of course. Or is she my mother? thought Janie. Is she Daddy's second wife? Did they steal me from my real mother? Or is it Daddy who is somebody else? Maybe they're not even married. Maybe they just—

"Your mother said to my mother, 'At least you can be proud of Megan, Lizzie, and Todd,' and then my mother said, 'That's true, three out of four isn't bad.' "

Nobody else in my family has red hair, thought Janie. I don't laugh like Mother and Daddy. My fingernails aren't shaped like theirs. "That's terrible," she said to Reeve. "They're being rotten, writing you off like that."

"I'll be lucky to get into the community college," said Reeve. He fiddled with the radio dials and the heater knobs. flicked the emergency blinkers on and off, and pawed through the cassettes he had in the Jeep.

"At least you have a Jeep to commute in," said Janie, but this was not a comfort to Reeve, who wanted to be brilliant, outstanding, impressive, and memorable, like his brother and sisters.

She opened her notebook. She tilted it and peered at the back of the milk carton. It was still her on there.

She had not allowed herself to read the name under the photograph. Now she read it.

Jennie Spring.

Her brain stopped being a color wheel and became an echo chamber—*Jennie Spring Jennie Spring Jennie Spring Jennie—*

"What have you got in there?" teased Reeve. He reached for the notebook to see what forbidden article was stashed in it. Janie jerked it back. "No, Reeve, don't," she said urgently, and he was startled, pulling his hand back as if maybe it were a scorpion inside the English notebook.

Reeve left the Scenic Overlook so fast they hydroplaned over the puddles. Then he gnashed the gears, roaring forward along the narrow, wet beach road, skidding purposely. He took each gear up to its highest RPMs so the motor screamed. He jerked left into the traffic on Route 1. Like a warrior he battled the cars and the rain, pedal to the metal, taking off from each stop sign like a chariot racer.

Janie touched her seat belt and said nothing. She would feel that way, too, if she were Reeve. While he was passing in a no-passing zone, Janie turned the milk-carton cover over again.

The little girl's name and birthdate, the 800 number to call if you recognized her, the place from which she vanished in New Jersey. None of it meant a thing to Janie.

I've always felt a year younger than Sarah-Charlotte and Adair, thought Janie. And if that's my birthday, I *am* a year younger. I'm not old enough to get my driver's license after all.

But it was too ridiculous. She had a family. A perfectly normal family. They loved her. She loved them.

"I don't feel like going home yet, do you?" said Reeve. He spoke in the voice people use when you have to agree or walk home. Besides, she did agree. She had hardly ever agreed with anything more.

"Let's get ice cream," said Reeve. He jerked the wheel hard, turned across traffic with far too little time, and just barely missed getting a pickup truck through the side of his Jeep. The trucker rightly leaned on his horn. Janie gave him an apologetic smile and the town wave.

The trucker grinned at Janie. She shook her red hair at him and the guy grinned even wider.

Perhaps I'm fascinating after all, she thought. That trucker forgave Reeve because I tossed my hair. He'd believe me if I said my name was Jayyne Jonstone.

"I don't have any money," she told Reeve. "And I can't have ice cream." But what if my name is Jennie Spring? she thought.

"I'll pay. Anyway, I saw you drinking milk for lunch. You've already broken the rules."

He saw me drinking Sarah-Charlotte's milk, she thought. Which I drank long after he waved. So he looked back. Checked me out a second time.

They went to a booth, passing two groups of teenagers she knew by sight but not by name. All

eyes landed on Reeve with Janie and drew conclusions. Janie was not sure she liked this. It was
not a date; poor Reeve was just having to admit
he was dumb; Janie was his trusty, rusty, next-
door neighbor.

Reeve ordered two hot-fudge sundaes on one
scoop each of vanilla and chocolate mint. For years
when they were little kids going shopping with
their mothers, this had been Janie's order. She
had changed preferences since the last time she
had had ice cream with Reeve; up till the lactose
intolerance discovery, she'd ordered vanilla with
butterscotch topping. She said nothing. She was
quite touched that Reeve remembered.

Reeve talked about first-quarter grades, which
were coming up in only a few weeks. He talked
about the horror of failing his senior year; of having to go to a lousy college when Megan, Lizzie,
and Todd went to such winners; the horror of all
school at all times.

The waitress brought the sundaes much more
quickly than usual and Janie thanked her. She
turned to look at her sundae.

The world shifted.

Friendly Ice Cream seemed to spin around her,
all its flavors, all its booths, tilting and screaming.

She was sitting with somebody else.

Sitting on a high stool—a stool that swiveled—
she was turning herself slowly and carefully by
holding on to the counter—her feet did not touch
the foot rest—she was little—she was admiring
her white cotton socks as she turned because
they had a little strip of lace—

21

*A woman was next to her—not swiveling—
long, straight hair cascading down the woman's
back, so pretty Janie had to touch it. The woman
kept her hand in the air behind Janie's back so
she wouldn't tip off the spinning stool.*

*Janie was having a sundae—whipped cream
on it—eating the cherry off her sundae first and
then one off the woman's sundae.*

They were laughing.

*Janie was little—the woman hugged her—
swung her around as the stool had swung—*

*—there was a hot wind—they were outside
now; in a huge parking lot; maybe the biggest
parking lot in the world—her dress, white with
tiny dark dots, blew in the air—*

"Janie?" said Reeve. "Are you all right?"

Janie's mouth was dry, her hands icy. She was
shivering all over. She could feel the tiny table
shaking from her shivers. Reeve was frightened.

"Are you getting the flu?" he said. He put his
hand out as if to stop her from crossing some
terrible road. "You're not really *seriously* allergic
to milk, are you? I mean, is your throat going to
close up or your heart stop?" She was aware that
he was calling her. Raising his voice. That people
were looking. "Janie? Janie, are you okay?" His
hand took hers and to her frozen fingers his hand
felt like a furnace, as if he were going to scorch
her.

"I'm fine," she said. "Dizzy."

She had always had control over her daydreams;
like the daydreams of Denim and Lace in which
she designed every detail to suit herself. She had

22

never had a daydream that dreamed itself, like nightmares. That crawled out of her brain like a creature of the dark.

A daymare.

Janie shuddered. "I'd better not eat the sundae," she said. Already the daymare was fading, leaving her flesh like jelly, but no pictures to remember it by. Woman, she thought dimly, stool, dress, hot wind.

It must be, thought Janie, that my life is boring. Deep down I must be as angry over the boredom as Reeve is over being dumb. He drives like a maniac to feel better and I fall into maniac daydreams. My parents are my parents. Nobody kidnapped me. I don't really remember the dress.

Reeve called to the waitress. "Could we have these to go?" He pointed at Janie. "She doesn't feel well."

"They'll be messy," said the waitress doubtfully. "The top will be on the bottom."

Tell me about it, thought Janie.

There were no cars in the driveway. Her father couldn't be coaching soccer in this weather so he would be pulling in any moment now. Her mother must be at the hospital—what day was this?—she volunteered two days a week.

The Johnsons' driveway was separated from Reeve's by a thin row of shrubs over which Megan, Lizzie, Todd, and now Reeve continually backed. Only hours ago Janie had thought joyously of the day when she, too, learning reverse, would flatten a few bushes.

"You sure you'll be all right?" said Reeve. "I could ask Mom to go over and sit with you."

"Please," said Janie, meaning no, and they both laughed. When Reeve's mother took care of a person, she took serious care—bed rest, chicken soup, and pillow fluffing. On school-nurse forms, Janie had always put Reeve's mother to phone in an emergency, and Reeve had always put Janie's mother. Reeve's mother always sat with Janie, rubbing her back, reading chapters from long books. Janie had to be in the mood for all that loving kindness. More often, when she was sick, she just wanted to be alone, in the silence and the nest of her bed.

How can I be kidnapped? thought Janie. I don't even have neighbors who understand evil, let alone parents.

She got out of the Jeep and dashed through the rain, putting her key in the side door. This opened onto a landing on the stairs between the cellar and the kitchen. Down in the cellar next to the gleaming-white washer and dryer, her folded jeans were stacked. Up in the kitchen lay a pile of mail, an overflowing brown paper bag marked for the Salvation Army, and the breakfast dishes.

She scraped the dishes and loaded the dishwasher. It wasn't full enough to run. There was a note on the refrigerator in her mother's pretty script: *Darling—don't forget class tonight, home by supper, love Mommy.*

Janie hadn't called her mother Mommy in years, though she still called her father Daddy. Class? she thought, trying to make sense of that reminder.

She walked through the house, touching. Same furniture: her mother liked deep, intense colors: the sofa and chairs were a blue so dark and rich they invited you like a deep sea to dive in. In the dining room two walls were glass and one was bright red; the only decoration was an enormous framed color photograph of Janie, age twelve, bridesmaid for a wedding. She was giggling in the picture, half bent over, trying to hold her tiara of flowers as it slid off her red hair. Janie disliked the portrait: she hadn't gotten her braces yet and the uneven teeth seemed to take over the entire picture. But her parents loved it. "How you adored that long dress!" they would say, smiling into the photograph's eyes, as if it were as alive. "How proud you were, being in the wedding party, dancing with the groom, staying up till dawn."

Janie climbed the stairs to her room, passing by the ascending wall of photographs. Her parents disliked albums; they immortalized Janie on the stairs. Janie at the beach, on skis, in a Scout uniform, in her first dancing dress. Janie on their trip to the Grand Canyon. Janie in gymnastics, Janie at the Middle School Awards Ceremony. Janie on the runway for the fashion show the hospital sponsored as a benefit.

I'm sick, she thought. Deranged. Imagine imagining they kidnapped me! I mean, talk about proof of loving family. From the folded laundry to the refrigerator note—

She remembered what the class was.

Her mother had decided that she and Janie needed An Activity to Share. She'd picked, of all things, cake decorating. In spite of their past record at arts and crafts—the failed needlepoint pillows, the abandoned quilt tops, the unfinished knitting—her mother was convinced that she and Janie could be like the rest of the world and do something creative with their hands.

The only thing Janie liked to do with her hands was put nail polish on them and dial phone numbers.

. . . phone numbers . . .

On the milk carton was a toll-free, 800 number to dial. *If you have seen this child . . .*

Janie froze three steps from the top. Turning her head slowly, like a patient becoming paralyzed, neck stiffening forever, she forced her eyes to search among the photographs.

There were no baby pictures.

She had asked why before. Because they never got around to buying a camera till Janie was five, said her parents.

But you didn't need your own camera for baby photographs. Every single store that sold baby clothes—from Sears to Bloomingdale's, from High-Fashion Tot to Toys R Us—had photographers; and special portrait prices.

Jennie Spring. Taken from a shopping center in New Jersey at age three.

But I should remember, thought Janie. Three years old is time to have memories. It's not as if Jennie Spring was three months old.

She entered her room. It was the largest bedroom in the house. Since her parents each had a small study, they had taken the little bedroom and given her the spacious master bedroom. Janie had a habit of leaping into hobbies with tremendous enthusiasm for a few months and then abandoning them forever. The walls and shelves were testimony to lost interests. There was the gymnastics display, when she had fallen in love with tumbling. There were the horseback-riding ribbons, from fourth grade when she practically lived at the stable. There was the music, when she had intended to be the world's foremost flutist. The last piece she had ever practiced still lay open on the pretty little music stand her parents had bought her for Christmas that year.

Janie did not share her mother's adoration of fierce, intense blues and reds. When she turned fourteen, they had redecorated the room by Janie's colors: ivory, pale pale rose, and faded lavender. The bedspread Janie had chosen was lace panels: all different shades and textures of white. It was too fragile to sit on. She folded the lace into a tube at the bottom of her bed and lay down on the plain, dark-rose wool blanket beneath it. She was as rigid as a board. The mattress sank down while Janie's spine remained stiff. She ordered her muscles to relax, forcing first her shoulders to go limp, then her neck, and her jaw.

At last she had sagged into the contours of the mattress. Now she tried to look inside her brain, to dip through her memory as if it were a card catalog at the library.

Nothing.

And yet—memory felt oddly bright—not dark— not scary or mysterious—light . . . easy . . . good.

There's somebody else down there, thought Janie.

She shuddered violently, picturing another tiny little girl living at the bottom of her body, begging to get out.

Janie wet her lips.

The silence of the house was suddenly unbearable. She leaped from the bed, pounded down the stairs, flung open the side door, and ran over to the Shieldses' house.

They were too close friends with the Shieldses to bother much with knocking. She opened the door, yelled, "Hello," and went on in. Mrs. Shields was watching *Lassie.*

"There's probably something wrong with me," remarked Reeve's mother, "but I adore all these old black-and-white reruns. They're so safe."

Safe, thought Janie.

"Is not safe," said Reeve, coming into the room. He had his physics lab book with him. The sight of Reeve with an academic text in his hand startled Janie. "Timmy and Lassie are always saving somebody from runaway trains or bottomless swamps or forest fires."

"Ah, but the kitchen!" said Mrs. Shields. "Nothing ever goes wrong in the kitchen. Have a chocolate chip cookie, dear," she said to Janie.

"Don't," advised Reeve. "She put icky things like oatmeal and bran into the cookies. Timmy," he told his mother, referring to Lassie's owner, "would never have had to gag down oatmeal and bran in *his* cookies."

Nevertheless Reeve took several of the largest cookies and flung himself into a chair. He was one of those boys who don't simply sit: they collapse, snapping the legs off chairs and breaking the backs of couches. Janie and his mother waited for Reeve to fall on through to the floor, but the chair held him once more.

"Mrs. Shields?" said Janie. "How long have you lived here?"

"Darling, I am that rara avis. A native. I was born here."

"I mean, in this house."

"Twenty-eight years. Bought it when we were married."

"Do you remember when we moved here?"

"I certainly do. You were the most adorable five-year-old who ever drew breath on Romney Road. And your mother was the strictest parent. I shaped up once she moved in, let me tell you." Mrs. Shields smiled, a private smile of memories kept within, to warm herself by.

"Why was she so strict?" said Janie. She had bitten off some cookie and now was unable to chew it. Little bits of dough and bran lay on her tongue and threatened to choke her.

"Because you were so bad." said Reeve immediately.

He and his mother laughed. "No, Janie was always sweet, good, obedient, and courteous," said Mrs. Shields. "I used to yearn for a Janie among my four wild animals."

Why was I such a goody-goody? thought Janie. Was I afraid? If they stole me, I should have been afraid of *them*, not the rest of the world. "Seriously," said Janie.

Mrs. Shields watched *Lassie*. Timmy's mother was wearing her apron. In old television they always had on aprons.

Janie fell into another nightmare by daylight. Her mind plummeted down into the nightmare the way Reeve's muscular body had fallen onto the upholstery.

Apron.

It was white; heavy; almost as heavy as canvas; it had a bib; her mother kept little hard candies in one pocket and Janie could stretch up and reach her baby hand into the pocket to take out one candy. With a cellophane wrapper that crinkled.

But my mother doesn't wear aprons, thought Janie.

"Life isn't like that now," said Mrs. Shields sadly. "Too many dreadful possibilities out there. And hardly any Lassies to save you. Mothers have nightmares about their babies, Janie—from drowning in a neighbor's swimming pool to snapping the spine playing football. I think all mothers fear that one dreadful accident—when the child dashes out in front of a truck. When some maniac snatches the child during the one second the mother isn't looking. Your mother has always felt that way, Janie. She's always been afraid."

"For what reason?" said Janie. She forced herself to swallow the dead cookie in her mouth. Reeve, becoming a host, which was almost as unthinkable as Reeve becoming a scholar, handed her a Coke.

"What mother ever needed a reason?" said Mrs. Shields. "I suppose because you were the only child. I had three earlier ones to take out my unreasonable fears on. Old Reeve here, I didn't worry about him much because I'd used up so much worry on the others."

She and Reeve began a teasing verbal battle about how much worry he had caused her in his

31

seventeen years, and was likely to cause in the next seventeen.

Janie stayed till the end of *Lassie*. The final scene was in the kitchen. Timmy of course had a glass of milk. Nobody in old television gave their kids soda. It ended happily ever after, with hugs all around and a barking collie.

"Oh, my goodness, I'm late!" cried her mother, throwing open the front door. Her mother never came in the side door. She liked to look around the front hall, with its graceful mirrors and slender, elegant furniture, and into the beautiful living room she had designed. "Janie, by any wonderful chance did you start supper? We have our cake decorating class tonight. We've got to leave in thirty minutes. What's in the freezer? Anything we can microwave? Did you do your homework? How was school?"

She gave Janie a big hug and a little row of kisses down her cheek toward her throat. "Daddy home yet?"

"No." Janie stared at her mother. She tried to imagine her mother as a kidnapper, rushing into shopping malls and jerking little girls off soda fountain stools. But her mother was elegant, formal. She could imagine her mother raising funds for a scholarship for this little girl—but actually snatching her? Mother liked to conduct her meetings properly, with much consulting of formal Rules of Order.

"Oh, dear, I hate it when we leave in the evening without seeing him. I hate not having dinner together. I read the other day that most families in America now have separate meals—each one just grabs a bite on the run, a pizza here, a frozen Weight Watchers casserole there. I think that's so sad, families no longer sitting down together every evening. And here we are, just like all the rest. I hate being just like all the rest."

Well, you're not, thought Janie. You're a kidnapper.

Her mother was beautifully dressed. She hung up her crimson wool coat and slipped off her high, slim heels. Her feet were very long and very narrow and finding shoes was a real trial. Janie's feet were short and wide.

There's nothing in me that's like her, thought Janie. Is it because I have none of her genes? Because she is not my mother?

She forced herself to think of Adair O'Dell, who was so sleek. Adair's mother was a fat, messy woman whose offspring you would expect to be total rug rats. So lots of times kids didn't resemble their parents. It meant nothing.

Her father charged in the side door, full of energy from soccer. "What a team!" he said. He launched his first bear hug at his wife, and Janie would normally have run up for hers, but she found herself edging out of reach. "What a season. I love my kids. They try so hard! We practiced in the school gym because of the rain. Can't stand that stupid principal they have down there. Good janitor, though. Big help. I can't wait for the next game. We have so much potential this year! Why are we having microwave pizza? Where are you

33

guys going? Don't I even get to talk to my girl?"
He pretended to kick soccer balls around Janie's
ankles.

"Daddy, stop it," she said.

"How can I embarrass you when there's nobody
around to see?" he countered. "Tell you what. I
promise to do this in front of all your friends one
day, just for comparison's sake."

"Thanks," said Janie.

"Cake decorating," explained her mother.

"Do you think it's the right sort of class for
somebody as weight obsessed as you are?" said
her father.

"I won't eat any of it," said her mother virtuously.

"Sure," said her father. "Listen, you two scarf
down those awful frozen jobs. I'll make myself a
real dinner after my shower. Love ya. Have fun.
Bring me some cake. I want the most frosting."
He charged up the stairs.

They talk more than I do, too, thought Janie.
They spout conversation continually, both of them.
I have more listening in me than talking.

The class was at the Y. The familiar hot-chlorine-
and-sweat smell of the pool met their noses.

"Remember your swim team?" said her mother.
"I was so glad you lost interest in swimming.
There I'd sit, with all the other mothers, waiting
for hours till your heat came up, and then I couldn't
even tell which one you were and it was over in
three minutes anyhow. Ugh. At least when you
took up riding, it was more fun. Why don't you go
back to riding?"

"I would have if I'd known the alternative was cake decorating," said Janie. "Mom, I'm dreading this. We've bombed out on watercolor, decoupage . . ."

"Well, you couldn't eat any of those. The taste tests will make all the difference." They took the stairs to the kitchen. The Y ran a soup kitchen by day (where her mother had not yet volunteered but surely would before long), but in the evenings the kitchen was available to cooking classes. Japanese, Chinese, Vietnamese, and French cooking each had a night. Cake decorating seemed backward and untrendy next to those cuisines.

"Think of all the calories. This is a dangerous hobby, Mom. Besides, you told Daddy you weren't going to eat any."

"I lied."

Janie and her mother burst into giggles.

There were nine in the class. Janie was the only one under forty and the only one not watching her pounds. "I'm going to like this," whispered her mother. "Next to you, I'm the skinniest person here."

They learned on cardboard, not cakes. They piped icing out of tubes, cloth bags, and paper cones. They used star tips and tube tips for flowers and ribbons. Janie could not keep the pressure on her tube even, so that for every attractive flower, she had a pitiful plop of icing instead. "Yours looks like a very faded bouquet," remarked her mother.

The instructor demonstrated flowers yet again. As Janie leaned forward to see the technique, she fell hideously into another daymare.

The conscious part of her thought: Am I falling into the cake? Will I be a pitiful fool in front of these women, my face covered with icing?

The daymare was white: white flowers, white whipped cream, white ice cream. *The pretty woman, the whirling stool at the counter. And white shoes: tiny, shiny white shoes.*

We were shoe shopping, thought Janie. But who is "we"? Who am I?

"Now you try," said the instructor, putting the tube in her hand. Janie struggled to make a flower, but there was no white icing in the tube. There was a thin line of blue gel instead. She stared at the demonstration cake and saw that while she had been lost in a dreadful white dream, they had changed from flowers to writing.

Her hand shook. She tried to write HAPPY BIRTH-DAY.

What was the birth date on the carton? she thought. When was Jennie Spring's birthday? Is it mine?

CHAPTER
4

She slept soundly.

If she dreamed, she did not remember when she awoke.

How strange, thought Janie. You'd think if anything would give me nightmares, it would be this.

She got out of bed. Janie loved nightwear. Sometimes she was in a pajama mood and she had flannel pajamas, silk shortie pajamas, and sweet cotton-and-lace pajamas. Sometimes she preferred nightgowns and she had everything from bridal-trousseau-type gowns to teddies. But recently she had gotten into sweatshirt stuff: this new gown was a soft pearl gray, like a sweatshirt to the floor.

She peeled the gown up and over her head and stared at herself, naked in the mirror. She liked her body.

Morning sun streamed in the window. It caught on the prisms Janie had been given for some elementary-school science project and never taken

down from their plastic strings. Miniature rain-
bows danced across the walls. She held out her
hand and "caught" one in her palm.

On the desk was a spray of reference books
given her over various Christmases and rarely
touched. The dictionary was a huge dark-blue Web-
ster's. She looked up nightmare. From Middle
English *niht*—"night"—and Anglo-Saxon *mare*—
"demon." Then she looked up "daydream." "A
pleasant, dreamy thought."

Below it, there actually was a word "daymare."
Defined as a nightmare taking place in the day.

Demon, thought Janie. That's what it was.
Some demon—some goblin or troll—forcing a
daymare on me.

In school the boys were particularly sophomoric.

Janie adored mischief, if she could watch rather
than participate. She was perfectly willing to cheer
the boys on as long as she ran no risk of getting
punished along with them.

Pete had a huge roll of masking tape left over
from an art project.

All the kids were attracted by the tape. Everybody wanted to rip off a piece and tape things
together. "We could tape Sarah-Charlotte's mouth
shut," said Jason, laughing, ready to do it.

"Tape the trash-barrel lids closed so nobody
can throw anything away," Adair suggested.

"Or tape Ellen Winter's braids to her back!" Nobody liked Ellen Winter. Nobody ever had, nobody
ever would. The poor thing would have nobody to
untape her.

"No, let's tape Janie's hair down!" cried Jason.

"At last I'll have breathing space during lunch. We'll just wind the whole roll around her forehead until her hair is finally under control."

Janie shrieked with mixed horror and delight, protecting her head with her arms. She considered whether to yank her sweater up over her hair and run screaming down the halls. Sarah-Charlotte shuddered, imagining this fate. "You'd never get it off! When we pulled the tape away, we'd scalp her! You sadist. Somebody lock this boy up. He's sick and twisted."

"I like that in a person," said Adair.

"I know," said Pete. "Let's tape all the desks together."

"Let's what?"

"Let's go into the ninth-grade wing. They're all at lunch. We'll turn every desk inward and tape them together. When they get back from lunch, they won't be able to get their chairs under the desks."

"Ooooh, that's a great idea," said Sarah-Charlotte. "What a gift from us to them. Think how they'll waste a whole period trying to untape desks."

There was silence while each debated whether the pleasure would be worth the pain, if they got caught, or whether they'd rather just sit there and have lunch, or if they'd be wimps if they didn't follow through on it now.

Adair, who was going for her driver's test the following Monday, and who carried her driver's ed book with her everywhere, was not interested. "Don't let's do that," she begged. "Somebody test me on stopping distance instead."

Janie flipped the book open and read aloud the

questions on stopping distances. Adair got them all right. She had the entire book memorized.

"I'm so afraid I'll forget something when I go for my test," said Adair. "What if they won't give me my license just because I didn't remember to bring my birth certificate?"

"Then we'd know what a dumbbell you are," said Jason. "If you're that dumb, you don't deserve your brownie, so give me your dessert."

Janie's body turned to ice.

I have no more control over my temperature than I do over the daymares, thought Janie. She said, "You have to have a birth certificate to get a driver's license, Adair?" Now her interior betrayed her: all the organs in her chest and abdomen shuddered and rippled.

I don't want to know, thought Janie. Because . . . because why? Does something deep inside me know already? But why now? Why haven't I known all along? How could you forget something like your real family and the moment you were taken from them? I know I'm making it up; it's a demon, the dictionary says so.

So why am I turning cold with fear?

"Three forms of identification," said Adair. "I'm bringing my birth certificate, which you have to have, my Social Security card, and my passport."

Jason laughed suddenly. "I remember the first time I saw my birth certificate," he said, "with its little raised seal and the gold lettering at the top, and it was so official and all: the real me: and it had the *wrong* birth date. I practically passed out. I thought—*I'm somebody else, I'm adopted, they switched babies at the hospital.* I sweated so much the paper got soggy."

Janie's mouth was so dry she could not ask questions.

"It turns out," Jason explained, his voice rich with relief, "that there are two dates: the day you were born and the day they register you on the records, which in my case was several days later. My eyes landed on the wrong date."

Janie seemed to melt, like ice cream in the sun.

She had no energy left, hardly even a mind. She pictured road surfaces in winter, ripped into potholes and heaves by the changing temperatures, ice one day, sunny thaw the next. Would the changing temperatures of her imagination rip through her, too? She had never seen an insane person. They don't mean to go insane, thought Janie. It happens to their surface, like freeze and thaw.

She had a sense that she must hold on to her sanity, the way in a crowd in the city you held on to your purse. That it would take both hands to stay sane.

Reeve did not give her a ride home.

She took the bus.

It stopped at the corner; she had a block to walk.

Theirs was an architecturally mixed neighborhood. Originally a street of substantial older houses with front porches, big attics, and trees that dumped a million leaves every autumn, each side lot had been built upon. Modern ranches and cute little Cape Cods lay between each brown-shingled old place. Her own house was an old one dramatically modernized with sheets of glass where once there had been dark, hidden rooms.

Janie walked through mountains of leaves in the gutter, waiting for the town crew to come with the frightening leaf-vacuum that sucked and then minced the scarlet and gold leaves. She had never been able to watch it.

She went in the side door. "Mom?" she yelled.

"In here, dear." Her mother was at her desk. Lists, folders, notations. All the stuff for her various causes and crusades. "How was school, darling?"

"Oh, you know. School."

"I had a great day," said her mother happily. "My Laotian boy. He's really made a quantum leap. He's not going to need me much longer." Her mother tutored English as a second language. The Laotian boy had one interest, and one only: sports. He wanted his terms straight so he wouldn't refer to "baskets" or "goals" for a baseball game.

"Mom?" said Janie, keeping her voice light. "I'm going to need my birth certificate for getting my driver's license. Can I see it now?"

Her mother's pencil stopped moving on the form she was filling out.

It seemed to Janie that her mother's knuckles tightened and whitened. Her mother said, "Darling, you won't be eligible for months."

"I know, but Adair's been talking about it and I got interested."

"It's in the safe deposit box at the bank," said her mother.

42

"Oh. Well, then, let's go open it."

"I'm very busy, darling."

"Let's go tomorrow then."

"Tomorrow's Saturday," said her mother quickly. "The bank's not open."

Janie felt like an executioner, escorting her own mother to the guillotine. "Monday then," said Janie.

Her mother said, "Jane Elizabeth Johnson, you do not give your mother orders, do you hear me? You may ask courteously, but you may not command."

"Why don't you want me to see my birth certificate?" said Janie.

Her mother turned a page in her notebook and stared at the blank paper. "Don't be ridiculous, Janie. Now let's have a snack. What do you feel like? I did a huge grocery shopping. New microwave and frozen stuff we haven't tried yet. And fruit juice popsicles for you instead of ice cream."

She doesn't want me to see my birth certificate, thought Janie. Because there isn't one? Because the dates are wrong? Or because she isn't in the mood to bother with the bank?

In the kitchen Janie looked in the breadbox and passed on doughnuts, fresh onion bagels, and raspberry coffee cake. She checked the shelves but did not feel like opening Double Stuf Oreos or Mallomars. She was not in the mood for the strawberry-vanilla yogurt or leftover pizza in the refrigerator. "I knew all along my snack would be in the freezer," she remarked.

But her mother had not come in with her.

Janie turned slowly, looking around the empty room.

Always, after school, if her mother was home, the two of them shared snacks, discussed their day, opened the mail together.

Her mother not only remained in her study; she had even shut the door.

Janie jerked open the freezer. Cold air bathed her cheeks. There was a quart of Wildberry Ripple Ice Cream, Flavor of the Month, for her father.

From the shelf she took her favorite bowl, a Peter Rabbit bowl she had had—since when? thought Janie. All my life? Or since I was—

She wrenched her mind away from it.

From the utensil drawer she took the ice cream scoop.

It was old, with a wooden handle now split from many runs through the dishwasher. The scoop itself was pitted with age.

Like a painting from the bottom up, another kitchen emerged in her brain. She saw the floor first—toys on it—yellow linoleum. She saw the legs of chairs next, and the legs of grown-ups. Then a tabletop—it was at eye level—she was the height of the table.

Janie panted like a child having an asthma attack.

She could barely keep her balance.

The painting grew, gathering color and detail.

. . . *not a large room . . . messy . . . two screaming babies, each in a high chair . . . the apron: that white canvas apron with the pocket of candy . . . a bag of Wonder Bread; she could*

44

remember the wrapper . . . her voice asking for
milk . . . but nobody heard her over the scream-
ing of the babies, so Janie got it herself, spilling
a puddle. She could remember mopping it up
with a paper towel, proud of herself for making
the mess and for unmaking it. . . . She remem-
bered being scooped up, hugged . . . laughter
. . . noise . . . mess . . . commotion . . .

The kitchen in which she really stood was large,
smooth, and empty. The counters and shelves
pounded in her head, like cartoon things taking
on life and rhythm.

Abandoning the quart of Wildberry Ripple, Janie ran outside.

Reeve was raking leaves in his yard. "Hi," he
said, "come to help? I've got an extra rake. It's
time you earned your keep, woman." He grinned.
His face was rather long and narrow, and the
grin was a surprise, because it took up so much
space—you were socked with joy when Reeve
smiled at you. A French-looking beret tilted on
his hair. He was thigh-deep in leaves. "I've got
to mow the lawn again," he explained. "That
grass went and grew some more. I don't know
how, under a foot of leaves. Here. Rake, Janie. I
need you."

She took the rake. Energy spilled out of her
like oil from a smashed tanker. Leaves were
flung into the air. She made immense, immedi-
ate progress.

Reeve stared at her.

She raked on and on, until the leaves were a
mountain in front of her and the lawn a green
swarm behind her.

Without catching himself, Reeve fell backward into the leaf pile and sank toward the ground, brown leaves sliding over his face and chest. "Janie, you have a problem? Come tell Uncle Reeve." He sprawled comfortably. The leaves crackled with every breath he took.

She sat next to him, cross-legged, looking down into his face. They were in a nest, hidden from the adult world. There was nothing like a pile of leaves to make you feel little again. "Reeve, do you think 800 numbers can trace a call? I mean, if you called an 800 number and didn't say anything, could they find out what phone you called from?"

"I take it you're not going to call *Time* magazine for a subscription," said Reeve, laughing. "Who are you calling? The Secret Service to report an assassination attempt?"

How did he get so close? she thought. Does he know something, too? Deep down, without admitting it, does he remember? He would have been seven, I would have been five. "I thought I'd call the Milk Council to find out about new research on milk allergies," she said.

Reeve shouted with laughter. "Oh, boy, they'll really want to trace that call, Jane Elizabeth. They'll figure they've got an escaped, drug-running Central American dictator on the phone for sure when you ask about milk allergies." He laughed and laughed, put both hands around her, and pulled her down into the leaves with him.

5

The kiss was long.

And serious.

Serious like my hair, thought Janie. She stared amazed at Reeve's cheek, which was pressed against hers, and with amazement brought her lips together to kiss him again—to start the second kiss, and to choose when to end it. She could feel his heart racing and then felt her own pick up speed and run with his.

Very slowly her hands crept around his face, finding the back of his neck where his hair lay thick over the pulse. His hand, rough-surfaced, gently touched her face. Moved her hair away. With the pad of his thumb he traced her profile.

"Reeve!" shouted his mother from the house. "Reeve, where are you? Phone call! It's Michael."

They fell apart, each lying back on crinkly leaves, staring at the sky. Reeve said, "Uh—Michael probably wants to know if—um—well—I better talk to him."

"Okay," said Janie.

She stood up first and began dusting the leaves off herself. She could feel leaf bits in her hair and down the back of her sweater. Reeve's eyes fixed on her hair and he moved as if to brush the leaves away for her, but then he looked down at his feet instead, mumbling, "See you," and ran into the house.

Janie's heart and lungs were working as if they were trying to power a city's electricity. She picked up the rake again. Their two bodies had left prints on the leaf pile, like angels in the snow. She raked the pile back together, until the prints were hidden, and the evidence gone.

Reeve did not come back from his phone call.

The sun went behind clouds and she was cold.

She went inside, remembering the ice cream on the counter and wondering if it had melted everywhere. But her mother had put it away. "That showed such discipline, Janie," her mother complimented her. "To get exercise instead of indulging in forbidden foods!" An I've-got-a-secret smile spread on her mother's face. "Look," she said. "I've been practicing. What do you think of it?"

From the refrigerator she took a large rectangular pan covered with aluminum foil, which Janie had thought was lasagne. Peeling back the foil, her mother showed off a sheet cake. The cake was iced in white, with purple piping on the sides—and a cute little purple football arching over purple goalposts in the center. "Tomorrow we're all driving up to the university for the football game," said her mother. "I'm doing dessert.

Usually I go to the bakery and order lots of chocolate surprises, but this time I thought I'd do a cake. What do you think of it?"

"It's so cute!" cried Janie. "Look, you even have the little team over here, painted in gel. And here's a cheerleader. Mom, I love her pom-poms. How did you do it?"

Each year they went for a tailgate picnic along with Reeve's family and Sarah-Charlotte's. The football game! she thought. I'll be with Reeve tomorrow. All day. Her heart raced.

"I was in a Grandma Moses mood," explained her mother. "I decided to do a primitive painting in purple tube art on a cake."

They giggled. For the first time in her life, Janie regretted that Sarah-Charlotte would be along, with her eagle eyes and endless chatter.

"I just hope the cake is edible," said her mother. "I haven't baked a cake in a hundred years. I used Duncan Hines mix, though, so I'm probably safe."

"There's no way to taste-test," agreed Janie. "Unless we cut off the goalposts and eat them tonight."

"Bite your tongue. This took me the entire day, Janie. My goodness, what's in your hair?"

"Leaves," said Janie. "I went out to help Reeve rake and he got silly and we fell over in the leaf pile like a pair of third graders."

With Janie sitting on a kitchen chair and her mother standing behind her, she brushed and brushed till the red hair was full of static and the floor covered with tiny brown bits of leaf.

Janie thought of Reeve. Those leaves on the

floor might be the only souvenir of her only kisses. When he ran away to take Michael's phone call, had he also been running away from the kiss he had given Janie? "I think I'll do my weekend homework tonight," said Janie, "since the football game will take all day Saturday." She took back her hairbrush and went upstairs to be alone with the memory of Reeve, and his lips, and his rough-soft hand.

Usually she passed her so-called homework hours on the phone with Sarah-Charlotte or Adair. There were also Gretchen, Doria, and Michelle to call if Sarah-Charlotte's and Adair's phones were busy.

Janie was almost overcome with the desire to talk about Reeve. *He kissed me, he pulled me down in the leaves, like somebody in a romance novel where the man is so frantic with passion he pulls her off the horse, or out of the carriage, and onto the bed. You should have been there! It was incredible.*

However, Sarah-Charlotte, who liked things nailed down on all four sides, would demand, "So did he ask you out? Are you dating? What kind of commitment did you get from him?"

So she wouldn't call Sarah-Charlotte. And maybe not Adair either, because Adair would hate the part about getting leaves in her hair. Adair was against anything messy.

Janie sighed and opened her book bag, dumping the contents on her bed. She never studied at her desk. She used the desktop for her cassette collection.

Her cheap, blue-cloth, three-ring notebook fell out on top of the math, biology, American lit, and world history books. It was the kind you wrote on in ballpoint pen: tic-tac-toe games, interlocked initials, and assorted doodles. Janie opened the cover. The back of the flattened milk carton stared up at her.

FLOWER DAIRY
"The dairy that cares"
100% whole milk
one half pint

She unclipped it.

Turned it over.

Jennie Spring looked up at her.

The 800 number was like a dart being thrown into her eyes. I could call, she thought. I could ask—

But what could she ask?

All the questions were unthinkable.

Besides, what would it do to her parents to find out their very own daughter was calling the authorities to announce she had been kidnapped? Her mother, who had spent the day baking a special cake, and was too tired to consider going to the bank . . . her father, who would come home from soccer full of victory or deflated by loss.

Janie picked up her phone.

She dialed 1.

She dialed 800.

She dialed 346-72—

She was gasping for breath.

With two digits to go, she hung up.

She missed the phone. It clattered, slid off the bed, and hit the floor with a crash as loud as trains colliding.

But her mother did not yell upstairs to see if Janie was hurt. Up here it was the world crashing in; downstairs nobody had heard a sound.

All right, get a grip on yourself, thought Janie. The dictionary is right: These are inspired by a demon. You have to destroy the demon. Or maybe it's just premenstrual syndrome.

Except she had never previously had trouble before, during, or after her periods.

I will think about Reeve now, she ordered herself, glaring at the inner demon. I will think of kisses and love and dating.

But she thought of Jennie Spring. Of parents somewhere in New Jersey who missed their little girl so much that all these years later they were still hoping, hoping by the thinnest thread they would somehow find their Jennie again, and Jennie would be safe, not murdered or raped or abused—

—or happy and ignorant with another family.

This, thought Janie, must be what heavy drugs are like: hallucinations whether you want them or not. Temperature-changing, personality-changing doses.

This time she dialed Sarah-Charlotte.

Busy.

Then Adair.

Adair had total-phone and gave Janie twenty seconds of her time. She was on the phone with

Pete, who, she said, seemed to be on the verge of asking her out. "Then what'd you answer my call for?" demanded Janie. "You might have cut him off at the moment he got the courage together."

"Normal persons," said Adair, "can never resist a phone call." She disconnected to go back to Pete.

Janie called Michelle, who did not have total-phone.

The phone rang twice. Somebody picked it up.

Janie disconnected immediately.

Rude! thought Janie. Why'd I do that? Because I can't talk to Michelle about anything. If I told Michelle about Reeve, the next day the whole school would think Reeve asked me to marry him. If I told Michelle about the milk carton, the whole school would know that I actually believe I was kidnapped. Guidance Department would hear the rumors. They'd summon my mother from her Bloodmobile. *Your daughter's hoping you're not her parents; your daughter is planning to call the FBI on you; your daughter is living in a sick, twisted, perverted daydream in which . . .*

Her body vibrated with a queer, frightening energy, as if she could have run all the way to New Jersey to that shopping center.

What if I can't get this horrible idea out of my brain? she thought. What if it sits there, and grows, like some terrible egg, splitting open and turning into something real?

In separate cars, the Johnsons, the Shieldses, and the Sherwoods drove upstate to the football game.

"Please let me drive," Janie begged her parents. "Sarah-Charlotte's family is letting her drive because she needs highway practice. And Reeve gets to drive the whole way."

"Reeve's had his license an entire year," said her father. "And Sarah-Charlotte's been practicing longer than you have."

"I've never driven on the highway," said Janie. "Please, please, please? This is a perfect day to start. Lots of sunshine, no rain, no ice on the roads, no summer-people traffic."

"All right," said her mother nervously.

"Certainly not," said her father.

Old times. Progressive mother, conservative father. Janie waited for the debate to commence, and for them to meet in the middle. They would probably let her drive part of the way.

"Oh, all right," said her father. "I keep not wanting to believe you're going to be sixteen soon. I don't like the year sixteen."

Janie giggled and took the keys from her mother's hand. Her parents clicked their seat belts firmly, as if to say, *we're sure going to need them this time.* "Have faith," said Janie reproachfully.

"Take off the parking brake," said her father.

"I was going to, Daddy, you just didn't give me time." She backed perfectly out of the driveway.

Not only did Reeve come out his door in time to see her drive, but so did his older sister Lizzie.

Lizzie was not one of Janie's favorite people. Lizzie had occasionally baby-sat for Janie in the past, but not because she liked kids. Lizzie rarely did anything except for the money. Lizzie was supposed to be safely in law school now, being as brilliant there as she had been in Princeton. Janie did not consider Lizzie's absence a loss to the neighborhood. How annoying to see Lizzie home. It would certainly tense Reeve up.

Even from the far end of the driveway Janie could see how straight Lizzie's spine was; how intense her face; how determined her jaw. It seemed unlike Lizzie to come home for a mere football game; Lizzie was opposed to frivolous waste of time. Lizzie was also opposed to Reeve, and had been all their lives.

But there was a silver lining to this. Reeve would be very eager to go off with Janie.

She wanted to wave to Reeve but was not coordinated enough to change gears, aim the car, miss the curb, and wave all at the same time.

Reeve did not act as if Lizzie had crushed him yet; he leaped around like a demented boy cheerleader, signaling with both arms and screaming syllables she could not hear.

"Look out for that car up there," said her mother.

"You're following too closely," said her father.

"Please," cried her mother, "not over twenty-five."

They were gripping the seats, the belts, and the armrests with white knuckles.

"How'm I doing?" said Janie happily. She loved driving. The power of it! Even diluted by her mother and father's panic, power filled her body. She, Janie, controlled destination, speed, passing, radio volume, and stopping time. She felt as if she had been born to drive, as if car designers had molded the driver's seat just for her. She loved checking the rearview mirror and watching the brake lights ahead of her and reading the route numbers on road signs.

For Janie it was a perfect hour and a half.

However, Reeve and Sarah-Charlotte, permitted to drive normal speeds like real drivers, had arrived first. When the Johnsons reached the designated parking lot for tailgate picnics, Sarah-Charlotte and Reeve stood on the pavement shouting, "You'll never be able to park it!" "Jinx, jinx!" "Try steering, woman!"

She parked perfectly. "So there," she said to her parents.

Her mother said, "This is an excellent weight-loss program. I'm sure I'm five pounds thinner than I was when I left home."

"You'll put it all back on eating your own pic-nic," said her father, dragging out the leg of lamb, the wine, the wild rice, and the sheet cake with the footballs. And that was just what the Johnsons had brought. Reeve's mother had a ham and Sarah-Charlotte's mother had all the classics: potato salad, coleslaw, macaroni salad, and fried chicken.

The weather was wonderful: sweater weather. In the shelter of their three cars, they ate till forced to rest their stomachs. "We'll need a tow lift to get us up into the stadium," joked Janie's father, who had had lamb, ham, and fried chicken.

Janie's mother played with the aluminum foil hiding the sheet cake while Lizzie discussed the constitutional law cases she was now analyzing. "If Lizzie laughs at my cake . . ." Janie's mother whispered to her.

"Or at you," Janie murmured back.

"We'll murder her," breathed Janie's mother.

"But then we'd need a lawyer," whispered Janie, "and we'd just have gotten rid of the only one around." They giggled.

Mr. Sherwood thought the kids should go away and explore the campus before dessert, thus giv-ing the adults some peace.

"We're not babies anymore," said Sarah-Charlotte irritably, "needing our diapers changed and our bottles heated."

"No, but you talk a lot more," said her father, "and we'd like our own conversation without you, okay? But I still love you. Kind of." Sarah-Charlotte made a face, claiming this lukewarm parental love meant she deserved her own car, insurance paid and gas supplied, of course.

"Uh huh," said her father dryly.

Reeve turned to his sister, grinning. "Come on, Lizzie," he teased. "They want the kids to leave. So they can have a mature conversation."

"I am the only one here who will bother with a mature conversation," said Lizzie. "They just want to gossip." She took a chicken leg, leaned back, and said to Janie's father, "Your turn, Frank."

Janie tried to imagine one day calling her friends' parents by their first names, failed, and fled with Reeve and Sarah-Charlotte. They wandered around the campus, talking about what college would be like ("If I get in," said Reeve gloomily) and how they yearned to live in dorms and be away from the confining rules of their parents.

Janie was lying.

College terrified her.

There was nothing she wanted less than to live on her own. The harsh glass-and-steel dorms the freshmen had did not look as if they could ever be home to anybody. They looked like cages for loneliness. Imagine five thousand freshmen you had never met.

Reeve said, "My parents and Guidance think I should take a postgraduate year, repeat some of my high school subjects to get better grades, and then go on to college."

"How humiliating," remarked Sarah-Charlotte.

"You're supposed to tell me nobody would notice," said Reeve.

"Of course they'd notice, it would be like staying back," said Sarah-Charlotte, who was not sensitive. "Jordan Feingold and Linda Lang stayed back in second grade and I never see them without remembering that."

"How comforting," said Reeve.

Janie wanted to hold his hand. The one whose thumb had drawn itself so lightly down her nose, bumping over her lips, landing on her chin. But she could not tell if Reeve was interested in this or not. He was full of energy. She and Sarah-Charlotte were sloths compared to Reeve, stumbling in his wake.

They had excellent seats: six rows up, left of center. Janie mostly watched the cheerleaders, who were heavy on gymnastics. They had tiny trampolines and were endlessly catapulting off each other's shoulders. She particularly liked how one tiny cheerleader with flowing golden hair stood on the palms of a boy cheerleader who could hold her easily at his own shoulder level.

With some ceremony, Mrs. Johnson opened her sheet cake for admiration and cut it up to serve during the second quarter. They ate it with their fingers, getting icing all over themselves and licking their fingers clean because nobody had remembered napkins.

"Lemme have another piece," said Reeve, nudging his hipbone into Janie's.

"You had two already," she said. "I'm cold, don't move away."

He didn't move away. She cut another square for him and something gave her the courage to feed it to him, bite by bite. His lips and tongue touched her fingers with every bite. Neither of them saw the second half of the game. They were both startled to find it had ended. People were on their feet. Sarah-Charlotte was saying, "We won, you two. You want me to write out the details so you'll feel as if you were here?"

Sarah-Charlotte spent the night at Janie's.

They rented movies—comedies they had seen before and knew they'd like. Sarah-Charlotte grilled Janie at great length about Reeve, analyzing the leaf pile and the football game. "He loves you," said Sarah-Charlotte.

"You don't have to sound so irritable about it," said Janie.

"I didn't want to be the one left behind. Pete asked Adair out and here's Reeve literally eating out of your hand, and who is there for me? Nobody." This led to the always pleasant activity of ripping apart the personalities of boys who had displayed no interest in Sarah-Charlotte.

They slept late and their sole activity in the morning was reading the Sunday comics.

Monday morning in Spanish the teacher passed out information on a winter vacation trip she was chaperoning to Spain. "Anybody who wants to may go," she said. "First come, first serve."

"Ooooooh, let's," breathed Sarah-Charlotte, nudging Janie.

"If you have any thoughts of going at all, and you don't yet have a passport, you need to apply immediately," said the teacher. "It can take months. You need your birth certificate and another piece of identification to get one."

The bank is open today, thought Janie.

In English they got back their corrected essays. Janie got a B. "Sweet sense of humor," Mr. Brylowe wrote, "although not what I had in mind." At the top of the page he had circled *Jayyne Jonstone*, adding, "Janie, you having an identity crisis?"

At lunch Janie got a wrist flick from Reeve, nothing more. She thought: He's not ready, or maybe not even thinking about doing anything public. She wondered what stages you went through to reach the moment when you could speak to each other in front of your friends, or refer to each other, admitting, *I like him.*

"I thought he was going to ask you out," said Sarah-Charlotte sadly. "Janie, he's so adorable with that moppy hair."

"He needs a decent haircut," agreed Janie. She didn't commit herself to anything more. She opened her lemonade carton. The rest opened their milks. She looked at Jason's milk. There was a different child on the carton.

A boy.

Nobody mentioned him.

Nobody referred to Janie's claim last week to have been the kidnapee. As far as Janie could tell, nobody even remembered; not even Sarah-Charlotte.

Adair had everybody's attention, having skipped first-period class to go to the Motor Vehicle Bureau for her driver's test. Flushed and proud, she displayed her brand-new license. Everybody politely agreed that she was recognizable in the photo, although she was not; nobody ever was.

Adair wanted to show off her driving skills. Everybody, she insisted, had to be passengers in her car and go to the mall that afternoon. "You coming, Janie?" said Adair, more excited than Adair ever allowed herself to be. Janie had not known that Adair's smooth finish, shiny as shellac, was an achievement Adair worked for.

But Janie wanted to go to the bank, not the mall. She said by way of excuse, "I'll have to call my mother and ask."

"Janie, you're still not allowed out by yourself?" teased Jason.

"Her mother is the strictest woman on earth," said Sarah-Charlotte.

"How come?" Jason wanted to know. "What terrible history do you have, Jane Johnson?"

CHAPTER
7

She came home to an empty house. Mondays were hospital volunteer days for her mother. Her father would be coaching at the middle school until dark. When did the bank close?

Janie went into her mother's study. She had a vague idea of finding the key to the safe deposit box and going to the bank herself.

The desk had two deep file drawers. The upper one was crammed with volunteer-related materials: all her mother's committees, boards, and causes. Girl Scouts (that was ancient history), Hospital Volunteers, Literacy Volunteers, Nature Conservancy Board (Janie had never even heard of this one), Parent/Teacher Association . . . in alphabetical order, the files went on and on. There was something very reasssuring about those files: full of her mother's time and energy and caring. Paper memories of meetings, fund-raisers, and suburban routines that made the world a better place to live in.

The frightening daymares of last week had not come back. Janie was more irritated than anything else, wanting to set aside the milk-carton idea; driver's licenses and passports were of much greater importance. If she could just see the birth certificate, she could extricate herself from this dumb idea. In the bottom drawer would be files marked Bills, Income Tax, Insurance Forms.

The bottom drawer was locked.

She found the lock strangely frightening. Her mother did not lock up jewelry, nor silver. So why lock a file drawer? What robber would care about her last-year's bills?

No key was mixed in the pile of paper clips and index tabs lying in the shallow pencil drawer.

Upstairs, Janie changed into old jeans and a sweatshirt. She found herself checking corners of her room for reassurance: Yes, her T-shirt collection was intact. Yes, her bumper-sticker collection was still in its shoebox. Yes, her Barbie dolls still lay silent in their carrying case at the back of the closet.

I should put them all in the attic, she thought. They're clutter. I want my room to be more streamlined than it is.

The attic.

Boxes and trunks. Whenever they went up those dark stairs for things like Christmas decorations, Janie would ask what was in those boxes gathering dust in the corners. "Junk," her mother always replied. "Someday we'll toss it."

Now it occurred to Janie that her mother—everybody's favorite chairwoman—was supremely organized. If she had intended to "toss it," or if it really were junk, it would never have gone into the attic; she would have donated it to the Salvation Army.

Janie opened the door to the attic stairs.

Cold drafts, like winter coming, sifted down on her face like dust.

The roof creaked.

She climbed the stairs. I've never been up here alone, she thought suddenly. If I ever needed my old Halloween costumes, or my last-year's winter boots, Mom went up for them.

At the bottom of the stairs, the draft made the door shut.

Janie whirled when it slammed.

Her heart was pounding.

She crept down the stairs, in case it was an intruder.

Of course it was nothing.

Putting books on each side of the door to hold it open, she went back up.

The attic was poorly lit. The previous owners had remodeled the kitchen, dining room, and bathrooms, but nobody had done anything up here, not even dust. The attic felt as old as time. Eaves ran down toward the floor and made dark corners.

On most boxes, her mother's neat handwriting spelled out the contents. *J—handmade sweaters*.

Janie smiled and opened that one. The sick scent of mothballs filled the attic. Child's sizes, long outgrown. The sweaters reeked of memory as well as mothballs: a Christmas-tree sweater, cream and green, brought back third grade in a rush of sound and color. That Christmas they'd gone to Disney World. She'd needed the sweater; it was cold in Orlando that year. She remembered sitting in the whirling teacup with her parents, clinging to her father's chest, shrieking in delight and dizziness. Billy Wadler, a big, mean fourth-grader, had teased her mercilessly all January about wearing a Christmas-tree sweater.

Billy Wadler had grown up into a really terrific guy. He took out his aggressions in sports now and was nice to girls. Sarah-Charlotte had always yearned for Billy.

Janie smiled and closed the cardboard box. It was hard to interfold the four cardboard pieces as neatly as her mother had done. She coughed from the mothballs.

The next box said *F—ski boots.*

Her father. Frank. She hadn't known her father skied. Maybe they'd do that this winter. She'd ask. She wondered why he'd given it up. Too expensive? Too dangerous?

The whole quest was beginning to feel quite silly. What a good thing that she had not explained anything to Sarah-Charlotte, nor asked anything of her mother.

Up against the very back, hidden by two neatly stacked rows of cardboard boxes, old jigsaw puzzles, and fishing equipment, a black trunk had been pushed. She remembered the fishing-equipment birthday. Her father had gone out twice, but he was not the fisherman type. He disliked solitary sports. How disappointed he had been when his only daughter preferred a social life to soccer!

She was smiling when she reached the black trunk. Probably my baby clothes, she thought. If Mom saved all my sweaters, I bet she saved all my baby clothes.

It was such a nice thought. Janie could hardly wait to see them: eensy, sweet, smocked things she loved to look at in stores.

The trunk was big and cheap, the sort you bought from Sears or Montgomery Ward, metal trim now tarnished.

It was locked.

A label was taped to the top. A single letter was written on it.

H.

Who was H? Her mother was Miranda, her father Frank, she was Jane. None of the four grandparents had been an H either.

An old Christmas-tree holder, three splayed feet and a cup for the trunk, lay gathering cobwebs. Janie wedged its metal foot behind the long, narrow lock-plate of the trunk and yanked.

The lock broke.

How old it must be, thought Janie. It's rusted through.

She lifted the heavy lid carefully, tilting it back against the wall. The trunk was filled with papers and photographs. She was immediately bored. Old school reports, old term papers, old fill-in-the-blank maps and quizzes. Somebody named Hannah. She had never heard of anybody named Hannah.

How could an unknown Hannah merit this stack of attention? Janie felt irritable and coughed again from the dust and the mothballs.

Beneath a sixth-grade report on "The Beginning of Mankind: Mesopotamia," and a sheaf of mimeographed maps where Hannah had wrongly penciled in *Germany* on France, was a school photograph. Janie recognized the cardboard folder immediately: the kind that offered your parents six different purchase agreements, so many wallet sizes, so many eight-by-tens.

She flipped open to see what Hannah looked like. A pretty girl—perhaps twelve or thirteen— looked back at her. Sweet, blond, mild. The kind Sarah-Charlotte would refer to as a Used Rag Doll. "Not much stuffing in that one," Sarah-Charlotte liked to say of girls who were short on personality.

The dust was annoying Janie's lungs. It would be the pits if it turned out she had a dust allergy along with a milk allergy. How would she survive in this world if everything made her choke and cough?

From behind all the papers a little piece of fabric stuck up.

White cloth.

Tiny dark polka dots.

With hands of ice Janie plucked at the material, shifting the layers of school papers until she could pull it up.

It was the dress on the milk carton.

CHAPTER

8

For supper her mother had made a pot roast, with potatoes, turnips, onions, and a rich, dark, thick gravy. Janie had no appetite. The smell, which ordinarily would have brought her into the kitchen with her father, moaning and clutching at things, pretending starvation and deprivation, made her ill. She ate nothing.

"Janie, honey, don't you feel well?"

She shook her head. "I'm fine."

"What can I fix you, then?" said her mother. "Would you rather have soup and toast?"

"I'd rather have a McDonald's cheeseburger," said Janie. "I hate this old-fashioned, heavy-duty, mom-in-the-kitchen stuff with gravy." It was like stabbing her mother. She had to look away from the hurt on her face.

"My child of this century." Her mother struggled to make a joke out of it. "Pizza Hut is better than my chicken potpie, and a McDonald's cheeseburger beats out my pot roast."

Her father had seconds and then thirds to make his wife feel better. He complimented her extravagantly on the texture and flavor of the gravy. Janie knew they were waiting for her to take the initiative and apologize, so they didn't have to tell her to.

"How was school?" said her father.

"Oh, you know. School."

Her father drew a long breath. "We had a great practice. I can't wait for the next game. Lincoln Middle School graduated all its competition, so we ought to slaughter 'em. Janie, I want you to come. You haven't seen my team play yet. How about coming to tomorrow's game?"

He was as eager as a little boy to show off his team.

I could put an ad in the Sunday classifieds down there in New Jersey, thought Janie. What could I say? *Need more details. Describe Jennie Spring. Who is Hannah?*

But that would give those New Jersey parents hope that I exist. That I am out here, and I miss them, and I want them.

I exist. But I don't want different parents.

I like everything exactly the way it is.

How can I have a mother—or a father—or both—that I don't miss and don't want? Am I some kind of monster?

But now that I know they're out there, how can I leave them hanging? Never knowing that I'm fine?

Why am I fine? How could Mother and Daddy do it? Are *they* monsters?

Her father pulled her thick red hair back into a ponytail and brushed his face with it. "Come on, Janie," he coaxed. "I need you out there cheering. Bring a crowd. Make all those high school kids come and yell for us."

"Daddy, don't pull my hair like that." She tugged herself free. Now she had hurt her father as well.

He loves me, she thought. How could love arise from a crime like kidnapping?

"There's a great movie on tonight," said her mother. "Want to watch it with me?"

"Can't. Too much homework." Janie left the table, clearing her entirely clean plate. She went up to her room, shutting the door firmly. She tried to put her parents out of her mind, but Janie was peace loving. The little fight stuck her like needles.

She calmed herself going through her clothes, deciding what to wear tomorrow. There was an Honors Breakfast. The marking period had ended; the first quarter was over. It seemed to her they were shooting through fall, rocketing toward winter, that Christmas would have arrived before she had even gotten her winter coat out. She was in the mood for an entire new wardrobe. She wondered if her mother would take her—

—*shopping.*

Shopping.

Memory struck like an ax. It was the clearest daymare yet, complete with dialogue.

They were clothes shopping.

(*They.* Who were they? She could not quite see them. But she could hear them.)

"No, you can't have that, Jennie, you've got loads of hand-me-downs."

"But Mommy—"

"Not now! Can't you see I'm busy with the twins?"

"But Mommy—"

"No! You don't need a patent leather handbag."

Jennie stomping off by herself. Finding that store with those high, swiveling stools. Sitting at the counter. Swinging herself in circles. Pushing herself by the edge of the counter.

The counter was a pale, greenish-flecked Formica; the napkins popped out of a little stainless steel box.

The woman with the long, shiny hair sat next to her.

Bought her a sundae.

Toward eight o'clock her father knocked on her door. "Kitten? May I come in?"

"Sure."

Who was the woman? thought Janie. My mother downstairs? Another wife of Daddy's? The shopping mother? She called me Jennie. And I answered. It was my name.

Her father entered tentatively, as if he did not know her or the room. "Something wrong, honey? Why are you mad at us?" He was a big man, lean, able to have seconds on gravy without a thought. He had gone gray early, but lost no hair. The mass of gleaming silvery hair was distinguished.

She said evenly, "Why would you think that?"

"Because you are. You're hostile and mean. What's going on?"

"You tell me." She wanted to force answers out of him, but she did not want to ask the questions. They screamed at each other, and theirs was not a screaming family. Janie could not remember when she had thrown ugly words at her parents.

But in the morning she had to rush to school for the Honors Breakfast: jelly doughnuts, orange juice, and coffee supplied by the Parent/Teacher Association for anybody with the grades. It was dumb and embarrassing but nobody ever missed it. You didn't get the rounds of applause for a B average that you got for playing football, nor the spotlight for a terrific term paper that you got for the jazz band. You had to settle for a jelly doughnut and one line in the newspaper listing.

Reeve was there.

"Reeve?" said everybody, staggering around, clutching their hearts, running to the principal to double-check the honors list. "This is Reeve? *Our* Reeve? Reeve whose arms have never been weighted down with those paper and cardboard things known as books?"

"Drop dead," said Reeve. But he was grinning.

Janie beamed at him. "Reeve, I didn't know you were doing so well," she accused him. "You made me think you were going to have to repeat your entire academic career."

Reeve shrugged like a little kid. "I wasn't sure I could get the grades," he admitted to her. "I never tried before. Grades are what Megan and Lizzie and Todd do, not me."

73

"Mr. McKane," Sarah-Charlotte said to the principal, "did Reeve pay you off? Or is he just a misprint on the honors list?"

"Reeve studied brilliantly," said the principal. "Reeve is becoming a fine, fine student, indeed, just like—"

Don't let McKane say *just like his sisters and brother*, thought Janie. It will ruin it for Reeve. Let this be Reeve's, not some spin-off. "Just like me!" she said, striking a center-stage pose and flinging her vast quantity of red hair around.

"Oh, yeah," said Sarah-Charlotte, "you who sneak in here with exactly point one percent above the minimum. Reeve, if you're going to imitate anybody, imitate me." She flirted madly with him, seizing his wrist and beginning to dance wildly. Reeve grinned.

Joyfully, the PTA president announced that it was time to sit down. "What a fine, fine chance for all you brilliant young people to get to know each other better and find new friends," she said, trying to make them talk to people they didn't want to talk to.

She had no success.

It appeared that nobody wanted any new friends. With much grumbling they tried to shuffle place cards and sit with their old friends. PTA mothers intervened. Janie ended up at a table with all juniors and seniors, none of whom she knew. She looked yearningly for somebody to switch with, but Reeve had landed with seniors who were giving him a ritually hard time for having joined academic ranks, and Sarah-Charlotte was lost in the crowd.

"Introduce yourselves to the person next to you," caroled the PTA mother. Janie was very glad her own mother had been president when Janie was in middle school, and she had been spared this humiliation. She knew who the PTA president's kid was just by checking out the hunched shoulders.

"Hi, I'm Dave," said the boy next to her dutifully.

"Janie," she said.

"Tell me about yourself," dictated the PTA mother, as if they were memorizing lines from a play.

"Tell me about yourself," repeated Dave.

"Well, I was kidnapped at age three from a shopping center in New Jersey . . ." Janie panicked. Had she said that out loud? Had those words really fallen out of her mouth? No, surely not!

"Just the basics," said Dave teasingly. "This isn't an autobiography for advanced comp. Where were you born, who are your parents, how long have you lived in Connecticut, that kind of thing."

The room shifted and the table slanted. She wondered why the coffee did not spill, why the doughnuts did not slide to the floor. Dave blurred when she tried to face him. Parents and Hannah, kidnaps and cars, drove through her eyes and crashed at the back of her brain. "I—uh—play tennis a lot."

"She's afraid of you," said a senior girl. "Gee, that's pretty neat, Dave. You're not only an honor student, you're a Big Bad Wolf."

The older kids all dropped their voices an octave. "You're biiiiiiggg," they drawled, pointing at Dave, "and you're baaaaaad, and—"

Janie's head cleared. She said, "I faint every morning if I don't have all the jelly doughnuts in sight. Somebody quick pass me a jelly doughnut."

"We ate all the jelly doughnuts," said the girl. "You have to have a plain one."

"She can have mine," said Dave. "Look. Chocolate icing. Now there's an energizer." He held it out of reach, so she would have to make an effort—touch his hand—lean toward him.

Dave was interested in her. *Interested*. That world of dating and movies and the backseats of cars. If she smiled back in the right way, one thing would lead to another. She wondered if Reeve was watching. If she flirted with Dave, would Reeve be angry? Jealous? Would he decide to speak up and claim her before Dave did? And Sarah-Charlotte, was she watching?

Janie looked more carefully at Dave, to assess his personality and appearance. She became aware that Dave had asked her another question. "Ummm," she said. "I—um—wasn't listening."

"I said," said Dave very clearly, "where are you from? I just moved here last year from Colorado."

She knew he was trying to start a real conversation. That being from Away—having First Impressions of This Part of the Country—was a classic opener.

But I don't know where I'm from, she thought. Or who I am.

The breakfast was over. Half the people at her table had already left. One of them was Dave.

Sarah-Charlotte came over practically hissing. "Janie Johnson, you could at least talk to the guy. What's the matter with you these days?"

"I don't know," said Janie. She tried to imagine herself telling Sarah-Charlotte the kidnap stories.

"It's not like he's asking you to sleep with him, you know," said Sarah-Charlotte.

Janie did not know why Sarah-Charlotte had to go so far in her plans for Janie. One kiss with Reeve and Sarah-Charlotte had decided Janie had a sexual history.

"And he was so adorable," said Sarah-Charlotte. "I never noticed him before. It's odd how you can be in school with people you never see."

School that day was a queer and floating place.

Janie filled her spot. She talked, wrote, wended her way from hall to class. But she was a mind floating in an ocean of confusion, battered against milk-carton photographs and attic trunks.

It was raining again that afternoon, so Reeve gave her a ride home. She wanted him to say *I love you*. Or, *Let's go to a movie*. Or, *Don't be friends with Dave, be friends with me*. But Reeve just poked the radio buttons endlessly, dissatisfied with every station. She wanted him to kiss her again and she wanted him to suggest it, or start it.

"I can't make small talk," she said. "Breakfast was awful. It was like filling out a form."

Reeve laughed. "I loved it. All the girls flirted with me."

Why did he say that? she thought, utterly miserable. I don't want to be the one who's jealous! "Dave kept asking me questions I didn't know the answers to."

"He asked where you were born," said Reeve. "You couldn't come up with that?"

"Reeve, I don't know the answers to questions like that."

Reeve moaned. "That sounds like my philosophy class. I hate that kind of thing. Don't you start it."

"Reeve, if I tell you something, will you keep it a secret?"

"The Johnsons have secrets? I don't believe it."

"I don't believe it, either. That's half the problem. I can't tell if I'm going insane, or taking drugs in my sleep, or if . . ."

"If what?"

But it was too preposterous to say. Especially to Reeve. He more than anybody would find it absurd: he knew the family too well.

"Janie," said Reeve loudly, as if saying it for the tenth time, "we're here. Get out."

She stared at him. Who was he? Had she ever seen him before? Her fingers fumbled for the handle. Her hands were stiff and numb, as if she were going into rigor mortis.

She remembered leaving the stool. The stool that could only be in that shopping center in New Jersey. Remembered hopping down from that green counter and leaving that half-eaten vanilla ice cream sundae. Remembered somebody taking her hand, saying, "Let's go for a ride now." She remembered herself laughing . . . delighted . . . and going.

I gave up my real family for a sundae? thought Janie Johnson.

78

She crossed the shrub barrier between their driveways. Both her parents' cars were there. She walked slowly, rain pouring on her hair and her face. Inside the side door she scuffed the bottoms of her wet shoes on the rubber mat.

Her mother had made a pot of coffee. Janie could smell it, filling the house like breakfast and warmth. She walked into the kitchen. It was like a child's scene built in a shoebox for second grade. Her father pouring milk in his mug; her mother filling the sugar bowl; the clock chiming; the snack they were having—a Pepperidge Farm cake—defrosting on the counter.

I will go mad if I don't find out, she thought. If I'm not already mad.

Still dripping from the rain, clinging to her book bag, Janie said, "I want to know why there aren't any photographs of me until I'm five. Even if you didn't buy a camera until then, you would have had a baby portrait done. I want to know who Hannah is upstairs in the trunk. I want to know why you won't let me see my birth certificate."

CHAPTER
9

A silence as long as some lives.

Janie thought she might fall over.

Her father's hand was molded to his coffee mug. Her mother's hand stuck to her spoon.

Janie could not step closer. She could not run away.

The demon had seized them all in his daymare.

Her mother sank very slowly into a chair. Her father very slowly raised his chin to look into his wife's eyes. Like puppets they nodded.

Screams rioted in Janie's skull.

She gripped the book bag as if she planned to throw grenades.

In syllables that dropped as softly as notes on a flute, her mother said, "Hannah is your mother, Janie. We are not really your parents."

No! cried Janie's soul. No no no no no—

"We are your grandparents. Hannah was our daughter."

Janie dropped the book bag. "Is that all?" she

cried. She flung herself onto her mother. "Is that all? I thought—oh, Mother, you just can't imagine what I thought." She could not stop repeating herself. She hugged her mother ferociously, feeling the strength of wrestlers in her arms. "Oh, Mommy, that's all it is?"

We're related, it's okay, she's all but my mother, there's no daymare, no nightmare, no demons. Hannah just had an illegitimate baby and it's me and that's all there is to it.

Her father came up behind her, gave her a ponytail, and pulled her backward by her red hair. His hug was also the hug of wrestlers, hanging on to her, as if they were in danger of falling over cliffs. She leaned on him, letting the horrible cliff of kidnapping out of her mind.

"We love you, honey. You are our daughter. Just not legally and biologically. We don't have a birth certificate for you. So we don't know what we're going to do about your passport and your driver's license and things like that."

"Who even cares?" said Janie. She found she was sobbing. Her hair was wet, her coat was wet, her cheeks were wet. Her mother peeled away the outer layer of Janie's clothing. "I'll fix you a snack," said her mother. She patted Janie, as if to dry her by hand. Her mother's teeth were chattering.

"Food solves all," agreed Janie, laughing through tears.

"The old Johnson family motto," said her father.

Janie pulled away from them. "But I'm not completely a Johnson, then."

"Nobody here is a Johnson," said her father. "It's a long story, Janie."

All three were breathing hard, as if from a long jog in the cold.

"Let's sit on the couch together," said her mother, forgetting snacks. "So we can hug. I've rehearsed this in my mind a thousand times, but now that we're here, I've forgotten my lines."

They sank together in the big velvet couch in the living room, Janie in the middle, a parent holding each hand. She was so tired from the assault of emotion she could hardly hold her head up. She rested against her father's shoulder.

"Our name is not Johnson," said her father. "It's Javensen. We've never come across the name anywhere else. It has a Scandinavian sound, but we really don't know much about my family."

Javensen, thought Janie. I like it, she thought. It's better than Jayyne Jonstone. Jane Javensen.

"Your mother and I . . ." Her father's voice staggered, like clumsy feet. "I guess I'd better say, your grandmother and I."

Janie shuddered. "No. Don't say that." She put a hand against his chest as if to trap those words.

"We'll call us Frank and Miranda, then," said Janie's mother.

And the story her parents told, line by line, agony by agony, was so sad that Janie wept for them.

Frank had a degree in accounting and Miranda had a degree in medieval literature. Frank went to work for IBM in marketing, they got married, and a year later a baby girl was born. They named her

Hannah, which meant full of grace. Hannah laughed and cooed and was happy her entire childhood.

"Hannah was my whole life," said Janie's mother. Her eyes fastened on a past Janie knew nothing of.

I'm your whole life! thought Janie, jealous and angry that somebody had come before her.

But Hannah had been an unusual child. Janie frowned when they described Hannah. She could think of no girl who even slightly resembled Hannah. Hannah had never wanted to do the things other girls did: she didn't play with dolls or ride a bike. When she was a teenager, she didn't care about boys or getting a tan or the radio. She worried about right and wrong. From the time she was very small, the inequities of life horrified Hannah. How could her family have so much and the world so little? Miranda could volunteer for a cause, do whatever a committee could do, and return home happy to a good dinner. Hannah never felt she deserved dinner.

"Hannah was beautiful," said her father, "in a haunting sort of way. Hannah always seemed to be looking at something else. In another age she might have become a nun and spent her life thinking of God. But we were not a religious family, and I don't suppose she even knew what a nun was."

The oddest thing was happening: Janie was falling asleep. The sleepless nights worrying about the milk carton and whether to dial the 800 number had caught up to her.

"Do you know what a cult is?" her father asked.

Janie shook her head, bumping his shoulder.

"A cult is a religious group with exceedingly strict rules for the people who join it. The Hare Krishna movement swept America like a prairie fire in the sixties and seventies, Janie. It attracted young and old, hippie and conservative, East Coast and West Coast. And it attracted Hannah. She met a group of young people who told her that if she became a Hare Krishna, she would be purified. It would no longer be her fault she had so much, because they would not let her have anything. She would be saved. When she was sixteen, she fell on her knees and begged to be allowed to be one of them."

Janie could picture none of this.

"They were scary people," said her mother. "They wore bright yellow robes, the men shaved their heads, they carried bowls and begged. You saw them everywhere in cities, in airports, chanting and demanding money. But where we tried to be honest with Hannah, saying, 'Nobody knows why some people starve and some people have everything,' the leaders of the cult had answers for all her questions. And what Hannah wanted, in the end, was a set of answers and a set of rules."

Yellow robes made her think dimly of *National Geographic* photos. But it evoked no memory.

"Sixteen therefore is a terrifying age for us," said her father. He tried to laugh. "That's why we're having such a hard time with you, Janie. We have to give up part of you. Let you drive; maybe take the trip with the Spanish class; go off to college; make your own decisions—but Hannah's decision! It ruined our lives and hers."

"Why didn't you tell me before now?" Janie asked.

Her mother was shuddering violently, from her teeth to her knees. "Because we were so afraid you'd want to find your mother, or maybe your father, and get sucked up in that cult, too! I can't go through that again. I can't lose another daughter. Janie—please—"

They need me, thought Janie. They need my comfort. "I wouldn't do that to you. You won't have to go through that twice. I promise."

Her parents kissed her on each side. Her mother took both her hands now and held them against her cheek, as if in prayer. "We tried everything to get Hannah out. We took her on long vacations, we sent her to live with my cousin in Atlanta, we tried traditional church. But she went to California to join the temple commune. There was nothing we could do. The law wasn't on our side, Hannah wasn't on our side. The cult even had armed bodyguards to keep parents like us from snatching our children back."

Snatching children, thought Janie. To think I actually thought Mommy and Daddy had snatched me! She could no longer keep her eyes open, but let herself doze against her father's warmth.

"We wrote continually," said her mother in a strangled weep, "but Hannah rarely wrote back. The few times we were allowed to visit, she seemed dulled. Like a silver spoon that needs to be polished. She spoke only when spoken to. All her responses were memorized. Our beautiful Hannah had stopped smiling forever. 'I'm very happy here,' she would say tonelessly, like a mechanical object."

"I was still with IBM," said her father. "I was transferred frequently. We sent Hannah every address change. Whenever I went on a business trip, I mailed her postcards. I suppose I thought I could entice her back into the world with pictures of waterfalls in the mountains or castles in Europe."

Janie tried to remember California.

Her mother whispered, "We *were* good parents, Janie, we *were*! We never knew what we had done wrong, or why she rejected everything we ever taught her. We tried everything to get her back. We sent police, we paid the cult off, we tried to debrainwash her when she visited. But she wanted to be in the cult. She was like a very tall, docile toddler: she simply obeyed her Leader; her mind was strangled. We wept on her birthday and that was all we had of Hannah."

Her father described the passage of years in which Hannah led a weird enclosed life with harsh, incomprehensible people.

"We got an official letter telling us she had been wed to a man in the cult. That was all they told. Not even his name. Then one day," said her mother, "the front door opened. I was making pound cake for the Women's Club bake sale. I was in the kitchen adding six eggs to the batter and the beaters were whirling. I had added the first four. I remember that so clearly. I had two eggs to

86

go. And there stood Hannah—holding you by the hand."

Her parents sat up. Janie was amazed by this mutual physical response of the emotions. Even their posture knew the worst was over. Her father leaned forward, resting an elbow on his knee and cupping his chin, so he could look at Janie. Her mother's voice lightened. She ran her hands through Janie's red mane, held both Janie's cheeks, and kissed the tip of Janie's tilted nose. "You were such a beautiful child!"

I was a resurrection for them, thought Janie. Hannah reborn.

"You were her little girl, by the man who had been chosen as her mate by the Leader."

"Mate?" repeated Janie. "What an animal term for the love between husband and wife!"

Her mother didn't hear her. "You had no clothes except the clothes you were wearing. I had the best time taking you shopping! We bought sweet little socks with ribbon trim, and the cutest little jacket with bunnies on it and a tiny little beret. It was so adorable against your red braids. You had the best time! You had never had so much attention. I suppose in the cult you were in some kind of day care. You often referred to the other children and asked about them."

Those twins, thought Janie. The spilled milk. It was just day care.

"We gave you your own bedroom and you thought that was the most exciting thing that ever happened."

"You know what would be exciting now?" said

her father. "Dinner. I am absolutely starving. Nothing builds an appetite like trauma."

Janie giggled. She felt warm and toasty and complete.

"Let's nuke the leftover pot roast," he said. "Are there any potatoes left, Miranda?"

"No, but I can make instant mashed if you want them, Frank."

"I love instant," said her father.

They went into the kitchen, as if leaving the bad parts of the story behind in the living room. Good things happen with hot food, thought Janie. "So, go on," she said when the pot roast was nuked. "Hannah came in the door and you bought me tons of clothes and then what?"

"Well!" said her mother excitedly. "Hannah had realized the cult was a terrible way to bring up her little daughter. So she escaped! She didn't even like you near the windows for fear the guards of the cult would be there, peering through the curtains. The second night of celebrating Hannah's return and your existence, we realized the cult could find us just as easily as Hannah had, because of course we had always sent our forwarding address."

Minutes ago Janie had been incredibly sleepy. Now she was incredibly hungry, eating as if she had never known food. Her hands shoveled the meat into her mouth. She felt like an animal. Her parents saw nothing. They were a tag team, rotating speeches.

"IBM knew all about Hannah and the cult because I was always flying west trying to extricate

Hannah. They not only transferred me immediately, they got us into a hotel that night under assumed names until they could pack our belongings for us. My senior vice-president even sold our house through a power of attorney for me so the cult wouldn't find our names anywhere. We had all mail forwarded through the company, never to our house."

She had no memories of the West Coast. This cult with its costumes, capes, and rituals. The woman and man who were Hannah and her designated mate. No memory of a cross-continental flight. Three years old. Wouldn't you remember planes and trains, cars and overnights, even if you were only three? thought Janie, disappointed.

Janie Johnson . . . a name to disappear under. A name without personality. Without trace.

"You had the best time, Janie!" said her mother.

For the first time Janie saw clearly how old they were. Much older than her friends' parents. And more tired, too. More used.

Hannah, what did you do to them? thought Janie. How could you have thrown them away like yesterday's newspaper? Your own mother and father, who tried so hard to give you everything; to get you back?

"We were fleeing, but you were in heaven, Janie, bouncing all over the place." Her mother painted a happy little Janie in the new houses—buying new clothes—teaching her to swim—Hannah standing blank-eyed—packing boxes never unpacked before the next flight—yet another different driveway—Janie dancing like a water sprite.

"But even though we did all we could," said her father, "Hannah eventually wanted to go back to the cult."

This time Janie entered the daymare willingly, as if it were a hallway down which she could walk if she chose. She felt that down that corridor she could find Hannah, find California, remember that nursery school. The laughter of children rang in Janie's head. Then something different—*a man's laughter—big and chesty—and she knew herself held in the air by this man—a red mustache— she was tugging the mustache and he was nibbling Jennie's fingers—she could even feel its texture, bristled like a paintbrush, same color as her own braids—she could remember the braids, remember the way the rubber bands yanked when—*

"Hannah was addicted to the cult the way some people are addicted to heroin. When Hannah insisted on going back, we let her." Her mother's voice grew urgent. "She wanted us to keep you, Janie. I've always cherished that. She loved you very, very much. You have to know that."

In the windows her mother's red geraniums still bloomed. Their lives in the sun were probably happier than Hannah's. Her mother's hands covered Janie, patting, needy. "She gave you up so you could have a real life. Your mother gave you the gift of freedom, Janie. It was the only gift she had to give. She left you with us when she went back to the cult."

Shortly after Hannah left, Frank and Miranda

90

had realized that the cult would want the little girl. Not to mention the father, whoever he might be. Hannah had no strength. One interrogation and she'd tell the cult where she had left her daughter. Their attorney advised them to change their name. Javensen was too unusual. So they had taken Johnson.

"We moved several times in one year," said her father. "Looking back, I suppose it was irrational. But whenever we let you out in the yard, we'd panic. So we kept finding a new yard. You loved it. You were always giggling, always the center of attention. It took you a while, but eventually you switched to calling us Mommy and Daddy."

Her mother beamed: a smile like the sun.

If I hadn't come to live with them, Mom would never have smiled like that again, thought Janie. *I am that smile.*

"And then we made the most painful decision of all," said her mother. "We never wrote to Hannah again. Our only daughter. Your mother. We never sent her an address. We never again telephoned on her birthday. We never chose and wrapped another Christmas present for her. We let her vanish into nowhere so that we could keep you safe."

They were no longer at the table, no longer eating. They had all gotten up, their bodies desperate for comfort. They were hugging each other, an oddly rocking trio. *"Oh, Mommy!"* said Janie. They cried together.

Her father did not weep, but then he never did;

he got tight; the muscles bunching in his jaw, no doubt also in his gut. Janie hugged him separately, and her father hugged her back, with affection so deep she could hardly bear it.

They are my mother and father, she thought. They raised me. They love me. I love them. Mother and Daddy are all I have, and all I want.

CHAPTER
10

She woke up as if attacked, ripped out of sleep.

Her body was drenched in sweat, and her thin nightgown clung damply to her skin.

Monsters and hideous, evil, sucking things scattered in her brain. She lay in the dark, clinging to the satin hem at the top of the blanket. *Just a dream, just a dream.*

She wanted to get up and get a glass of water. Find another blanket. Turn on some lights.

But she was caught in an old childhood fear of things under the bed: the silly fear that kept her even now, at nearly sixteen, from sleeping with her toes hanging off the edge—something might nibble them, drag her down.

Slowly she curled tighter and tighter under the covers, bracketing her spine with her pillow, protecting her heart and soul with tucked-in knees.

It was a nice story they had told last night. But what about the Springs? What about the milk carton? Hannah was real. The trunk in the attic full of her geography papers proved it. But the milk carton was real. Jennie Spring was real and so was that 800 number. New Jersey was real. And that shopping center.

I remember a friendly kitchen with lots of kids. I remember shoe shopping. I remember . . .

Memories swirled dimly. She held herself still, trying to pull them in, like a fisherman with a reel. The cult did not sound like people who took their nursery-school class shopping in malls for shiny white shoes.

The white apron? Was it Hannah's? Why did she remember a white apron and not yellow robes? California and cults should make a deeper imprint on a child's memory than a sundae and a swiveling stool.

Janie's made-up versions slipped and slid like cars on ice; they crashed into what few dim memories she had—or had created. But one thing was true and certain: the dress in the attic matched the dress on the carton.

In the dark of her bedroom an idea misted in her brain like fog: dank and sour and thick.

Had Miranda and Frank Javensen, their minds warped from losing Hannah, decided to replace her? With a new little daughter?

Had they gone for a drive? In the heat and the sun and the dusty wind? Had they landed in a shopping center in New Jersey? Had her mother—a different, younger mother—twirled on a stool beside a little girl named Jennie Spring? Bought her with nothing more than ice cream? Taken her home forever?

A real kidnapping.

Her dear, sane, good parents.

Janie's notebook faded in and out of her brain like the shadow of a migrating bird, with the flattened milk carton clipped to the cover. She could show them the milk carton. She could say, "I know the truth."

But then what?

She didn't want the truth to be true any more than they did.

She wanted to be their daughter, too.

Janie lay awake the rest of the night, sifting her brain, finding nothing certain.

In the morning, they had breakfast together. This was unusual. Her father normally left for work before Janie got up; her mother liked to be solitary in the morning and sipped coffee alone in her bedroom, reading the morning paper, while Janie had a glass of orange juice and a croissant.

They were as nervous as strangers waiting to have their teeth drilled. They drank orange juice as if it were spiked with cyanide. They buttered toast and abandoned it.

How had her parents slept? Janie wondered. Were their hearts on Hannah this morning? And my heart, thought Janie, where is my heart?

Janie was too exhausted for speech. In her head the daymares clamored for attention: toddlers in high chairs pounding spoons on the tray, laughter richocheting off kitchen walls, car doors slamming. The faces of her mother and father at the breakfast table seemed to crawl over and through the daymares.

Her father set his untasted coffee next to his untouched toast. "Janie, honey, are you all right?"

"Sure, Dad."

Her father's smile was pasty and peculiar. "You don't look as if you slept."

"No. There was a lot to think about."

"Do you have any questions?" her father said nervously.

She had a million questions. But they would answer in lies and she could not bear it. Her father—whom tax clients and soccer teams adored and respected? Her mother—who cared so passionately about the hospitals and the illiterate and the schools? Telling lie after lie after lie because in fact they were criminals?

Perhaps they don't even know anymore, she thought. Perhaps for them, too, the daymare has blended with the daydream, and the truth is lost.

"You and I should spend the day together," said her mother. "I'll phone the school. I'll cancel my meeting in Hartford."

"No, I have an important test. Anyway, I want to talk to Sarah-Charlotte."

She would never tell Sarah-Charlotte. She would never tell anybody. What words were there? *My parents are insane. They lost a daughter and kidnapped another, except that they probably didn't; I'm probably their granddaughter with a demon inside.* "Go to your meeting. I'll see you at supper."

Her father said, "Maybe it's best to try to keep things normal. Regular schedules. That sort of thing."

Normal, thought Janie, choking back hysteria.

Her mother turned into a whirlwind, gathering papers while she snatched up clean stockings from the drying rack, telephoning another board member while she wriggled into her crimson suit. She always looked so authoritative in that suit.

Her father wanted to kiss her good-bye. His arms seemed to hang inside his jacket as if they had been stapled there. He had a hard time lifting them toward Janie. Her father, whose perfect co-ordination came from years and years of sports. This morning his silvery hair hung on his fore-head like a grandfather's, not a father's.

He's afraid I won't love him as much, thought Janie. But I do. I don't care what they did. I love them just as much. How can that be?

"I love you, honey," said her father desperately. "I'm sorry about—about all of it. But—"

"I love you, too." Janie tacked on her brightest smile, allowing him to leave. He hugged her, but she did not hug back, and he knew it and was afraid.

"Janie," he said, "we did the best we could. With you and with Hannah."

"I don't care about Hannah," said Janie, which was certainly true.

Her mother came rushing back. "Do you think this pin looks good?" said her mother anxiously, touching the silver brooch she had fastened to her scarf. Her mother didn't feel comfortable with pins. She was always sure they had drooped or turned themselves backward. "It looks fine," said Janie.

She looked out the window. Pouring again. What

was with all this rain? At least she could ride with Reeve this morning instead of waiting for the bus. "Good-bye, Daddy," she said, forcing herself to hug him. "I hope your meeting is good, Mom."

Her father said, "You'll telephone me at the office if—if you're upset or anything, won't you?"

Outside in the rain, Reeve honked his horn.

"Have a good day at school, sweetheart," said her mother. "I—maybe I should stay by the phone in case you want to call. Or—I could call you from Hartford."

"Mom," said Janie, "everything's fine. Don't worry. See you later." She grabbed her coat, her books, her bag lunch with its nonmilk drink, and flew out the door. Reeve had given up on her and reached the end of his driveway. Screaming, she ran after him. "Reeve! Here I am!"

He saw her, grinned, reversed, and waited for her. "Thought you took the bus after all," he said. "Did you sleep late? You look frantic."

She laughed hysterically.

"That's just how I feel," he agreed. "Here I make a hit by getting on honor roll and the very next day I don't finish my homework and I have to go make an ass of myself with an oral presentation in English."

"I wish we could cut school," Janie said.

"Okay. Let's," said Reeve. "There's nothing I want in that building."

They were heading into town; they were on the overpass of the interstate. Janie said, "Get on the highway, then. Head south."

Reeve's jaw dropped. "You serious? Janie of the sweet, obedient personality wants to cut class?"

"Yes. Turn. Hurry up. You'll miss the entrance."

Reeve got on the highway and turned south.

The windshield wipers clicked rhythmically. The rain thudded metallically on the roof. Reeve turned the radio up louder; they were listening to KC-101 Rock. Janie had never heard KC-101 at this hour; she was always in school.

The miles went by.

They passed a turnpike rest stop and gas station.

Their speed dropped. They were in rush-hour traffic. A thousand cars throbbed around them.

"We can't turn back now," said Reeve, waving his watch. His grin tested her, to see if she was serious.

Buddy, thought Janie, you don't know how serious I am.

"We're officially late," said Reeve. "We go to school now, we have to get late passes from the vice-principal and they telephone our parents."

"It doesn't matter," said Janie. "We're going to New Jersey."

CHAPTER
11

They spent two hours on the Connecticut Turnpike. Janie read every blue and white highway sign as if it were immortal literature and she was going to be tested.

On the New York Thruway they paid a toll and turned north for White Plains, where they headed for the Tappan Zee Bridge and crossed the Hudson River. The river was very wide and flat, the same gray color as the sky. A single barge floated downstream.

All that water, thought Janie, and no traffic on it. She stared at the apartment buildings and houses on the riverbanks and pretended to choose a place where Jayyne Jonstone would live. Jayyne Jonstone. She had planned Jayyne to be mysterious and sensual and full of flair.

She had always thought of mysteries as exciting curtains, to be tugged aside to reveal intriguing pasts. But her mystery was sick and vicious. Was she even now driving on the very road that

Frank and Miranda Javensen had driven down when they made their horrible decision to replace Hannah? Had they ever talked about it? Out loud? Ever said to each other, "Why don't we kidnap somebody?" Or had it just happened of its own accord, without plan, and then somehow had seemed right to them, instead of hideously, evilly wrong?

"Janie," said Reeve, "it's impossible."

Janie held up the milk carton.

"I see the milk carton," said Reeve. "But that isn't you. How could you recognize you after all these years?"

"I don't recognize me. I recognize my dress. Reeve, this dress is in the attic! In Hannah's trunk."

"Come on, there must be a trillion polka-dotted dresses that little girls wore once. My sisters probably wore that stuff. So big deal."

"It is a big deal, Reeve."

She could feel that Reeve wanted to drive a hundred miles an hour and was angry with the traffic and the law for keeping him back. "And who could this Spring family be?" demanded Reeve. "Maybe it's a conspiracy the Springs dreamed up to destroy your mother and father. They'd go to prison, you know, if they really kidnapped you." Reeve looked right at her. "Which they didn't," he said.

Prison. Another dark and vicious word. She had never seen a prison, except on TV cop shows. Her mother—stripped, searched, locked up, and tormented?

Mommy! Janie's heart cried.

But out loud she said calmly, "Okay, I've been studying this map of New Jersey." She was glad driving took so much of Reeve's attention. He did not have much turnpike experience; the heavy, truck-filled traffic kept Reeve's eyes ahead, or on the mirrors, but rarely able to meet Janie's eyes. "It's a good thing that gas station was stocked with maps. We want to get off in seventeen more exits, and then turn south. The town where the shopping center is will be halfway between—"

"What are we going to do when we get there?" Reeve demanded.

She said nothing. She did not know yet.

"Janie, how'm I going to explain to my parents where we've been?"

"Why do we have to explain to anybody? Let's say we went—um—just driving around—killing time—we felt like skipping school."

Reeve said uneasily, "They'll figure we found a motel room or a nice private beach. They'll figure it's sex we wanted, not getting out of a test or an oral report."

Janie swallowed. Normally a natural, unnoticeable task, swallowing had become almost an athletic event. It's too cold for a beach, she thought. She pictured herself and Reeve on hot sand, nothing but a string bikini between them. She said, "It's a long way. New Jersey is a much bigger state than you think it is."

A double truck passed them, spraying such a puddle of water over the windshield that they were blinded. For a moment they were as isolated as if they were trapped in a tin can. Reeve turned the wipers up to high. The water was whacked away. "Though anybody less interested in sex and romance than you would be hard to imagine, Janie. You're a little scary. You're like this hard, sharp, pointed *thing*."

He doesn't like me, thought Janie. I'm in the car with my best friend. I guess he's my best friend, and not Sarah-Charlotte, because it's Reeve I've told. He wants not to be here. He doesn't like this person in his passenger seat. "I've got to find out," she said.

"Why don't you just ask your parents?"

"Reeve, what am I supposed to say? 'Daddy, stop telling me these cute little stories about Hannah's childhood. Admit you kidnapped me.' It would hurt their feelings."

Reeve laughed hysterically. "But Janie, if they did kidnap you, who cares about their feelings?"

"I do. They're my parents and I love them."

Reeve said, "I think we're a little confused here."

"Wouldn't you be?" demanded Janie.

They drove on and on. New Jersey seemed to last forever. Signs for Philadelphia began to appear. That's Pennsylvania, thought Janie. She knew nothing of Philadelphia except the Revolutionary War and the Constitutional Convention. Now I'm sliding into a time warp as well as a kidnapping, she thought. I've lost my parents, I've lost my name, I'm losing my century, too.

Reeve found the silence intolerable. He began telling her more than she had ever known about his own childhood. About how Lizzie and Megan

103

were so impressive in everything: music, sports, academics, even housework. How Lizzie and Megan were virtually an opposing team of two in the Shieldses' household, each determined to get all the blue ribbons. How Todd, born the year between them, struggled endlessly to be seen and heard in that aggressive sandwich of sisters. How Reeve, born years later, had merely stared at all these superachievers, doing nothing much himself but making the occasional Lego building or turning a TV channel.

I lived next door to them, she thought, and I hardly noticed. How much does anybody ever notice?

She found herself thinking of Sarah-Charlotte, who had not noticed any change in Janie. Janie's life had collapsed. Sarah-Charlotte nevertheless telephoned each night, giggled each lunchtime, and did not notice.

They had long since lost KC-101 on the radio. Reeve tuned endlessly, trying to find a station he would like as well. When he had nothing more to say, he turned the radio up so loud they could no longer hear the rain.

"Say something," said Reeve.

"It's this exit," said Janie.

Reeve turned to look at her for so long she was afraid they'd go off the road. Briefly, this seemed quite reasonable. Forget finding answers. Abandon life instead.

He expected me to say something about his childhood, she thought. About all those painful confessions he just made. But I'm too deep in my own painful confession. I am a bad person. I was a bad daughter. Because a good person, a good daughter, would have noticed she was being kidnapped! She would have remembered her real parents. She would have wept and sobbed and fought and tried to get home. She wouldn't just trade them in. And certainly not just for an ice cream sundae.

"Janie, what if we find these people? These Springs?"

Her mind was so cluttered with confusion she had not actually planned to look for the Springs. She had planned to walk through the shopping center and see if it triggered any memories. See if she could find that stool in front of that green Formica counter. See if she could remember, instead, Hannah and the cross-country flight.

Reeve got off the New Jersey Turnpike.

We're here, thought Janie. Fear seemed to throw water up over her eyes, the way the truck had thrown it on the windshield, and she was canned inside her fear.

"Spring is an unusual name," said Reeve. "There might be only one Spring family in the phone book."

There was an International House of Pancakes at the side of the road. Reeve swung suddenly into their parking lot, and they jolted in the air as he leaped over the sidewalk. "Let's have pancakes and think about this," he said. "They could be home. We might find them. What are you going to say when you ring the bell? 'Hi, there. Am I your daughter?' "

Janie shivered. I don't want to be their daughter. I want to be Mommy and Daddy's daughter.

Reeve parked, opened his door, circled the car, opened her door, and took her hand. She still had her seat belt on and it jerked her back in. When Reeve undid the seat belt catch, Janie began to cry.

"Don't do that," said Reeve, horrified.

"Whaᴛ else is there to do?" She imagined herself at some unknown doorway, some unknown woman answering it—would it somehow be Hannah?—a twelve-years-older Hannah?—would there be other children? But years had passed. The high chairs would be gone.

She crumpled against his chest. They stood in the rain, Janie hugging his middle. He was more solid than she had expected, and she could listen to all his inner parts: his heart beating in double thumps, his lungs filling in rhythm with hers.

"Janie, the thing is, I think they would call the police. That's what I would do. Janie, think! Can you imagine the scandal? If you made all of this up, they're going to put you in a mental institution and give you counseling and shrinkage forever. Your parents will be wiped out. Wiped, Janie. Off the map." Reeve tilted back from her and held her face up off his wet jacket. He slid his hands back along her cheeks until his fingers were tangled in her hair. "How would they face a whole town, all those soccer parents, all those volunteer ladies, and say 'yes, our daughter accused us of kidnapping her?' " He looked into her eyes and she thought: He loves me.

She could actually read it in his eyes. But she did not know what kind of love it was. Compassion? Neighbors? Older brother?

Reeve tried to lead her into the restaurant. She remained rooted to the spot. "So," he said, trying to kid around. "Not in the mood for pancakes? How about a cheeseburger? I see golden arches in the distance."

Janie shook her head.

"Janie, what if you're right?" His voice was shaking. "The police won't let you go back to your parents—well—to Mr. and Mrs. Johnson. They'll—" Reeve sucked in air. "Something will happen, I don't know what. Social workers and newspaper reporters and TV cameras and—"

"We won't actually go to the door," said Janie. "We'll just drive by."

Reeve pointed to a telephone booth across the street at a Mobil station. They pivoted to face it, staring as if at the Great Pyramid in Egypt. Then they got back in the Jeep. Reeve circled the ugly A-frame restaurant with its slick brown roof. Janie was gasping for breath. Her head hurt savagely. Her hands hurt even worse. She looked at them, to see if she had slammed them in the door or something, but they were clasping each other so hard she was trying to snap her own bones. She made herself let go. Reeve crossed traffic and pulled into the gas station. He maneuvered until he had her passenger door right in front of the phone booth.

She prayed the phone book would have been stolen.

But it was there, hanging in a metal case by a metal cord.

Her life, her soul, her history, her genes.

She got out of the car and stood again in the rain. The rain was a known quantity. It seemed as safe as Reeve's chest.

Then she went into the booth and looked up Spring.

There was one listing, and one only. How ordinary it sounded. How suburban and middle class.

Spring, Jonathan Avery . . . 114 Highview Avenue.

She walked into the gas station. A youngish man in need of a shave and a good weight-loss program sat in filthy blue coveralls behind a greasy table and leered at her. She said, "Would you please tell me how to get to Highview Avenue?"

For a moment she thought he would refuse. That would be a sign, wouldn't it? That she was not meant to know. That even total strangers knew better than to let Janie Johnson near Highview Avenue.

But he said, "Long way, baby. South on this road about two miles, left on Mountain Road, it's down Mountain somewhere. Read the street signs. Easy to miss. Good luck."

She got back in the Jeep, dripping wet. Reeve turned the heater blower up high to dry her off. "South on this road," she told him.

"Janie, I think we should go home." He was white and pinched. "I thought when you said skip school together you really wanted to do something neat with me, Janie. I didn't know you just

needed a chauffeur for something like this. I don't
want to be part of it. No matter how much you
want to know, I don't want to know at all! I was
thinking that you—" He broke off.

He was thinking that I liked him, she thought.
I do like him. I adore him.

Her head pounded on and on. She had never
had a headache like this. Hammers and spot-
lights behind her eyes.

She touched the cuff of his shirtsleeve where it
stuck out of his jacket and then very softly, nervously, touched the skin of his wrist. She traced
his wrist on each side of his watchband. She
wanted to kiss his wrist, and the golden hairs
that almost invisibly caught in the spiral tension
of the band. If he had not been driving, she would
have yanked him toward her, kissed him forever.

Reeve said, "Janie? In the leaves? That day?"

But the part of her not suffering a headache
and the part of her not aching with love was
reading street signs. "There's Mountain Road,
Reeve. Turn right there."

They got caught behind a school bus.

"What time is it?" said Janie, frowning.

Reeve held up his wrist for her but she couldn't
read upside down. "Two o'clock," he said. "They
must get out early here."

Two o'clock in the afternoon! she thought. We
won't get home till after dinner. What am I going
to tell my parents? They'll be so mad at me! They'll
never let me—

She had to take her hand away from Reeve's

wrist and put it over her own mouth to stifle hysterical laughter.

The yellow school bus stopped once. Stopped twice.

The third stop was for Highview Avenue.

The one hundred block.

It was a development, perhaps twenty years old: mostly split-levels with identical front bay windows opening into pleasant yards and thick shrubs. Each house had a two-car garage, and most had hedges between them. The similarity among the houses was rather comforting, as if this were a neighborhood where you could predict what would happen next, and be safe.

It had momentarily stopped raining. Enormous puddles attracted the children as they leaped off the school bus. The boys jumped square into the puddles, soaking their sneakers, splashing mud on the girls, who screamed happily and threw things, like lunchbag apples they hadn't eaten.

Reeve stopped the Jeep while the children crossed the street.

Two boys, about sixth-graders, went to number 114.

Spring, Jonathan Avery . . . 114 Highview Avenue.

The boys had red hair. The color of Janie's.

She subtracted the years she had been gone. Had they sat in high chairs in that kitchen once while she spilled milk on the floor?

We had a dog, thought Janie. *A big dog. Yellowish. I used to hug the dog and she'd lick my face and my mother would yell at me. Honey was the dog's name.*

The front door on number 114 began to open for the redheaded boys. They were not latchkey kids. Somebody was home to welcome them. The inner wood door was bright red. A hand reached to push open the storm door. Janie covered her eyes and sank down in the seat. "Drive past, hurry up, Reeve, drive past."

There were too many children dancing on the sidewalks, wild with release from school, to drive fast. He drove about ten more houses and parked the car. "The woman who opened the door has red hair, too," he said.

"It's not true!" said Janie. She could not tell if she was whispering or screaming. Her skull was vibrating as if dentists' drills had gone crazy inside her. "I refuse to have it be true. Reeve, take me home. You were right. We have to make up a good lie, we can't tell anybody about this."

From the other direction came a second yellow school bus. It stopped quite close to them at the intersection of the two-hundred block. It was the high school bus. A handful of teenagers got off, none interested in each other, going their separate, bored ways.

A tall, skinny boy, from whose right shoulder swung a nearly empty book bag and a pair of enormous sneakers, headed toward them. "Now those are serious feet," said Reeve admiringly. "I hope the rest of his body grows to fit. Look at the size of those feet."

Look at the red hair, thought Janie Johnson. *That's my brother.*

The boy never saw her; he checked out the Jeep, and he checked out Reeve, but was not interested in the passenger. The sneakers, hanging by tied laces, banged his chest as he walked. She turned very slowly in the seat and watched him. He crossed the street; he glanced in a newspaper cylinder. He put his right hand on the fender of a parked car and used it for leverage to toss himself over a hedge. He leaped into the air to touch the sagging, leafless branch of tree. The branch snapped back and jittered. It began to rain again, as if the twig had punctured the cloud.

The boy went in the front door of number 114.

The drive home took forever.

They had not known there was this much traffic in the entire world, let alone New Jersey to New York to Connecticut. Reeve was exhausted. His hands gripped the wheel, his eyes darted around. He would never have admitted it, but the pressure of the racing cars, the huge trucks inches away, the endless turnpike entrances where cars nudged his fenders, trying to squeeze in, visibly frightened him. Neither one had driven anywhere but their own safe, slow corner of the world.

Janie kept looking at his watch.

"Should we call them?" she said nervously. "Tell our parents we're fine, but we're going to be late?"

Reeve said, "Well, if you can think of anything to say to your parents, go ahead and call. I'll stop at a McDonald's on the Connecticut Turnpike.

But I know what my parents are going to think. They're going to think you and I went to a motel to learn about sex. My sister Megan did that with her second boyfriend. His name was Philip. My mother still gets a fever whenever she hears the name Philip."

They crossed the Hudson River and hurtled on toward Connecticut. There seemed to be no way out of the traffic; it had a nightmarish, eternal quality; as though they might be doomed to race wheel to wheel with the rest of the world, never reaching any destination.

Janie said, "A motel." She tried to think in terms of romance. Or at least sex. Both were certainly easier subjects than kidnapping and another set of parents. Spring, Jonathan Avery, whose family consisted of at least three brothers.

And a missing daughter.

The radio brought traffic reports. Highways they had never heard of were jammed for miles; bridges they had never crossed were impassable; alternate routes with preposterous names were suggested.

Reeve's hands suddenly loosened on the wheel. "It's not too late," he said.

"For what?"

"For the motel."

The speed in their lane never slowed. Nobody had ever heard of the fifty-five mile per hour limit. Anybody driving fifty-five would have been crushed beneath the wheels of a thousand automobiles, each flattening them a little more, till there was nothing left in the road but the metallic gleam of a car that drove too slowly.

She could touch him in places she had never touched another human being. She could lean on a chest not covered by layers of wet jacket and buttoned shirt. "I don't think I could concentrate," she whispered, wetting her lips.

"Maybe if I concentrated enough for both of us?" said Reeve.

CHAPTER
12

They were in Connecticut. They passed the beautiful suburbs from which commuters went daily to New York City, then hurtled through the ugly mill towns and smog-rimmed cities that lined the shore farther east.

Reeve took an exit.

"Are we out of gas?" said Janie.

Reeve shook his head. Down the exit ramp they went, and the sudden release from traffic and noise was like taking off heavy coats. Janie felt thin and easy again.

Reeve turned left at the stoplight, went back under the turnpike, and there in front of them was a motel.

The motel was nasty: flat-roofed, crouching rows of cheap pinky-yellow doors. "How will you pay for this?" said Janie.

"I have my father's American Express card."

They both registered. Reeve wrote in his tall, cramped handwriting "Reeve Shields."

She took the pen and froze up. *I have no name. I am not Janie Johnson nor Jayyne Jonstone nor Jane Javensen nor Jennie Spring.*

The clerk saw her hesitation and gave her a sick, sly grin.

She wrote "Jane Johnson."

The clerk turned the registration card around and read the names out loud. "Jane Johnson?" he repeated, smirking. "Big imagination, lady."

Reeve's fist came out, terrifying them all.

The clerk leaped backward.

Reeve grabbed the key instead of decking the clerk. His hand locked on Janie's arm and he hauled her outside. They stood panting in the smoggy, rain-laden air of industrial Connecticut. She said, "Reeve. I can't."

She expected an argument but she got none. He just nodded. He looked for a while at the cement blocks that were peeling with old vanilla-colored paint, and the rain puddling through rusted gutters. They both knew if he had gone to a different sort of place, with a safer, richer, cleaner feeling, they could have. Would have.

Reeve shrugged. He stuck the key in the motel mailbox and they went back to the Jeep.

Janie said, "When we do it for real, Reeve, it won't be like this."

"When?" said Reeve softly. His long face seemed thinner than ever, and his open mouth a stranger's. Then his wonderful joyful grin split his face, and he turned back into Reeve, her trusty, rusty next-door neighbor, and he grabbed her waist and swung her around, then stood very still, kissing her.

116

It was a full-length kiss; she felt him down the entire length of their bodies, through their clothes, through their coats. The ice of her fears was replaced by a shimmering heat. A heat that was Reeve.

"I don't think I can drive," said Reeve when they were in the Jeep.

"Well, I can't, not in this traffic."

"You want driving experience, take it."

Neither of them wanted driving experience. It was another experience altogether they wanted. "Start the motor," said Janie.

"Believe me, it's running," said Reeve, and they giggled desperately.

"What time is it?" said Janie. She blew a long puff of air upward, lifting her hair off her rain-wet forehead.

"Late," said Reeve. "I don't know why we worried about New Jersey calling the police. If we don't get home soon, our parents will be the ones to call the police." He touched her hair (hair he had yanked a million times when he was nothing but an annoying brat next door) as if she might refuse him permission; as if he were touching gold. He took a breath so deep she thought his rising chest might split his shirt, and then he fell back against his own window instead of against her.

"Reeve, we registered. There's going to be a bill. It'll come through on your parents' American Express next month. Your mother will talk about Megan and Philip," she said. She gripped the seat belt when she wanted to be exploring him.

"I don't think my mother wants to go through that a second time," said Reeve. "I always planned to keep it a secret from her when it was my turn. Why does my turn always come so much later than Lizzie's and Megan's and Todd's turns?"

They managed to talk. He managed to drive. Neither of them, radio addicts though they were, remembered to turn on the radio. The car was filled with rhythm and rock of their own thoughts.

The journey that had lasted so long rushed by toward the end. They fell silent. He took their exit. Drove through their town. Passed the houses of their friends, the streets of their childhoods.

"Janie," said Reeve suddenly. His voice shocked her in the quiet of the car. "Your parents have been my parents, too. They raised me as much as my own. Whenever Lizzie and Megan and Todd were driving me nuts, I'd be at your place. I haven't figured out the truth in this New Jersey stuff, but Janie, we can't jump to conclusions."

"Oh, okay, sure," said Janie. She was sick with nerves. "Just because they have my hair and I remember the dog Honey and it's my dress on the carton, we won't jump to any conclusions."

"Okay, so the conclusions are there staring us in the face. The fact is, your parents are going to be there staring us in the face in about a minute. What then, Janie?"

I promise, you'll never have to go through this a second time. She herself had said that. And meant it. But Janie had not quite realized she would have to go through it, too. And not just once. All her life she would be part of whatever had happened in that shopping center in New Jersey.

Reeve drove up their hill.

The lights of both the Shields and Johnson houses were on from attic to cellar, as if their parents had been searching for bodies in hidden corners.

"This is it," said Reeve.

"I don't want to go in alone."

"I don't want to go in at all."

But there was no need to go in.

Four angry, screaming parents came out instead.

CHAPTER
13

It was wonderful to be yelled at. It was so parental.

Her mother's face, taut with worry and rage, was a mother's face. Her father's hands, rigid with wanting to shake her by the shoulders till her teeth rattled, were a parent's hands. They loved her. Parents who loved you bothered to get mad.

Once years ago, furious at Sarah-Charlotte, Janie had stomped on Sarah-Charlotte's glasses and purposely broken her friend's retainer. When her parents saw the pink plastic splinters on the sidewalk, Janie thought they would kill her. And that time she cheated on the math test in sixth grade. That occasion was memorable first for the screaming, and second for the failure her parents had insisted she get for the entire marking period, even though the teacher was willing to forgive Janie. And of course the time she and Sarah-Charlotte, aged ten, decided to see whether it was true what they heard at a slumber party, that you died when you had Coke and aspirin at the same time. The time her mother said Janie was old enough now to do her own laundry and ironing, and Janie replied, "Forget it. You do it or I'll stay dirty."

Ah, the yelling.

They're my mother and father, Janie thought. That's why they're so mad. That's what mothers and fathers do.

"Janie! How could you do this! No matter how upset and angry and confused you were, you know what a telephone is."

They yelled and she basked in it; it was like sunshine in summer, seeping into her pores.

"You could at least show some remorse," shouted her father, "instead of smiling at the driveway!" while next to him Mr. Shields bellowed, "Reeve! How could you have done this! Did you know about this Hannah nightmare? And yet you purposely the very next day whisked Janie off so her mother and father had to go through it again? That was horrible of you! What kind of person are you?"

Those people in New Jersey are just people in New Jersey, thought Janie. I don't want them and I don't care about them. "I'm sorry, Mom," she said. "I'm sorry, Daddy. We decided to cut school so we could talk. We just drove around for hours. Nothing happened."

"Nothing happened?" repeated her father. He had aged. Tonight he was indeed a grandfather. Lines creased his cheeks as if he had slept on a pile of books. The distinguished hair was just a tired gray. "We paced the floor for hours in complete panic. Wondering if you'd ever come back. Wondering if you'd bother to let us know. And you dare tell me nothing happened?"

Reeve simply stood still, waiting it out. Boys did that.

Janie's mother, exhausted from worry and relief, burst into tears. "Janie, why didn't you tell us at breakfast you were that upset? Why did you lie and insist everything was fine? We would have done anything. Hannah ran away like that! I thought you were—"

"We weren't running away," interrupted Reeve. "We were talking. That's all. I know we should have called and said we were fine, but we didn't. I'm sorry. Everything's fine."

"You have a very strange concept of the word 'fine,' " said Reeve's father. "Let me assure you, you are not fine right now. You are about to get the punishment of your life. Get in the house."

Reeve and Janie looked at each other. They won't let us see each other again, thought Janie. I won't be able to ride to school with him. His father will ground him the rest of senior year. "But Reeve helped me," said Janie desperately. "I needed him and he was there."

The yelling stopped.

Their parents stood quiet and limp. Nobody had touched. Nobody had reached out to forgive or hold.

Reeve's mother surprised them all. "Then I'm proud of you, Reeve," she said huskily. "Frank and Miranda told us about Hannah and the cult.

It must have been a terrible shock to you, Janie. It certainly was a shock to us. Now that you're back, and we know you're safe, I suppose I can admit that helping Janie work this out was much more important than a day at school."

Reeve changed gears as fast as a race car. "We could talk about it again tomorrow, Janie and I," he suggested brightly. "It was probably enough shock to skip school all week."

"I think not," said Reeve's father.

Inside the Shieldses' house, the phone began ringing. "It's Megan," said Mrs. Shields. "Or Lizzie or Todd. We called to see if you had run away to one of them."

Reeve stared at his mother. "Megan's in California," he said.

The adults nodded. "So is Hannah, presumably," said Janie's father, looking old enough for canes and nursing homes.

"Oh, Daddy!" cried Janie, hurling herself on him, as if she were three years old instead of nearly sixteen. *But I'm not nearly sixteen. Jennie Spring on the carton has a different birthday altogether. She's six months younger than I am.* "I'm not going to join some creepy cult. I'm not running away. Daddy, I'm sorry," Janie linked arms with her elderly father and trembling mother.

Her parents made a sandwich around her. They were both taller, and she was tucked between them like a child. "We don't know where Hannah is. We don't even know if she's alive," said her mother, weeping afresh. "Cults went out of fashion. I haven't seen any Hare Krishna in years.

Hannah could be wasting away on some forgotten commune in California or she could be a bag lady in Los Angeles. Who knows?" Her mother rocked Janie back and forth, but she was really rocking herself, or baby Hannah. "You promised last night we wouldn't have to go through this again," said her mother. "And twelve hours later it began."

Her mother's voice changed to begging. *Don't hurt me, Janie.* "Janie, please," said her mother. Raw, bleeding.

Mr. and Mrs. Shields and Reeve went in to tell Megan, Lizzie, and Todd that the lost had been found.

Janie helped her parents inside. Consoled them. Made promises. She knew that she would never talk about New Jersey to them. They could not endure it.

New Jersey. What a nice, catchall phrase for the mess that had erupted in her life. It rounded up the chaos into a neat rectangle below New York, leaning onto Pennsylvania and waving out over the Atlantic Ocean. "I'm sorry," she said again. She began crying harder than her mother.

And her mother, being motherly, recovered somewhat. "Don't cry, honey. It'll be all right. I love you. Daddy loves you."

Her father stared at the wall, his jaw clenched to prevent weeping. His eyes were saddest, laden with grief he chose not to shed. And whether he was thinking of Janie next to him, or Hannah gone forever, she did not know.

Think of *me*, Janie thought. *I'm* your daughter.

*   *   *

The nightmare came like mud: thick. Oozing filth. The mud hung on to her feet and her brain. It was filled with reaching hands and cackling laughter. Car wheels spun in the mud and fingers pointed. Janie ran but her feet did not move. Trucks tried to run her over, and when she screamed for help, her parents were busy with other things.

She woke up. The bed was drenched with her sweat. What time is it? thought Janie, groping for the clock. If only it could be dawn, so she could go downstairs and start coffee, be done with this horrible night.

But it was two A.M.

She wept briefly. Her mother had said, "We love you. It'll be all right." But did love conquer all? Could love conquer the theft of a child?

It will never be all right, she thought.

She did not turn on the lights. The room was entirely dark except for the faint-blue glow from the digital clock. Yet she knew every object in the room; everything around her was normal. She did not feel kidnapped. She felt chosen. Adopted. Needed so desperately by Frank and Miranda that perhaps they didn't even know what they'd done to acquire a second daughter. Temporary insanity.

But if it came out, thought Janie, it would be permanent insanity. For all of us.

New Jersey must vanish. Jennie Spring must never be.

She resolved to be Janie Johnson with all her heart, mind, and soul.

She fell asleep feeling better but the dreams

came again, and this time they were of falling. Bottomless falls. Evil below. Evil above. When she woke up, she was hanging on to the pillow with a grip so tight she had ripped the lace trim off the pillowcase. She went silently into the guest room and retrieved more pillows, which she arranged around herself in bed like walls. Huddled in a white percale fortress, she managed to sleep a couple of hours.

In the morning, breakfast was desperate and silent.

Her mother drove her to school, as if Janie might escape otherwise. "Mom," said Janie. "I promise. Okay?"

Her mother nodded shakily. "I'm staying home," she said. "I've canceled everything. If you need me—if you feel upset—if you think even for a minute about running off again—Janie, promise you'll telephone me." It was cold with the beginning of winter and the car heater had not yet begun to warm the car, but her mother was perspiring. She looked as exhausted as if she had just mowed several acres of lawn with a push mower. She looked old.

"I promise," said Janie. "But I'm not going anywhere except class. Today's your hospital day. Go to the hospital."

"It's my tutoring day."

"Then tutor."

"I don't want to tutor."

They giggled. "We sound like two-year-olds slugging it out," said Janie.

Her mother took Janie's hand, turning it over, examining it, as if she might never see the hand again and needed to memorize the texture and shape.

"Mom!" said Janie. "I promise."

"Okay."

"Okay. Have a good day." Janie bolted before either of them broke down.

"Earth to Jane Elizabeth Johnson, Earth to Jane Elizabeth Johnson!" trilled Sarah-Charlotte. She was elegant today: long knit skirt, heavy blouse with a wide dramatic belt, and long coppery earrings that reached her narrow shoulders.

Janie felt at least five years younger than Sarah-Charlotte. "I'm right here," she said. "Stop making a spectacle of yourself."

"I beg your pardon," said Sarah-Charlotte frostily. "You are the one acting crazy."

"What do you mean by that?" Janie tried to occupy herself unfolding a paper napkin for lunch.

"I mean you are out in space today. What's going on in your life that you aren't telling me about? I resent this, Janie. I mean it. What aren't you sharing with me? There is nothing in your life that you are allowed to keep private." Sarah-Charlotte took Janie's napkin away. Janie said nothing. In a more irritable, more honest voice, Sarah-Charlotte added, "Your mother and father telephoned four times yesterday looking for you. Now where were you? What was going on? I can't stand it that you didn't tell me."

"She's in love," guessed Katrina.

Automatically Janie's eyes flew across the cafeteria to locate Reeve.

Every other kid peered or stood to see where she was looking.

"It's Reeve!" said Jason. "I knew it. The old boy-next-door trick."

Reeve waved at her.

"You toad," said Sarah-Charlotte. "You've been doing stuff with Reeve and you didn't call me up and tell me. Our friendship is over, Janie."

A strange, flighty mood was keeping Janie aloft. "That's okay," teased Janie. "I have a replacement over there in the senior section." She felt truly strung out, as if she were a rubber band being stretched, vibrating with pressure.

"Blow him a kiss, Janie," said Adair. "Let's get this romance on the road."

Janie blew Reeve a kiss.

Reeve blew one back.

"Okay, I'm begging," said Sarah-Charlotte. "We're still best friends. Now I want details. All of them."

Jason, Pete, Katrina, Adair, and Sarah-Charlotte swiveled their heads in unison and leaned forward into Janie's face. "You may have my overcooked mushy canned peas if you tell," offered Jason.

"You can have the bottom half of my biscuit, too," said Adair. "It's hardly burned at all. It's supposed to be black like that."

Taking her thick auburn hair with both hands, Janie stacked it in a huge mop on top of her head. She waved her hair at them and said pertly,

"No," and they all giggled. Sarah-Charlotte discussed her belt instead and where she had found it and how many shops she had been to before finding the perfect one, and what the earrings had cost.

After lunch a sick heaviness settled where the silliness had been. Janie's head began pounding. When she tried to swallow, nothing happened. Her throat thickened and went dry.

Fifth-period history the teacher passed out a list of permitted choices for the winter term project. Sarah-Charlotte said in a high-pitched, British *Masterpiece Theater* voice, "Shall I look into changing world opinion on the dropping of atom bombs on Japan, my dears, or shall I examine the personalities of Soviet leaders from Stalin to Gorbachev? I feel slightly faint from the excitement of it all."

The teacher ignored Sarah-Charlotte and sent them all to the library. "You're to do preliminary research. Read articles on subjects that interest you so that you may make an informed decision about a topic you will be investigating for many weeks."

The class charged to the library. "From the pace we're setting," observed Sarah-Charlotte, "you would think we actually wanted to do this."

The librarian, Mr. Yampolski, was everyone's best buddy. He never gave detention to boys who stood on the library tables using newspapers for wings while they played Superman. He never yelled at people who had forgotten how to use the card catalog. He never suggested you should peruse

The Wall Street Journal when what you wanted to do was look at the movie stars in *Teen* magazine. "Hey, Janie, babe," he said. "How's Mom?"

"She's great. Probably can't wait till next summer so she can help you with inventory again." How plausible I sound, thought Janie. Perhaps I will get used to lying, and it will turn real, the way my parents' lies have turned real for them.

"Listen, inventory's the light of my life since your mother started doing it with me. So what's the term paper, kid? Lay it on me. Let's get your reference books out here."

Mr. Yampolski was always twice as excited about your project as you were; if you were fascinated by cowboys, he'd be sure to locate a book about cowboys in Argentina or a *National Geographic* article about cowboys in the Ukraine, and then he'd want to sit with you and exclaim over the pictures. There was nothing Mr. Yampolski enjoyed more than sharing knowledge.

"We're here to look at the prom issue of *Seventeen*," said Sarah-Charlotte.

Even Mr. Yampolski might have argued with that, but too many classes were pouring into the library for him to fight her.

"Why the prom issue?" said Janie. "It's only November."

"You're bound to be going to the senior prom with Reeve," said Sarah-Charlotte.

"He hasn't asked me."

"Of course he hasn't asked you. Boys never think farther ahead than the next meal. But you have to plan, Janie. Especially with your red hair.

You can't wear just any color. Now what do you think of this white gown?"

"Too wedding-y," said Adair, turning the page immediately.

"I hate sharing anything," said Sarah-Charlotte. "Especially magazines. When you hold it, I can't see, Adair. Let's get all the prom issues going back as many years as the library has. Then I won't be subjected to all this sharing. Mr. Yampolski!" she yelled.

"Sarah-Charlotte!" he yelled back.

"Do we have back issues of *Seventeen*?" she yelled.

"Why doesn't anybody ever want my back issues of *The New York Times*?" he yelled.

"Because nobody cares about garbage strikes in New Jersey!" yelled Sarah-Charlotte, triumphant.

Seventeen lay open to a particularly repulsive dress, with layers of tacky lime-green ruffles and ribbon trim. The words "New Jersey" paralyzed Janie momentarily. She felt that the whole room had turned around and was pointing at her, silent mouths shouting, "You, you, you!" the way they would for fouls at basketball games. "*The New York Times* covers New Jersey?" Janie said. Her heart was pounding so hard she could actually see the vibrations of her blouse. "I thought it was for New York City."

"You're so ignorant, Janie," observed Adair. "And no, you cannot appear in public in a neon-green dress. Turn the page."

"*The New York Times* covers the world, my dear," said Mr. Yampolski. "With special emphasis on news events of the greater metropolitan area of New York."

A thin, wispy shudder ran through Janie, like a little snake tunneling. Kidnappings are news events, she thought. "How many years do we have?"

"Twenty. Microfilmed. Want some? I'm offering an especially good price today."

"We'd rather have a good price on a prom dress," said Sarah-Charlotte.

Soviet leaders were bound to have been doing something twelve years ago. Janie walked up to her history teacher and asked to do Stalin through Gorbachev. He was truly thrilled, as if this request meant that teaching was worthwhile after all. Janie felt guilty. She would have to do an extra-good job on the term paper now or he would suspect something. But there was no way she would look up New Jersey here at school, where Mr. Yampolski would read over her shoulder, soaking up knowledge along with her.

When the final bell rang, she left the building immediately, climbing on a different bus from the one that went to her street. People spoke to Janie, demanding to know why she was trespassing on their bus, but she did not hear them. She got off at the town library and went inside.

The librarian there showed her how to use the many-volumed index to the *Times*. Showed her how to find the spool of film in its little file drawer, how to thread it in the viewing machine, how to print out the page if she wanted a copy instead of taking notes.

132

"Thank you," said Janie, waiting for the librarian to leave her alone. She had read somewhere that when doctors told their patients they had cancer and were dying, the patients invariably ended the conversation by saying "thank you." She felt the cancer of madness inside her brain, the demon of her daymares: its little fingernails scraping.

She turned to the index for twelve years ago. Looking over her shoulder to be sure nobody was watching her, she looked up "Spring, Jennie." It was listed. It was real. It had more than one entry. Day after day they had followed the case of the stolen three-year-old.

She walked toward the microfilm drawers as if she were buying dirty magazines. Opening the shallow drawer, she read labels on white boxes until she found the right date, then took her spool of film.

Over by the window a potted tree had grown huge and lofty. Nobody had expected it to flourish in the dry library, but now nobody wanted to cut it back. Leaves hung into the science fiction books and one branch curled over the microfilm viewer. Janie ducked beneath the bright green leaves and sat on the metal stool. She wound the film on the machine, turned on the lights, and watched *The New York Times* appear on the screen. She had thought they would save only the important articles, like what the president was doing, but no: everything was there, from classified ads to fashion photos. She spun the knob, leaping past one day, and into another. It was difficult to focus, confusing to operate.

What if Sarah-Charlotte or Adair comes up behind me and wants to know what I'm doing? she thought.

She was out of breath. Her brain had ballooned into a misshapen thing filled with demons, while her lungs had contracted, like flat tires, and she was suffocating in the library stacks.

And then, quite suddenly, her own picture stared back at her. The same one that had been on the milk carton. *No ransom has been asked for little Jennie Spring*, read the caption. *Hope that the three-year-old wandered away and would be found has diminished as National Guard units give up the search.*

She read about the shopping mall, the lack of clues, the search. She read quotes from neighbors and police. At the bottom of the column, in a different typeface, it said, "Continued on Page 34."

Janie scrolled around to page 34. A three-column photograph appeared on the screen. It was a family portrait: parents, grandparents, and children lined up, babies on laps, smiles on faces.

She closed her eyes. *It's them.* If I look at them, they'll exist. If I read page 34, I'll know their names. They musn't become real. Mother and Daddy are real. I don't want New Jersey to be real.

She kept her eyes closed and fumbled for the light switch. When she had turned off the machine and the page had vanished, she rolled the film back up and put it in its box. She had to hold on to the edge of the table to find sufficient strength to stand up.

Reeve was beside her.

She stared at him, still struggling for breath.

"I followed you," he said. "In my Jeep. I wanted to give you a ride home. I wanted you to ride with me every day. Always. And you got on the bus."

Janie was so aware of his maleness. They had shared nothing except a kiss in the leaves and another on the sidewalk. "Are you in trouble with your parents?"

Reeve rolled his eyes. "My father wanted to know where I got the money for the trip. See, they think the first step in preventing drug abuse is preventing access to money and they knew I didn't have much. So like a jerk I said I charged it all to American Express and my father took the motel receipt out of my wallet."

"Oh, yikes," said Janie. "You don't think they'll tell my parents, do you?"

"They promised not to. They said your mother and father have enough to worry about already."

"Did you tell them we didn't actually do anything?"

"Yes."

"Did they believe you?"

"What do you think?" said Reeve. "Would you believe your seventeen-year-old son if he—"

A body came between them: thick, middle-aged, female. The librarian here was not as understanding about flirtation in the stacks as Mr. Yampolski. In a dry, sarcastic voice she said, "Are we doing a term paper? And if so, may I inquire as to the subject?"

"Cults," said Reeve without missing a beat.

"The Hare Krishna. How they went from being an idealistic organization of peaceable hippies to major-league crime like drugs and kidnapping."

He had said "kidnap" out loud. Janie felt truly endangered, as if somebody would notice—call the police or the FBI or arrest her mother. "Oh, no, Reeve!" she gasped. "Quick, give me a dime! I have to call my mother. I'm not home! She'll be worried. I have to tell her I'm here."

Janie could hardly punch the pay phone buttons to put the call through. What if her mother had already panicked? Already gone to the school—found Janie had not taken her own bus?

"Hello?" said her mother.

"Mommy!" Janie was sick with relief. Lunch threatened to return. "Don't worry. I'm at the library. I'm looking up a term paper. I meant to call you before I came. Sarah-Charlotte says I've been in outer space all day. Were you worried? Are you all right?"

"I'm fine," said her mother.

"Is that true?"

"No, it's a lie. I'm a wreck. And your father's at a soccer game so I couldn't call him to say you were missing again."

"Mommy, I haven't been to a game of his yet. Reeve's here. He'll drive me. I'll meet you at the soccer field, okay?"

CHAPTER
14

Her father's team won the soccer game.

"It was probably because you and Reeve screamed so loud," he said. "That and running up and down the field to follow the action." He was so glad she had attended his game that she was overwhelmed with guilt for not going before. He introduced all his little players to her, and then to Reeve, and the pride in his voice swamped her.

"What's for supper?" said her father when they were all heading for the cars to go home.

"Is that always your primary concern?" teased her mother.

"It sure is high on the list," he said. "Not much but soccer and daughters come ahead of it." He kissed his wife on the mouth to show that she was also ahead of food. He looked younger. The lines weren't as deep as last night.

"Actually we're going out for pizza," said Janie's mother.

Janie, Reeve, and Mr. Johnson raised eyebrows.

Mrs. Johnson felt that fast foods divided the family. She served old-fashioned meals that always deserved the adjective "solid." The pizza was an offering. *See, Janie, we'll even get you the food you want. Anything—just don't leave the way Hannah did.*

They offered me ice cream once, she thought, and I let them buy me off with that, too.

She did not know if she could even gag pizza down. But there was more to swallow than pepperoni and mushrooms.

Her parents made it clear that it would be thoughtful of Reeve to go on home. He left reluctantly, after Mrs. Johnson agreed that Janie could ride to school with him in the morning. The Johnsons drove to Pizza Hut, making silly, flippant conversation about soccer and Janie's love life.

When the waitress had brought a pitcher of Coke to the table and they were back from the salad bar, her mother said, "I've arranged family counseling at the Adolescent Trauma Center."

"I won't go," Janie said immediately. "I want to think things out for myself." She was already protecting herself from the penetrating eyes of friends and parents. Now she had to keep her lies going in front of psychiatrists who specialized in adolescent trauma?

"I don't want to go either," said her father. "I hate talking about personal things to strangers." He shoved half the objects on the table to the far side—salt, Parmesan cheese, Sweet 'N Low—as if pushing away the invasion of their privacy.

"Besides," added Janie, "we're doing fine."

A complete untruth.

She would never again be honest with her mother and father. She would carry her milk carton around, photograph down. She would lie. She who had never had secrets would carry New Jersey around like a tray, spread in front of her, invisible to all eyes but Reeve's.

Janie stared at her father, trying to imagine him going to New Jersey to steal a child.

With trembling hands, her mother distributed extra napkins. "I think we could use counseling." Her husband and daughter looked away. "We'd all go," whispered her mother. The whisper gave intensity to the simple words. She sounds as if she's praying, thought Janie. She must have prayed for Hannah.

Memory surfaced.

Janie tried to stomp on it. Her feet actually moved, kicking away the memory. The memory came anyhow. Not a daymare. More like a sound track.

She, who lived in a household without religion, knew a prayer.

> Bless this food
> Bless this house
> May all my brood
> Be quiet as a mouse.

We recited that at dinner. There were so many of us and we made such a racket. He wanted us to be quiet for just a little while. He . . . my real father . . .

No, no, no, no, no, no!

*I want to be Janie Johnson, not Jennie Spring.
Go away! Drop dead! Leave me alone!*

"Janie, what are you thinking about?" said her mother.

She surfaced from New Jersey. It was like swimming underwater, having to shake your head before you could see again. "Oh, nothing," she said. The brightness in her voice was so false even the waitress paused and took notice.

Janie tried to do homework.

It was impossible.

She walked around her room, touching, wishing.

On top of a stack of papers lay a small, square, spiral notebook with a silver glitter cover and silver-rimmed pages. Every September, Janie started the new school year by buying an assortment of pretty notebooks from various gift shops. She always intended to write assignments in one, keep a diary in another, copy interesting poems or phrases in a third, and so forth. She rarely made more than a page of entries before the assignment notebook was misplaced or the diary became dull.

She opened the silver notebook. Only two pages had been touched. Janie ripped them out and flipped to the middle, where it looked safe. She began to draft a letter, to help herself think about the unthinkable.

Dear Mr. and Mrs. Spring,

In the school cafeteria I took my friend's milk carton and on it was a photograph of your little girl who was stolen from a shopping center in

140

New Jersey all those years ago. It was me. I recognized myself. But I knew it could not be true, because I have a wonderful mother and father already, and a wonderful life, and I have always been very happy. So I could not have been kidnapped. It really wasn't me.

She was too tired to write. Her hand shook and the six sides of the pencil hurt her fingers. That's when you know you're weak, she thought. When pencil surfaces wound you. She closed the notebook and put it under the clip in her three-ring notebook along with the milk carton.

In the morning, she fell asleep during math.

During English, when Mr. Brylowe was discussing modern European literature, she opened her silver glitter notebook and wrote again.

Every time I look at that carton I have another memory: of a kitchen and spilled milk, high chairs, and a dog named Honey. A table blessing about mice.

And there's the dress. It's in the attic. Tomorrow when my mother is out of the house I'm going to get it out and iron it. I'll hang it in the back of my own closet where I can see it.

Mr. Brylowe said, "Janie?"

She looked up, startled and unfocused.

"Everybody else has left for lunch, Janie."

The room was entirely empty.

Mr. Brylowe said, "Janie, is there anything you would like to talk about? Anything you'd like to share with me?"

She shook her head.

141

The classroom door seemed terribly far away. Hard to find. And lunch, even though Reeve would be there, hardly seemed worth the effort it would take to reach the cafeteria.

She got halfway there and had to finish her thoughts.

Had to write.

It was like a druggie stabbing his vein.

She stopped right in the hall, holding the silver notebook against the wall for a desk, and writing vertically.

You must promise not to go to the police or even to get mad at my parents. Because they are my parents. They are my mother and father. I love them.

The most terrible thing about this is that I forgot you. I am very sorry. I don't know how or why I could have, but until I saw that photograph of me on the milk carton, I never thought of you.

You can stop worrying. I am all right. I have always been all right. But the thing is, I have not told my parents. I don't know how to tell them that they were part of kidnapping me. I haven't decided yet whether I want to meet you. I know that sounds awful. But I have a family and I love them and I don't know you.

Three times a week after history she had typing. They were learning to do envelopes. Since they had to use up envelopes anyhow, the class was doing a mailing for Students Against Drunk Driving. Janie had twenty-five to address.

The class was filled with the clicking of keyboards, the moans of students making errors, and the continuous demand for replacement envelopes when somebody goofed up too much to use the old one. Everybody wanted to be using the computers instead of the typewriters because you could correct your errors so much more easily.

The afternoon sun came strong and golden through the windows. Both students and teacher were half-asleep. Janie's own mistakes had nothing to do with the heat of the sun. She kept putting her own return address on the envelope instead of SADD's. But the envelopes were still perfectly useful, so she stuck them under the clipboard in her blue-cloth notebook.

For the hundredth time she checked both sides of her milk carton. It was still her.

I'm like a toddler with my blanket, thought Janie. I can't get very far from my carton. Pretty soon I'll be sucking my thumb again.

After school, Reeve caught her so she couldn't take off for the library. "Or points unknown," he said. "Or Sarah-Charlotte's."

In his Jeep they went to the Scenic Overlook and watched the couples for whom it was a Sexual Overlook.

"I can't," said Janie miserably. "No matter what is happening my mind slides around to New Jersey."

"I wish I could say the same," Reeve said. "No matter what is happening, my mind slides around

143

to you. It's consuming my whole life. I don't even have a life except thinking about you."

She was not sure if he meant thinking about Janie, or thinking about sex with Janie.

They kissed each other, but Janie turned away almost before it began and his lips brushed her disappearing cheek instead. He said, "You're losing weight, aren't you?"

"I'm too nervous to eat."

"Tell me."

"Reeve, I want them not to exist! New Jersey, I mean. I don't want them to be down there. Waiting. I feel as if they're going to pop up somehow and leap into my life and I won't have any choice. I want my parents, not them."

He nodded. His cheek brushed against hers and it was a sensation she had never had before: an unshaven cheek.

"Besides," she whispered, "it makes me realize what a horrible little girl I was. Reeve, I'm so afraid to find out what happened. What if I gave up those brothers and sisters, and the father who shouted blessings, just for an ice cream sundae?"

He said, "I suppose you did, Janie. Maybe it was pretty neat to be the center of all that attention. Driving fast and laughing and singing and having ice cream, and new parents and new clothes and a new bedroom."

"I would have been three and a half," cried Janie. "Kids that old know how to use the telephone. They have their phone numbers memorized."

"But would it have occurred to you to call up New Jersey? You wouldn't have felt kidnapped.

You were having lots of fun. When they said, 'Pretend you're our little girl'—gosh, Janie, you'd be great at that. You always have some fantasy running in your head. Like that whole Denim and Lace thing."

"I never told you about Denim and Lace," said Janie, embarrassed.

"No, but Sarah-Charlotte did."

"You talked about me last year to Sarah-Charlotte?"

"Yeah. Now do you feel like kissing me?"

She did.

They did.

And it was good. "I love you, Reeve," she said. How easily it came out. How true it was.

"Maybe they were mean to you in New Jersey," suggested Reeve.

"No," said Janie. "I can remember that much. Nobody was ever mean. You know, in a way I'd like to go to that Adolescent Trauma thing and ask a doctor about memory loss. How come I didn't remember?"

Reeve said, "I don't suppose you needed to remember before. Everything was fine. If you hadn't seen the milk carton, it would still be fine."

"I hate that dairy. I'm never drinking Flower Dairy milk again."

"Good. Because you have a milk allergy."

They leaned on each other, snuggling for the best fit. Janie thought that nothing could be nicer than getting comfortable on Reeve's chest. She was aware of his scents: Reeve himself, the faint soapiness of his shirt, a slight perfume from his shampoo.

If it hadn't happened, she thought, I would not be me. I would be somebody else entirely.

It horrified her that she had once daydreamed of being somebody other than Janie Johnson. Jayyne Jonstone, indeed. How precious her own name and address seemed now.

Reeve had supper with the Johnsons. Nobody discussed Hannah or grandparents or the skipped day of school. After dessert (Reeve had Janie's as well as his own; Janie's mother did not seem to see how little Janie ate) they studied together. Reeve was done in three minutes and wanted to know what he was supposed to do for the next two hours.

That night, along with checking her milk carton, Janie checked her SADD envelope, where her real address was so professionally typed. It seemed to her that they might offset each other: the carton and the envelope.

CHAPTER
15

Soccer season was nearly over. Cake decorating was drawing to a close, and her mother wanted to take pottery next.

Janie had taken the polka-dot dress out of the trunk, washed and ironed it, and hung it in the back of her closet. Every morning and every night she touched it, as routinely as she brushed her teeth. She had made dozens of entries in the silver notebook. Writing cleansed: it removed the badness from her mind and kept it safely on the paper.

Autumn had all but vanished. One maple hung on to a few yellow leaves, and a hedgerow was wine red behind the house. On Saturday the sky was indigo blue: like new jeans. The wind was soft and warm, as if it had news to spread.

"Let's go for a drive," said Reeve, who was having breakfast with the Johnsons. He liked breakfast there on weekends because Mrs. Johnson, who ignored weekday breakfast, got excited on

Saturdays and produced waffles, bacon, and melon slices. Reeve's mother just said she had been making breakfast for twenty-seven years and anybody who wanted breakfast again this year knew where the cereal was.

"It's perfect weather to head into the horizon," said Janie's mother, looking out the window.

"It's funny how you feel that tug only in the fall," said her father. "No other season. In the autumn you want to go. Drive. Have a journey."

When had Hannah decided to leave? Janie wondered. Out loud she said, "Where shall we go, Reeve?"

"Anywhere. I have a full tank of gas and I earned money last week cleaning out the McKays' garage and cellar. I'm rich. We can eat lunch anywhere." He grinned at her.

Friday when she got home, Janie had dumped her book bag on the kitchen floor. Now, getting up for more orange juice, she shoved it out of the way and the books fell out, spreading across the linoleum.

"Janie," said her mother crossly, "how many times do I have to tell you to carry your book bag directly up to your bedroom?"

"Six million," said Janie.

With his shoes, Reeve pushed the books into a pile to pick up.

"Reeve," said Janie, "how many times do I have to tell you to handle school property carefully?"

"Six million," he said. "Thanks for the waffles, Mrs. Johnson. Maybe Janie and I will drive to

Vermont and get you more maple syrup." Together he and Mrs. Johnson began picking up the books.

"Vermont!" said Janie's father. "That's four hours away."

"We'd still get back before dark," said Reeve.

Janie's mother scooped up the books nearest her chair. The load was too heavy for her hand and dropped back on the floor. The blue-cloth English notebook fell open.

The milk carton lay exposed.

Janie lunged forward, slamming the cover shut, grabbing her books.

Her parents stared at her.

"Sorry," said Janie with a bright, crazy smile on her face. Her heart was throbbing, her horrible headache had begun again. She already knew tonight's nightmare: the carton falling out, her parents seeing it, New Jersey exposed and waiting.

She put the books back in the book bag, zipped it shut, and ran upstairs with it. Clattering back down, she grabbed the jacket Reeve tossed and slipped her arms in the heavy sleeves. "Let's go, Reeve."

"Telephone if you're going to be out after dark," said her father.

Reeve promised. He took Janie's hand and swung her around like a dance partner. They ran out of the house.

He was in a great mood. He talked steadily. Janie loved to listen to him. In Reeve's childhood, Megan, Lizzie, and Todd had done all the talking. Reeve's delight when at last both sisters and his brother were away came through in his speech: for a change, Reeve could have the audience.

I must have wanted an audience, too, thought Janie. I was only three and a half and I wanted a bigger audience.

Reeve did all the driving. She had not had another driving lesson with either parent. They would have to talk about licenses if they did, and the birth certificate problem, and she was afraid of screaming, "But I know my real birthday! I can make one phone call and they'll send me my real birth certificate!"

She was trying to fence off all the dangerous places, where things might cave in, where they would know that she knew. She kept having the sense that if she could steer her life right, the way Reeve was steering the Jeep right, they would avoid ever hitting the kidnapping.

"I looked up the kidnapping in *The New York Times*," said Janie.

She had interrupted him. Reeve stopped his story and drove on, looking straight ahead, his body stiff.

He thought my mind was on him, Janie thought, and now he knows it wasn't. "I'm sorry. What were you saying?"

He shrugged. "I thought you were going to stop worrying about New Jersey," he said.

"I was."

"So what happened?".

"I can't."

He said, trying to be lighthearted, "I'm not enough distraction for you, huh?"

The only thing anybody wants is to be the center of a universe, she thought. Reeve had to wait for Megan, Lizzie, and Todd to go away before he could be the center. I wanted the center so much I traded my family for an ice cream sundae. She said, "You're not a distraction. You're the light of my life."

She thought he would make a face at this Valentine's-card sentiment, but he said, "Really?" His face relaxed somewhat.

"Really," said Janie. His face relaxed completely.

Reeve stopped at a restaurant. It was too early to eat anything when they were still waffle-stuffed. He ordered Cokes. Reeve chewed ice.

"Don't do that," she said, "you might crack your teeth."

"There are parts of me I wish you'd pay more attention to than my teeth," said Reeve.

They flirted.

She loved the silly sentences, the innuendo. Sarah-Charlotte may look older and act older, thought Janie happily, but I'm the one doing older things.

When Reeve paid for the Cokes, she studied him. How he enjoyed looking in his wallet, seeing the thick wad of money, leaving a generous tip because he was glad to be driving away instead of waiting table. He liked getting her jacket from the peg where he had hung it up, and he liked holding her hand as they left.

I love you, she thought, and she kissed him

just as they were going through the doors, so she got caught in the glass, bumping into a patron trying to enter.

If New Jersey hadn't happened, thought Janie, I wouldn't have my own parents or my house or school or Sarah-Charlotte . . . or Reeve.

They never reached Vermont.

They saw a sign for a state park and drove in. A narrow road wound among thick, dark hemlocks and emerged at a cascading waterfall where boulders were surrounded by mountain laurel. The sun glittered on the leaping water, and when they parked, the sun's rays turned the interior of the car into a heated sunroom.

"I love you, Reeve," she whispered, lying against him. "You know what?"

"What?"

"If I ever get in touch with New Jersey, I'll have to say, 'Luckily for me, I got kidnapped.' Of course, I'm not getting in touch. I never think about it anymore. I wrote it all down and spiraled it away."

Reeve took a very deep breath. She giggled when his chest lifted her like an escalator and then sank her back down.

"I called my sister," he said. "Lizzie."

Janie snuggled under Reeve's throat and felt it vibrate when he spoke.

"I told Lizzie everything," said Reeve.

"You what?" screamed Janie. She flung herself backward. She would have thrown things if there had been anything loose in the Jeep.

"I had to, Janie. You need advice. And what do I know? She's a lawyer. Or she's going to be."

"How dare you?" screamed Janie. "How dare you tell anybody without my permission. I haven't even told my own mother and father and here you are telling Lizzie, who I can't even stand!" She was so frantic the Jeep was rocking.

Reeve put on the parking brake. "Listen, Janie, I told her everything you told me and she said—"

"Whatever Lizzie said, I don't want to hear it. I'm sorting this out in my own mind and—"

"You're losing your own mind, Janie."

His voice was so soft she could hardly hear it. Inside her head was a terrible racket: the crying and laughing of the voices of the past. She felt like a snow flurry: she was coming down fast, in tiny wind-whipped particles. "No, I'm not losing my mind," she said desperately. "Am I?"

He held her again. She did not feel like a person in his arms but like a small, scared animal. That word for Hannah's chosen husband, a *mate*, like an animal. Am I really Hannah's daughter? Could that be the truth? Will I turn out weird like Hannah? Am I already weird?

"Lizzie looked up the kidnapping in *The New York Times*, too, Janie, all the subsequent articles and all the follow-ups. Janie, are you ready for this?"

"I'm not ready for anything."

"Lizzie thinks it's Hannah who kidnapped you. We all agree that Mr. and Mrs. Johnson just wouldn't do that. Couldn't do that. Isn't it much more reasonable that Hannah really did run away from the cult? Stopped at that shopping center in

153

New Jersey? Maybe she had stolen a car or the cult guards had nearly caught up to her. She was afraid. She ran inside and there was this sweet little girl who would hold her hand. Lizzie thinks maybe Hannah took you along for company. And Hannah was such a lost soul maybe she didn't even know she was kidnapping you. But if she did know, she sure wouldn't tell her mother and father when she got to their house."

Peace settled on Janie. She felt heavier, as if her weight might press on Reeve till his ribs broke. She said, "Mother and Daddy aren't bad, then."

"Well, we don't know anything for sure. But that way, your parents' story is entirely true. Lizzie and I can't believe they would have been part of anything criminal or evil."

"Hannah was the evil criminal." Janie was so lethargic she could not imagine moving again. How wonderful to place the crime on a woman who no longer counted in anybody's life.

The sun fondled her lovingly. Or was it Reeve?

In an odd way, she felt even more like an animal: soaking up the sun, no worries, no cares, no concern for the future: just affection and warmth.

"I don't know," said Reeve. "I don't think Hannah sounds evil or criminal. I think she sounds like a scared, cult-blinded automaton. Even at three you were a hand to hold, somebody to talk to in the car, somebody to give Hannah courage until she reached her own mommy and daddy and was safe again."

Janie liked it. It meant that her parents had told no lies. Were sane and good. Really did consider themselves her grandparents. Or parents. "There are too many parents in this," she said to Reeve.

"Tell me about it. And now I've thrown in Lizzie, who is tougher than any four parents anyhow. Lizzie sees kind of a problem, though, Janie. If we tell anybody about it, see. Kidnapping is a federal offense no matter how many years have gone by. Like murder. You can still be tried. So if we say anything at all, the FBI would have to locate Hannah. To prove or disprove our theory."

It took too much effort even to lean on Reeve's chest. She managed to lie down, her head in his lap, her feet on the passenger seat, her back full of gear shifts.

"Isn't that uncomfortable?" said Reeve.

"Yes, but I'm too tired to sit up."

Reeve reached awkwardly into the backseat and retrieved a stadium blanket. "Let's sit out there by the waterfall." He had to uncurl her from the gear sticks. They staggered into a spot of sunshine and he spread the blanket on a rock hot with sun.

"Can you imagine the publicity?" said Janie. "All those horrible newspapers in grocery store racks. Talk shows where everybody else on it has trans-bi-cross sexual habits." She shuddered. "I can hardly wait to be among them."

Reeve said, "I'd settle for any sexual habit at all, Janie."

"I want to finish this topic first."

Reeve sighed. "Lizzie says if you're going to get in touch with New Jersey, you'll have to handle it privately."

"I suppose Lizzie thinks she's the best person in the world to handle it."

"Lizzie has always thought she's the best person in the world to handle anything," said Reeve.

"I've never liked that trait."

"It's even worse when you have to live with it. And when Megan and Todd are exactly the same."

"You know Megan and Lizzie and Todd," said Janie. "You grew up with them. I didn't grow up with my brothers and sisters. Do you think they ever talk about me at supper? Or keep my picture on the wall? Or say to each other—she'd be a sophomore in high school now?"

"I'm sure they do," said Reeve. He was kissing her everywhere. He had unbuttoned nothing, was feeling through the fabric. His mind was definitely not on New Jersey.

"One bad thing is still true though," said Janie, starting to cry.

"What?" He kissed her tears and she kissed his lips, tasting the salt of her own weeping.

"I'm still a rotten little kid who wanted more attention and was willing to be kidnapped to get it."

Reeve laughed. "You can't have been too rotten if they're advertising on milk cartons to get you back."

We're both frantic, she thought. His heart is

racing for me. My heart is racing for fear. She said, "There are only two choices."

"Right. Either we do it or we don't. I vote we do it."

"Wrong. Either I get in touch with New Jersey or I don't. I vote I don't."

"I vote that, too. Who needs another family?" Reeve shifted half on top of her. His weight was warm and convincing.

CHAPTER
16

The following Saturday they rented movies.

Sarah-Charlotte brought Jason and the potato chips. "He's kind of a potato chip himself," she whispered to Janie.

"Hush," said Janie, "I like Jason."

"I do, too," said Sarah-Charlotte, "but he isn't romantic. He's just Jason."

Janie nodded. "I got the romantic in the crowd," she said. "See my little pumpkin pin? Reeve gave it to me on Thanksgiving Day."

"That's so neat!" cried Sarah-Charlotte.

Mrs. Johnson brought in an immense bowl of popcorn.

The four of them sat in a circle on the rug arguing whether the popcorn or the Trivial Pursuit board deserved the middle. Jason said since he had rented the movies, he got to choose the first one. Reeve said somebody would have to sit with his back to the movie if they were playing Trivial Pursuit at the same time, and it wasn't going to be him.

"Bets on who will win Trivial Pursuit," said Sarah-Charlotte, inelegantly stuffing a fistful of popcorn in her mouth.

"Not me," said Reeve. "I never know anything except Sports."

"Not me," said Janie, "I never know anything."

"Oh, good," said Sarah-Charlotte, "I love playing with dumbos. I always know everything. Your go, Janie."

Janie rolled the dice and chose Geography.

Sarah-Charlotte took a card and read the question. "Did Reeve give you the milk carton as well as the pumpkin pin? Does the carton have some sort of romantic significance?"

Janie choked on her popcorn. Reeve slapped her on the back. "Sarah-Charlotte, read the real question."

"But we're all dying to know, Janie," said Jason. "You open your notebook twenty times a day and stare down into that milk carton. Come on, admit it. What's it all about?"

Her mother brought in a platter of turkey sandwiches on rye and two liters of Coke. "I wondered about that, too, darling," she said. "That Saturday you practically had a heart attack because your notebook fell open. All I saw was 'Flower Dairy.'"

Sick fear enveloped Janie like fog. Not here, she thought. Not in front of Jason and Sarah-Charlotte. Not when Mom is the happy hostess and good mother. In fact, not ever. I voted not to have New Jersey.

"Since when is it anybody's business but ours?"

said Reeve. He rolled over against Janie, and kept rolling until he had flattened her. From beneath him she made strangling, let-me-have-air noises.

"Uncle," whispered Janie.

Reeve rolled off onto the carpet again. He lay on his back and said to the rest, "Young lovers deserve privacy."

Sarah-Charlotte looked twice as interested.

She knows where my carton is, thought Janie. She'll study that till she's figured everything out. "Back in a minute!" Janie cried. She ran upstairs into her room, ripped the carton out of the notebook, and rushed into the bathroom. Locking the door behind her, she started to shred the carton to flush it down the toilet.

But she could not tear herself in half.

The milk carton was all that existed of herself.

She walked back into her bedroom and slid it between the mattress and the bedsprings instead.

There had been a week of peace. A solid week without nightmares or daymares.

In the silver notebook Janie wrote all theories and all possible variations. Then she began condensing and choosing the most likely for final drafts.

"What do you want a final draft for?" said Reeve irritably. "What's the plan now? You're going to mail some anonymous notebook to New Jersey?" He was very tense with her. He had taken her twenty miles to go to a very popular, expensive pizza/video place and had bought dozens of tokens. They were sitting together playing a war

160

game, and he wanted to laugh and be silly and win. New Jersey was interfering.

"Of course not," said Janie. "It's just for me."

Reeve said, "It's Pandora's box, isn't it? The myth. The minute you opened that milk carton, it was all there: every evil thing. And you'll never be able to put it back. It's out now."

"The only evil," she said, "is that I don't mind that it happened. I like my life. You see—"

"I can't tell you how tired I am of New Jersey."

"I just want to finish my thought, okay?"

He looked at the screen. He counted the tokens in his palm. He shrugged. "Okay."

She stabbed a game button. "I'm gonna beat the pants off you, boy."

He laughed. "Any time, girl." His bombers attacked her tanks.

She continued her thoughts in the silver notebook. If Reeve was tired of New Jersey, the notebook was all she had now.

Why didn't Frank and Miranda see the newspaper coverage of the kidnapping? It was on the television news for days, too. I suppose they were pretty distracted that week. Hannah returned, complete with granddaughter, and they fled—who had time for a morning paper?

If they had bought a paper the day after Hannah came—Frank would have seen the photograph . . . would have called the police himself . . . taken the Spring's little girl home. Hannah would have been imprisoned; the Johnsons' lives—no, back then they were still Javensens— would have been completely different.

161

Grimmer. Emptier.

*I would have no memory of the Johnsons
instead of no memory of the Springs.*

That night she went to an awards banquet at
which her father as coach received a trophy. It
was a typical banquet meal: gravy, red meat, and
wilted salad. Her father even made a little speech,
thanking not just his team and the team parents,
but his beloved wife and daughter. He wanted
Janie to take the trophy for him.

Janie smiled back at her father, tall and perfect. The after-school athlete was an odd match
for the dedicated, formal, elegant committeewoman
he had married. They smiled at her, and she knew
they had forgotten Hannah right then: she was
their daughter. She was their love.

She stood up in the banquet hall and hun-
dreds of little soccer players and their parents
applauded for Janie, who had done nothing whatsoever. She stood up and a mother nearby whispered, "Look at that wonderful red hair! Isn't she
a beautiful child? The Johnsons are so lucky."

They were photographed as a trio. It would be
in the sports pages. Her mother whispered, "I'm
glad you wore the purple sweater. Nobody believes
a redhead looks great in purple until they see you,
Janie."

The photographer shouted, "Smile now. Smile
everybody."

Janie smiled.

She thought, if I do not tell New Jersey that I
am safe, I am *still* the spoiled brat. Still the rotten

162

daughter who didn't care about the family she had left behind.

The only way to be the good daughter is to tell.

They left the banquet to the handshakes of parent after parent, thanking Mr. Johnson for all the hours, all the sportsmanship, all the encouragement, all the positive thinking, he had given their sons and daughters.

That night Janie lay on her bed holding the telephone in her arms like a teddy bear, dialing the 800 number. This time she let it ring.

It rang once.

Twice.

Three times.

They're not home, thought Janie. How can a toll-free 800 number not be home?

Four times.

Adair's parents have each remarried since the divorce. So Adair has four parents. Two mothers, two fathers. It's not so unusual. I can do it, too.

Five.

There was a click. Her heart slammed upward in her chest. The carefully rehearsed sentences vanished from her head. Her mouth was so dry her tongue scraped. *Oh, my God, what have I done?* her head screamed. I've betrayed my mother and father—I—

"You have reached . . . " began a recording.

The voice asked her to leave her name, number, and a brief message after the tone, and they would get back to her. After the tone, Janie hung up.

The phone rang in her arms.

Its shrillness invaded her heart, making her leap from the bed, scattering books to the floor. *They tapped my phone! They're calling back: they've got me.*

"Hi. Sarah-Charlotte," said Sarah-Charlotte, who always spoke as if she were phoning herself.

"Hey, girl, what's up?" said Janie. She was slippery with sweat; she even smelled of fear, and tasted it in her mouth. It was like biting metal.

"You know Reeve's best friend, Michael?"

"Not very well."

'Better than I do. I adore Michael. Do you think you could ask Reeve to ask Michael to ask me out?"

Janie could hardly get through the conversation. She had to plan every sentence, figure ahead the possible answers to possible questions. It was harder than homework.

Sarah-Charlotte babbled on and on about Michael, and boys, and friendships between boys. Usually Janie could pass an hour, even two hours, on these precise topics. "Don't you and Reeve ever do things with Michael? He and Michael used to be inseparable. Isn't Michael always over at Reeve's house?"

Janie struggled to listen. Her mind exploded with loyalties and parents. She could not seem to put Sarah-Charlotte into the framework of her life. She could not figure out the conversation they were having.

"What kind of friendship is it when the only words you say now are yes, no, maybe, and mm-hmm?" said Sarah-Charlotte. "I'm sick of this,

Janie. You aren't any fun anymore. You don't even like any of us anymore."

She tried to find an explanation that did not include New Jersey. "That isn't true," she whispered, but Sarah-Charlotte had already hung up.

Reeve drove straight for the Scenic Overlook. She knew by his driving. It was more physical, more excited.

I want to be a nice person, she thought. I want to be the kind of little girl who would have screamed for help when she got kidnapped. I don't want to be somebody who thought it was neat. But I don't want to be Jennie Spring.

"Reeve, pull over."

"I can't stop here, Janie."

"Pull over."

He yanked the car to the edge of a road that barely had passing room anyway. Behind them a car honked. Janie opened her door, leaned out, and threw up into some unfortunate person's shrubbery.

If I can't write it out of my mind, she thought, I guess my body is going to throw it out instead.

She refused to go home.

Reeve drove to a diner miles away because she refused to go anyplace where people might recognize them. In the bathroom she mopped herself up with paper towels. Her complexion was like kindergarten paste: white and gluey.

Then she dragged Reeve back to the car. She couldn't sit in the diner. People might look at her.

Reeve said, "Janie, I thought you could just forget about it, but obviously that isn't working.

165

So you have to tell them. You have to talk about it with them."

"No."

"Janie! You are losing it. Literally."

"Fine."

"No, it isn't fine. You've got to have your parents in this with you."

"No, because the minute I do that, I have to trade them in again for another set."

"No, you don't. Nobody would make you."

"That other family—those people in New Jersey —you think I could just call them up and say, I'm fine, so stop worrying and don't bother me, either? They'll be in court, they'll call the FBI, they'll get lawyers. And I"—Janie's voice turned so ragged it no longer sounded human—"I'll have to admit what happened at that shopping center."

"Janie!" shouted Reeve. "What happened was, a pretty blond woman took a pretty little girl for a ride in her car and they had a great time."

"And the little girl never looked back," said Janie. "I hate her. I hate that little girl." She began to cry. The tears made no noise and took no effort, but they burned fiercely, as if they were the acid remains of her horrible deeds.

She wouldn't let Reeve touch her. She wouldn't answer anything he said to her. They went home, finally, Janie crouched against her door, and Reeve driving with a stiff precision.

A mile from home he said, "I'm sick of this. Now tell them."

"No."

"Tell them," said Reeve, his voice hard and loud, "or I'm not seeing you again."

"I'm not ready to tell anybody."

"You're being stupid. Either wise up or I don't want to be bothered."

"Fine!" she said. "Don't be bothered." She jumped out of the Jeep, slamming the door. Her foot caught on a loose pavement brick and she stumbled, blinded by tears. "This is my life we're talking about!" she shouted at him. "And you don't want to be bothered anymore."

Reeve got out of the Jeep more slowly. "Janie," he said.

"Drop dead." She ran in the side door and slammed that, too.

Inside the house, the tears ripped through her with even more force. How could she have done that? Why be mad at Reeve, the only one on her team, the only one who knew?

Her sobs made a racket, ripped out of her lungs even as she tried to choke them down. It brought her mother and father running. "What's the matter?" they cried, enfolding her.

"I broke up with Reeve," she said, praying it was not true.

CHAPTER
17

The following week was bright with pain.

Life flickered in Janie's face like flashbulbs going off.

No matter where she looked, Reeve was there, but he neither looked back nor waved. In the mornings when she got up, he was already gone. She could not bear to take the school bus again— that public declaration: yes, I lost him. Her mother drove her to school every morning. Afternoons Adair dropped her at home unless she took the bus that passed the town library.

You know life is pretty grim if reading about Stalin and Krushchev beats all the other options, thought Janie. She tried to make herself laugh, but nothing in life was amusing.

Five days after her scene in the driveway, Reeve drove home with a senior named Jessica. Janie knew Jessica by sight, a tall, thin, dark girl with very short hair and a brittle smile. She had thought nothing could be more painful than New Jersey.

She was wrong. Reeve's arm around Jessica kept her awake as many hours as New Jersey ever had.

"If that isn't a classic," said Sarah-Charlotte. She was enjoying her role as comforter. It had made them best friends again. Although she was no longer the best friend Janie wanted. I want *Reeve*, she thought.

"Everybody knows," said Sarah-Charlotte, "that Jessica sleeps around. Was that his reason?" She looked intently at Janie. "Did you go all the way with Reeve or not?"

Janie shook her head. They had come close. All that they had done she had loved. Would always cherish. Would never describe to Sarah-Charlotte.

"Clearly," said Sarah-Charlotte, whose knowledge of sexuality came entirely from talk shows, "that's the only thing that mattered to Reeve in the end."

What mattered to Reeve, thought Janie, is what matters to everyone. Being first in somebody's life. I put New Jersey first. He took it for a long time, considering.

During study hall, Janie opened her silver spiral notebook. Losing Reeve had made one thing clear. If she also lost her parents, she would die.

Never, never, could she get through that.

She had condensed the facts and theories of the kidnapping to four pages. She tore them out of her glitter notebook, folded them, and stuffed it all into an envelope under the clip. She missed having the carton there to look at. She licked the stickum and closed the flap. There, she thought. I'm done thinking about it.

She would pin the envelope and the milk carton to the inside of the polka-dot dress and put all three back in the trunk in the attic. That would store the problem for another season.

Later on in the class, feeling spooky, she put the Springs' address on the envelope. *Mr. and Mrs. Jonathan Avery Spring, 114 Highview Avenue.* It made her heart pound to write it. Did I know that address by heart once? she wondered.

She slid the envelope under the clip in her notebook. This afternoon her mother would be tutoring. Plenty of time for a solitary trip to the attic. She would study Hannah's photographs. And then lock the trunk.

She had to sit at lunch with Jason, Sarah-Charlotte, Adair, Katrina, and Peter instead of with Reeve. She felt like the most conspicuous person in the cafeteria. She did not know where to focus her eyes. She wanted to look at Reeve. Only Reeve. Always Reeve. But Reeve was sitting with Jessica. Laughing.

We didn't laugh enough, thought Janie. I haven't had any laughter to spare since the milk carton.

She wondered if she could learn how to laugh again. If there would be a time, living next door to Reeve, when she would smile in an ordinary way at the driver of that Jeep?

Sarah-Charlotte wanted to have a Pity Party for Janie.

"I'll invite only girls," she promised. "Let's see. Adair, Katrina, Jodie, Linda, Hilary. Who else do you want? Should it be a sleep-over? We'll sit around and talk about how rotten boys are and Reeve in particular."

Jodie.

Memory slugged her.

Jodie.

One of my sisters is named Jodie. "I don't want a Pity Party," she said, starting to cry.

Jason and Pete suddenly had to get extra desserts. They fled the table.

"Well, they won't be back," said Adair. "Boys collapse when girls cry."

"That sounds like Shakespeare," said Sarah-Charlotte.

"Embroidery on pillows," agreed Adair.

The bell rang. Janie walked between Adair and Sarah-Charlotte as they battered their way out of the cafeteria and back to English. Don't let me be in the doorway the same time as Reeve and Jessica, she thought. Please.

One prayer answered. But only one.

English ended.

History poked along.

Passing period following passing period.

Janie went to her last class slowly, not because she was dawdling but because she felt weak. I haven't eaten in days, she thought. Pretty soon my mother won't just have me at adolescent trauma counseling, she'll have me at the anorexia clinic.

The halls swayed and grew in the middle and clapped their sides against Janie's head. She touched the lockers to steady herself but was knocked from the wall by a bunch of worthless boys. Druggies and scuzzies, all.

I'm a scuzz, too, thought Janie. Tossing out my family like last week's newspaper.

The halls were empty. She did not know how that had happened. A moment ago she had been one among a hundred kids.

She fumbled with her blue English notebook.

She needed to see the carton.

Dimly she remembered the carton was no longer there. It was between the mattress and the box springs.

But her silver notebook was there.

No, it wasn't. It was in her book bag.

But the envelope was still there.

No, it wasn't.

There was nothing under the clip.

The clip was broken.

She had used the clip so often that the cheap little spring had snapped. The envelope was gone.

I addressed it, she thought. To New Jersey. It was one of the SADD mistakes with my real return address on it.

But no stamp.

It can't go anywhere without a stamp.

Unless some Good Samaritan stamped it for me.

Unless the post office delivers it and charges the postage to the Springs.

If it's been mailed, it will be read.

They'll know.

In two days, the Springs will know who I am and where I am.

How am I going to save my mother and father now?

Her thoughts stabbed her separately, knife after knife of fear.

Past the offices, past the school library, past language labs Janie walked. Reeve had last-period chemistry. She found the room and opened the door, walking in. Juniors and seniors looked up, startled. She could not see their faces. Reeve was somewhere among them but her eyes would not focus.

The teacher was writing on the blackboard as he lectured, his back partially to the class.

"Reeve," Janie said, plowing across the room like a tractor.

The teacher turned, chalk in hand. "Uh—miss?" he said.

"Reeve, I need Lizzie's phone number," said Janie, walking steadily toward Reeve, although there were desks and knees in her path.

Reeve unfolded from his desk. Took her shoulder, turned her around. "Be right back," he said to his teacher.

"And just where do you think you're going?" said the teacher.

But they were out of the room and the teacher did not bother to follow them.

"You're pushing me," said Janie.

"I'm walking at a regular speed," said Reeve. "You're trying to walk while standing still. Pick up your feet. Are you on drugs or something?"

"I don't think so. I need Lizzie's phone number. Reeve, you won't believe what I've done. How stupid I've been."

"I think I could believe that," he said.

She talked. He drove her home. "I hate to play psychiatrist with you, but you didn't lose that letter by any accident, Janie. Any more than you wrote it and put it in an envelope and addressed and sealed it by accident. You had to get out of this somehow, and that's the route you took."

The house was empty. They went into the kitchen where Janie stared at the wall phone and Reeve automatically checked her refrigerator for something to eat. It embarrassed him and he shut the door without taking anything.

He wrote down Lizzie's number for her. "Do you want me to call her first?" he said.

She shook her head. She was starting to cry. Now she could see him clearly: Reeve, whom she adored. No wonder he had walked her out of chemistry; she must have looked completely demented, storming desks to get at him. She could imagine the class snickering. Telling Jessica. Preparing to humiliate Reeve when he got back.

His fingers, full of car keys, rested stiffly on the counter. She would have to give him permission to go. Reeve would force himself to be neighborly to the end. She bit the insides of her cheeks. She did not want to blackmail him by crying. "Thank you for the ride home," she whispered. "You don't have to stay."

The empty house seemed very noisy. The freezer

hummed. The furnace buzzed. The clock ticked. Her own pulse throbbed in her forehead. She managed to look at Reeve.

"Janie," he said, "I'm sorry."

She nodded behind the blind windshield of her tears. "Me, too. It's okay." She turned away from him. Think about Lizzie, she ordered herself. One disaster at a time. Think how you're going to beg Lizzie to call New Jersey before they get the letter and call the police.

"No," said Reeve, swallowing audibly. "I mean, I'm sorry and I want to make up. That kind of sorry."

CHAPTER
18

In their place," said Janie's father, "I'd move heaven and earth to ruin the people responsible."

Lizzie sat quietly, having laid out the circumstances so easily, so clearly, that Janie marveled. It had taken Janie weeks of daymares to work her way to the end of this; Lizzie reached the end in ten minutes. Lizzie's green wool dress had a narrow waist and very full skirt. Sitting primly on the edge of the coffee table, her skirt draped to the carpet, she looked like a tent in which tiny children would want to play house.

"The Springs might understand," said Janie. She was soaring. There was no burden left. She felt like dancing, laughing, throwing confetti. It's over, she thought, dizzy with relief.

"I wouldn't understand," said her father. "I'd have the police and the FBI, SWAT teams and old college roommates, all surrounding this house to get *my* daughter back." His hands knotted into fists, as if he, too, would gladly have a fight with somebody; anybody.

"Can't you imagine the SWAT teams surrounding the house?" said Reeve, starting to laugh.

"Unfortunately, yes," said Janie's father.

Janie and Reeve began giggling, acting out SWAT teams with submachine guns peering in their windows. "You know what?" said Janie.

"What?"

"I am starving. I haven't eaten in two weeks, I've been so nervous. I could eat my shoelaces. What is there to eat, Mom?"

"Let's order a pizza," said Reeve.

"Especially when you talk like that," said Janie's father, "you feel like my daughter. Food first." His control broke; tears suddenly made little gleaming rivers on his face, like gold in rocks. He put his arms around Janie. "Hannah would have faded away under this much stress."

"I thought about it," said Janie, "but I reconsidered. I'm tough." She gave her parents an impish grin. "I was well brought up."

Her father managed half a smile. "What am I going to say to those parents?"

"Maybe they'll be nice about it," said Janie.

"Maybe they won't," said her mother. On her mother's lap lay the flattened milk carton. The stolen child who was Jennie Spring, who was Janie, smiled back over the years.

I don't need to see it again, thought Janie. It's over. I'm safe.

Reeve said, "Pepperoni? Mushrooms? Sausage?"

The telephone rang.

Everyone but Lizzie jumped. Shrill rings penetrated their hearts, like surgery. Nobody crossed the room to answer it.

"Probably my mother wondering where I am," said Reeve, but he looked white and afraid of the phone.

"Sarah-Charlotte," said Janie. "She's mad at me."

Her mother's laugh quivered. It was not really a laugh at all; it was a splintered soul. My nightmares laughed like that, thought Janie. "Or New Jersey," said her mother.

The phone rang eleven times. A determined caller. Janie's mother had one hand on her mouth, the other on her throat, as if to contain her fears.

"Getting worked up," said Lizzie, "is not going to help us design our approach."

"Lizzie, have you ever been worked up over anything in your life?" said Reeve.

Lizzie ignored him. He was merely a pesky baby brother. She said, "We have the weekend. They can't possibly get the letter before Monday."

Janie's mother said, "I can't believe this is my life."

Lizzie waited two seconds to pay tribute to this sort of emotionalism and then continued, "But as long as the situation has arrived, Janie, we should deal with it. I'll call the Springs."

"Wait a minute," said Janie's father. "I would take bets that the letter didn't get mailed. The more logical assumption is that it's in the trash at the high school. The janitors swept it up with candy wrappers and discarded quizzes. Which means no one in the world knows but us. We don't have to take any action."

Janie's mother raised a haggard face. "Oh,

Frank," she said. "If we don't take any action, then we *have* kidnapped her. We *have* stolen her." Her mother slumped, defeated and afraid.

All I suffered since October, Janie thought, Mom's getting slapped with tonight. "But you are my parents," said Janie. "That's why I didn't do anything. I know who I am. Janie Johnson."

Her mother whispered, "It seemed so logical at the time. Oh, Frank! Frank! Do you think Hannah really did say this was her baby, our granddaughter? Or do you think we decided on that ourselves, because we needed her so much?" She began sobbing uncontrollably, stretching hands toward her husband. The thin fingers of her left hand glittered with her diamond engagement ring, her gold wedding band, the ruby twenty-fifth-anniversary ring. He took the hand with the rings and held it between both of his. He sank to one knee, and his wife, still holding his hands, bent over it. They looked as if they were proposing to each other.

"I'm yours," said Janie desperately. "Don't cry." She was excluded from their pain. She felt as if she had caused it, would always cause it; that while Frank and Miranda were a unit, she had no family now; neither here nor in New Jersey. "Mommy?" said Janie, as if calling her mother back.

Together, dimly, her parents looked up; they were ten years away.

They can remember it, thought Janie. I have found a few scraps of memory, but to them it is bright: the day Hannah brought a little girl to fill their lives.

"Don't be mad," Janie mumbled. "Please don't be mad."

Her mother pulled Janie down onto the chair with her; there was no room; Janie sat on her mother's lap. She had to curl her spine to fit in the soft, safe spot above her mother's breast. When she wept, she could not tell whose tears were on her cheek. "If I could have any wish," whispered her mother, "it would be that no parent on this earth ever suffered a missing child. And I made it happen to another mother."

"Well, if I had any wish," said her father, "it would be to keep Janie."

"You will," said Janie. "I'm not going anywhere."

"The courts and the Springs may have different ideas."

"You could run away again," suggested Reeve. "After all, you know how it's done."

"Reeve," said Janie's father, "you are getting tiresome."

"Sorry."

Janie was faintly surprised that Reeve and Lizzie were still there. It seemed to her that she and her mother and father had gone where no one else could go: some ghastly voyage of past and present, guilt and anger.

"Maybe we should telephone them right now," said her mother. She frowned uncertainly at the chair, as if unsure that any seat could be safe.

"What would you say?" asked Janie. "Hi, this is your stolen daughter's mother, who thought she was her grandmother, who didn't mean this to happen, and please don't get mad at the kidnapper, because she was a lost soul herself and only wanted company while she ran away from *her* kidnappers."

"They'll think we're insane," said Janie's mother. "The Springs are not going to believe that normal people could have gotten themselves into such a grotesque situation. They'll never let you stay with us, Janie."

The discussion had acquired velocity. Janie felt as if she were hurtling, brakeless, toward yet another cliff. "Lizzie will handle it," said Janie loudly. I just got away from the edge, she thought. Don't shove me over again. "Lizzie will tell them to let it go. Stop worrying and let us be."

"*Stop worrying?*" repeated her mother. "Do you think I have ever stopped worrying about Hannah? Do you think there's been a night in my life when I haven't prayed for her safety? When I haven't wondered if we did the wrong thing, letting her vanish forever? Janie, no mother ever lets go."

"You pray for Hannah?" said Janie, amazed. "You never said you believe in God."

"I have no beliefs," said her mother. "Only hopes. They'll have to meet you, Janie, these Springs. We'll have to meet them."

"No! They aren't real right now. I don't want them to be real. I want them to go away."

"They've waited long enough," said Janie's mother. "I know what it is to lie awake year after year, never knowing what happened to your little girl. I know what it is to cry out on her birthday, *If only, if only!*"

Even Lizzie's eyes were wet.

"Lizzie could meet with them first," said her mother. "We have to protect Hannah. I wonder if they would promise—no, we can't ask that."

"Don't ask, Lizzie. Tell. Tell them either they're nice about it or I won't see them," said Janie.

Lizzie was taking mental notes. "Then you will see them if they agree not to try to find Hannah or prosecute anybody?"

Janie found herself pushing her parents together to make a shield against the enemy. This is how Hannah felt, she thought. The world caved in and she had no hiding place.

"Maybe after Lizzie sees them, it'll be over," said Reeve.

Lizzie's voice was calm and factual. "It'll never be over."

Never over, thought Janie. This isn't a term paper; I won't pass it in. This isn't high school; I won't graduate. *This will never be over.*

Lizzie stood up, the tent of her skirt rearranging itself gracefully; she was lean and elegant and clever. "I'll telephone the Springs. I will arrange Saturday or Sunday for a preliminary meeting. I will suggest to the Springs that the meeting with you, Janie, take place later in the month without your mother and father there."

"I suppose you'd be the best escort," said Janie. She was crushing her mother. She stood up. Her mother stood with her. Her father moved closer. They were like children in a camp race: legs tied together, stumbling to the finish.

"Of course," said Lizzie, who had never had trouble being modest.

"I want to go, too," said Reeve.

"Nonsense," said Lizzie. "What do you think it is, a movie and popcorn? It's going to be very emotional."

Her mother let go and walked shakily to the cherry table where the library books and the Kleenex sat beside a bowl of yellow and blue dried flowers.

"Then I'm not going," said Janie. "I've had enough emotion. I just want this to end happily ever after."

"Not everything does, Janie," said her father. "Hannah didn't. I don't see how this can."

He was so weary it terrified her. So old she was afraid for his life. "It has to!" cried Janie. "Tell the Springs, Lizzie. Tell them it has to end happily ever after."

Her plea echoed in the living room. The deep sofa was just furniture; the scarlet and blue just colors. The room felt no difference; it would be as lovely after Lizzie saw the Springs as before. Reeve was watching Janie sadly. Her father was unfolding a handkerchief to blot his tears. And her mother had not, after all, crossed the room to get a tissue. Slowly, hypnotically, she was dialing the telephone.

"Mommy?" said Janie. She could not catch her breath. "Mommy, who are you calling?" She tried to see the spinning numbers.

Her mother dialed another digit.

"Mommy, are you calling for pizza?"

Her mother dialed beyond seven digits. She was calling long distance. Out of state. *New Jersey.*

"A mother," said her own mother, "would need to hear her baby's voice." Her mother's face was so soaked in tears it might have been raining.

"I'm not Jennie, though," whispered Janie. A split personality, she thought: I am truly two people. I have to choose. A good daughter or a bad one? But I have two sets of parents. How can I be good to both of them?

The dialing ended.

In the velvety silence of the room Janie, Lizzie, Reeve, her mother, and her father listened to the telephone ring in New Jersey.

Was it ringing in the kitchen? Where the twins had sat in high chairs? Where a laughing father had said a homemade blessing? Where a little girl once spilled milk?

The phone rang a second time. A third time.

Happily ever after, thought Janie. *Please be nice people.*

With numb fingers Janie took the phone from her mother. I should have had something to eat, she thought. I'm so hungry I'm dizzy.

It rang once more.

In New Jersey somebody picked up the phone.

"Hello?" said a woman's voice.

Janie clung to her mother. She said, "Hi. It's . . . your daughter. Me. Jennie."

184

CHAPTER

1

After their sister's kidnapping, Dad not only took Stephen and Jodie to school every morning, he held their hands.

Not once—not once in a hundred and eighty days a year, kindergarten through sixth grade— were the remaining Spring children allowed to take a school bus. Not once had Jodie been allowed to walk in or out of the elementary school without her father there.

The children would get out of the car. Dad would take Jodie's hand in his right hand and Stephen's hand in his left. Then they would walk across the parking lot, into the building and down to Jodie's classroom where he would transfer Jodie's hand to the teacher's. His eyes would scan the halls, as if kidnappers were lurking beside the winning poster from the science contest. When Jodie was safely in her teacher's care, Dad would continue on with Stephen.

For years, Jodie thought this pattern was normal.

But when Stephen was in fourth grade, he said

if anybody ever held his hand again, he would bite it. He said if anybody had planned to kidnap another Spring child, they had given up by now. Stephen said he would carry a knife, he would carry a submachine gun, he would carry a nuclear bomb, and he would blow away all would-be kidnappers, but never again would he let anybody hold his hand.

From his fourth-grade heart had come the hidden rage they all felt and never dared say out loud.

"I hate Jennie!" Stephen had screamed. "I hate my sister for ruining our lives! The least Jennie could have done was leave her body there for us to find. Then we could bury her and be done with her. I hate it that we have to worry every single day. I hate her!"

Stephen was seventeen now. Jodie could remember that meal as if it were yesterday. Mom and Dad had sat as tight and silent as wind-up dolls. More vividly than anything else, Jodie remembered that nobody yelled at Stephen for saying such terrible things.

Years of worry had torn the family's guts apart, like a tornado peeling the house walls away. Worry had separated them from each other, so they were not six people knit close in tight, warm threads of family, but travelers accidentally in the same motel.

There had been a long, long silence after Stephen's outburst. Even the twins, who had been thick and annoying all their paired lives, knew better than to speak.

At last Dad had extended his hands from his

sides, straight out, like a Roman slave being cruci-
fied.

The whole family held hands every evening to
say grace before supper. That was what Dad intended, and yet the stiffness of his arms, the awful
lines around his mouth, did not look like grace.

Jodie had been scared, because she was between Dad and Stephen, and she would have to
take Stephen's hand, and she was pretty sure Stephen really would bite her.

But he didn't.

He cried instead. Stephen had cried easily when
he was little and the humiliation of that had left its
mark; nothing would have made Stephen Spring cry
now that he was seventeen. Where a ten-year-old
had exhibited tears, the young man used fists.

So they had held hands, and Dad had prayed.
Not grace. He didn't mention food. He didn't mention shelter. He said, "Dear Lord, tonight we are going to bury Jennie. We love her, but she's gone and
now we're going to say good-bye. Thank you for the
time we had Jennie. The rest of us have to go on
living. Thank you for making Stephen tell us."

Jodie was only nine. Only a third-grader. Jodie
had needed to take her hands back from Stephen
and Daddy so she could wipe away her tears, and
Jodie never admitted to anybody that they were not
tears of grief for her missing sister, but tears of relief
that they were going to put Jennie on the shelf and
be done with her.

"Give Jennie a guardian angel," said Dad softly
to the Lord.

Usually during grace, Jodie felt that Dad was

talking to his children, ordering them to behave and be thankful. Not this prayer. Dad was talking to the Lord; Jodie thought if she looked up she would see God, and that was even scarier than having to hold Stephen's hand, so she didn't look up.

"Take care of Jennie, Lord, wherever she is. Help us not mention Jennie again. Help us be a family of six and forget that we were ever a family of seven." Dad squeezed Jodie's hand.

Jodie squeezed Stephen's.

The squeeze went around the circle, and the Lord must have been there, because the lump in Jodie's throat dissolved, and the twins began to talk about sports—even when they were babies they talked about sports, they had been playing with basketballs and footballs and tennis balls from birth—and Stephen showed his B-plus geography paper; he had gotten forty-two of the fifty state capitals right.

The family sealed up, like a perfect package. Things fit again. Everything from the number of chairs around the table to the toppling stacks of presents under the Christmas tree. The Spring family had six people in it now. The seventh was gone.

Mom and Dad didn't even telephone Mr. Mollison again. Mr. Mollison was the FBI agent who had been in charge of the case. For a while he had been as much a part of the family as Uncle Paul and Aunt Luellen.

The next year, nobody talked about Jennie on her birthday. Nobody sobbed on the anniversary of the day Jennie went missing.

Mr. and Mrs. Spring were still more careful

than any other parents in the state of New Jersey, but the children were more careful, too. It was not because Jodie and her brothers were worried that they might be kidnapped, too. They were worried that their parents would be worried. The Spring children were always lined up at telephones to let Mom or Dad know where they were. They were never late. They were children who knew, too well, one of the horrors of the world.

The thing Jodie could not get over, now that her sister Jennie turned out to be alive and coming home, was that *there had never been a horror.*

They had imagined all of it.

Jennie had not died.

She had not been tortured.

She had not been cold or lost or drowned or raped or even frightened!

Jennie had been just fine all along.

It was incredible, when Jodie thought of the lancing fear the rest of them had endured for eleven and a half years. In most ways, of course, worry and fear vanished. When she was small, it vanished because Jodie believed in Daddy's deal with God. If Daddy and the Lord both said Stop Worrying, well then, who was Jodie to worry? But as Jodie moved into her teens, the reality of her sister's kidnapping often surfaced. When she brought a library book home . . . and the heroine was a redhead named Jennie. When Stephen had his first date . . . and her name was Jennie. When the late movie on television was about a kidnapping. When Jodie went in the post office and saw those black-and-white photos—HAVE YOU SEEN THIS CHILD?

She'd feel it again. The panic like burning acid, making it impossible to think of anything else. And the rage: the terrible, terrible anger that their lives had been so brutally interfered with.

Brian and Brendan were babies when it happened, still sitting in the double stroller, getting everything sticky. (Jodie's relationship with her twin brothers began by steering around them lest they smear her with melting lollipop or contaminate her with Oreo-cookie crumbs. Somehow it had continued that way. Keeping clear was Jodie's major activity with her little brothers.) But Jodie had been in kindergarten and Stephen in first grade, old enough to have memories, old enough to understand what had happened.

Well, no.

Not quite. Nobody had ever known what happened that day at the shopping mall. Nobody had ever known where Jennie was taken, or who took her, or for what purpose.

But all too well Jodie understood what happened to her family because of it.

It was so confusing and astonishing to find that all along, Jennie had been happy and healthy and warm and everything else that was good. The Springs had never needed to worry.

Mom and Dad were weak with relief and joy.

Jodie mentally laid her history of nightmares out on the bed, like laundry to be put away, and studied them, understanding less than ever.

Stephen, of course, was angry. Stephen didn't even have a fuse; he just continually exploded. Stephen yelled that Jennie ought to have suffered, since the rest of them had.

"Don't talk like that once she comes," warned their father. Dad was wildly excited. He and Mom kept bursting into shouts of laughter and hugging each other and hyperventilating. That was Jodie's new word—hyperventilate. Jodie did not want her family getting overly emotional, or too noisy. She felt it was time to drop the hand-holding at dinner and the saying of grace. Jennie would think they were weird. "Don't hyperventilate," Jodie begged constantly. But her family was the hyperventilating kind.

When Mom thought nobody was watching, she would rearrange the dining table, seeing where the seventh chair fit best. The chair her missing daughter would sit in when she came home. Then Mom would do a little tap dance around the chair, fingertips on the wood. She looked so comic, a forty-three-year-old, getting heavy, going gray, wearing sneakers that squeaked on the linoleum instead of tapping.

"We'll all have to work hard," Mom warned every night. "Jennie's grown up with another family. Different values, I suppose. This won't be easy." Mom burst into laughter, not believing a word of it. This was her baby girl. It would be easy and joyful. "We may have a hard time adjusting," she added.

This was for Stephen's benefit. Stephen was not a great adjuster.

Jodie planned to be the buffer between Jennie and Stephen. Jodie knew that she would not have problems. This was the sister with the matching J name. They would be like twins.

Brian and Brendan never noticed much of anything except each other and their own lives. Jodie thought it was such a neat way to live, wrapped up and enclosed with this secret best friend who went with you everywhere and was part of you.

That was how she would be with Jennie.

At night, when they were each in their own beds, with only a thin little table and a narrow white telephone to separate them, they would tell each other sister things. Jennie would tell Jodie details about the kidnapping that she had never told anybody. And Jodie would share the secrets of her life: aches and hurts and loves and delights she had never managed to confess to Nicole or Caitlin.

Jodie was cleaning her bedroom as it had never been cleaned before. Nicole and Caitlin said it was impossible to share a room this small. Two beds had been squeezed in, one tall bureau and one medium desk. Another person could never fit in her share of sweaters, earrings, cassettes, and shoes. Jodie was seized with a frenzy of energy, folding and refolding her clothing until it took up only half the space it used to; discarding left and right; putting paper grocery bags stuffed with little-used items in the attic.

She had spent her allowance on scented drawer-liner paper from Laura Ashley. It was a lovely, delicate English-looking pattern. Its soft perfume filled the room like a stranger. Jennie would be pleased.

Mom loved matching names. Jodie and Jennie

went together. Of course the twins, Brian and Brendan, went together. Stephen was the oldest, and Mom and Dad had always meant to have a sixth child, who would be named Stacey whether it was a boy or a girl. So there'd have been Jodie and Jennie, Stephen and Stacey, Brian and Brendan.

Of course, after Jennie went missing, nobody could consider another baby. How could any of them ever have left the room again? Nobody could have focused their eyes anywhere else again. They'd all have had heart attacks and died from fear that somebody would take that baby, too.

Jennie was only twenty months younger than Jodie. As toddlers they had fought, Jodie pairing up with Stephen. Over the years, Jodie had thought of this a lot. If she, Jodie, had been holding Jennie's hand at the shopping mall the way she was supposed to, nobody could have kidnapped Jennie.

When she got to know this new sister, should she say she was sorry? Admit that it was her fault? If the new sister said, don't worry, everything's fine now, I'm home and happy, Jodie would be safe telling about her guilt. But if the new sister said, I hate you for it, and I've always hated you for it—what then?

Jodie put the hand mirror that said J E N N I E down on the piece of lace she had chosen to decorate the top of the bureau.

Jodie's mother loved things with names on them. The four kids had mugs, sweatshirts, bracelets, book bags, writing paper—everything—with their names printed or embroidered or engraved. Mom wanted to have a house full of J E N N I E items for the homecoming. It was a popular name. They had had no trouble at the mall finding tons of stuff that said *Jennie*. They bought so much they were embarrassed. "We'll have to bring it out one piece at a time," said Jodie, giggling.

"She'll know we love her," said Jodie's mother.

But behind the hyperventilating and the laughter lay the years of worry.

Mom was trembling. She had been trembling for days. She was actually losing weight from shivering. You could see her hands shake. Nobody had commented on it because everybody else had shivers, too. Everybody was worried about everything. What to serve for dinner on the first night? What to say to the neighbors? How to take Jennie to school. How to hug.

Would she be afraid? Would she be funny? Would she be shy? *What would she be like—this sister who had grown up somewhere else?*

Jodie opened her bureau drawers and looked at the empty halves. She was so proud of herself, opening up her life, just like a drawer, to take Jennie in.

I have a sister again, thought Jodie Spring. She isn't buried. She isn't gone. She wasn't hurt. Her guardian angel did take care of her. And now he's bringing her back to us.

Tomorrow.

"Once upon a time," he repeated helplessly, stuck in horrible repetition of that stupid phrase.

And then talk arrived, like a tape that had come in the mail. For Reeve Shields really did know a story that began with "Once upon a time."

"I dated a dizzy redhead. Dizzy is a compliment. Janie was light and airy. Like hope and joy. My girlfriend," he said softly, into the microphone. Into the world.

"You know the type. Really cute, fabulous red hair, lived next door. Good in school, of course, girls like that always are. Janie had lots of friends and she was crazy about her mom and dad, because that's the kind of family people like that have."

Never had Reeve's voice sounded so rich and appealing.

"Except," said Reeve, "except one day in the school cafeteria, a perfectly ordinary day, when kids were stealing each other's desserts and spilling each other's milk, Janie just happened to glance down at the picture of that missing child printed on the milk carton."

His slow voice seemed to draw a half-pint of milk, with its little black-and-white picture of a missing child. It was almost visible, that little milk carton, that dim and wax-covered photograph.

"And the face on the milk carton," said Reeve, "was Janie herself."

He deepened his voice, moving from informative into mysterious. "They can't fit much information on the side of a half-pint," said Reeve, "but the milk carton said that little girl had been missing since she was three. Missing for twelve years.".

In radio, you could not see your audience. Reeve could not know whether he really did have an audience. Radio was faith.

"Can you imagine if your daughter, or your sister, had disappeared twelve years ago? Twelve years have gone by, and yet you still believe. Surely somehow, somewhere, she must be waiting, and listening. You haven't given up hope. You refuse to admit she's probably dead by now, probably was dead all along. You believe there is a chance in a million that if you put her picture on a milk carton, she'll see it."

Beyond the mike, Reeve imagined dormitories —kids slouched on beds and floors, listening. Listening to him.

"Well," said Reeve, "she saw it."

SOME SECRETS AREN'T MEANT TO BE KEPT. . . .

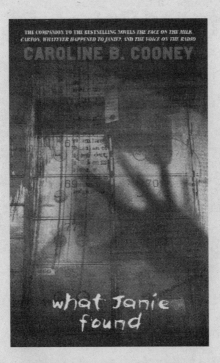

The thrilling conclusion to the bestselling novels
*The Face on the Milk Carton, Whatever Happened to
Janie?,* and *The Voice on the Radio,*
by Caroline B. Cooney